Witch Moon

The Hollows: Book 2

Tom Horn

Published by Purple Parrot Publishing.
Printed in the United Kingdom.
First Printing, 2022.
ISBN: Print: 978-1-7397857-8-9
          Ebook: 978-1-7397857-9-6

Purple Parrot Publishing
www.purpleparrotpublishing.co.uk
Edited by Viv Ainslie

Acknowledgements

My small circle of Beta readers have once again spent countless hours reading every draft of this book on its path to publication. To give so freely of your time is truly a blessing to me. You have my love and my sincerest appreciation and thanks for your undying support. (I know how hard it can be to set aside your valuable time in order to help me make this book as good as it can be.) You are my heroes.

It's been a very long time since I was in High School, and certain elements of this novel required several attempts to get it up to par. Though I never was too far off, subject matter experts kept my nose to the grindstone until I got it right. (You know who you are!)

Still, none of this would be possible without the dedication and tireless work of my Editor, Vivienne Ainslie. She sits atop the Parrot Cage where Birds of a Feather scramble for their voices to be heard. I will always owe you my gratitude for all that you do. Our Skype sessions have always been one of the highlights of my week. You are a true inspiration and with your simple queries you help my imagination to soar. You have my love and respect, always.

Writing has always been a dream for me since a very young age. If it is yours, don't stop, keep scribbling away. Dreams don't have to stay that way.

—TH
March 2022

Dedication

To Nati Snow

You've always been willing to help, and I thank you.

Contents

Prologue: In the Beginning 9

Chapter One: The Attack 13

Chapter Two: Hollows High 25

Chapter Three: Battle Lines 37

Chapter Four: The Dawning 59

Chapter Five: Tucker's Invitation 69

Chapter Six: Ari 75

Chapter Seven: A Little Good News 83

Chapter Eight: Drawing Down the Moon 89

Chapter Nine: Over the River adn Through the Woods 97

Chapter Ten: Okwaho Tekahionwake 103

Chapter Eleven: Confrontation 109

Chapter Twelve: Grandpa's Return 115

Chapter Thirteen: Aunt Abigail 123

Chapter Fourteen: Spirit Quest 133

Chapter Fifteen: Keegan Rourke 139

Chapter Sixteen: Two Girls and An Appaloosa 147

Chapter Seventeen: Gotcha! 155

Chapter Eighteen: The ay to a Man's Heart 165

Chapter Nineteen: Millie's Revenge 175

Chapter Twenty: Betrayal 189

Chapter Twenty-one: Down in Numbers 193

Chapter Twenty-two: The Collingsworth Manor 207

Chapter Twenty-three: Tucker's Warning 213

Chapter Twenty-four: The Bradford's Home 217

Chapter Twenty-five: Consequences 225

Chapter Twenty-six: Dilemma 237

Chapter Twenty-seven: The Raven 241

Chapter Twenty eight: Incident at the Morgue 253

Chapter Twenty-nine: Answers 265

Chapter Thirty: A New Ally 271

Chapter Thirty-one: Gram's Warning 261

Chapter Thirty-two: Sons of the Raven 297

Chapter Thirt-three: There Are Worse Things to Be 309

Chapter Thirty-four: Sinister Plans 315

Chpater Thirty-five: A New Lease on Life: 319

Chapter Thirty-six: An Unexpected Encounter 327

Chapter Thirty-seven: Trouble in Paradise 337

Chapter Thirty-eight: The Beast Within 347

Chapter Thirty-nine: Distressing News 351

Chapter Forty: Blood Moon Ritual 357

Chapter Forty-one: A Visit to The Hollows 359

Chapter Forty-two: Return to School 367

Chapter Forty-three: Shelby's Denial 385

Chapter Forty-four: Magic in the Air 389

Chapter Forty-five: Girl's Night 399

Epilogue: Transcendence 407

Mohawk Pronunciation Guide 413

About the Author 417

Prologue

In the Beginning

Life in The Hollows is different now. Sebastian Barrister has managed to turn my already crazy world completely upside down. He is a vampire, and he has turned my grandmother into one as well. She in turn, has also turned one of my friends into a creature of the night–Tucker Morrison. I had watched in horror, unable to do anything, as she drained his blood in front of me. All he had wanted to do was help me, to help her, and she brutally killed him. I don't blame her; she had no real control over her actions. She was a newly turned vampire, and as such her thirst for blood was ravenous. She attacked him in order to sustain herself, to survive. *So can I really fault her?* I choose to blame Sebastian Barrister instead. This was his doing.

Now a completely changed Tucker Morrison is out there. He too would be hungry just as Grandmother had been. Now, not only was Tucker a vampire, he was also a lycanthrope, a member of my own wolf pack. How has this unlikely merging changed him? We couldn't possibly know. Fact is: Werewolves and vampires don't get along. They have always been immortal enemies. Now Tucker is caught, somewhere, in between. He may not even be fully aware of all that has happened to him, the conflict growing within him. We need to find him as quickly as possible. Help him, if we can.

But how?

If he is suffering, can we do what is necessary? Will we be able to kill one of our own? I honestly don't know. I wish Grandpa were here, but he's not. He went off in search of Keegan Rourke, hoping that he might help us deal with Sebastian Barrister. It's been months, and we've not heard from him. Fortunately Barrister and the Coven have also been quiet, no doubt plotting something nefarious. In Grandpa's absence I have assumed the role as pack leader—not because I wanted to, but rather that no one else stepped up to the plate. Now they are looking to me for leadership. The Alpha has to make the decisions about what to do about Tucker Morrison. I don't know if I am up to making that call.

I'm not even certain what the right call is!

The truth is, I've got enough on my plate without having to make decisions for the Pack. My Grandmother is a damn vampire for Heaven's sake! My little brother's best friend is the ghost of a young girl who died in 1884. My Aunt Abigail is a witch, shunned by the local coven that's involved with Sebastian Barrister. My Grandpa, a werewolf, is trying to enlist the aid of the man responsible for killing his wife and making him a lycanthrope in the first place. And to top it all off, school starts soon. This is all way too much for a girl of fifteen to deal with. Girls my age normally only worry about their grades and catching the eye of a cute guy. But since the death of my parents, my life has been anything but normal.

Fortunately, I have an incredible best friend to help me deal with all this madness. I don't know what I'd do without Millie

Bradford to help me. She has been my lifeline to reality through everything so far. And to be honest, she has helped me deal with all the supernatural events that have happened to me since coming to Wellington House. Without her assistance I would've lost Bobby to the past. I would not have survived any of it without her. I should really thank her more.

Attending an actual school is going to be a new experience for my six year old brother, Bobby and me. Until the death of our parents we had always been homeschooled. Most of our friends were the friends of Mom and Dad; we had very few that were actually our own age, and those were mine; Bobbybear didn't have anyone even close to his age. The only friend Bobby has that is close to his own age now is Sara Robinson. The problem is, she died in 1884. She's a ghost. At least I have Millie and the Wolf Pack.

Since coming to The Hollows I have made enemies, more than I have friends. Trouble is, I don't know who they all are yet. The coming days, weeks and months are going to prove interesting to say the least. We are facing an all-out war for The Hollows. It is one that I'm not sure that we can win but I am certain that we have to win it. It is the only way that we can save all the innocents that would end up being collateral damage, and ourselves. We cannot allow the vampire to triumph and carry out his nefarious plans.

Chapter One

The Attack

The car sped along the dark mountain highway traveling faster than the speed limit. The man behind the wheel didn't really care, it had been a long day and he was tired. He just wanted to find a hotel where he and his wife could stop for what remained of the night. They still had a long drive ahead of them before they reached their destination. They had seen a sign a few miles back stating that lodging was available in the town of The Hollows; hopefully there would be a vacancy. He really didn't want to drive any further.

It was a black, moonless night. There were no stars that could be seen due to the thick clouds that hung over the forest, threatening more rain. He had his high beams on so that he could see better; the road was deserted so he didn't have to worry about blinding anyone before he could dim the headlights. "I wish you would slow down, you're scaring me," his wife said, there was a hint of nervousness in her tight voice. She thought he was being reckless; the road was wet and slippery.

"I just want to get there," he said, slightly irritated, as he glanced at her. The car sped toward a bend in the road. He was going faster than he should on the wet asphalt and took the turn wider than he intended, causing the car to straddle the middle of the road. There was no oncoming traffic, but in the center of the highway a huge wolf was feasting on its recent kill, a large buck.

The woman screamed, instinctively grasping her husband's bicep. "Look out!" Her eyes were wide with panic.

He jerked the steering wheel to the right to avoid an accident, but his rear tire struck the deer's antlers. The tire popped, causing the car to whip out of control. The driver fought with the wheel as he braked. He managed to bring the car to a stop on the right hand shoulder of the mountain road. "What the *Hell* was that?" he said, looking around franticly.

"Some animal, I think," she said.

"Are you okay?" he asked, concern in his voice. Both were breathing heavily. They had come so close to disaster, and they knew it.

She nodded. "Yeah, I'm fine. You?"

He sighed as he unbuckled his seatbelt. Nodding, he said, "Felt like we popped a tire."

She had a worried look in her eyes. "Maybe we should call for roadside assistance. I don't want you out there changing a flat if there's wild animals close by."

He glanced at his phone; she had a good point. Besides, there had been something big feasting on the dead deer. He shrugged. "No signal."

She pulled her phone out of her purse, checking. She shook her head. "Me neither."

He pressed the button on the lower left side of the dash, popping the trunk open. He switched the car's hazard lights on. "Guess I'm changing the tire. I'll need you to hold the flashlight on your phone so I can see, it's really dark out there."

She grabbed his arm as he opened his door. "Can't we just stay put? Someone's bound to come by."

He smiled. "We could be here all night." He squeezed her hand reassuringly. "It'll take twenty minutes, max. I'm perfectly capable of changing a tire on my own." He pulled her to him, kissing her lightly upon the lips. "We'll be fine. I promise."

He slid out of the car and looked at the driver's side rear tire; it was badly shredded. He glanced down the road where the deer lay; he could see steam rising up from the animal's exposed stomach. It had obviously been a fresh kill. The antlers were mangled where the car had struck the beast's head. He could've sworn that there had been a dog, or perhaps a wolf, feeding on the deer, but there was no sign of it now - likely it had been frightened off. Bits of rubber from the tire littered the asphalt. He glanced at the surrounding woods on both sides of the highway, a thick gray fog rose up from the ground filling the gaps between the pines, but he saw little else. Whatever had been feasting in the middle of the highway was probably long gone now.

He scratched his chin thoughtfully and then went to the trunk and sighed. He would have to take their luggage out to get to the spare tire. He pulled his wife's suitcase from the trunk, grunting as he did so. He shook his head. "Did you pack everything you own in this thing, Jess?"

"Not everything," Jessica said with a smile. "Just the essentials."

He pulled a smaller case out; it was half the size of hers, and nowhere near as heavy. He raised it into the air, trying to make his point. "I packed lightly," he said.

She rolled her eyes. "They're your friends and family, Richard. I want to make a good impression."

He grinned. "You've already done that. You married me!" he chuckled at his own joke.

"When did you get to be so funny?" she asked with a roll of her eyes.

He pulled the spare from the trunk and placed it on the ground near the ruined tire and went back for the jack. He saw Jess walking up to the dead deer. She was using the flashlight on her phone to better see it. He shook his head. "You really don't want to see that." He knew what she would find; it wasn't going to be a pretty sight.

"Ew! It's gross!" she said, clearly it held a morbid fascination for her.

He started jacking the car up. "I told you it was pretty grisly. How about you bring that light over here?" He shook his head with a grin. Jess had always had a love of the macabre. That was one of the things that had attracted him to her.

Though it sickened her, Jessica found it difficult to pull her eyes away. Half of the deer's head, thanks to their car, was a mangled mess. The animal's one remaining eye seemed to stare at her. She could see Richard changing the tire reflected in the lifeless eye of the deer. She could feel herself being drawn in; the blinking on the hazard lights adding to the spell. She was suddenly startled, the hypnotic enchantment instantly broken as what appeared to be a large wolf attacked her husband.

Richard tried to scream, but the wolf ripped out his vocal cord with a single, rapid swipe; blood seemed to spray everywhere, turning his scream into gurgling nonsense.

Jessica turned away from the reflection in the deer's lone eye so she better could see what was happening. She aimed her flashlight on the wolf that was continuing to rip Richard apart; her husband's blood was splattered on the left rear quarter panel of the car like careless graffiti. Her pulse matched the on-off flash of the blinking lights. Horrified, she screamed. The wolf dropped what was left of Richard's corpse and faced her; she could see her husband's blood dripping from the beast's jaw.

The wolf growled as he slowly took a step in her direction.

She couldn't move; her fear had her rooted in place. The wolf seemed to stand on its hind legs, changing—morphing—as it moved slowly toward her. Ebony skin glistened with sweat and blood as a naked man replaced the beast. He was now slowly coming for her, each step accentuated by a flash of amber light. He grinned as his fiery eyes gleamed hungrily.

Jessica took a step backwards, and tripping over the dead deer, she fell to the ground coating herself with blood and guts. She quickly started to scramble away, trying to gain purchase with her hands and knees. Somehow, she rose but quickly slipped on the gore and fell again. Crying in fear and desperation she managed to rise without falling. Her ankle twisted and she lost a shoe as she limped away. She took off her other heel finding it easier to run without it. She could hear the sound of the man's naked feet slap the pavement and his laughter drawing closer.

In her panic she fell down the embankment at the side of the highway and landed on her butt. It was the only reason she didn't completely tumble. She could hear him laughing at her. Sobbing as she gulped for air, she struggled to her feet, and ran through the forest, screaming for anyone to help her. The pine needles were slick and she fell again, slamming her chest against the hard-packed ground, forcing the air from her lungs. Terrified, she climbed to her feet and took off running, leaving her other shoe lying in the mud.

She glanced over her shoulder and was surprised that he was no longer following her. She stopped, leaning against a tree she tried to catch her breath. *Where was he? Had he given up?* She didn't think so. She was a complete mess; blood, deer innards, mud, pine needles and grass clung to her. The horrid stench was almost overwhelming. Pushing herself off the tree she started to walk as quietly as she could. Her eyes searched the darkness. She knew she couldn't remain where she was; it just wasn't safe. She cursed softly; *somewhere* along the way she had lost her phone. She needed to make it back to the car. She could lock herself in, perhaps keep the wolf out. Anything was better than where she was now.

She risked another look over her shoulder as she continued to walk as quietly as she could. She slammed into something hard and unmoving. Strong hands gripped her upper arms, lifting her off her feet. Turning, she stared at him in disbelief. "How?" she asked in a tremulous voice, wondering how he had gotten in front of her.

He grinned, exposing his teeth. She could see his canines growing. She tried to shrink away, but she couldn't. He lowered his mouth to her neck and she felt the sharp stab of pain as he bit into her flesh. *'Oh God…'* she thought. She wanted to scream but she couldn't. After a few moments she no longer cared what was happening to her. She smiled, taking pleasure in the vampire's embrace.

§

"Bobby! Hurry up! We don't want to be late our first day!" I said as I frantically ran around the cottage trying to shove things into my backpack that I might need for school. Bobbybear was taking his time eating his cereal. He still had to finish dressing and brush his teeth; he seemed in no hurry at all.

Aunt Abigail was sipping her coffee with a bemused smile on her face. She wasn't helping. She seemed to be enjoying my frenetic pleas to goad my brother into getting it in gear. I stopped and glared at her. "You know, you're not helping at all."

Aunt Abby rolled her eyes. "Relax, Kat, you still have plenty of time. Brock isn't even here yet."

I shook my head. "That isn't the point. Bobby is wasting time; he needs to get his butt moving!" I glared meaningfully at him; he seemed not to care as he shoveled another spoonful of Cheerios into his mouth. Smiling all the while. The little booger knew he was irritating me, and he was enjoying it!

The rumbling sound of the old Chevy pickup could be heard coming up the drive even before Brock blew the horn. I raised an exasperated hand in the air. "He's here, finally!" Brock was running later than we had agreed; we were going to have to push it to get to school on time.

"You can go ahead and leave if you want," Aunt Abby said. "I talked to your grandmother last night, Harrison is driving Bobby and I to school."

"I don't want him to be late on his first day," I said again. I glanced at my mother's watch that I still wore on my left wrist.

"I'll get him there on time. Don't worry; his class starts an hour later than yours. He won't be late. Trust me," she said. She turned to Bobby. "You do need to finish your cereal and then get dressed, sweetie."

I glanced at the watch and sighed. I felt rushed. Brock's late arrival wasn't helping to right things. "Fine. I'm counting on you!" I walked up to Bobbybear and kissed him on the forehead as he crunched upon the last of his cereal. "Have a good day, Bobby. Remember what Dad always said about first impressions!"

He had lifted his bowl up to his mouth and slurped the last of the milk; setting it down on the kitchen counter he belched loudly; totally ignoring the milk that dribbled down his chin. "First impressions are lasting impressions," he said, quoting our father.

"And you know what that means?" I asked as I slung the backpack's strap over my shoulder.

He made a point of rolling his eyes. "I'm gonna be seven soon. I'm not a little kid, I know what that means."

I turned and gave him a last look as I opened the front door. Trouble was, he was six going on sixteen, already very mature for his age. "I love you bunches, Bobbybear."

He grinned as he pointed his fingers at me, pistol-fashion. "Right back atcha!"

I glanced back at Aunt Abigail sipping her coffee. She still had that amused smirk on her face as she watched me. "I love you, Aunt Abby. Have a good day."

She saluted me with her coffee cup, a sly smile curving her lips. "Oh, I intend to."

I didn't have time to wonder what she meant; Brock had just pulled the old Chevy to a stop and was leaning heavily on the horn. I shot him an aggravated glance as I closed the cottage door behind me; he just seemed to ignore it as he hit the horn one last time, grinning. *What is with everyone today?'* I shook my head, wondering.

As I opened the door of the truck and tossed my backpack onto the seat, I glared at Brock. "You know the whole horn thing wasn't necessary; I could hear you coming up the road a mile away."

He shrugged. "No worries. It's not like it'll wake the dead or anything." He gave me a lop-sided grin. "How is your grandmother, anyway?"

I knew he didn't approve of me allowing my grandmother-turned-vampire to continue to 'live', but I was quickly growing tired of his stupid jokes. They just weren't funny; maybe at first they had been a little amusing, but now they were old and a bit much.

I sighed as I climbed in, slamming the door of the Chevy. "She's undead, so I suspect she's sleeping just fine." He didn't seem to have a response for that, which made me smile. I leaned close to him and gave him a quick kiss on the cheek.

He returned my little peck and smiled. "What about Bobby?"

"Aunt Abby is taking him in the Bentley. She has some errands to run. Why are you running so late this morning? You know I don't want to be late on my first day."

"No worries, we've got time." He frowned after a moment. "There was an incident on the highway late last night. Cops are combing the area."

I frowned. "What kind of an incident?"

He shook his head. "You'll see. I doubt that they've got

everything cleared by now. Things happen kinda slow here in The Hollows."

I chuckled softly. "I've noticed." The Hollows was your typical sleepy mountain town. Things moved at a much slower pace than in the city.

Sure enough, police were still on-scene at the incident on the mountain highway. A pearl-white Mercedes-Benz S580 Sedan was on the right shoulder of the road, trunk open and the left rear wheel was lifted off the ground so that the flat tire, which was practically torn in shreds, could be removed. A splattering of red blood stood out on the rear quarter-panel of the vehicle, the early morning sunlight seemed to gleam across it. A body lay upon the ground, covered by a white sheet that allowed the blood to stain through. The torn carcass of what appeared to be a deer with its antlers horribly mangled was sprawled across the center of both lanes. The Highway Department had a vehicle blocking the left shoulder of the road while two workers stepped out to clear what remained of the buck. I didn't envy them their task. It was absolutely gruesome. The threat of losing my breakfast forced me to look away.

Brock shook his head as he stopped the truck, waiting for the opportunity to continue down the road. He slipped the stick shift into neutral and engaged the emergency break with his foot. "It doesn't look like they've done much." He glanced at me. "They've covered the body, and that's about it."

Three of The Hollows' seven-man police force were on the scene, carrying out their investigation. One of which was a young-looking female. She looked like she should still be in High School. She smiled brightly as she approached the truck. "I thought that was you that went by here earlier," she said to Brock.

Brock grinned at her. "Good morning, Tiffany. How's the job?"

She glanced over the highway as she leaned against the truck door. "We've had a bit of excitement this morning, as you can see."

"What happened, officer?" I asked, hoping for some insight.

She turned her attention toward me, as though seeing me for the first time. "Accident," she said noncommittally. It was impossible to read her expression behind her dark, tear-shaped sunglasses. After a prolonged moment of staring at me, she turned back to Brock and smiled. "Who's your little cutie?"

Brock chuckled softly, prompting me to poke him in the ribs with my finger. He turned and frowned at me, and then said, "This is Katherine St. Claire. She's the granddaughter of Mrs. Wellington."

"Is that right?" she asked, turning her gaze back at me. She lowered her glasses down the bridge of her nose to get a better look, and smiled. "So Elizabeth Wellington is your grandmother, huh?"

I nodded. "Yes." We had a real winner here. Hadn't she heard what Brock had just said?

She straightened up and returned her sunglasses to their proper position, as she smiled at Brock. "You should be able to continue on in just a few minutes." She took a step back.

"So," Brock quickly said at my insistence, "was it a careless driver, or what?"

Officer Tiffany looked around as though to ensure that she wasn't overheard. She stepped closer. "Near as we can tell from our preliminary investigation, the driver of the Mercedes came upon the dead deer and tried to avoid a collision. The approaching vehicle had, evidently frightened off whatever was feasting on the road kill. It seems to have returned and attacked the man while he was changing the tire. His female companion, likely his wife, hasn't been located yet. We're just beginning to search the woods. That's all I can say right now. Nothing is official yet."

"What kind of animal?" I asked.

She glanced at me briefly and then looked at Brock. "My guess is that it was a wolf. A rather large wolf." Her lips curved slightly. *Did she know?* I wondered.

Chapter Two

Hollows High

Officer Tiffany stepped away from the truck and spoke to one of the men from the Highway Department. "Rick, you wanna move your truck so these kids can get by? We don't want them late for their first day of school. Besides, I think that the little girl is a bit squeamish."

I started to say something but Brock put a calming hand on my arm. He whispered with a smirk, "Let it go, Kat. Tiff's just trying to get under your skin. That's all."

"Who the hell does she think she is? She's not that much older than we are!" I was more than just a little mad. For some reason I was pissed! The nerve of her calling me a *little girl!*

Brock chuckled. "She used to be one of the head cheerleaders back when she was in school. She was a senior my freshman year. Very sweet girl, though."

I shook my head. "I'm *not* squeamish, and I'm *not* a little girl! I bet I could show her something that would make her squirm."

Brock laughed. He was clearly enjoying this. I punched his arm.

The Highway Department moved their truck so that we could pass. Officer Tiffany smiled sweetly at Brock as we drove by. He waved with his fingers as he kept both hands on the steering wheel. He blushed with a grin. I shook my head. "She seemed into you. Isn't she a little old to be flirting with you?"

He laughed. "Not really. She's only 19."

"Still, she's older than you are. You're only 16."

Brock laughed again. "What's that got to do with anything?"

I shrugged. "Nothing, I guess. I'm just surprised that they'd let a cradle robber on the police force."

He grinned at me, his dimples in full evidence. "I can't believe that you're so jealous." He laughed. "There's really nothing to be jealous about."

"Why would I be jealous? It's not like I didn't have boyfriends back in the city," I lied. I'd never dated anyone before. Being homeschooled I didn't even know any guys close to my age. Not until I'd been forced to move to The Hollows, anyway.

We rode for several miles without talking. I was watching the trees zip past. Finally, Brock broke the silence. "Look, Tiffany is not my type. I'm not interested in her at all."

"She sure seemed interested in you though," I said. The tone of my voice left no doubt that I was still a little angry about the whole thing. I didn't want him to even know how upset it had made me.

He nodded. "Tiffany was the head of the cheer squad. When I got into High School and became the captain of the football team, she thought we should be together. We went out on a couple of dates, but nothing happened. She's not my type at all."

"Oh?" I looked at him. "Just what is your type?"

He reached up and twisted the rearview mirror so that I could see my reflection staring back at me. "*That's* my type!"

I slid over against him and as he wrapped his arm around me, I smiled and said, "You're so sweet!" He laughed again as I readjusted the mirror for him.

"Besides, Sam has always encouraged us to be on good terms with the police department, but until Tiffany got on the force it hasn't been easy."

"So you're saying this flirtation between the two of you is my grandpa's fault?" I asked with a raise of my brow.

Brock just shook his head and sighed, and then he laughed. "I didn't say that."

Silence once again descended around us. I frowned, my thoughts returning to the incident on the highway. "Do you think it was Tucker that attacked that man?"

Brock sighed. "Well, it wasn't any of our guys, that's for sure. And if another wolf was stalking prey in these woods I'm pretty sure that we'd know about it."

I looked up at him. "So you do think it was Tucker?"

He shrugged. A brooding frown caused lines to appear on his forehead, as he seemed to consider it. "Who else?"

"Well, my grandpa was going to seek out this Keegan Rourke to help us with Sebastian Barrister, maybe it was him. From what I've heard, he's pretty ruthless." I sighed. "We need to be certain. We can't just accuse Tucker solely because he isn't a part of the pack anymore."

Brock nodded. "Me and the guys will take a run out in the surrounding woods after school, see if we can find anything that the police may have missed. We'll be able to determine if it was Tucker or some other lone wolf." He glanced at me with a raised brow. "You comfortable enough to take the truck home?"

I raised both my brows. "I've driven the truck before. I can handle it."

He chuckled softly. "Yeah, okay."

I poked him in the side with my finger. "Watch it!" I warned with a grin. I was determined now, more than ever, to prove him wrong. I knew that if I took my time and didn't try to rush things, I would do just fine. I could handle the Chevy; I'd done it before.

We rode the rest of the way in silence, which I was grateful for. I needed to watch Brock work the pedals and the gearshift, hoping that when the time came I could mimic his actions and drive the pickup truck home without difficulty. It looked easy enough, but my wild ride through the woods with Millie haunted my memory. But in hindsight, even then I hadn't done so badly. We reached our destination, or would have had we not run out of gas; and we had survived. Easy peasy.

We pulled into the parking lot of Hollows High. I was surprised at the number of vehicles that were present. *Did everybody drive?* I wondered. Brock turned off the Chevy's ignition and handed me the keys. "Take good care of her," he said.

I looked at him, but I couldn't see any sign of sarcasm in his eyes, and he sounded genuinely concerned. "I will," I said, snatching the keys from his hand. I wasn't sure if I should be irritated or not.

He grinned looking toward the school. "Are you ready for this?"

I forced my lips into a smile that I didn't really feel. I was incredibly nervous. I had never attended public schools before. Mom and Dad had insisted on home schooling Bobby and I out of concern for safety, ours, as well as everyone else's; lycanthropy was in our genes; though I hadn't known it until I got to The Hollows.

I slid out of the truck behind Brock and as I did my toe somehow got hung up on the floorboard and I very nearly fell. Only Brock's quick reflexes saved me from a face-plant on the asphalt. If I had been hoping for a grand entrance on my first day at Hollows High that was quickly dashed. A group of girls had been standing nearby and had seen my near fall from grace. I heard their laughter and I could feel the heat of my own embarrassment rising to my cheeks.

Brock chuckled softly. "Are you okay, Kat?"

Physically I was, but inside I felt humiliated, and his snickering didn't help matters. I quickly brushed him off as one of the girls, her auburn curls bouncing about her shoulders, approached. Two other girls followed her, one a strawberry blonde, the other a brunette. They were all sporting wide grins, no doubt at my expense. The first girl arched a brow and grinned. "Helping the disabled I see; that's very thoughtful of you Brock." The others giggled; I didn't find her the least bit funny.

Brock had a spurt of laughter until I punched him on the arm. He recovered quickly. "She's not disabled," he said with a hint of amusement still in his voice, as he rubbed his arm where I'd hit him, "she can walk just fine."

"Can she?" She glanced at me with doubt in her green eyes and shook her head. "Where are my manners? This is your first day at Hollows High! I'm Shelby, and this is Sherrie and Cindy." She swept a hand at the blonde and then the brunette.

I swept an errant strand of hair out of my eyes, and forced another smile. "I'm Kat," I said.

Shelby smirked and held her right hand up in the air, her designer nails poised to strike like feline claws. "Meow!" she giggled; the others laughed, again.

I could feel the tiny hairs at the base of my neck begin to prickle. Fortunately for Shelby and her friends I was wearing my talisman that Aunt Abby had enchanted to keep the wolf within at bay. "Funny," I said without any trace of emotion. I could feel the fire beginning to smolder in my eyes.

Shelby gave me an amused look and raised her eyebrows slightly as she batted her eyes. She obviously knew that she had struck a nerve, but she clearly didn't care. She smiled. "You should try out for the cheerleading team. We have a spot open since Carla Johnston graduated; you're about the same build as she was. I think you'd be a nice fit."

I was astonished; completely blown away; I hadn't expected this. "I… I wouldn't know what to do." *Me? A cheerleader?* The idea was so unexpected it sounded crazy!

Brock nodded. "That's an excellent idea! You'd be great!"

"Of course she would!" Shelby said; a huge smile stretched across her face. "And since I'm Captain of the squad, I can already guarantee your spot!" She looked into my eyes. "You're not afraid of heights, are you?"

"I'm not afraid of anything," I said with a slight raise of my chin. To be honest, I didn't have a clue what heights had to do with cheerleading but I wasn't about to show any fear to Shelby and her friends.

"Fantastic!" She turned to her companions. "Come on girls, I want to talk to Brenda and Mel before the bell rings."

I leaned back against the pickup my head still spinning from the unexpected invite to join cheerleading. "Not how I expected today to go." I shrugged. "They seemed friendly enough," I said as I watched Shelby and the other girls walk off.

Brock chuckled softly. "You do know that they are all daughters of the Coven members, don't you?"

I could feel my jaw drop slightly. "Are you serious?"

He nodded, clearly having fun at my expense. "That is Shelby Collingsworth. Her mother is Marybeth Collingsworth, the witch that took over your grandmother's Coven."

I slapped his arm. "No way!"

He rubbed the spot where I'd hit him. "You've really gotta stop doing that. I might bruise."

"But why would they want me to try out for cheerleading? Surely they know who I am."

He shrugged. "Well, you know that they say, 'Keep your friends close and your enemies closer'."

I bit my bottom lip as I nodded and I continued to watch the group of girls. As they reached the building Shelby turned and flashed a winning smile in my direction. "They do say that, don't they," I said. Maybe it would be a good idea to join the Cheer Squad after all. After taking a few steps toward the school, I stopped and put a hand on Brock's arm. "You really think they see me as an enemy? I mean I've never done anything to them. We've only just met."

He chuckled as he wrapped his arm around my shoulder and started walking me toward the school building. "You're a Lycan, what more can I say? Besides, didn't you threaten Marybeth that night?"

I had. "But she was twisting Bobbybear's arm, hurting him. I had to make her stop."

Brock nodded. "And you can bet she told the Coven all about it, including her daughter."

I frowned. "I only growled at her."

I furrowed a brow and glanced up at him. "You're a Lycan too, but they seemed pretty friendly with you." It just didn't add up. I never cared for double-standards.

He chuckled again. "What can I say? Sometimes it pays to be the local football hero."

I shook my head. "That is so not fair."

"Welcome to High School," he said, shrugging his shoulders. The smug look on his face made me want to slap him again, but I didn't.

We found the rest of the Wolf Pack huddled together in the school courtyard near the side entrance to the main school building. Silas had his arm wrapped around Millie's shoulder, and she was grinning happily. Cho Ming had one hand shoved into a pocket of his jeans, and was turning an apple in the other, taking another bite; the boy was always eating, always hungry.

"There was a wolf attack on the road early this morning, at least one fatality," Brock said pointedly.

I nodded. "A woman is still unaccounted for."

Cho tossed the apple core toward a garbage bin as though it were a basketball hoop; it landed in the center of the container. "Nothin' but net!" he said pumping his fist.

Silas frowned at Brock. "You think it was Tuck?"

Millie had a horrified look on her face.

Brock shrugged. "Could've been. We'll know more once we take a look for ourselves."

The guys stepped away leaving Millie and I on the outside. I heard Brock telling them that they were going to do a bit of recon after school. I smiled at Millie. "Looks like you and Silas are still getting along."

Her glasses had slipped down her nose again and she shoved them back into place. "We are!" she said excitedly, practically jumping up and down as she grabbed my arm. "I have a feeling that this year is going to be my best yet! I'm so glad that you're here now."

I laughed; her enthusiasm was contagious. "I certainly hope so. I need to go check in with admin, could you show me the way?"

Millie looped her arm through mine. "Hollows High is not that big, but I'll be happy to take you there. But first there're some people I'd like you to meet. They're kinda friends of mine. We used to eat lunch together last year. They were outcasts like me until I met you, and before Silas and I were a thing." She quickly put a hand on my arm as a huge, happy smile spread across her face. "That seems so weird to say that Silas and I are a thing. Makes me feel all giddy inside!" She giggled with joy, somehow resisting the urge to jump up and down again.

I was truly happy for Millie. After the library in The Hollows had burned down Millie had seemed so distraught, she loved working there as much as she loved old books. Silas had convinced the Wolf Pack to help her rebuild. But, in order to finance the renovation someone needed to pay for it. It had been surprisingly easy to persuade Grandmother to finance the restoration, especially when I told her that I suspected the Coven were responsible for its destruction. She and Marybeth Collingsworth were not on good terms after Marybeth took control of the Coven; Grandmother did not like being displaced. Could it be that Grandmother was a new ally for the Wolf Pack? Only time would tell.

Stranger things had happened.

It was easy to see why Millie's friends were outcasts from the rest of the school; they didn't look like everyone else. Both the boy and the girl were a deep caramel color, with jet-black hair and dark eyes. At first I thought that they were brother and sister, but clearly they were not. Millie introduced them as Manuel Rodriguez and Warise Tekahionwake, or Manny and Ari as they liked to be called. He was Hispanic and she was from the Mohawk Nation. Both seemed reserved and guarded; hesitant. It was almost as if they were reserving judgment. Who could blame them?

I smiled after the introductions. "I guess you can tell that I'm kinda nervous. Today is the first time I've ever attended a public school. Mom used to home-school my little brother and I back in the city. I hope that we can all be friends." I had almost forgotten to breathe.

Manny smiled as he shook my hand, his dark brown eyes twinkled brightly. "Welcome to The Hollows, then." A thick lock of his straight, dark hair fell across his face and he shoved it back up out of the way only to have it fall again.

I glanced at Warise; she seemed to be studying me with her very dark eyes. I saw a slight rise to her brow as she slowly nodded. "Yes. Welcome to The Hollows. I think I've seen you around in the woods."

"Oh?" I was surprised. "Where?"

She locked eyes with me. "Up near Valen's Ridge."

I felt the small hairs on the back of my neck begin to prickle. I had been up near the Ridge only a time or two. The first time was by accident, having lost my way; the second was when I led the Wolf Pack in search of Sebastian Barrister's lair. I hadn't seen anyone either time, other than the guys. The wolf in me hadn't sensed anybody else either. How then, had she seen me and I not seen her? I couldn't escape the feeling that there was more to Ari than she was letting on. She had definitely sparked my curiosity.

I touched Millie's arm and smiled. "It was really nice meeting the both of you, but I need to run; I've got to check in with Administration. Millie?"

Millie jolted causing her glasses to slip down her nose. "Oh! Right! I was gonna take you, sorry!" She blushed slightly as she gave Manny and Ari a little wave. "See you guys at lunch?" They nodded.

As we got out of earshot, I pulled Millie close. "How well do you know them?" I asked in a near whisper.

Millie frowned. "What do you mean?"

I searched her eyes. "There's something about Ari that I can't quite put my finger on."

"What do you mean?" she asked, glancing back the way that we had come.

I shook her arm. "Don't look back, she'll know we're talking about her," I could see that it was already too late. Ari was staring at us with a knowing look on her face. She crossed her arms over her chest and continued to watch us; a single brow arched.

I could feel my own frustration starting to build. I sensed the pull of the wolf deep within me. She knew that I loved to run through the woods when I was stressed or just needed to think. I'd give anything if I could do just that, but right now I couldn't. It was out of the question.

Distracted, we started walking again, and that was when we

slammed into a brick wall. As it turned out it wasn't an actual wall, it was Tucker Morrison. Had he not grabbed our arms we might have fallen off-balance. His grip was strong, almost to the point of hurting. Millie was struggling to keep her glasses on, and I could see her eyes had widened into huge, round orbs from her obvious fright.

"You need to watch where you're going," Tucker said, squeezing our arms a bit more, "you might get hurt."

I tried to push his hand off, but his grip only tightened. "Let go! You're hurting me." Tucker was wearing dark shades so I couldn't see his eyes, but I could nonetheless tell he was amused. He had a big grin across his face. He seemed to be enjoying this way too much.

He squeezed a little more before letting go; clearly he had a cruel streak running through him. This was new. He had always been so nice. "We wouldn't want that now, would we?"

I took a deep breath, trying to compose myself. Millie quickly turned and ran back the way we had come; clearly seeing Tucker had spooked her. I forced a smile. "Tucker, I'm surprised to see you." I swallowed.

He cocked his head to the side. "Why's that? Isn't it the first day of school? Why would you think I wouldn't be here?"

I shook my head. "I… I just thought with all that happened… with all that you've been through…"

He chuckled softly. "I know what you really mean, Kat. You didn't expect to see me in the light of day because of what your grandmother did to me. I get it, I do. But I've got it covered."

I reached out and touched his arm with the tips of my fingers. "No, Tuck, that isn't it at all." I could only wonder what he meant by *having it covered.*

He laughed. "Sure it is. I can tell by the way you're looking at me that you think I'm some kind of a monster. Your little friend sure seems to think so, she disappeared like a frightened little rabbit." He licked his lips. "A nice, plump little rabbit."

I squeezed his arm. "Hey! Be nice." I searched his face. "I'm worried about you Tuck. We all are. We want to help you, that's all." This attitude of his was new. The old version of Tucker Morrison was a sweetheart.

He brushed my hand away and laughed again. "Well isn't that sweet. Truth is, I don't want or need your help. I'm fine."

I swallowed. "I don't believe that, Tucker. I don't know how you could be, with what happened to you. Let us help you."

"How are you going to help me?" he grasped my shoulders and snarled. He opened his mouth and I could see his canines grow, extending into sharpened points. I gasped as I struggled against him, but it was no use. He was strong—much stronger than before. I felt a stab of white-hot fear jolt through me. I was helpless.

Chapter Three

Battle Lines

"Let her go!" It was Brock coming to my rescue. I could tell by the sound of the footsteps that he wasn't alone; Silas and Cho were there as well. Millie hadn't just disappeared; she had gone for help. I knew she wouldn't simply desert me, no matter how frightened she'd been.

Tucker gave me a little shove as he released me, and I fell backwards into Brock. Thankfully he kept me from falling completely. "What are you gonna do, Brock?" Tucker's tone was taunting. Menacing. Full of challenge. It was almost as if he were daring Brock to try something. Silas and Cho stepped forward ready to join the impending battle. Tucker wasn't alone; four guys joined his side. "You want to do this here? Now?" Tucker hissed. He seemed eager.

A crowd was starting to gather.

I put a hand on Brock's arm. "Let it go. There's no harm done. I'm fine." I could feel the tension in the air. It was thick, almost palpable. The faces on those that had formed around us were smiling, hankering for something more to happen. They obviously had no clue as to the danger that they were in.

Shelby Collingsworth stepped forward. "This is not the place." She smiled suddenly. "Besides, the bell is about to ring."

As if on cue, the high-pitched ringing of the school bell echoed throughout the courtyard, dispersing some of the crowd, but not all. There were those still hoping to see the conflict escalate as they lingered at the fringe. A booming male voice sounded as the bell stopped. "All right people, you heard the bell. You have places to be. Move along. Mr. Morrison, Mr. Jacobins, in my office!" Principal LaRoche was standing with his hands on his hips, glaring at everyone. "Move it people!" he repeated his demand.

Millie stepped up beside me, her hand touching my elbow. "I didn't know what else to do. I figured I'd best get the guys."

I smiled at her. "You did right, Millie. I just hope we can avoid a massive conflict. I don't want to see anybody get hurt."

Shelby stepped up to us. "Guys can be such jerks, can't they?" She placed a hand upon my arm. "Well, don't forget Cheer practice after school. It'll be fun!" She turned and walked away, followed by Sherrie and Cindy along with one other girl that I hadn't yet met.

Millie's eyes went wide. "You're not seriously thinking about joining cheerleading, are you?"

I shrugged. "Why not?"

She gave me a look as though I had just betrayed her. "They're all Daughters of the Coven, why on Earth would you want to hang out with them?"

I rolled my eyes. "It's not like that, Millie. Shelby offered and it sounded like it might be fun." I shrugged, "If nothing else it'll be a good way to keep tabs on them. And besides, Shelby seems like she doesn't want things to get out of hand any more than I do. Maybe if we work together, we can avoid an all-out war."

Millie pushed her glasses up the bridge of her nose. "Well if you ask me, I think it's a big mistake. Those girls are nothing but trouble. I should know, they've treated me awful for years."

"Come on, Millie, that isn't really fair. They seem really nice, I'm sure they're not like that anymore. People can change."

Millie shrugged, shaking her head. "I… I've gotta get to class." Her voice sounded hurt, clouded with disappointment.

"You're not gonna take me to Administration?" I was a little surprised at her reaction.

"Just go through those doors," she pointed. "You can't miss it."

"Millie…" I reached out to her but she merely shook her head and walked away. It looked as though her eyes were brimming with unshed tears. She seemed completely devastated. What had I done? The courtyard grew empty, leaving me all alone. I sighed as I turned and entered the main building in search of Administration.

The clerk in Administration was sweet and friendly. Knowing that the first period bell had already rung, she quickly entered my name into the school record book and went over my class schedule. She smiled as she touched her brow with her fingertips, her eyes growing wide for a second as she scanned everything one last time, making certain that she hadn't forgotten anything. "And I believe that you're all set. I'll just walk you to your first class."

As she was about to step around the counter, another girl walked into the office. "Morning Norma," the girl said with a smile. "I was doing stuff for my dad. Am I gonna need a tardy slip?"

Norma Shelton batted a hand in the air and gave her a quick wink. "Oh, I think you'll be fine without it, Mel. Say, could you do me a favor? This is Katherine St. Claire; she's new. Could you be a doll and take her to class with you? You'd save me a trip."

Mel smiled with a quick nod. "Sure thing, Norma, anything

to help." She turned to me and stuck out her hand. "Hi, I'm Melissa LaRoche, but you can call me Mel; everybody does." She was shorter than I was, but not by very much. She wore her hair short, in a pixie style, with a sprinkle of blonde highlights.

I returned her smile as I shook her hand. "Call me Kat."

"So, where are you from Kat?" she asked as we stepped back into the hallway. The throng of students rushing to class had already greatly dispersed.

"New York City," I said. "Originally."

"Wow, the Big Apple huh?" She crinkled her brows. "What brings you to The Hollows?"

I sighed. "My parents were killed in a car accident less than a year ago. My brother and I were brought to live with our grandmother."

She pouted. "Sorry to hear about your folks. Who's your grandmother, if you don't mind me asking?"

"Elizabeth Wellington. But we no longer live in Wellington House, now we live with my Aunt Abigail in her cottage."

She stopped walking and stared at me. "Oh, so you're a Wellington?" she sounded shocked.

I nodded. "We're related."

She frowned suddenly. "I didn't know that."

I could see her mind working. I arched a brow. "Is that a problem?"

Mel seemed lost in thought for a second. She appeared to jolt out of her stupor as she blinked. "No, it's not a problem, I guess. I just didn't know; that's all." She started walking again. "We should get to class."

We walked the rest of the way in silence, our pace quickened. I got the feeling that Mel was in a hurry to be free of me. Why, exactly, I wasn't sure; but I trusted my instincts.

As we entered the classroom there were two vacant seats, one beside Millie and the other beside Shelby. After I handed my attendance slip to the teacher, Mrs. Crombie, I turned to find that Mel had taken the seat that Millie had been saving for me. I couldn't help but smile at the helpless look that Millie gave me. My gut was telling me that Shelby had maneuvered things to keep Millie and I apart.

The first three hours of classes seemed to drag by. Each one, English, Math and Science seemed like a rehash of what I'd learned during my homeschooling with Mom and Dad. Certainly there wasn't anything new, and I deliberately withheld the knowledge that I already knew what the teachers were discussing; I didn't want to come across as a know-it-all. That wouldn't be good, especially on my first day. But, when called upon by the teacher, I didn't hold back, either. I wasn't going to play stupid just to fit in.

Finally, lunchtime came. I was looking forward to spending time with Millie and just talk; I wanted her to understand my reasons for joining the Cheer squad. Shelby and her friends had managed to keep us apart in every class; it had irritated me and I could tell that Millie was miserably unhappy. Our lockers were on opposite ends of the hallway, so we didn't even have time between classes to hang out.

Who knew that high school could be so stressful?

The cashier at the head of the lunch line gave me my change that I didn't bother to count. I picked up the plastic tray, which held my meal in separated compartments, and stepped away from the line and stopped, scanning the crowded lunchroom for Millie. I could see her sitting in the far corner at a round table; she was with Manny and Ari. Sighing with a sense of relief, I headed in her direction.

As I placed my tray onto the table, I started to sit. Millie gave me a frosty look. "I thought you'd be sitting with your new friends," she said coldly. Her words held a definite edge to them and I could see the tightness of her jaw and the hard glare of her eyes magnified behind the round lenses of her glasses. She was angry with me that much was clear.

I hesitated for a second, caught off guard by her words. I sat down in the unoccupied chair and touched her arm. "Millie, I haven't done anything wrong. Besides I am just as upset as you are that they've kept us apart."

"Yeah, right" she practically snorted as she spoke the word, giving her head a little shake.

I glanced across the table at Ari and Manny. He was pretending not to listen but she was staring at me with a straight face, showing no emotion, no hint at what she was thinking. I turned back to Millie and squeezed her arm. "Can we please talk about this?"

She slammed her milk carton onto the table causing milk to spill from the straw. She shook her head with fervor. "There's nothing to talk about. You'd rather hang out with your new friends, be my guest!"

"Millie, I'm here with you, aren't I?"

Tears filled Millie's eyes and she abruptly stood up, shoving my tray into my lap, covering me with what passed for meatloaf. She turned and stalked away, leaving me to wonder what the heck was going on.

It was obvious that Manny had a big heart. He blushed, ignoring his lunch items he quickly jumped up and ran after Millie. Ari sat there, staring at me with an arched brow and a slight curve to her lips. She was obviously amused. It only made me mad.

"None of this is funny!" I said heatedly as I slammed my tray back onto the table and began to pluck a chaotic mixture of meatloaf, mashed potatoes, creamed corn, and fruit cocktail from my lap.

Ari chuckled. I must've been a heckuva sight. And, to top it all off, I was flustered. *What had made Millie so upset? Surely not the fact that I was joining Cheerleading...*

After a moment, Ari crossed her arms and leaned back in her chair. "You have to understand what Millie has had to endure.

The Daughters of the Coven have tormented her for years, and now her best friend seems to have joined them."

"But I haven't!" I insisted, flicking a kernel of corn onto my tray.

She shrugged. "She doesn't know that. All she knows is that you seem to have easily fallen in with them. She's understandably hurt."

I sighed gruffly. "How can I fix this? She won't even talk to me."

Ari smiled. "Sometimes actions speak louder than words."

I shook my head. "What do you mean?" I asked with a roll of my eyes. Everyone in The Hollows was so cryptic!

Ari stood, gathered her tray, Manny's and Millie's, and stacked them together. She smiled a tight little smile. "That is what you need to figure out."

I plopped a chunk of meatloaf onto my tray as she walked away. "Great," I said with a frown. "Just great."

Millie continued to avoid me for the remainder of the day. Every time I tried to talk to her, she'd turn and walk away, not wanting to hear anything that I had to say. *How was I supposed to fix this if she wouldn't give me the chance to explain?* I was beyond frustrated!

After the final bell rang, I tried to stop Millie but she simply disappeared in the hallway mob of students bustling to leave. I sighed as I turned toward my own locker. As I was putting my textbooks away, Shelby leaned against the locker next to mine, smiling. "You ready for Cheerleading practice?"

I grabbed my backpack out of my locker and slung it over my shoulder as I shook my head. "Look, I appreciate the offer, but I don't think it's such a good idea."

Shelby frowned with a massively exaggerated pout. "Why?" she asked.

I shrugged. "After school just doesn't work for me. I have to pick up my kid brother and take him home." I didn't bother telling her about Millie.

Shelby quickly nodded. "I get it. How about we practice first thing in the morning? Can you get here; say an hour early every day? I'm sure the others wouldn't mind."

I sighed. "I have a friend, she's kinda feeling left out."

"Millie?" Shelby's brow furrowed. "Have her come too. It would be good for her, and maybe she could lose some weight in the process; she's really cute. She'd look great if she lost a few pounds."

I lightly shook my head. "I don't think she'll want to try out for Cheerleading; especially considering her history with everyone involved."

Shelby placed a hand on my arm. "I totally get it, I do. I'm trying to extend the olive branch here. I know we've been unkind to her in the past, but I want to change all that. All I'm asking is that she meet us half way."

"I'll talk to her," I said. "But I wouldn't get my hopes up."

Shelby smiled brightly. "Great! I hope to see you both tomorrow!" She turned and walked off. As I watched her go I could only hope that she was being sincere.

When I walked over to the elementary school to get Bobbybear I wasn't prepared for what I'd find. My kid brother, so sweet and innocent, was sporting a blackened eye and a split lip. He had obviously been in a fight. "What happened, Bobbybear?" I asked as I knelt down in front of him. I was searching for any further signs of injury.

He scowled at me as he slipped my grasp of his arm and pushed me away. "I hate school!" he said with a pout. He stomped away, leaving my head spinning.

"Bobby!" I quickly scrambled to my feet and went after him. I gently grabbed his arm, bringing him to a stop. "Bobbybear wait! Please tell me what happened. Did you get in a fight? Are you hurt? Who did this to you?"

His heavy sigh and tear-filled eyes nearly broke my heart. His bottom lip was still fixed firmly in a pout. I hadn't seen him this sad in a very long time – not even after the death of our parents. "I can't fix this if you won't tell me what happened," I said softly.

As tears rolled down his round cheeks he looked away, his lip quivering. "I just want to go, Kat."

I hugged him tightly. "Okay, Bobbybear. Let's go home." Maybe Aunt Abigail could get him to talk about what had happened. It was obvious that he didn't want to discuss matters with me. I lovingly rubbed his back as we walked toward the parking lot where the old Chevy pickup waited.

Bobby quickly glanced up at me when he saw Grandpa's truck. "Who's gonna drive us?" He had expected to see Brock, but he and the rest of the Wolf Pack were already gone.

I smiled down at him as I jingled the keys. "I am." I couldn't quite keep the pride out of my voice.

He stopped walking and stared at me with surprised eyes. "You're gonna drive?"

I feigned shock. "I can drive."

"Since when?" Bobby asked skeptically.

"I learned last year," I said slapping him lightly upon the shoulder.

He looked at me with those big, puppy dog eyes of his, so full of innocence and wonder. After a brief moment a slow grin appeared across his face. "Can I drive?" he asked, sounding hopeful.

I laughed as I reached out and tousled his hair. "Not on your life, kiddo."

I opened the door of the pickup and he grabbed the seat and climbed in. I closed the door behind him and then walked around and got in as I fished the keys out of my pocket. I blew out a breath of air, hoping that I didn't make a fool of myself in front of everybody that was still around; Bobby would never let me live it down. Fortunately the Chevy fired right up. I glanced over at him with a proud gleam. He wasn't impressed. It took me a minute to get it into reverse, the grinding of the gears seemed louder than it actually was, but soon we were on our way.

Bobby gave me a curious stare. "We're not going home?" he asked. He was expecting me to turn left out of the school parking lot, but I'd gone right.

I nodded. "We are, but first I want to see if we can catch up with Millie. She had a rough day and I just want to make sure that we're both okay. She was a little upset with me."

He smiled for the first time. "I like Millie."

I grinned back at him. "I know you do kiddo. And she really likes you too."

So far things were going rather well. I was pleased that I remembered how to shift gears and keep the pickup driving smoothly, unlike my first experience behind the wheel where Millie and I had a wild ride through the woods back to Wellington House. Yet, even then we had survived unscathed. Bobby pointed. "There she is!" The excitement in his voice was undeniable. He did truly love Millie, and so did I. She was my best friend, despite what she might be thinking to the contrary. But I meant to fix that, to get our friendship back on track. We couldn't allow one screwed up day at school destroy what we'd built over the past several months since our first meeting in The Hollows Library. I refused to allow that to happen. I slowed the truck to a crawl.

Millie glanced over at us and rolled her eyes. "What do you want?" She tried to sound angry, but I could tell she wanted things back to the way they were as much as I did. Despite her best efforts she couldn't hide the twinkle in her eyes. She was happy to see me. Or it could be she was pleased to see Bobbybear. But either way, she couldn't stay mad; it was against her nature.

"Thought you might like a ride," I said through Bobby's open window.

She pointed down the street. "I'm almost home." She stopped walking.

I stopped the truck and gave her a pleading look. "Millie, I'm sorry for today."

Bobbybear pouted at her. "Hi Millie."

Seeing Bobby's face, she quickly stepped closer to the truck and touched his arm. "What happened to you, Bobbybear?" She gave me a scathing look as though his appearance was my fault.

He shrugged. "I was in a fight."

She glanced back at me and then looked at my brother. "I can see that. Are you all right?"

He sniffled, wiping the back of his hand across his nose. "I'll be okay. But I don't think I want to go back to school anymore. People are mean. Will you let us take you home?"

She stepped back. "I'm within walking distance now," she said as she pointed at her house. "I'm practically in my front yard now."

Bobby pouted again. "You don't like us anymore?" he asked. He was really laying it on pretty thick. Millie didn't have a chance against him. He was the best at making one feel guilty so that he could get his way. Where he had learned this particular art of manipulation was beyond me.

"Oh Bobbybear, of course I do! Don't ever think that I don't. You guys are the most important people in my life!" She smiled, "Next to Grams, of course."

"What about Silas?" Bobby asked. "Don't you still like him?"

She laughed. "Yeah, I still like Silas. But you, kiddo," she stepped forward, reached in and tousled his hair, "are still my first boyfriend!"

He beamed joyfully.

She opened the door and Bobby happily slid into the middle

of the seat. She climbed in and stared at me silently as she wrapped a protective arm around Bobbybear. Finally she spoke, her voice tense, "Are you really joining Cheerleading?"

I nodded. "It's a great way to keep an eye on the Daughters of the Coven, for one. And Shelby seems to want to fix things as much as I do. No one wants an all-out war. Maybe it's up to us. Besides, she wants you to join Cheerleading too. She wants to make amends for all the bad things that they did to you in the past. She sounded really sincere."

Millie seemed shocked. "Me? A cheerleader?" She shook her head. "That just sounds crazy!"

Bobby grinned at her. "I think you'd be a good cheerleader!"

"You do?" Millie seemed surprised.

He nodded. "Yep!" After a moment he frowned. "What is a cheerleader, anyway?"

Millie and I exchanged glances and then burst out laughing.

I pulled up in front of Millie's house and waved to her grandmother who was sitting on the front porch, knitting. She returned my wave and then went back to her task without missing a beat. "I love your grandma!" I said, smiling.

Millie climbed out of the truck and gave Bobbybear a kiss on his cheek. She looked over at me. "If you're really gonna go through with this Cheerleading thing, then I guess I'm in. I won't just throw you to the wolves —" she blushed, realizing what she said. She shrugged in embarrassment, and with a roll of her eyes she added, "You know what I mean."

I couldn't help but chuckle. "Thanks, Millie. I appreciate it. It'll be fun, I promise."

"Pick me up tomorrow, then?"

I nodded. "They want us at school an hour early, so I'll be here bright and early."

She sighed as she shook her head and turned away from the truck. "This is crazy," she said. "Hey, Grams, I'm going to join cheerleading!"

I couldn't hear what her grandmother's response was, but she seemed shocked.

"Okay, Bobbybear, are you ready to go home?"

He nodded. "Can I drive now?"

I slipped the truck into first gear and pulled away from the curb. "No, you can't drive. Nice try, though."

He chuckled. "Maybe one day can I drive?"

I laughed. "Maybe. You'll have to wait until your feet can reach the pedals first."

He crossed his arms over his chest and pouted as he glared down at his feet dangling in the air. "I hate being short!"

§

Aunt Abigail greeted us at the front door of the cottage, all smiles, and eager to hear all about our first day of school. Her good mood instantly evaporated upon seeing Bobby's black eye and split lip. She was absolutely furious; threatening to teach all of Bobby's antagonists a lesson they'd *never* forget.

Bobby's eyes were wide; he'd never seen Aunt Abby quite so furious. "Can I go over to Grandmother's? Margaret promised there'd be cookies next time."

I had to calm Aunt Abby down, and it wasn't going to be easy. Bobby loved being over at Wellington House when Grandmother awakened. He seemed not to mind that she was a vampire. He actually thought it was 'cool.' I knew that Grandmother would never hurt him. I looked at Bobbybear and quickly nodded. "Don't eat too many cookies, they'll spoil your appetite."

As Bobby ran off, I followed Aunt Abigail into the basement where she kept her spell components. I needed to make her see reason before she did something we'd all regret. She glared at me. "You do realize that most of the teachers at Bobby's school are Coven members don't you? There's no doubt in my mind that they allowed this to happen." She pulled a jar from the shelf; it contained something dark and frightening looking.

"Aunt Abby, we need to think long and hard about this. We don't want to make matters worse." That wild look in her eyes was starting to scare me. It kind of gave credence to the *'Crazy Abby'* claims that Grandmother had once mentioned.

She sighed heavily as she put the jar back onto the shelf. "Then what would you suggest?" Her eyes were moist with unshed tears.

I shrugged, shaking my head. "I don't know." I indicated the shelf of ingredients with a wave of my hand, "But this isn't the answer. It can't be!"

She sighed again. "God I wish Sam were here. He'd know what to do."

"Still no word from Grandpa?" I asked.

She shook her head. "Nothing. I'm starting to get a bit nervous. I don't like Keegan Rourke. I don't trust him."

I could tell that she was worried. She had every right to be. Grandpa had gone off in search of a deadly enemy that he hoped could be persuaded to become an ally against the vampire Sebastian Barrister. Without some assistance Barrister and the Coven might easily be too much for the Wolf Pack to handle – especially since we had already lost one of our own. Tucker was apparently working with the Sons of the Raven, which were staunch supporters of the Coven; most of their members were either sons or siblings of the witches or the Daughters of the Coven.

Aunt Abigail ran a hand through her hair and smiled weakly. She appeared to have given up on casting a spell to remedy Bobby's situation. "We should head on over to Wellington House. Mother is expecting us for dinner at six; we don't want to be late."

I nodded as we climbed the basement stairs. "Why wasn't anyone contacted by the school when Bobbybear was hurt?

Someone from administration should've reached out to either you or me."

She practically snorted. "You're kidding, right?"

I shook my head. "Isn't it protocol, or something?"

Aunt Abby let out a huge, frustrated sigh. "The principal of The Hollows Elementary School is none other than Belinda Michaels. She's a priestess in the Coven. The teachers there are all either Coven members or are seeking their favor. I'm sure that they just turned a blind eye to the whole thing."

"That can't be legal," I said in protest. "The state of New York has laws to protect against things like this."

She nodded. "That may work everywhere else in the State, but this is The Hollows. We don't exactly follow all of the rules of a normal society. It would be impossible, really. But don't worry. They'll get what's coming to them. I promise you that."

I couldn't help but shiver. Aunt Abigail could be terrifying if she set her mind to it. I was eager to change the subject. "I saw Tucker at school today."

I could see her shoulders tense up as she paused at the top of the staircase. She turned to face me, a single brow arched expectantly. Clearly she wanted to hear more. "That is surprising."

"That's what I thought. Does the fact that Tucker is now a vampire-werewolf hybrid allow him to be out in direct sunlight? Is that it, do you think?"

Aunt Abby frowned. "I wouldn't think so." She pursed her lips together. "Tell me more."

I shrugged. "He is different now, much stronger than before."

"How so?" she asked.

I couldn't help but blush. I couldn't really tell her that he had at one time snuck up behind me and picked me up. I had been spying on the guys swimming in a pond. Everyone was naked, including me. It was one of those moments that I would just as soon forget. I shook my head. "That isn't really the point, but trust me, I know. Anyway, he was wearing dark sunglasses all day, even in the classroom. You don't suppose that is all it is, do you?"

She shook her head. She tapped her lip with a finger. "I wouldn't think so. That may protect his sensitive eyes from the bright light, but it wouldn't do anything to protect his skin from the sun's rays. Tell me, was he wearing long sleeves?"

"No, not at all. He was wearing a tight, form-fitting black t-shirt. When Brock and the others came up to assist me, these guys stepped up beside Tucker. I found out later that they are the Sons of the Raven. I think they are working together. If Principal LaRoche hadn't interfered there might have been an all-out war in the courtyard. Shelby Collingsworth stepped in and helped to diffuse the situation. She seemed to want to avoid a fight as much as I did."

Aunt Abby's frown deepened. "That surprises me, actually. Marybeth Collingsworth has taken control over Mother's Coven, why would her daughter side with you?"

I shrugged. "I don't know. But Shelby seems really nice. She's invited Millie and I to join Cheerleading."

Aunt Abigail's eyebrows shot up her forehead. "You and Millie are going to be cheerleaders?" She sounded amused. A small smile began to twist one corner of her mouth. It was impossible for me to know what she was thinking. She chuckled softly.

I crossed my arms over my chest as we headed out of the cottage. "Does that sound crazy to you?"

She blinked. "Not at all. It's just that I didn't think either of you were the cheerleading type."

"Well, if you must know, I'm doing it so that I can keep a closer eye on the Daughters of the Coven. You know, keep your enemies close, that kinda thing."

"And Millie?"

I shrugged. "Shelby seems to want to make amends for the way they've treated her over the years. It's kind of an olive branch. Besides, I think Millie and I will make great additions to the squad. We might even have fun."

She chuckled, shaking her head. "I just hope you know what you're doing."

"Well," I said, "look at it this way: If Shelby is truly serious about wanting to de-escalate matters between the Coven and the Wolf Pack then this might be a step in the right direction. It wouldn't hurt to start building a friendship with her."

"I guess it'll be good that Millie and you are joining together. You can watch each other's back. I don't want either of you getting hurt."

"Did you ever try out for cheerleading when you were my age?" I asked, suddenly curious.

Aunt Abigail laughed. "God no!" She shook her head. "I never had time for all that silliness. Your mother did though. That's how she caught your father's eye."

"Really?" I said. The thought of my mother as a cheerleader brought a smile to my lips.

As we walked along the path toward Wellington House, a light breeze blew through the pines; you could hear the needles whispering softly in the air. The sun was already sinking from the sky, and sounds of the approaching night were beginning. The chirp of crickets, somewhere off the path, could be heard; the croak of a bullfrog even further out. I could feel the tug of the wolf within me; it would be a good night for a run. It made my thoughts turn to Ari, and her claim that she'd seen me in the woods up near Valen's Ridge.

"I met one of Millie's friends, two of them actually; but one said something that made me pause. Ari said that she'd seen me in the woods." I shook my head, "But I've never seen her. Especially not up near Valen's Ridge."

"Who is she?" Abby asked.

I shrugged. "Her name is Warise Tekahionwake; Ari for short. She's a Mohawk Indian."

Aunt Abby nodded. "Well, that would explain why she saw you up near the Ridge. The Mohawk have a settlement just north of there on the other side of the river."

"But why didn't I see her? Surely the wolf would've sensed her, or something."

"Not necessarily."

I reached out and touched her arm, stopping. "What do you mean by that?"

She studied me for a moment and then smiled. It was more of a sly grin. "Not everything in The Hollows is as it seems. I thought you knew that by now." She started walking toward Wellington House again, leaving me standing there.

I rolled my eyes and started after her. "There you go again with your cryptic little sayings. I don't know why people can't talk more plainly." I could hear her softly chuckle ahead of me.

§

Aunt Abigail glared across the table at Grandmother as she watched her take a forkful of peas to her mouth; clearly she was not pleased about something. Grandmother didn't seem to care; she lowered her fork to her very rare steak, joined it with her knife, and cut off a bite. "Seriously, Mother," Aunt Abby said, "Why do you even bother with the charade?" her voice was thickened by the merlot.

I touched Bobby's sleeve. "Why don't you run along and play, Bobbybear?" I could sense a confrontation brewing and I knew that he didn't need to be a part of that. Both Grandmother and Aunt Abigail could get quite worked up when there was an issue that they had a difference of opinion about. Clearly this was one of those times. Aunt Abigail had been sending glares toward Grandmother all night.

He glanced from me to Aunt Abby, and then to Grandmother. Uncertainty filled his eyes. I could see the lump in his throat as he swallowed.

Grandmother smiled at him. "Run along, Robert. I believe Margaret has more of those fresh-baked cookies in the kitchen. Why don't you have a couple for dessert?"

After Bobby had left, closing the door behind him, Grandmother placed her knife and fork onto her plate. She picked up her cloth napkin from her lap and patted it upon her lips, and then tossed it over her plate. Her eyes were cold as she met my aunt's gaze. "I believe that you have perhaps had too much wine, my dear. You seem to have forgotten your manners."

Aunt Abby's hand tightened into a fist as she placed her napkin onto the table. I was afraid that she would say something that we'd all regret, so I gently touched the toe of my shoe against her shin. She glanced at me and nodded, returning her eyes to Grandmother's disapproving stare. "Perhaps I have, Mother. Please excuse me."

I was duly impressed.

Grandmother smiled. "That's more like it." She pushed her plate away. "If you must know, I find the food completely without taste. But I want young Robert to have a meal with his family. A bit of normalcy, perhaps. The poor boy has been through quite enough, don't you think?" she arched a brow as she waited, daring either of us to contradict her.

Aunt Abigail nodded. "Of course." She shook her head after a moment. "I just don't know why you bother."

"Would you prefer if I merely sat and watched everyone eat? Perhaps maybe I could have a goblet of blood to quench my appetite. Or maybe I could have a guest over, drain them as you ate. Would that be more pleasing to you, Abigail?"

Aunt Abby closed her eyes tightly and shook her head. "No, Mother, of course not. You are right, of course." She took another sip of her wine and added, "As always."

Grandmother glanced from Aunt Abby to me. "Can either of you please explain to me why my Grandson is sporting a blackened eye and a split lip?"

"He was bullied at school," I said, my voice tinged with anger. "Apparently the staff just let it happen." I was still pretty upset by the whole thing. Incidents like this shouldn't happen.

Grandmother arched a brow as she looked from me to Aunt Abby. "Doesn't Belinda run things there at Robert's school?"

Aunt Abigail nodded, finishing the last of her merlot. "She does."

Grandmother nodded. "Well then, problem solved. I shall speak with her."

"Do you honestly believe that speaking with her will solve anything?" Aunt Abby said with a hint of doubt and sarcasm mixed.

Grandmother smiled. "Oh, I can be quite persuasive, I assure you." She stood. "We should take this conversation into the parlor. A sherry would be nice." She smirked. "Merely a habit that I am still quite fond of," she added as an afterthought.

A crackling fire was glowing in the fireplace; evidently Harrison Beckett had been instructed to keep it going for warmth. These days Wellington House always seemed so cold and drafty. Grandmother took a sip of her sherry as she looked at us over the rim of her glass. "I suspect that there is more to this than your disapproval of my dining habits, Abigail. Let's not beat around the proverbial bush." She paused. "Out with it."

Aunt Abigail stood and crossed the room, standing near the hearth. She crossed her arms, rubbing warmth into her biceps. "I just wonder where you stand in all this. Sebastian Barrister and Marybeth Collingsworth intend to destroy the Wolf Pack, which will include your Granddaughter. Barrister has made it clear that he has nefarious plans for Bobby. I will fight against them, of course. I will do all I can to see that they are kept safe. But, I can't help but wonder, where does your allegiance lie?"

Grandmother placed her sherry on the end table. "I promised Katherine that I would allow no harm to come to either her, or her brother. I fully intend to keep that promise. It may come as a surprise to you, Abigail, but I do not want any harm to come to you, neither."

"Will you join us, then?" Aunt Abigail asked. "Can we count on your assistance to fight them?"

"I will do all that I can. But you must understand, as my maker, Sebastian Barrister holds considerable power over me. Going against him will not be easy. Extreme care must be taken."

"Then how can you possibly help us?" I asked.

She picked up her glass of sherry and took a small sip. "There are those in the Coven that are still loyal to me. Perhaps I can regain control and keep them out of the fight. Without the Coven's support, Sebastian Barrister is much weaker."

"Marybeth will not relinquish control of the Coven without a fight; she has support there as well," Aunt Abby said. "And it seems to be growing."

Grandmother almost laughed. She drained her sherry. "If it is a fight that Marybeth wants, then I will give her one. She will rue the day that she crossed me."

As we made our way back to the cottage, I noticed Bobbybear was holding the revolutionary toy soldier in his right hand. I recognized it as the one that I had first seen in the portrait of Sara Robinson up in the attic storage room. "Where did you get that?" I asked innocently.

Bobby shrugged. "Sara. She said I should take it to school."

I glanced quickly at Aunt Abigail, "I'm not sure that's such a good idea, Bobbybear."

Aunt Abby frowned. "On the contrary, I think it is an excellent idea." She seemed to know something that I didn't.

I still wasn't convinced. "What if those boys that bullied you take it away? It would be a shame to lose Sara's gift."

"They won't take it from him," Aunt Abby said confidently, a smile twisting her lips.

I frowned. "How can you be so sure of that?" I asked, shoving my hands into the pockets of my jeans.

Bobby gave me a small smile. "Sara said that it would protect me. As long as I had it with me they'd leave me alone."

I knelt down in front of him. "Bobbybear, it's just a silly toy. It can't protect you from those bullies. It's not a real soldier."

Aunt Abby scoffed. "Don't be so naïve, Kat. The soldier won't protect him, Sara will. She will watch over Bobbybear and see that no harm will come to him. The toy is just a way for her to stay connected with him."

I stood and looked at Aunt Abby as Bobbybear continued to walk along the path. "I don't want Sara hurting anyone."

Aunt Abby batted a hand in the air. "Oh, please. Those boys deserve whatever they get! Besides, I don't think she'll actually hurt anyone. I'm not sure she can."

"You don't know her like I do. Sara Robinson can be pretty scary, trust me." She had definitely given both Millie and I a pretty good fright months ago when we contacted her through Millie's Spirit Board. It still gave me chills just thinking about it, causing me to rub the goosebumps on my arms.

Bobby looked back at us as he waited for us on the path. He shook his head. "She promised she wouldn't hurt them. She'd only scare them."

I still didn't like the idea of Sara's interference.

Chapter Four

The Dawning

The following morning I gave Bobbybear a hug and kissed his forehead. Aunt Abigail wanted to take Bobby to school herself, and have a word with the elementary school administrator about the events of the day before; she was certain that she could prevent another altercation if the proper people were involved. I could only hope that she was right. Aunt Abigail was definitely a force to be reckoned with, especially when she was angry. I certainly wouldn't want to cross her.

Bobby simply shrugged and said that everything was already taken care of. Sara wouldn't allow any more harm to come to him; she'd promised. I wasn't convinced that the ghost of a girl who had died in 1884 could be that helpful; but what did I know? This was The Hollows, after all.

I tousled his brown curls and gave him a steady look. "Promise me you won't let Sara hurt anyone."

He nodded. "She won't. I already made her promise. She's

just going to have a little fun with them, that's all."

I sighed, giving my brother another kiss on the top of his head as I hugged him against me. "Okay. Wish me luck!"

He wrapped his tiny arms around my waist and grinned. "Good luck, Kat! Tell Millie I said 'good luck' to her too!"

I chuckled softly as I glanced at Aunt Abigail. "I will."

She winked over the edge of her coffee cup as she took a sip. She was never very talkative before she'd had at least one cup of strong coffee to get her going.

I left the cottage and went out to the pickup, tossed my backpack onto the seat and climbed in. This was the first time that I was in the truck alone, but I wasn't too worried. At least if I made any mistakes shifting gears, no one would know. I was getting pretty good at driving the truck, and didn't really think I'd have any problems; but I'd never driven in darkness and it had me slightly apprehensive.

The Chevy fired right up, but the headlights weren't on and I could barely see anything outside the truck. It took me a few minutes to find the knob that controlled the lights, and pulling it out, I was instantaneously rewarded with two yellow beams of light illuminating the road ahead of me. "Easy peasy," I said to myself. I took a slow, measured breath and let it out as I shook both hands in the air before grasping the steering wheel. I shifted the truck into gear and headed out.

As I drove past the garage of Wellington House, I could see Harrison Beckett preparing the Bentley to take Aunt Abby and Bobbybear to school. He waved a hand in the air greeting me, and I could read his lips wishing me a good morning. I waved back, quickly returning my hand to the steering wheel.

Ever since Sebastian Barrister had bitten Grandmother, Harrison Beckett had undergone a drastic change; even Aunt Abigail had noticed it. He seemed nicer now. It made me wonder if Grandmother had done something to him that caused this unexpected change. He was more likable now, at least I thought so; Aunt Abby said he was only more infuriating. I think she just missed their old verbal sparring. Even Margaret was different now. She seemed more docile than ever, and nervous all the time, which only led me to believe that Grandmother had done something to the household staff of Wellington House. I had to admit that living with a vampire under your roof couldn't be easy.

It was the only thing that made any real sense. She had to have done something to exert more control over them, otherwise they likely would have left once Grandmother had been turned into a vampire; but I hadn't noticed any bite marks on their necks… *How then, was she controlling them?* I wondered. I wasn't well versed in all this supernatural stuff, not like Millie. She was my mystical guru. I made a mental note to ask her about her thoughts on the matter. She might have better insight.

I slowed the old Chevy, downshifting into second gear as I neared the blacktop highway. I turned the steering wheel to the right; and then picked my speed back up as I shifted into third and then fourth, once I'd left the dirt road behind. The creaking of the undercarriage lessened as the pickup sped along the paved mountain highway. I couldn't help but smile; I truly was getting pretty good at this whole driving thing.

I slowed the truck down as I neared the bend in the highway where the accident had occurred. I could still see the massive blood stain in the center of the road where the deer had been ripped apart. The pearl-white Mercedes was gone from the side of the road, but I could see a dark splotch of red where the owner had fallen and bled out after being attacked by the wolf. Why I did it, I don't know, but I steered the Chevy onto the shoulder of the road and stopped. I turned off the ignition and just sat there, staring off into the woods.

I felt the hairs on the back of my neck begin to prickle. *Had I just seen a woman walking in the forest?* Without really thinking, I opened the door and slid out. Swallowing, I went around the back of the truck and walked down the slope and into the woods. I had to navigate the dew-covered embankment carefully so that I wouldn't fall. I called out. "Hello? Is everything all right? Do you need any help?" I could only imagine that the wife of the victim was terrified by what she'd seen happen to her husband, and possibly she was even hurt herself. She had to be cold, hungry and frightened beyond belief.

Why hadn't Tiffany and the other deputies found her yesterday? And if not them, the Wolf Pack? Brock had said that he and the guys planned on searching the woods after school; surely they would have found her. *Could she have hidden from them, somehow?* They had probably searched the woods while in wolf form. *But why hadn't they sensed her? Smelled her fear, at least.*

I could feel my heartbeat quicken as I stepped deeper into the forest. There she was, standing with her back to me, leaning against a tree for support. She must be cold. I could hear her whimpering. I reached out to her and lightly touched her shoulder. "It's okay. I only want to help you."

She straightened, and turned around to face me. I stumbled backward, and tripped, falling to the ground. I gasped in fright at the sight of the woman before me. Her skin was deathly pale and I could see two small puncture wounds from a bite on her neck. Dried blood was caked upon her skin and stained her shoulder and part of her chest. Her eyes were a fiery orange-red, as her mouth opened and I saw her sharp fangs extending; she was hungry. Ravenous.

I scrambled on my rump as best I could, digging my heels into the soft earth and pushing, the palms of my hands doing the same; I was desperate to get away. She took a step toward me and stopped, indecisive. Angry, she growled in frustration. Why she hadn't pounced on me, I didn't know; I was at her mercy. But then I felt the warmth of the golden rays of sunlight touch my skin and I looked back at where she had stood, but she was gone. Vanished.

I quickly stood up and ran back to the highway. I climbed into the truck, and turned the key in the ignition, but in my haste it wouldn't start right away. I was breathing heavily and my hands were shaking. I was furious at myself for never having considered the possibility that she had been turned. I forced myself to calm down and then I tried again to start the truck. The Chevy rumbled to life and I was on my way. I looked back at the woods in the rearview mirror but saw no signs of her. The sunlight had driven her away. I shook my head, berating myself. *How could I have been so stupid, so reckless?*

As I drove toward The Hollows my mind was racing through a myriad of possibilities, but only one made perfect sense. Officer Tiffany had stated that the man had been attacked and killed by a large wolf; my encounter this morning by the female vampire was most likely the man's wife. She had been bitten and turned by a vampire. It could be merely a coincidence and the two attacks were completely separate, but I didn't think so. It stood to reason that the attacker of both the husband and the wife were done by a single assailant: Tucker Morrison. If my suspicions were correct, clearly something would have to be done. Tucker was out of control.

I pulled up in front of Millie's house and she was on the porch talking with her Grammie. When she saw me she kissed her Grams on the forehead and bounded toward me, smiling happily, her eyes twinkling brightly. Mrs. Bradford waved at me with her knitting. She was a very sweet lady with a warm, kind face, nothing at all like my own grandmother. "You're certainly in a good mood this morning," I said as Millie climbed into the truck.

She chuckled softly. "I could barely get any sleep last night. Just thinking about being a cheerleader has got me feeling all giddy inside. I always thought it would be loads of fun. And if the Daughters of the Coven are actually extending the olive branch, who am I to push it aside?"

I raised my brows, smiling. "Okay. Breathe!"

Millie giggled breathlessly. "I know, right?"

She cocked her head at me and reached up and pulled a pine needle from my hair. Her brow crinkled with her curiosity. "You go out for a run this morning?"

I shook my head and rolled my eyes. "It wasn't intentional, believe me. I saw something in the woods on my way into town. When I went into the forest to investigate, I slipped and fell." I really didn't want to elaborate any further; Millie would only chastise me for being reckless, and I wasn't in the mood; I really didn't need anyone to point out how stupid I'd been. Besides, if she told Brock and the others I'd never hear the end of it. I figured it was best left unsaid. I had already learned my lesson.

We pulled into the parking lot and I turned off the ignition. I glanced over at Millie nervously. "Are you ready for this?"

Smiling she quickly nodded her head and giggled as she pushed her glasses back into place on her nose. "I'm nervous! I'm not sure what to expect. What if I flub up horribly?"

I smiled. "You'll be fine. I'll probably be the one to screw up. I've got two left feet."

Millie giggled. "Are we crazy for doing this?"

I raised both my brows, grinning. "Probably!"

We got out of the Chevy and headed to the gym to change into shorts. We were supposed to meet the others out on the ball field for practice. We were running slightly behind, time-wise, thanks to my little jaunt into the woods earlier, but that couldn't be helped.

As we left the locker room and stepped out the side door of the gymnasium Shelby spotted us and came skipping over, full of energy and all smiles. "Great! You made it! We were beginning to think you'd changed your mind!" She gave me a big hug and then looked at Millie. Shelby seemed truly pleased that she was there. "I'm glad that you decided to join us! This is going to be so much fun!"

Millie's smile grew. "I have to admit I wasn't sure about this."

Shelby flashed her a warm smile. "Look, I know that we've been kinda terrible to you in the past, and I am awfully sorry about that. We were mean and hurtful, just silly little schoolgirls. We've all changed now." She wrapped her arms around our shoulders and herded us toward the others. "Shall we get started?"

After nearly twenty minutes of grueling routines, involving jumps, twirls and high kicks, both Millie and I were starting to get the hang of things. We were actually enjoying ourselves; everyone seemed to be. Shelby called for a water break and headed to the ice chest and started handing out ice-cold water bottles.

Millie tilted her bottle against mine in a little toast. "This is so much fun!" she said happily. "I can't wait until Silas gets to see us perform!" I couldn't help but giggle at her unbridled enthusiasm. I had rarely seen her this happy. "I wonder when we'll get uniforms?"

Shelby tossed her empty bottle onto the ground near the ice chest. "We have time for one more routine before we need to call it quits. It'll be awesome if you two are willing to give it a try," she said looking at Millie and I.

Shelby gathered all of us together and eyed us critically. "Okay, I think we can make this work. Everyone is close to the same size. Millie is the shortest, so she'll be the top of the pyramid!"

I couldn't believe it. "Wait. What? A pyramid?" This didn't sound good. I didn't think Millie and I were ready for something that sounded so complicated.

Millie nodded nervously. "It'll be fine." I could see the frightened look in her eyes, but she obviously wasn't going to let her fear stop her. I had to admire her for that.

Shelby began to organize the girls. "Melissa, Sherrie and Kat will form the bottom rank. Cindy, you and Brenda will be the middle, and Millie can climb to the top."

I touched Shelby's arm. "I'm not so sure about this. Are you sure we're ready for something so complicated?"

Shelby flashed me a huge smile. "Relax, everything will work out. You just stand in between Mel and Sherrie. Hold onto Cindy and Brenda's legs once they stand on your shoulders; Mel and Sherrie will help. Cindy and Brenda will support Millie. It'll be fine. We've done this hundreds of times. We've got you."

"What about you? Where will you be?" I asked.

"Oh, I'm the Team Captain. It will be up to me to make sure everyone is doing their part. And once everyone is set, I'll take the picture."

I glanced over at Millie. "Are you certain you want to do this?"

She nodded with a grin. "Come on, Kat. It'll be a hoot!" she seemed eager. The encouragement from the other girls seemed to alleviate her earlier fears.

After a couple of miscues, we finally were able to get the pyramid formed. Shelby clapped her hands together and grinned. "That's perfect! Okay girls, do your thing." In the next instant I felt Melissa and Sherrie push me backwards, and I lost my grip on Cindy, and Brenda's legs; but it didn't matter, they were already jumping off my shoulders, letting go of Millie in the process. I heard Millie scream in fear.

As I fell backwards onto the ground I realized that there was nothing I could do to save my friend from harm. She fell awkwardly to the ground, and I heard the loud snapping of bone, followed by Millie's agonizing screams.

Shelby pressed a foot against my shoulder, holding me onto the grassy field. "Oh, by the way," she said with contempt, "you and your fat friend are off the team!"

As I scrambled to get to Millie's side, I saw the five Daughters of the Coven running across the field toward the gymnasium. All of them were laughing. Clearly it had all been a ruse to hurt us.

By the time I was able to get help for Millie, the bell had already rung. Millie's injuries were more than the clinic nurse could handle, so they were going to have to take her to the next town over, where Doctor Pendleton could set the broken bone in her leg. I was instructed to go to class; they wouldn't let me accompany her.

Instead of going to class, I went straight to the Principal's Office; something had to be done to punish the Cheer Squad – they couldn't be allowed to get away with this. When I got there, Shelby and her friends were just leaving. Shelby pouted as she leaned in and touched my arm. "It's a shame what happened out on the ball field. I never should've allowed someone as inexperienced as Millie and you to attempt the pyramid routine. Neither of you were ready for that. I hope she's okay." She spoke just loud enough for everyone in the office to hear. The evil grin on her face said it all.

I felt my blood beginning to boil. "You did this to Millie! You meant for this to happen. You planned it!" I was furious that we had been so duped.

She feigned astonishment as she placed a hand over her chest and gasped. "That's a horrible thing to say! And it's just not true at all." She indicated her friends with a grin, "We've already told Principal LaRoche what really happened." She mouthed with a smirk: 'Five against one.' There was no way that he would take my word over theirs, especially since one of them was his darling daughter. I knew I couldn't win.

I grabbed Shelby's arm tightly and pulled her against me. "This isn't over," I said.

She just smiled and hissed in a whisper, "You may have been the top dog back where you came from, but this is The Hollows. We do things differently here." She jerked her arm free. "Best you remember that, *dog*!"

After they had left, I barged into the Principal's Office and glared at him. "Whatever they told you is a lie. They intentionally hurt Millie!"

He frowned. "Of course they didn't. They all agreed that it was a tragic accident. Put this nonsense behind you. You need to get to class, young lady."

I didn't move.

"Go," he said with a hint of anger.

Chapter Five

Tucker's Invitation

The first chance that I got to talk to the Wolf Pack was at lunch. I wasn't hungry so I skipped the lunch line and went straight to their table. Silas gave me an anguished look. "What happened this morning? We've all heard about Millie's injury; it's all over school."

I glared across the cafeteria where Shelby and her friends were laughing and having a good old time, as if they'd done nothing wrong. It only made me angrier. "They did this to her," I said.

"Come on," Brock said. "They claim it was an accident. These things happen all the time."

I shook my head. "It wasn't an accident." I glared at him, fire in my eyes. "I can't believe you'd even say that."

He spread his hands. "Why would they intentionally hurt Millie? It doesn't make any sense."

I slammed my hands down onto the table. "Come on,

Brock! Open your eyes. It was intentional. They were sending a message. They hurt Millie simply because they could. She was an easy target." I glanced over at Silas apologetically. "If I hadn't convinced her to join cheerleading with me, she'd be fine right now. It's my fault. I should've seen this coming."

I could tell that Silas was upset. He seemed near tears. "I'm gonna go check and see if the office has any word on Millie."

Cho reached over and grabbed Silas's tray. "Go man, I'll take care of this for you." He slid his empty tray out of the way and started eating from the one that Silas had abandoned. The boy was always hungry.

I sighed heavily as I watched Cho eat. I ran a hand through my hair and smiled weakly at Brock. "I'm sorry, I didn't mean to snap at you like that. It's just been a crazy day."

He rubbed the back of my neck. "It's cool, don't worry about it."

"So," I said, stealing a French fry from his tray, "what did you guys find in the woods yesterday?"

"We found a couple of drops of blood. Footprints were all over the place, but that's about it," Brock said with a shrug. "The police seem to have done a pretty thorough job searching the area. We definitely caught Tuck's scent everywhere."

Cho swallowed. "Most of the footprints we saw probably belonged to the cops that searched the woods before us."

Brock nodded. "That's what we figure, anyway. We also found a couple of barefooted prints. One belonged to a male, the other a female. That's where we found the drops of blood. They didn't really lead anywhere; they just kinda disappeared."

I related my little experience in the woods this morning, and added, "She's probably the wife of the guy that was killed. Probably has a safe place to wait out the day somewhere close by." I looked across the cafeteria again. The Sons of the Raven and Tucker had joined the Cheer squad. "Have either of you talked to Tuck today?"

Brock glanced at Cho and then shook his head. "Nah, we haven't had the opportunity. Besides, he made it pretty clear the other day where he stands."

I sighed. "That isn't the point. We need to find out if he was responsible for killing those two. If he didn't then we may have an even bigger problem on our hands."

Cho shrugged. "It's not like he's gonna just come out and admit he killed those two."

Brock nodded. "I agree." He shook his head as he glanced in Tucker's direction. "Besides, it doesn't really matter. Tucker's become a loose cannon; we need to deal with him sooner, rather than later."

"What do you mean by that?" I asked.

Cho drew a finger across his neck, and both he and Brock just stared at me.

I felt the shock jolt me. "But guys, he's part of our Pack. He's our friend!"

Brock had a dark look on his face. He shook his head. "Not anymore. He knows us too well. We can't take the chance that he'll use that information against us."

Cho nodded his agreement. "It's either him or us."

I couldn't believe what I was hearing. They had all been as thick as thieves just a short time ago, and now they were ready to turn on him. "I'm not ready to just give up on him. I don't think that my grandpa would be either."

Brock and Cho exchanged brief glances, and then they both stared back at me. Brock's brow furrowed as he sighed. "Sam's not here," he said. "So it's up to me to decide what's best for the Pack."

I shook my head. "No. No, it's not. You guys made me Alpha. Remember? So I decide."

Brock stood up abruptly and grabbed his tray. "That's just great. Well, you let me know what your big plan is when you figure it out. I'm gonna get ready for my next class." He glanced at Cho. "You coming, Chow Mein?"

Cho looked at me sympathetically and shrugged. He placed his tray on top of the one Silas had left behind and followed Brock out of the cafeteria, leaving me at the table all alone to clean up after them. I sighed heavily; this day couldn't get any worse.

I had been so lost in my own thoughts that I hadn't seen Tucker approach. "Trouble in Paradise?" he asked as he took a seat beside me, grinning.

I felt my skin begin to prickle as he stared at me from behind those dark sunglasses. He must have been able to read the unease in my expression, because he chuckled softly. He reached out and placed his hand over mine. I gasped sharply. His hand was cold against mine. I swallowed, slipping my hand out from under his. Surprisingly, he allowed it. He sat there with a knowing smirk written across his lips. "We don't have to be enemies, Kat."

I swallowed. "I don't want to be your enemy Tucker. I still want you as my friend."

He pursed his lips in an amused smile. "Good to hear. Will you join us, then?"

"Us?" I indicated the group sitting across the cafeteria, "You mean them?"

He followed my gaze and then, looking back at me, he nodded. "Us."

I almost laughed. I shook my head in disbelief. *How could he ask me that?*

He placed his hand over mine and lightly squeezed. "I've always liked you Kat. I could make you a hybrid like me. We could run this town. We could have so much more. We would be unstoppable!"

My breath caught in my throat. I couldn't believe what he was saying. I shook my head again. "No. I won't abandon my friends."

He applied pressure to my hand. It was starting to hurt. "Don't be a fool, Kat. You don't know the power you're turning down. I am so much stronger now. Surely you can feel it? You can have that too. Join me." He pulled his sunglasses down his nose and looked at me over the rims. His eyes glowed with a frightening reddish-orange intensity. I felt like I was being drawn into their assurance of warmth and security… the promise of power. It was becoming increasingly more difficult to look away. I felt myself slipping, my free will beginning to dissolve. I was drowning in the fiery pools of his eyes…

I blinked. It took every ounce of strength that I had to resist his hypnotic gaze. Finally, closing my eyes tightly, I was able to pull my hand from his grasp. I looked away. I was breathing heavily as I kept my head down and my eyes averted from his. Panic and fear filled me. I wanted to scream and run, but I couldn't even do that; something was preventing me. His will was keeping me here. It was as though I were suddenly helpless.

I heard him chuckle as he stood beside me, running his hand over the back of my head. He leaned in close, his lips barely an inch from my ear. His cold breath sent chills down my neck. "It's the only way that I can keep you safe, Kat. You've got to think about what is best for your brother. Together you and I can keep him safe from Sebastian. You've got a week to decide. After that…" he sighed with a slight shrug, "well, things will get difficult for you, and him."

I closed my eyes tightly, feeling tears run down my cheeks. For the first time I was afraid.

Chapter Six

Ari

The bell rang, signaling the end of the lunch period but I continued to sit in the cafeteria, unable to move. I felt rooted to the spot, breathing hard as though I had been out for a strenuous run. The ultimatum that Tucker had delivered was unthinkable. I could never join him, betraying all those that I cared about. I wouldn't. I'd rather die. *But then what would happen to Bobby?*

My mind was racing. He promised things would become difficult for me in a week's time if I didn't agree to his insane proposition. The Daughters of the Coven had already struck against us, and Millie had paid the price. Tucker was likely responsible for the attack on the highway; the Pack had found his scent everywhere, which left little doubt as to what he was capable of. I knew next to nothing about the Sons of the Raven. And then there was Marybeth Collingsworth and the rest of the Coven to contend with, not to mention Sebastian Barrister. We were in serious trouble. The odds were stacked against us and our chances of survival were bleak. I could only hope that this Keegan Rourke that Grandpa was looking for, could help us.

A hesitant hand reached out and touched my shoulder, causing me to jump. It was Manny. "Easy there, Chiquita," he said with a smile, "We're friendlies."

Ari slid into the seat across from me and gave me a steady look as she crossed her arms over her chest. Her eyes were dark, steely, and impossible to read. "Maybe we are, maybe we're not," she said stoically, her head cocked slightly to the side as though trying to decide.

Manny seemed genuinely shocked by his companion's remark. He looked at Ari with concern. "She didn't have anything to do with what happened to Millie!" he insisted, sounding flabbergasted.

"Did you?" Ari asked bluntly, her eyes locked with mine.

I sat back in my seat and crossed my arms in front of me. "I would never do anything to hurt Millie," I said. I could feel the unexpected emotions flooding my voice and my eyes. I willed myself not to shed a tear, but I guess I wasn't that strong; I could feel them rolling down my cheeks, anyway.

Ari uncrossed her arms and leaned forward. "So what are we gonna do?"

I shook my head. "I'm not sure what you mean," I said.

Manny placed his hands on either side of the narrow table. "She means what are we gonna do to avenge Millie. We can't let them get away with this."

"I went to Principal LaRoche," I said.

Ari shook her head and rolled her eyes. "And how did that work out for you?"

I shrugged. "Not good. It was five against one. I couldn't really prove anything."

Manny frowned at me. "You do know that Melissa is the principal's daughter, don't you? He'll side with her and her friends every time. We haven't a chance against them."

I sighed. "I know that now. But it was worth a shot."

Ari watched me, her eyes narrowing to slits. "Where does Tucker Morrison stand in all this? He seems to be hanging out with a new crowd this year. He used to be so friendly, but now he hardly ever smiles, and when he does it's chilling."

She certainly had that right. I shook my head. "Tucker is a problem." I wasn't certain how much I should tell them about what I knew of Tuck. I didn't know how much they already knew. I had only recently met them, but I knew that they were friends of Millie's, or at least they had been last year. Since she had started hanging out with Silas, I wasn't sure where that left them. Were they okay with Silas, or did they resent him for taking Millie away from them? I couldn't be positive, so I decided to skip details.

Manny shook his head with a bemused smile. "What's with the dark glasses, anyway? Is he trying to act all cool or something?" He looked from me to Ari as though he were uncertain, and shrugged. "I mean, I had always thought he was a pretty cool dude. He was always nice to me. But now… he just seems… I don't know… different."

Ari continued to stare at me. She nodded slowly. "Did he have some kind of a falling out with his old friends? He seems awfully chummy with the Sons of the Raven now. They are a bunch of assholes."

The cafeteria manager stepped out from behind the service line. "Don't you kids have someplace you need to be? You can't stay here. Get out before I call Principal LaRoche."

"Shoot!" Manny said as he glanced down at his watch. "We're late already." He gathered up all the trays from the table and hurried off.

Ari gave me a look as we stood up from the table. "Shall we go?"

I sighed. "I'm not really in the mood to go to class," I said.

I just wanted to get away and think, clear my thoughts. I felt as though things were starting to spiral out of control.

She grinned suddenly. "I wasn't really talking about heading to class. I just figured we could go someplace and get away from all this craziness for a while."

I gave her a strange look. "What do you have in mind?"

Ari indicated the side door to the cafeteria with an inclination of her head. "Follow me."

She led me along the outside of the building, ducking low underneath a window of the classroom in which we should be in, and into the trees at the edge of the school campus. She grasped the chain-link fencing and pulled it toward her, revealing an opening into the woods beyond. I hesitated, and she gave me an insistent look. "Hurry before someone sees us."

I quickly ducked under the chain-link and stepped into the trees a few feet away and waited. Ari slid through the opening and joined me a moment later. "Where are we going?" I asked. I could feel an excited smile stretching across my face.

She took the lead. "There's a great spot nearby where we won't have to worry about getting caught. Stay close and follow me."

Ari led me through the thick clump of pines that skirted the edge of the schoolyard and deeper into the woods that hugged the southern end of The Hollows. I had never been in this part of the forest, but it seemed to be a normal wooded area, not much different than any other that I'd been in. I could only marvel at how she navigated through the forest. She moved silently, with a cat-like grace that left me feeling slightly envious. It was clear to me that she was at home in the woods, and I wondered if her silent steps across the ground were from years of practice or perhaps something else. Other than the sounds of nature, I was keenly aware of my own heavy movements. We went down a slope, up another, and then down again. Crossing a small creek that wasn't more than three feet wide, we climbed onto the top of a large, flat rock that stretched back over the stream.

Ari took her backpack off her shoulder and plopped it down. She sat upon the rock; her feet stretched out in front of her and leaned back on the palms of her hands. "This is one of my favorite spots," she said as she closed her eyes and took a deep breath.

I could immediately see why. The heavy scent of pine hung in the air all around us, the sounds of the small babbling brook offered peaceful tranquility, and birdsong filled the air. I plopped my backpack down and sat next to her, facing her. Smiling, I studied her silently, not eager to disrupt the quiet that surrounded us.

"It's so peaceful here," she said after a while.

I smiled. "It is," I agreed with a slight nod. I frowned as a thought came to me. "You said when we first met that you had seen me in the woods up near Valen's Ridge. But I never saw you…"

She chuckled softly, and shook her head. "Why would you? I wasn't there."

I crinkled my brow in confusion. "I don't understand. Why did you say you saw me there if you weren't even there? Are you some kind of a psychic or something?"

Ari bit at her bottom lip as she studied me, smiling through it all. She seemed to be enjoying this far more than I. After a moment she lightly shrugged and said, "My Grandmother is a Mohawk Medicine Woman, a Shaman really. My *akhsótha* has taught me many things. She has taught me to see through the eyes of others."

"So, what… you saw me through the eyes of one of my friends?" My confusion was only growing.

Ari chuckled again. "No. I cannot do that." She blushed slightly and grew silent as she looked away.

I reached out and touched her knee. "Then how? Help me to understand."

Ari sighed as she sat up, folding her legs in front of her. She frowned as she seemed to search for the right words, and then she looked into my eyes. "My *akhsótha*, my grandmother, is very in tune with the world around her. She is a very spiritual woman and can communicate with those that others cannot."

"Wait. You mean she can speak with the dead?"

Ari smiled and continued to speak softly. "That is only a very small part of what she does. She can communicate with animals and even the plants and trees of the forest. You see, my people, the Mohawk, believe that everything around us has a living spirit. Mother Earth is very real to us. Akhsótha believes in many gods, not just the one. Through her teachings I have learned much. She calls me *kanatakón:ha*."

"What is that?"

"It means sparrow. Akhsótha has taught me to be one with the little bird during a *Spirit Quest*. I can see through its eyes, even experience what it feels. That is how I saw you up near Valen's Ridge, I watched you from up in the trees."

"You were a bird?" I could feel my eyes grow wide.

Her smile slowly disappeared as she studied me. It was almost as if she were trying to decide something important. Finally, she smiled shyly. "I was the little bird, yes. I have been taught to transform into a sparrow, much like you are an *okwáho*, a wolf. I also know about the others. I've seen you in the woods a lot, actually."

"The guys?" I could only nod. "They're part of my wolf pack. My grandpa is the Pack's leader."

Ari touched my arm; she had a sly smile on her lips. "Yes, those too. But really I actually meant the others, the Gray and the White. The ones with the *spirit light* around them."

The shock of her words sent an unexpected jolt right through me. I felt all tingly as the goosebumps appeared on my arms. "You know about them? What can you tell me? Please, I need you to tell me everything!"

Ari chuckled softly. "Another time, perhaps. We should be getting back to school. I have a bus to catch and you need to pick up your little brother." She was right, the time had flown by and soon the final bell would sound; we were just going to make it back in time if we hurried.

Chapter Seven

A Little Good News

The last bell rang and the hallways were filled with bustling students as we re-entered the main school building and headed to our lockers. I didn't want the day to end, I had so many more questions that I wanted to ask Ari, but now there wasn't any time, and she had already disappeared in the thick sea of people rushing to leave the day behind.

Silas met me at my locker just as I was closing it. He took my backpack from me and inclined his head toward the exit. As we started walking it was clear that he wanted to talk. "Any news about Millie?" I asked raising my eyebrow, too impatient to wait for him to start the conversation.

He nodded. "Norma Shelton was a little reluctant to tell me, but I eventually won her over. She said that Doctor Pendleton's office called the school and said that Millie had suffered a compound fracture of her lower leg. They had to set it and they ended up putting a cast on her. She'll likely have to wear the cast for about eight weeks; but she should be good as new after that. She should be home now. I was wondering if you wanted to drive over to her house, after you picked up Bobby?"

I smiled at him and quickly nodded. "Of course I would! Why don't you come along and we can go together?"

He smiled. "That'd be great. I was hoping you'd ask."

We walked out to the parking lot and climbed into the Chevy. I fired it up and we drove the short distance down the street to the elementary school parking lot. We could see Bobby waiting for us behind the fence. Silas opened the passenger door and slid out with a grin. "How you doing kiddo?" he asked.

Bobbybear greeted Silas with a wide smile. "I'm doing good!" he said as he gave Silas a bear hug. "I wasn't expecting to see you."

Silas laughed as he gave Bobby an assist into the pickup. "You guys are giving me a ride to Millie's."

Bobby's brow furrowed. "Where is she?"

I placed a hand on Bobbybear's arm as Silas climbed in beside him. "Millie was hurt at Cheerleading practice this morning. She broke her leg and has been out all day."

Bobby's eyes went wide. "How did she break her leg?"

I sighed, "It was an accident."

Silas snorted with a roll of his eyes. I glared at him; my kid brother didn't need to know all the details. "Anyway," I continued, "maybe Millie will let you sign her cast."

Bobbybear's face brightened. "Wow! That'd be cool!"

"Did you have any trouble today with those guys that bullied you?" I asked as I drove back out onto the street.

Bobby chuckled. "Nope!"

Silas frowned. "What's this about?"

I shook my head. "The other day Bobby got into a fight with a couple of schoolyard bullies." I glanced down at my brother, almost certain that he wasn't telling me everything. "So?" I pressed. "What happened?"

Bobby shrugged. "They left me alone."

"Really? Just like that?"

Bobby chuckled again. "Yeah! Sara made their pants fall down to the ground, underwear and all! Everybody was laughing at them and they started crying like little babies. It was awesome!" Bobby's enthusiasm had Silas and I laughing right along with him. My side was beginning to hurt.

As we pulled up in front of the house that Millie shared with her grandmother, both she and her Grams were sitting out on the front porch, chatting. I could see sunlight flash on the metallic knitting needles as Mrs. Bradford continued to work on whatever project she was involved in. Almost as quickly as Silas had the passenger door open, Bobbybear was scrambling across his lap and descending onto the curb. "Millie!" his squeal of delight sounded.

She waved a hand in the air, seeming equally enthusiastic. "Hello boyfriend!" she blushed. "Hi Silas!" she added.

Silas chuckled as he shot me a look. "I've already been replaced."

I nodded as I came around the front of the pickup. "He was her first!" I frowned, scrunching my nose. "That didn't sound right."

He laughed. "No, it didn't."

I slapped him on the arm. "You know what I meant."

By the time that Silas and I got up to the front porch Bobby was already crawling onto Millie's lap and giving her a huge, comforting hug. I could see joyful tears wetting Millie's eyes as her glasses slid down the bridge of her nose. "Oh my!" she said, sounding overjoyed.

Mrs. Bradford got up and placed her knitting aside. "I'll leave you kids to it." She kissed the top of Millie's head. "I'll be inside if you need anything."

Millie smiled at the plump old woman. "Thanks, Grams."

Frowning, Bobby looked down at the cast on her leg and

pouted. "I've never seen someone with a cast before." He rapped upon the plaster with his knuckles. "Does it hurt?" he asked with a scrunched face.

Millie nodded. "It kinda does. But certainly not like it did when I fell. And when Doctor Pendleton reset it, well, let me just say, that really, really hurt!"

Bobby gasped, quickly drawing his hand away from the cast. "How did they reset it?" he asked.

"Well," Millie answered, "he had to pull on it to line the bones back up so that they would heal properly."

Bobby's eyes went wide. "Golly! Did you cry?"

She nodded. "I did. I could've used somebody strong like you to hold my hand."

He pouted again. "I was at school and didn't know, or I would've been there for you." He slipped his hand in hers. "But you can hold my hand now, if you want."

She hugged him and kissed his cheek. "Oh thank you, Bobbybear. You're here now and already I feel a whole lot better! Say, would you like to be the first to sign my cast?"

"Wow! That'd be cool! Can I sign it anywhere?" Bobby said as he hopped off her lap.

Millie giggled. "You certainly can, little man!"

I tousled Bobby's hair and said, "I think I have a *Sharpie* in my backpack. It's in the back of the truck."

Silas held out his hand for Bobby and winked at Millie and me. "Come with me and we'll dig through your sister's things!"

"Cool!" Bobby said enthusiastically.

As the Boys headed for the truck I knelt down in front of Millie and looked at her apologetically. I reached out and touched her arm tentatively; I guess I was afraid of hurting her further. It was silly, I know. "I'm so sorry for this, Millie. I never should have trusted those girls. You were right all along."

Millie shrugged. "It wasn't just you, Kat. I let myself get carried away too." She chuckled suddenly. "Literally, I mean. I was carried off the field." At least she could joke about it; that was a good sign.

"I went to the principal's office but Shelby and her horrible friends had gotten there first. He doesn't believe that they purposefully hurt you." I shrugged, feeling suddenly emotional at the anger rising within me. "There's nothing he'll do about it."

She shook her brown curls. "Of course not. His daughter is one of them. His little angel wouldn't purposefully hurt anyone. You were crazy to even think otherwise. Guess I was crazy to think Mel was different from the other girls."

"Manny and Ari have asked about you. They're both really concerned. Ari and I had a long talk after lunch. We kinda skipped out on the rest of our classes. She's really very nice. I like her."

Millie's eyes went wide behind the round lenses of her glasses. "You skipped school?"

I chuckled and batted a hand in the air. "It's not a big deal, honestly."

The guys were still at the truck. Silas was standing along the side of the pickup while Bobby was in the bed, hunched over my backpack. "Don't make a mess of my stuff!" I called out. "Geez. That was a mistake." I shook my head with regret. No telling what I was gonna find.

Millie giggled. And then she looked at me with a frown as she pushed her glasses back up the bridge of her nose. "So, you still gonna be on the cheer squad?"

I laughed out loud. "Yeah, right." I glanced at her and shook my head. "Shelby kicked us both off the team."

Millie sighed. "Oh thank God! I was afraid you were still gonna hang out with them!"

I shook my head. "Nope. Not gonna happen. You're stuck with me, kiddo!"

Tears rolled down Millie's cheeks and her bottom lip quivered as she spoke softly. "Honestly, there's no one I'd rather be stuck with. I was afraid I was gonna lose you."

I leaned in and gave her a hug. "That'll never happen!" I promised.

Millie giggled. "That's the best news I've heard all day!"

Once we got home, Aunt Abigail greeted us with a broad smile. She knelt down in front of Bobby and asked. "How was your day, sweetheart?"

"Great!" he said with a huge grin. "I got to sign Millie's leg today!" he stepped around her and ran into the cottage.

Aunt Abigail stood and gave me a curious look. "What was that all about?"

I sighed. "It's a long story. Did you talk to Belinda Michaels?"

She nodded, frowning. "I did. I don't think Bobby will have any more difficulty at school. It seems that your Grandmother paid Belinda Michaels a visit last night. She was very cooperative this morning when I spoke with her. As I stood in front of her she put a hand to her neck as though she were worried I might bite it or something. She stayed like that the whole time we talked."

"That sounds odd. You don't think that Grandmother bit her do you?"

Aunt Abby shook her head. "I didn't see any marks. But I'm certain that my mother threatened her with that very possibility if she allowed the bullying to continue. Your grandmother can be a very frightening person – especially now that she's a blood-sucking vampire."

Chapter Eight

Drawing Down the Moon

Friday seemed to take forever to arrive, and then the day dragged on at a miserably slow pace. I couldn't wait for the school day to end. I had promised myself, promised the Wolf within me, that tonight we would go for a run in the woods. It had been far too long since we had enjoyed that freedom. Neither of us would be denied. Besides, I needed time to think and I could best do that alone, surrounded by nature. And what better night than that of a full moon? I was only all too aware that time was quickly evaporating. Tucker would come soon for my answer.

Brock and Cho were being elusive and I couldn't get over the feeling that they were plotting something that they were keeping from me. Even Silas was being left out of the loop, and that was strange; usually the guys were thick as thieves. But, it really wasn't that unbelievable, really. Silas was spending a lot of his time doting on Millie, waiting on her hand and foot, and carrying her books to and from each class. Obviously, she couldn't be happier.

I, in turn, was spending more and more time with Ari and Manny, attempting to know them both a little better. Manny was a very shy guy, which is one of the reasons he had such few friends. He was extremely nice, slender of build and kinda geeky, not athletic at all. He was more obsessed with his grades than anybody I had ever known, and he always had either his math or science book open. He claimed his father would kill him if he didn't get straight 'A' marks in each subject. I could tell by the looks he gave Ari that he had a major crush on her, but she seemed not to notice. When she spoke, he hung on every word. Yep, to me it was obvious that he had it bad!

I could never tell if Ari enjoyed all the attention he was giving her, or if she was merely tolerating him just to be kind. She was definitely a hard nut to crack. She refused to give up anything about herself that would help you get to know her better unless she wanted to. I could only wonder why she was always so secretive. It had me wondering if she also was shy, or perhaps just very guarded.

Manny glanced down at his watch and gasped as he stood up from the table, hastily grabbing his lunch tray. "I need to get to class! I have a couple of things to look over. I think we're having a pop quiz today! Catch you both later," he said as he hurried off.

"Is he always like that?" I asked with a smile.

Ari had a slight grin twisting the corner of her mouth. "Always. Ever since fifth grade."

I studied her for a moment as I considered mentioning the fact that he had a crush on her. I finally decided to let it slide. She probably already knew. I just wondered how she truly felt about him. Were they merely friends in her eyes? Or did she hope for more, and was just waiting for him to get up the nerve to ask?

"Any big plans for the weekend?" she asked.

I felt the smile grow upon my face. "I figured I'd take a run in the woods. Nothing major. A little me time."

She glanced at me and nodded, biting her bottom lip. "You should take a run up near *Valen's Ridge* tonight. I hear there's a little *Wiccan* ceremony taking place. You might find it interesting."

I was shocked by this revelation of hers. "A *Wiccan* ceremony? How did you hear about that?"

She had a sly grin, which quickly disappeared. Her dark eyes continued to sparkle, giving her away. She spoke softly, "I keep quiet, keep a low profile, and I listen. People don't seem to notice me much, or they just don't care. It's almost as if they forget that I can speak and understand English." She shrugged. "So I hear things. Sometimes things I'm not supposed to."

I knew that tonight was a Full Moon, and that the witches of the Coven believed that the various phases of the moon held magical energies. Grandmother had recently told me that the New Moon helped the witches to begin certain tasks, conjure new spells; the Full Moon could bring their powers to fruition, while the Dark Moon could be used for intense *Spirit Travel* and *protection magic*. It all sounded a bit like *hocus-pocus*, but I knew that Grandmother was a firm believer in the mystical properties of the moon. It certainly pulled on the Wolf within me, always beckoning her to come out and play.

"Sounds like it might be interesting," I said. I continued to watch her closely.

"Good," Ari said as she crossed her arms over her chest. "Maybe I'll see you there."

Surprised, I slid my hand across the table towards her. "Wait. Are you attending the Wiccan ceremony?"

She had a pleasant sounding chuckle as she shook her head.

"No, not at all. I figured I'd watch it from a distance, if you know what I mean."

After dinner, I stepped into the parlor with Grandmother and Aunt Abby. Bobby had already run off to play with Sara; it was my chance to find out more about the ceremony that Ari had mentioned. Grandmother and Aunt Abby exchanged looks as they sipped their sherry. Finally Grandmother looked at me and smiled. "What is on your mind, dear girl? You've been chomping at the bit this entire evening."

I smiled sheepishly. "Was I really that obvious?"

Aunt Abby shook her head with a smile. "You're as bad as your mother."

I took a deep breath as I glanced from one to the other. "Tonight the moon will be full," I swallowed, "and I heard that a little ceremony is planned by the Coven." I paused, continuing to watch them both closely. Aunt Abigail stiffened as she placed her glass upon the mantle of the fireplace; she turned toward me with a furrowed brow, obviously uncertain where I was going with this; clearly she didn't like it.

Grandmother had a slight smile turning one corner of her mouth, her right brow arched noticeably. "The *Drawing Down the Moon*," she stated matter-of-factly. "It is a harmless ceremony, really."

"Unless the ceremony is tainted somehow," Aunt Abby said as she stared at Grandmother.

Grandmother practically snorted. "Honestly, Abigail. I cannot believe some of the things that come out of that mouth of yours. The ceremony is meant to pay homage to the *Triple Goddess*." She smiled at me. "It really is quite harmless."

"The Triple Goddess?" I asked. I had never heard of her before.

Aunt Abigail downed her sherry quickly, as though she had something distasteful in her mouth that she wanted to wash away. She winced. "In the Coven she is symbolized by the three phases of the moon; the crescent, full and dark moons."

Grandmother scoffed, shaking her head. "There you go again, spouting your nonsense." She turned to me. "The *Triple Goddess* merely refers to the waxing, full and waning moons. There is absolutely nothing sinister to be found."

Aunt Abigail shook her head and rolled her eyes as she took a seat beside me, placing a hand upon my knee. "That may once have been true, but now, with Sebastian Barrister's influence upon the Coven I doubt it seriously. He brings darkness upon us all. The man is vile and corrupt. He is turning the Coven into a dangerous enemy. No one is safe."

Grandmother slammed her glass down upon the table beside her. "Am I your enemy as well?" she asked sharply.

Surprisingly, Aunt Abby remained calm. She took a deep breath before she spoke. She looked at Grandmother and said, "Mother, you have lost control of the Coven. Marybeth Collingsworth is not the strong priestess that you once were. She is far too easily manipulated. Her hunger for power draws the Coven down a very dark path. She will allow Sebastian Barrister to destroy everything. Everything that you have built, she will see it fall into ruin just to gain his favor and to please him. Her lust for power could be the Coven's downfall. You, at least, had some common sense."

I could see Grandmother's grip on her cane tighten. She knew that what Aunt Abby said had merit. And if she was right... The shake of her head was barely noticeable. She kept her silence. I could see that her jaw was clenched.

After a moment I cleared my throat. "May I be excused? I have to meet a friend."

Grandmother nodded absently, still lost in her own thoughts. "Of course, dear."

Aunt Abby gave me a warning look but said nothing. I stood and looked at her. "Will you see Bobby gets home safely?" She nodded. I closed the parlor door as I stepped out. It was a little after seven. I needed to hurry if I wanted to get up to *Valen's Ridge* in time for the ceremony.

Leaving Wellington House, I followed the path toward Aunt Abigail's cottage. Once I had the cabin in sight, I veered off into the woods and found a secure spot to strip out of my clothes. There was a slight chill in the air and I could feel the goosebumps starting to rise on my skin. I pulled the waterproof bag out of its hiding spot in the twisted pine, folded my clothes into the bag, and returned it all back to the shielded little nook. I could tell that the Wolf was excited. She was ready for a bit of freedom. I turned toward the north and began to run, morphing into the Wolf as I leapt over a fallen log…

The Wolf pulled against my mind wanting complete control but I pushed back, denying her wish. I needed to maintain the ability to revert back into human form if the need arose. Experience had taught me not to give into the Wolf's desires fully – she was reluctant to give control back and if I allowed her, she would wander for hours on end. Tonight I had a singular purpose in mind. I felt that I needed to witness the *Drawing Down the Moon* ceremony. I needed to maintain a certain amount of control.

The Wolf slowed as the human sounds broke through the natural tranquility of the forest. Up ahead we could see the flickering light of torches and the excited chattering of human females gathering together. I urged the Wolf closer, eager to witness the unfolding milieu taking place. It was a large clearing that was surrounded by tall Northern Pines. Torches burned from sconces mounted on long poles stuck into the ground at the outer perimeter of the circle of white-robed women. The firelight only aided my approach, making it difficult for them to see more than a few feet into the woods; the flickering flames would blind them to anything beyond that. Clearly, they were not expecting company. I edged closer to a position that gave me a good view of the Coven members. Their gowns seemed to glow like flimsy, delicate gossamer in the firelight.

It was a star-filled night, noticeably absent of clouds of any kind. The great sphere of the moon hung high above the clearing, full and majestic in radiant silver splendor. Excitement was in the air; it truly was a magical setting to behold. I heard a fluttering in the boughs of the pine above me. A Great Horned owl gazed down at me with bright, yellowed eyes. "*Whooo?*" it called as if expecting an answer from the Wolf.

Turning my attention back to the Coven, I could see the members swaying side to side, their bare feet barely making a sound as they twirled about, their hands reaching toward the stars. Someone was singing a tune in a language that I couldn't understand; others began to softly join in, adding their voices to the first. I could hear the soft plucking of harp strings from somewhere nearby. Marybeth Collingsworth was sitting upon a wicker throne, looking resplendent in a deep blue, sequined gown that caught the firelight. To her right was Sebastian Barrister. He almost seemed out of place wearing his dark, pinstriped suit. Both were smiling as if sharing some dark, sinister secret.

I followed Marybeth's gaze, she was staring at the center most group of girls, the Daughters of the Coven, and her pride was clearly evident. Shelby looked stunningly beautiful; her gown seemed to float in the air as she danced. Her hair was adorned with small white flowers that reminded me of baby's breath in a bouquet of deeply red roses.

Marybeth stood and held her hands into the air, gazing up at the heavens she spoke in a reverent voice, "O Divine One, Goddess of the Night, the Stars and the Moon, You have been known in many lands, since the time of the Ancients, by many names, yet You are Constant and Universal. In the dark of night shine down upon us and bathe us in Your light and love."

The Daughters of the Coven seemed to dance away from Shelby, leaving her alone in the center of the ring. She spread her feet apart, about shoulder width. Her arms rose up into the air, out away from her body. I could feel an unexplained surge of energy taking place. Shelby spoke in a voice that rang out, full of power, clearly not her own. "I am the vessel from which All Things spring forth. The One who watches over all. I am the wind in the sky, the spark in the fire. Honor Me on this night of the full moon. I crash the tides upon the shore; I shine on the mighty trees of the forest. Honor Me and receive My Blessing!"

The witches all responded, "We honor Thee, Bless us one and all."

The Coven turned toward Shelby, arms raised high overhead they seemed to bend towards her in supplication, their voices singing a melodic chant with words that I did not understand. Shelby lowered her gaze and stared right at me; her eyes seemed to shine with a brilliant green light as a smile slowly appeared across her lips. Her right hand lowered and pointed towards me. "We are not alone!" she said.

Instinctively, the Wolf backed away slowly as though she were startled; I could feel the hairs on the back of her neck stand on end. The Great Horned owl dropped from the tree above me. It seemed to flutter anxiously in front of the Wolf. "*Whooo!*" it screeched loudly as if urging me to follow. It darted through the forest, low to the ground.

Members of the Coven were rising, turning toward me with angry faces.

Chapter Nine

Over the River and Through the Woods

The Wolf continued to chase after the owl, desperate to distance herself from the danger the Coven represented. I tried desperately to seize control of the Wolf but my mind was still reeling. Afraid, she refused to relinquish herself to me. Fear had strengthened her and she pushed back fiercely against all of my attempts. In the distance I could hear the familiar voices of the Sons of the Raven. Though I hadn't seen them at the ceremony, they were pursuing me now. I wasn't worried about them as much as I was of whom else might also be chasing me. I knew I could outrun the Sons of the Raven easily enough. It was the others that I was most fearful of.

If the Sons of the Raven were present at the *Wiccan* ceremony, as well as Sebastian Barrister, I was certain that Tucker Morrison was there too. I feared him most of all, even more than I did the vampire. I wasn't ready to face him all alone. I knew that Tucker and Barrister would be much harder to evade than the others;

they could fly, and Tuck had the honed instincts of a wolf.

The Great Horned owl continued to fly low to the ground, allowing the Wolf to follow. *"Whooo!"* it screeched again. *Was this Ari?* I couldn't be sure, but the owl seemed to be guiding the Wolf through the forest.

We crossed a stream, and once on the other side, the Wolf stopped and searched the forest we had just gone through. The Great Horned owl turned and swooped in front of the Wolf and fluttered in midair. *"Whooo!"* it insisted. The boys hadn't yet given up their pursuit, and still in control, I urged the Wolf forward, deeper into the woods, following the owl.

I had never been this far from Wellington House, and I had no idea where I was. The path we were following started climbing higher and then seemed to level out. The Great Horned owl landed on a branch of an old knotted pine and seemed to study us with its large yellow eyes; clearly it would lead us no further. Sounds of pursuit were farther off now and I hoped that they had finally given up. But the thought that if Tucker was among them greatly disturbed me. *Would he give up so easily?* I had my doubts. *And what about Barrister?*

The Wolf glanced up at the large owl and barked once. The owl seemed disinterested as it tucked its wings in close to its body. *"Whooo?"* it responded.

I could see that the moon seemed to be encircled within a large blue ring, like a halo in the sky. I heard the chirp of crickets, as the forest seemed to settle around me. Looking up at the moon I saw a large bat flying. Fear gripped me. The snap of a branch brought my vision back to the ground; a large dark wolf was emerging up the path. Panicked, I turned and urged the Wolf to run, frantically dodging trees and rocks.

I could hear the larger wolf's pursuit, and glancing up I could see the bat still flying above me, angling to cut me off. I was in serious trouble. Without the Wolf Pack to help me I didn't stand a chance. Then the owl flew across my path, not once, but twice. *"Whooo!"* it seemed to beckon for me to follow. With little other choice, I did.

It turned toward what I thought was slightly northwest, through a thick strand of Eastern White Pines, with long, horizontal branches that seemed to spread out toward one another. The owl glided through the limbs, keeping fairly low to the ground. Eventually the trees parted and it landed on a wooden post that was driven into the ground. Two other slats of wood were nailed to the post, stretching upward forming a V shape. There appeared to be two skulls at the top of each upward point of the V. One skull was canine in appearance, the other quite human, or near enough. The Wolf stopped, eyeing the Great Horned owl with trepidation. The Wolf seemed to be waiting for me to make a decision as the owl blinked and called out yet again, *"Whooo?"*

I heard the large wolf stop behind me as well as the sound of something from above touching down upon the ground. I could hear the shifting of canine bones morphing into human form. Turning, I saw Tucker standing naked beside Sebastian Barrister, his ebony skin glistening with sweat. "Hello Kat," Tucker said with a leering smile. They both stepped forward.

The Wolf sensed the danger we were in but she also knew that it was senseless to try and out run our enemies. Still, I sensed in her a reluctance to abandon me. She lowered her head, spreading her front paws upon the ground, her back hunched as though ready to spring. A vicious growl escaped the Wolf, warning our enemies not to come any closer.

Sebastian Barrister chuckled without humor as he glanced at Tucker. "She is a feisty one, I'll give her that. No wonder you want her so badly."

Tucker gave a sideways glance at Barrister and then faced me, his smile disappearing. "Time for you to decide how this ends, Kat."

Barrister reached out with his right hand, halting Tucker

where he stood. "She's not alone," he hissed, suddenly sounding angry.

Emerging out of the woods to my left, two wolves, the Gray and the White, shrouded in their ghostly aura, joined my side. Both snarled viciously, threatening my enemies to come no closer.

Sebastian Barrister glared at the three of us. "This isn't over." A second later he turned to mist and simply vanished.

Tucker took a deep breath, curled his lip into a snarl. Clearly he was unhappy that he had been abandoned. "This isn't over!" he repeated as he turned and morphed back into his wolf form. He disappeared back down the way he had come, thrashing wildly through the forest undergrowth. The Great Horned owl blinked once, spread its massive wings and took flight.

The Gray and the White wolves turned to the northeast and sauntered off a short distance. They turned back to me and barked once more before they continued through the forest. Evidently I was expected to follow. I hesitated for a moment, looking back up at the skull adorned V. It was only then that I noticed that the human skull actually had two extended incisors on its top row of teeth. Was this mysterious signpost a warning for vampires and wolves? The White returned and barked again, this time it sounded more insistent. The White and the Gray had never led me into a dangerous situation before; they had only sought to help me. I urged the Wolf to follow, and she seemed eager to go.

As we moved through the forest both the White and the Gray continued to stay just ahead of me, but not too far. They always made sure that I could easily see one or both of them. It was almost as if they were insuring me safe passage through the woods. Whenever one moved out of sight, the other would drift back closer to me. It gave me a good feeling knowing that they were watching over me. I had felt a kinship with them ever since Bobby and I had first seen them outside the hospital when

Mom had died.

That had been back in the City. Now we were further north in the mountain community of The Hollows where strange things were the norm. Bobbybear had asked when we first saw the wolves with the ghostly light if they were Mom and Dad. At the time I didn't think it was possible. But now, I wasn't so certain. These wolves had traveled back to 1884 and helped me to save Bobbybear when he and Sara Robinson were attacked. They seemed to always be watching over both my brother and I.

The scent of woodsmoke seeped through the forest and apparently the White and the Gray were leading me right to its source. As we crested a small hill, I could see a log cabin nestled amongst the trees below. In front of the cabin was a clearing of sorts. Both the White and the Gray bounded down the hill as an old Indian woman stepped out of the cottage. I hesitated on the top of the hill, uncertain.

I watched in fascination as the old woman held her hands out to the wolves, palms downward. Both wolves brushed her weathered hands with the tops of their heads. She spoke to them, but I couldn't make out the words; they were in the old woman's native tongue. A moment later the bluish-white glow seemed to move up the woman's arms, until she was completely encompassed, and then it faded from her, remaining solely around the wolves. I saw a familiar figure emerging from the cabin. Ari started walking towards me, carrying a large, thick blanket.

She smiled at me as she offered the blanket. "I see that you made it. This is for you. Come, my akhsótha wishes to speak with you."

Chapter Ten

Okwaho Tekahionwake

I morphed back into human form and was immediately grateful for the blanket that Ari had brought me. It was hand-made, thick, warm and inviting. I glanced at Ari as we began to walk toward the cabin. "Were you the owl at the ceremony, the one that led me here?"

Ari chuckled as she shook her head. "No. I told you that I can only take the form of a sparrow. Tonight I was using the eyes of the *tsihrtékeri* to see. I was also telling her that she needed to lead you to safety when it became necessary. You were wise to follow."

"I was followed," I said with a shiver. I knew that I had come extremely close to a horrible fate. Sebastian Barrister had already threatened to kill everyone I cared about, including me, and then saving Bobby for a special fate. Tucker had given me an ultimatum to join him, to become a hybrid, or suffer the consequences. Neither was appealing. Just thinking about how close they had come to achieving their goals tonight, caused tears to fill my eyes. I just wanted to curl up into a ball and escape.

Ari looked at me and nodded slowly. She placed a hand on my arm, and then seeing the troubled look on my face, she pulled me into a firm hug. "You are safe here."

I believed her. With the warmth of the blanket I was feeling better already.

By the time that we reached the cabin, the Gray and the White wolves had slipped off into the forest. Ari's grandmother, her *akhsótha*, had already entered the cabin and was waiting patiently. With a hesitant glance at Ari, I went through the door that she held open.

There were very little furnishings in the main room of the cabin, no actual furniture to speak of, other than a single shelf and a couple of large, plush pillows sitting on a hand-woven rug that surrounded a small metal brazier where hot coals glowed an orange-white. I was surprised that such heat was being put off by such a small source.

The old Mohawk Medicine Woman watched me with wizened eyes as she extended her offer to sit with an outstretched hand. "I have long awaited this night," she said as her eyes sparkled and the corners of her mouth turned upward. "Sit," she said, "we have much to discuss." She glanced at Ari, "*Kanatakón:ha*, prepare for the *Spirit Quest*."

I looked from the old woman to Ari, and then back again. "Spirit Quest? I'm sorry, but what is this about?"

The old woman waved Ari away with a brush of her hand in the air. She smiled at me as Ari left the room. "Relax, little one. I know you have questions. I will do my best to see that the answers find you."

"The two wolves that led me here," I swallowed as I looked at her closely, "can you tell me about them?"

Her eyes seemed to sparkle in the dim light of the cabin as

she silently watched me. It was almost as though she were sizing me up; for what, I didn't know. Finally she lifted her shoulders slightly and let them drop again. "This is not the first time that they have come. This is *Sacred Ground*. My people have lived here since the beginning. Mother Earth has been kind to us, and we in turn, respect Her and all Her children."

"I've seen the two wolves before. The night my parents were both killed in a car accident, my brother and I saw them outside my mother's hospital room."

She said nothing. She just continued to watch me in silence. There was something reflected in her dark eyes, sadness, it seemed. But it was fleeting and soon was gone, leaving me to wonder if I had actually seen it at all.

"I'm almost certain it was the same two wolves," I added nervously.

She nodded. "Perhaps. Time and distance means little in the Spirit World."

Ari returned with an earthenware bowl of what looked like finely crush herbs. She placed it down beside the brazier, close to her grandmother. She glanced at me and smiled shyly, before looking away and concentrating on her task. She stood and silently left the room and returned a moment later with a long match. She placed it beside the bowl and then departed once again, drawing a curtain closed behind her, leaving me alone with her grandmother.

The old woman picked up the match and lit it from the hot coals in the brazier. She looked into my eyes and said, "It was no accident that killed your parents, my child."

I felt the shock jolt me as though I had been struck in the chest with something hard. I was having trouble breathing for a moment. Finally, I was able to recover, gasping for breath that didn't want to return. "What do you mean? Are you saying that my parents were murdered?"

Her eyes locked with mine. "Your father was meant to die in

the crash, not your mother."

My mind was racing. If what this old Mohawk medicine woman was saying was true, that meant that someone had wanted my father dead, and my mother was just collateral damage. The ramification of what she had said led me to only one possible answer, and I didn't like it: Grandmother!

Tears filled my eyes, blurring my vision. I could feel them rolling down my cheeks, dripping off my chin onto the thick blanket. I had a sick feeling in the pit of my stomach. There was no other explanation. Grandmother had somehow orchestrated the vehicle accident in order to kill my father. *But what could she hope to gain by his death?* And then I knew.

With my father out of the picture, Mom would have little choice but to return to The Hollows with my brother and I. Living in the City would no longer be an option she could afford. She would have to return to Wellington House. Grandmother would have her family back. That's how Grandmother knew to send Aunt Abigail to the City for Bobbybear and I. It had all been part of her plan. The only flaw, was that Mom succumbed to her injuries as well. That's when she devised the diabolical plan to send Bobbybear back in time to kill my grandfather, thereby preventing my mom from ever becoming a wolf. With Samuel St. Claire dead, my dad would never have been born. There wouldn't be a reason for my mom to leave The Hollows in the first place. It all seemed so very clear to me now.

The only question remaining was what to do with this information?

I quickly got to my feet, casting the thick blanket aside. "I need to go," I said.

The old woman's eyes sparkled. "But the *Spirit Quest…?*"

"Another time, perhaps…" I said as I turned and left the cabin. Stepping outside I put a trembling hand over my mouth, resisting the urge to puke. I could feel a huge knot in the pit of my stomach. I morphed back into the Wolf as soon as I was clear of the porch.

Ari stepped from the cabin and called out to me, but I refused to listen. My mind was full of thoughts tripping over themselves. *How could my own Grandmother be so cruel?* I couldn't allow her to get away with this.

Chapter Eleven

Confrontation

I ran from the cabin hoping that the Wolf's sense of direction would take me where I wanted to go. The old woman's revelation had me completely rattled. All thoughts of Tucker Morrison and Sebastian Barrister were nowhere in my mind. I could only hope that in my present state that I didn't come across either of them. I was a mess. The realization that my grandmother was responsible for my parent's deaths had completely floored me. *How could she be so heartless? So cruel? Did she even feel any remorse for the vile act that she had orchestrated? Did she even care? How could anyone be that selfish?*

I was angry. I was glad that the Wolf was in control. I was feeling reckless, which could easily land me into serious trouble, especially with so many of my enemies in the woods. My rage had blinded me to rational thought. All I wanted to do was confront my grandmother with everything that I knew. I was ready to end her unnatural existence. Hopefully, the run through the forest on my way back to Wellington House would give me the opportunity I needed to calm down before I did anything that I'd later regret.

By the time I returned to the spot where I had stashed my clothes I was exhausted. I was no longer set on driving a stake through my grandmother's heart, but I was still pretty upset. I briefly considered putting my little talk with grandmother off, but quickly changed my mind as I dressed. If I waited until tomorrow evening, Aunt Abigail would immediately see that I was upset about something, and she would demand to know why. She would undoubtedly already be curious about where I had been tonight, especially after inquiring about the *Wiccan* ceremony.

I returned my mother's watch to my wrist and noticed it was just past 1:30. Margaret and Harrison would most likely already have turned in for the evening. Grandmother would still be up, I was certain. But where in the manor I'd find her was another question altogether. I figured I'd start with the parlor.

As I entered the front door of Wellington House I was surprised to see Grandmother descending the stairs. She smiled down at me, "Katherine, what an unexpected surprise." The look she had on her face clearly said that she wasn't surprised at all. It was almost as though she were expecting me.

I swallowed as I took a deep breath to calm my heightened nerves. My fists were clenched tightly at my sides, my nails digging into the palms of my hands. I had to do something to hold my rage inside. "Good evening Grandmother. I was hoping we could have a little talk, just the two of us."

As she stepped off the staircase she swept a hand toward the direction of the parlor. "Shall we adjourn to the parlor? I have a feeling that a glass of sherry might be in order, and you can warm yourself by the fire."

I nodded and turned toward the left, heading to the parlor. I could hear the tap, tap, tap of her cane upon the flooring as she followed along behind me. I wanted to scream. I wanted to cry my eyes out in despair. My emotions were in turmoil. I could feel her eyes upon me, boring into the back of my head. The crackling of the fire sounded warm and welcoming, it had been a chilly night, and without the thick fur of the Wolf the cold seemed to cut right through me.

I held the doors to the parlor open, allowing Grandmother to enter ahead of me. She went straight to the decanter that held the sherry and poured a glass. She sat down in her chair with a slightly amused expression lighting her eyes and a small smile on her lips as she watched me cross to the hearth. Finally, she said, "Tell me, dear, did you witness the *Drawing Down the Moon* ceremony? I assume that is where you ran off to."

"You know what they say about assumptions, Grandmother."

The smile left her face and her eyes grew cold as her jaw tightened. "Do not continue with this snarky attitude of yours. I do not like it, and it certainly won't be tolerated in Wellington House."

I nodded, suddenly ashamed by my rudeness. "I'm sorry Grandmother. This isn't how I wanted this to go." Truth was, I wasn't entirely sure what I was hoping for. I guess I wanted her to convince me that she wasn't involved in my parents' death; offer another plausible explanation. But deep down I knew that wasn't in the cards. There was very little she could say to convince me that what I already knew was merely a fabrication.

She placed her sherry down onto the small table next to her chair. "You're spending entirely too much time with Abigail, picking up her cryptic sayings. Why don't you cut to the chase, Katherine? What is this really about?"

I knelt in front of the hearth and extended my hands toward the flames. My hands were shaking. I sighed in disappointment; the fire gave me little warmth. Inside I still felt incredibly cold and angry. I could feel tears welling up in my eyes. I clenched my jaw tightly as I stood and faced her. "How did you know to send Aunt Abigail for Bobby and me?"

Her eyes narrowed. "I received a call from the State Police informing me of the accident."

I shook my head and stared up at the ceiling for a moment. "That couldn't be true, Grandmother. There wasn't enough time. And even if it were, Aunt Abby could not have gotten there so soon." I stared at her as the tears ran down my cheeks. "Why would you lie about something like that?"

Her eyes flashed in anger. "I'd be very careful about what you say, my dear. I do not like to be called a liar, especially in my own home."

I shrugged as a humorless laugh escaped me. "Then don't lie!" It couldn't be any simpler than that.

She stood quickly, the fire behind her eyes blazing white-hot. "I don't know where you are getting your information, but it sounds absolutely ludicrous. I will not be treated in this manner by you, nor anyone else!" Her eyes turned red as they drifted down to my neck where I could feel my pulse throbbing. "I suggest you leave while you still can!" she hissed.

I could see her incisors growing long and pointed. I took a faltering step back, my hand going to my neck, instinctively. *Would she really do this to me – her granddaughter?* I had no reason to believe that she wouldn't. She'd already killed her own daughter and son-in-law.

"Go, Katherine!" she said, seemingly ready to pounce. Her fury had fueled her hunger.

I nodded and managed to squeeze past her. I quickly left the parlor and ran out of Wellington House. I didn't care if I never returned; I just wanted to get away. Blindly I ran around the corner of the old Manor and collided with Harrison Beckett, causing him to drop his liquor flask onto the ground as he grabbed my arms to keep us both from falling.

Tears filling my eyes, I swallowed. "I'm sorry, I wasn't watching where I was going."

The whites of his eyes seemed tinged with red, his voice was thick, heavy with drink. He chuckled softly. "Been to see your grandmother, eh? Taking quite a chance aren't you? She hasn't gone out to feed yet." He chuckled softly, as if sharing a joke.

"Please, let go of me," I said, brushing his hands from my biceps. "I need to be getting back to the cottage, Aunt Abigail is expecting me."

He looked me over, swaying slightly. He wiped his mouth on his sleeve. "Pretty little thing like you shouldn't be wanderin' alone out in the woods this time of night. There's all kinds of horrors lurking in the shadows." He grinned at me. "Maybe you should let me take you home." He smiled. "I could protect you."

I could feel the hairs begin to prickle upon my skin. The look in his eyes warned me that he didn't truly have my safety in mind, far from it. I tried to step around him. "I'll be fine."

He grabbed my arm and pulled me against his chest. I could feel his breath on my face; smell the bourbon. He chuckled again; I almost gagged. "Don't be in such a hurry," he said, a slight edge to his voice. "I'm just tryin' to be nice."

"Take your hands off my granddaughter!" My grandpa came out of nowhere. He pried us apart and slammed Harrison against the side of the Manor; I could hear his skull smack upon the side of Wellington House. How he managed to remain conscious, I'll never know. Perhaps he didn't hit as hard as I had thought, but it certainly sounded that way. "If you ever lay a hand on her again it'll be the last thing you ever do!"

Harrison Beckett raised both his hands into the air and said. "Take it easy. I was only trying to help her get home safely. You should thank me."

Grandpa quickly grabbed him by the collar, and seemed close to hitting him. I put my hand on his arm and stopped him. "Please, Grandpa. Just let him go." I just wanted to get back to the cottage.

Grandpa sighed heavily and then roughly flung him aside. "I'll make sure she gets home. You'd best get out of my sight."

He kept his eyes on Harrison Beckett until the man had disappeared in the direction of the garage. He turned to me and placed a hand on my elbow. "Are you okay, kiddo?" he asked.

I threw myself against him in a comforting bear hug. "I am now. Thank you."

Chapter Twelve

Grandpa's Return

Aunt Abigail practically flew off the porch of the cottage and into Grandpa's chest as we approached. I had to quickly step to the side to avoid being hit by her outstretched arms. "Oh Sam! I'm so glad you're finally home!"

He chuckled softly as he hugged her tightly, lifting her feet up off the ground. He twirled her in a circle before setting her down, planting a big kiss on her lips. "Did you miss me?"

She slugged his shoulder. "What do you think?"

"So," he asked as they both stepped onto the porch, holding hands, "did I miss anything important?"

I looked at Aunt Abigail and then at my Grandpa. He had missed so much. She looked at him and motioned for him to take a seat on one of the rocking chairs sitting on the porch. "Have a seat, and we'll tell you all about it."

He frowned. "How's your mother doing? Did she survive the attack from Barrister?"

Aunt Abigail's right eyebrow shot up her forehead as she pushed him toward the rocker. "Let me get you a whiskey first."

He took her hand, preventing her from slipping away. "Don't bother. I think I'd like to hear this straight, if you don't mind."

Aunt Abby nodded. She quickly reached out a hand and prevented me from slipping into the cottage. "Stay, Kat. You can help me bring your Grandpa up to date."

I shrugged. "Sure," I said. Feigning exhaustion wasn't going to get me out of this one no matter how convincing I was. I yawned anyway. I was actually very tired, but I knew with everything that was buzzing through my mind, I'd have difficulty getting to sleep.

Aunt Abby started pacing as she organized her thoughts. I plopped down in the other rocking chair and waited, giving Grandpa a sheepish little smile. Finally, she stopped and faced him. "We couldn't save Mother. She succumbed to the bite."

I saw Grandpa tense up. "Did she… did she turn?" he asked.

Tears filled my aunt's eyes, and as she nodded, they trickled down her cheeks. Her bottom lip actually quivered slightly. "Yes, and in the process she fed off one of the boys. Tucker. She drained him."

Grandpa looked over at me with furrowed brows. I sighed and then added, "Tucker's been changed. He's some sort of hybrid. He's stronger now, a lot stronger. He showed up for the first day of school like nothing had ever happened. But I could tell he was different."

Grandpa shook his head as he gripped the arms of the rocker. "How is that possible? You said he was some sort of hybrid; does that mean he is a vampire now too? Does the wolf in him enable him to be out in the sunlight?"

Aunt Abby ran a hand through her hair. "I don't believe so."

He glanced from her to me. "Then how does he manage it?"

I shrugged. "We haven't quite got that part figured out yet."

Aunt Abby looked at us both. "He could have on some sort of Talisman that protects him. The Coven priestesses could easily enchant a piece of jewelry, much like I have done for you and Kat."

I quickly nodded. "That makes perfect sense. Tucker was wearing a ring with a dark red stone. I'd never seen it before. It looked a lot like the one that I saw on Sebastian Barrister."

Grandpa sighed heavily as he arose from the rocker and stood beside Aunt Abby. "That's just great. Now we have to face vampires in the light of day. Seems we can't get a break." He exhaled and shook his head. "So where does your Mother stand in all of this? Is she still against us?"

Aunt Abigail shook her head. "I don't think so. She regrets what she has done to Tucker; but there is nothing that she can do about it now. He has the support of both the Coven and the Sons of the Raven."

He frowned. "But if your Mother is his maker, can't she control him?"

"Sebastian Barrister has forbidden it, and she cannot openly oppose him. Mother wants to attempt to regain control over the Coven. If she can do that, it will mean one less enemy facing us. The Daughters of the Coven are starting to make things difficult for Kat at school. Even Bobby has had his fair share of trouble. Coven members run the elementary school. Mother had a little *talk* with Belinda Michaels, the administrator of the elementary school, and she seems to have fallen in line somewhat. I don't expect he'll have any more trouble there."

Grandpa nodded. "I'll gather the rest of the Pack tomorrow and hear what plans Brock's put into place since my absence."

Aunt Abigail glanced at me and then, placing a hand on his arm, she said. "That won't be necessary. The guys relinquished control of the Pack to Kat. She's been acting as the Alpha while you've been away."

He had a surprised look in his eyes and a smile growing on

his face as he looked at me. "Is that right?" There was a hint of pride in his voice.

I nodded. "Somebody had to carry the mantle while you were away. They were all reluctant to lead, so I wasn't left with much choice, really. I'll gladly relinquish the title back to you. You're better suited for everything that is to come."

"Did you find Keegan Rourke?" Aunt Abby asked. I could tell the thought didn't please her in the least.

He chuckled softly. "Oh, I found him all right."

"And?" she asked.

"Will he help us?" I added.

Grandpa shrugged. "He was reluctant at first, but I think that I finally convinced him to join us. We'll know in a day or two, I guess." He wrapped his arm around my aunt and pulled her against him.

She sighed heavily. "I wish we didn't need him."

Grandpa had a faraway look in his eyes as he stared up at the stars. His nod was barely perceptible. "Me too, sweetheart. Me too."

I stood up from the rocker, deciding to give them a little privacy. I wasn't certain it was the best time to tell them what I had learned about the accident that had killed both my parents, nor of my suspicions about Grandmother's involvement. Already they had enough on their plates to worry about. Did I really want to add to it? I stretched my hands up over my head and forced a yawn. "Well, I am exhausted. It's been a very long day. I'm glad that you made it home in one piece Grandpa. Bobbybear has really missed not having you around. We all have."

He pulled me into a hug with his other arm and kissed the top of my head. "I've missed all of you as well. Thanks for holding down the fort for me kiddo."

Aunt Abigail pushed an errant strand of hair out of my face with her fingertips and she looked at me searchingly. "Did you go up to Valen's Ridge and check out the Wiccan ceremony? I assume that's where you went."

I glanced briefly at Grandpa before I nodded. "I did. It was pretty interesting really. I actually could feel a mysterious energy once the ceremony started."

"Oh? What ceremony is this?" Grandpa asked.

"It's called 'Drawing Down the Moon'. Harmless really," Aunt Abigail said. She stared into my eyes, "At least it is supposed to be. It can be easily corrupted though. Was Sebastian Barrister there?" she asked.

I swallowed. "He was," I said with a nod.

"Oh Kat, you shouldn't have gone there alone," she said, placing a hand on my arm.

"I wasn't alone," I said quickly. "I had a friend there."

"One of the Pack?" Grandpa asked.

I shook my head. "No. It was a friend from school."

"No more of this risky nonsense," Grandpa said firmly. "These people aren't playing around."

Tears burst from my eyes and I sobbed before I could regain my composure. "Tucker threatened me at school the other day. He gave me an ultimatum. He wants me to join him. Become like him. A hybrid. He said that if I don't, things would go badly for everyone. He was there tonight too. He and Barrister actually chased after me. I barely got away."

Grandpa angrily slapped the porch post. "Damnit! No more crazy stunts like this! No more solo runs in the woods. It's far too dangerous! We cannot afford to lose anyone else!"

"I needed to see what we were up against," I said defensively. Grandmother said that the ceremony was harmless."

He waved a hand in the air. His voice was full of scathing sarcasm, "Oh, Grandmother said it was harmless. Well, there you go then. That makes all the damned difference. We should all take comfort in the fact that a blood-sucking vampire says it's harmless."

"Sam! Stop it," Aunt Abby said matching his anger. "Kat has been doing a remarkable job keeping the ship afloat in your absence. Don't you dare belittle her; she deserves your support. She's earned it. I don't see the rest of your Wolf Pack stepping up to the plate."

I cleared my throat and wiped the tears from my face. His unexpected words had stung, but Aunt Abby's defense emboldened me. "Tuck's a loose cannon. He has apparently attacked a man and a woman on the highway not far from here. He killed the husband and turned the woman. I saw her in the woods on my way to school the other day. I went into the woods to check on her, thinking she may only be scared and alone. I wanted to help her but when I got close, she attacked me. If the sun hadn't begun to rise I don't know what would've happened."

Aunt Abby gasped sharply, her eyes going wide. This was the first she'd heard of my little escapade into the woods.

"See?" Grandpa went into another angry rampage. "That kind of reckless behavior is going to get you killed, Kat."

I nodded. "I know. It was stupid. But until I got close I didn't know she was a vampire. She was crying and I only wanted to help her."

"That's the whole point—"

Angry, I cut him off. "The point is, she's still out there. She's probably ravenous by now. We need to find her and stop her before she turns anyone else. Brock and Cho want to kill Tucker before he can build an army. That may be the right thing to do, I don't know. I tried talking to Tucker at school, but he's absolutely thrilled with all the new power he has. I think it's gone to his head. He wants to turn me so that we can rule over The Hollows together. He has no qualms about trying to increase his following. He needs to be stopped." I looked up at my Grandpa and crossed my arms over my chest. "Now that you're back, you can deal with him. You're the Pack leader; I suggest you do something while you still have a Pack left. I'm going to bed." I turned and stomped toward the door, desperate to get away. I was exhausted. I didn't want him to see me crying again, but I couldn't stop the tears. I was seething with anger.

I paused as I opened the screen door. "Oh, there's one more thing that you should be aware of. I don't think the wreck that killed my parents was an accident. I think Grandmother had something to do with it. I can't prove anything at this point, and she's denying any involvement. But I thought you both needed to know."

Aunt Abigail and Grandpa exchanged looks of shock. I left them standing there and went into the cottage. I felt empty inside. Exhausted.

Chapter Thirteen

Aunt Abigail

It was late in the morning when I finally crawled out of bed. I could hear voices coming from the kitchen. Bobbybear was telling Grandpa all about school and how Sara had turned the tables on those who were bullying him. Though I was still slightly miffed at Grandpa for the way he had spoken to me, the sound of his laughter filled the cottage with love and warmth. We all had missed him terribly. I was glad he was home.

That thought made me smile. Home. The sounds outside my bedroom door were actually starting to sound like home. When Bobby and I first came to The Hollows I thought we had lost our home. I didn't think that I'd ever be able to accept this place. Mom and Dad were both gone. These people had been complete strangers to us. I had absolutely hated the fact that Aunt Abigail looked so much like my mother. The fact that they were almost identical twins had always infuriated me, the only difference was the strand of pure white in my aunt's hair. I wanted my mom, not a doppelganger.

But to her credit, Aunt Abigail wasn't out to replace Mom, she never had been. She had merely reached out to us with her unconditional love and support, offering my brother and me a safe harbor in the unrelenting storm that had swooped in threatening to destroy our lives. Now, when Bobbybear would slip and call her 'Mom,' it only brought a smile to my face instead of the intense anger that had consumed me early on.

I owed a lot to my aunt. She had been there for me from day one, though I hadn't known it at the time. I had been angry, lost and completely absorbed by my grief. I wasn't ready to raise my baby brother, and I knew that I certainly couldn't do it on my own. Aunt Abigail had been my guiding light in the dark chaos that surrounded me. Though I fought against her with all I had, she had remained steadfast; a lifeline that I could hold on to. She taught me how to be at one with the Wolf. Without her help, I never would have made it. I would have lost Bobbybear in the process.

She had saved me. She saved us both.

I stepped out of the bedroom that Bobby and I shared and smiled at the three of them sitting at the kitchen table like a happy little family. It brought a stab of nostalgia quickly to mind. Grandpa had enough similarities to my father and With Aunt Abby looking so much like my Mom it would be all too easy to think that I was still back in the city with Bobby and our parents. I forced a smile to my face as I made a beeline for the coffee pot.

Grandpa smiled at me. "Good morning sunshine. Uhm… about last night…"

I waved a hand in the air and shook my head as I took a mug off of the countertop mug tree. "Don't worry about it. We're cool."

He glanced at my aunt, then back at me his relief clearly

evident and said, "You sure?"

I nodded. "Absolutely. I know it was a lot to take in all at once." I added just a small amount of sugar to my coffee to blunt the bitterness just a bit and then took a sip. I could feel the burn all the way down; it was a small wonder that I hadn't scalded my tongue or the roof of my mouth.

Aunt Abby ran a hand down my back, giving me a loving caress. "I was wondering if you'd like to accompany me today? There are some herbs that I want to harvest. They only grow deep in the woods."

I glanced at Grandpa. "Sure, if we're allowed."

He rolled his eyes and sighed. "I would rather no one wander off alone. Especially knowing that Tucker is a powder keg waiting to blow. He's dangerous, and until he's dealt with it isn't safe. I'd prefer it if you didn't even walk to Wellington House without someone with you."

Aunt Abigail gave me a little wink. "He won't let me gather my ingredients alone. I'm going to need to restock my supplies for what's coming. He's agreed that if you go with me, he'll allow it. Meanwhile he's gonna reconnect with the guys."

"What about Bobbybear?" I asked. I wasn't thrilled with him being left alone.

She reached out her hand and tousled his brown curls. "He's gonna spend the day playing with Sara."

Bobby nodded enthusiastically. "We're gonna play Hide and Seek in Wellington House!"

I almost spit my coffee. "You're gonna play Hide and Seek with a ghost?"

He giggled. "She cheats, but it's still a lot of fun!"

I shook my head in disbelief. "Just don't make a mess of the place!" I warned.

He slid out of his chair and hugged everyone. "In fact, I'm gonna head over there now. There're a couple of places I wanna check out before Sara appears." He trotted out the door and into the yard.

Grandpa called out to him. "Hold up, Bobby. I'll walk you over."

We could all hear Bobby's disappointed sigh as I saw him bend and pick up a stick. He started whacking the brush at the edge of the path as he waited for Grandpa to escort him to Wellington House. I was happy he had the chance to still be a kid. I had feared that after the death of our parents he'd be forced to grow up too fast.

Grandpa glanced at Aunt Abigail and me as he stood up from the table. "You sure allowing him to play with a ghost is a wise idea?"

I nodded. "As long as that ghost is Sara Robinson, I am. She'd never hurt Bobbybear. Nor will she allow anyone else to harm him."

Grandpa sighed. "Okay. If you're all right with it, I guess it's fine. You don't think Bobby will have any more trouble with these bullies?"

"No," Aunt Abby replied. "Between Sara and my mother I don't think it'll happen again."

"Oh?" he asked. "What did your mother do?"

She raised her eyebrows and sighed. "Mother had a little chat with Belinda Michaels, the principal. She scared her pretty good."

Grandpa chuckled. "I can imagine." He leaned in and kissed my aunt. "You two have fun. I'm gonna see Bobbybear safely to Wellington House and then head on out and gather the guys for a little run, see what we can find." He leaned in and kissed the top of my head. "I am sorry about last night. You've done a good job in my absence."

I smiled. "Thanks Grandpa."

Aunt Abby and I climbed into the pickup with her behind the wheel. I could only wonder where we were heading; she seemed awfully secretive. I thought we were just going for a little stroll in the woods, I hadn't realized that we were gonna need the truck to get wherever we were headed. At my inquisitive glance she smiled over at me. "We're going a little out of the way," she said simply, refusing to shed any more light on the situation. I could tell that she was enjoying the mystery. She was always so cryptic, so mysterious. I guess that's why she made such a good witch.

We drove past Wellington House, down the long drive to the highway. We turned in the direction of The Hollows once we reached the main road. I still didn't have any clue where we were going. Finally I couldn't take the silence any longer. "It's good to have Grandpa back home. I was beginning to worry about him," I said, sticking my arm out the window. I started doing a little wave motion with my hand. I liked the way the wind flowed over the top of my hand, and how it pushed up upon my cupped palm. My fingertips were streamlined, cutting into the oncoming wind with little resistance.

She nodded. "I was too. I just wish we didn't need Keegan's help."

I twisted upon the seat to get a better look at her. "Do you really think that one man, one extra wolf, is going to make a lot of difference?" I had my doubts, if I was being honest. What good could one additional man accomplish, really?

She shrugged. "Sam seems to think so."

"You don't like him. Keegan Rourke, I mean."

She shook her head. "I don't really know him. I just know of him. I know what he's done in the past. I know how much he hurt your grandpa. I don't think I'll ever fully trust him, even if he does help us. The sooner we're rid of Keegan Rourke, the better."

"I don't get it," I said with a shake of my head. "Why does Grandpa keep contact with him after all that he's done? I mean, seriously? Why bring one of your oldest enemies to help you fight your new enemy? I'd be afraid that they'd join forces and simply attack me. It just doesn't make any sense. I wish we'd talked about it more before he ran off to find him."

She sighed heavily. "I know right? It's never really made any sense to me, either. But you know how your grandpa can be. Once he gets an idea stuck in his head there's no way you're gonna get it out of there. You just have to kinda strap in and hang on. Your dad was a lot like that."

"That's just plain dumb," I said. "Talk about reckless…"

Aunt Abby nodded. "Yup."

"Why do guys always have to plunge in without thinking things through?" I asked, giving her a small smile and a shake of my head.

She laughed. "And yet they claim that we women are the irrational ones."

"It's crazy," I said.

I looked out my window as we passed by the turn off for Grandpa's cabin. "Where are we going? The Hollows?" I furrowed my brows together.

Aunt Abigail chuckled softly as she shook her head. "No, Valen's Ridge. There are some herbs that grow near there that I've not found anywhere else."

"Are we looking for anything in particular?" I asked out of curiosity.

She nodded. "Yes. *Angelica*, also sometimes called *Archangel* or *Masterwort* by the older wiccans. It is a very powerful protection herb. It can be used in healing, and even exorcism too." She chuckled softly. "Some witches even believe that it can be burned in order to bring a lost love back to you."

I looked at her in astonishment. "Are you planning an exorcism?"

"Hardly. But we may need its protective powers."

I laughed and I really didn't know why. We took a wide turn in the highway and Aunt Abby began to slow, pumping the breaks she downshifted, slowing the truck. She steered the Chevy onto a dirt road that cut off to the right. It was in a little better shape than the one leading to Grandpa's cabin; but still I thought the old pickup was going to shake apart. Finally we came to a stop and she cut off the ignition. The surrounding forest was quiet and serene. She turned to me, placing a hand on my arm as I started to climb out of the truck. "Hang on a second. I want to talk. You said something last night that I need you to explain in greater detail; about the accident that killed your parents. You said you thought your grandmother was involved. Where is this coming from?"

Tears filled my eyes and I couldn't look at her without losing it. I shook my head and stared out the windshield. "Nothing about what happened makes any sense."

"That's why they are called accidents, Kat. They are random events. Completely unplanned."

I shook my head and faced her. "That's not it, Aunt Abby. How did you know to come to the hospital when you did? In order to get there when you did you almost had to have left The Hollows *before* the accident occurred. Tell me how that's possible!"

She leaned back against the seat as though she had been pushed. The shock on her face told me all I needed to know. She had never questioned it before, but now the absurdity of it all had struck her full-force, just as it had me. There was no denying it. Grandmother was involved. She had orchestrated everything! Finally Aunt Abigail looked at me, tears forming in her eyes. "Where is all this coming from? Why now, out of the blue?"

I swallowed. "Ari's grandmother may have mentioned it. I don't have a clue how she even knew about all this. But she seemed pretty certain of her information. She told me that Mom wasn't supposed to die in the accident, only Dad."

Aunt Abigail nodded, biting at her bottom lip as she thought about what I had told her. Finally, she looked at me and said, "Keep this between us for now. I need to have a talk with your Grandmother. She has a lot of explaining to do."

I shook my head. "That won't do much good. When I confronted her about it she got very angry. I thought she was going to attack me for a minute. Her fangs had sprouted and she couldn't take her eyes off my neck. I was terrified. She's dangerous."

"We're not far from where the *Wiccan* ceremony was held," Aunt Abby proclaimed as we climbed from the truck. "I'm sure you'll recognize your surroundings soon enough."

She was right. Even the smell of the woods was instantly familiar. As we climbed out of the pickup I knew that fifty yards deeper into the forest was the clearing where the Coven had held the *Drawing Down the Moon* ceremony. I shivered uncontrollably which elicited a chuckle from my aunt. "It's not funny," I said with a roll of my eyes.

As we stepped further into the forest I could see several footprints that belonged to a variety of people, mostly women, probably Coven members. Occasionally I could see a deeper, longer imprint that belonged to the Sons of the Raven or either Tucker or maybe even Barrister. The absolute fear I had felt when they pursued me through the woods came back to me. I could even feel the anxiety of the Wolf within me. I glanced over at my aunt. "Can we please leave this place?"

She led me deeper into the forest, heading further north by northeast. She seemed to know exactly where we were going, but I didn't have a clue. It wasn't until we came upon the babbling brook that I recognized where I was. Across the stream and a little bit further was the mysterious totem with the two skulls. We were approaching the sacred ground of the Mohawk. A bit further in the woods was Ari and her grandmother's cabin.

Aunt Abigail crossed the stream by stepping on large rocks that were spaced perfectly for a human adult's stride. The tops of the stones were flat and extended a good two to three inches out of the water, so they weren't slippery at all. I followed her across, and then we turned slightly upstream, heading away from the babbling brook. Birds were chirping high up in the trees and I couldn't help but wonder if Ari was watching us.

"Here we are," Aunt Abby said as she stopped. Reaching into her pocket she pulled out some latex gloves and handed me a pair. "It's best if you put these on. Some plants can be toxic to the touch, the *wild angelica* won't kill you but it can cause your skin to become very sensitive to sunlight."

"Good to know," I said as I blew into the gloves making them easier to put on.

Aunt Abby pointed to the plants we had come for. Some were nearly seven feet tall. Large umbrella-like clusters of white flowers, forming a ball-like appearance, sat upon thick, purple stems. Some of the stems were quite dark, while others were a shade of lilac. She grasped the stem in both hands, and snapped it apart. I was surprised to see that the stems were actually hollow on the inside. "The leaves are very similar to the leaves found on *poisonous hemlock water dropwort*, so it is good to know your plants," she continued. "If you are interested in learning more about them, I have a Herbal Grimoire back at the cottage. It was passed down to me by a very kind Wiccan priestess. She was what you might call a Green Witch. She took a liking to me before I left the Coven. She actually encouraged me to leave and practice on my own. She was a very wise woman."

"Plants aren't really my thing," I said. "But Millie would love to take a look at it, I'm sure."

I noticed that the stems were glossy with the lower part a purplish color and some of the upper parts a bit more reddish. The hollow stems were fluted and snapped easily if you twisted your wrists. I was starting to get the hang of it. The leaves of the plant were a bright green and divided into many leaflets, which appeared to have a bit of a serrated edge. You had to take great care not to get scratched by the fine teeth of the plant. I found that the latex on my gloves came close to tearing on more than one occasion.

We placed our harvest of *angelica* into a large wicker basket, similar to a picnic basket. After a few minutes more, Aunt Abigail smiled. "I think we've enough. While we're here, why don't we drop in for a visit with some friends."

I gave her a surprised look. "You know Ari and her grandmother?"

She chuckled softly. "Of course I do."

Chapter Fourteen

Spirit Quest

The cabin was much as I had remembered it from the night before. It was nestled in a thick clump of northern pine, with a relatively large clearing in front of the cottage. The welcoming smell of wood smoke coming from the chimney wafted through the trees towards us as we emerged from the woods. As we approached the cabin, Ari and her grandmother stepped outside, waiting our arrival.

Aunt Abby smiled and waved at the pair of women. "Hello," she said.

"Shé:kon," the old woman said, returning the greeting with a raise of her hand.

After Aunt Abigail placed her basket upon the ground she stepped forward and gave Okwaho a warm hug. "It is good to see you. You are looking good."

The old woman nodded. "Hen:,wakata karí:te." she said in a raspy voice.

Aunt Abby looked to Ari. The younger Mohawk smiled, with a nod. "She says she is doing well."

"That is good," Aunt Abby replied. "I have brought Kat, as requested."

I quickly looked at her with a raised brow. "What's going on? Who requested you to bring me here?"

Ari chuckled. "Do not fear, my akhsótha requested that you return for your *Spirit Quest*. She claims that you have very powerful enemies converging upon your path. It is good that you know whom your allies are. She can help you with that."

Aunt Abigail put a hand on my arm. "It is going to be all right. You can trust her."

I smiled weakly. "You're gonna be here, aren't you?"

She glanced at Ari and the old woman. "No. Ari and I are going to go and gather some more herbs, but there is nothing for you to worry about. Okwaho will guide you along. You really are in excellent hands."

Ari put a hand on my shoulder giving it a comforting squeeze. "There really is no one better to guide you upon your quest. My akhsótha knows these woods better than anyone."

The old woman touched my arm. "Ká:ts," she said, sweeping a hand toward the door of the cabin, beckoning me inside. The room was no different than it had been before. There was no furniture except a narrow wooden table located on the back wall. Four big, plush pillows sat on each side of a brazier containing glowing coals. She indicated one of the pillows. "Sátien tanon," she said as she took a seat upon a pillow across from the one she had indicated for me. We sat down with our legs crossed beneath us.

The old woman could tell that I was nervous. She smiled at me, reaching out a hand and lightly touching me upon my knee. "Ioiá:nere' ohstón:ha okwáho," she spoke softly, in a soothing tone.

"I'm sorry," I shook my head, "I don't understand."

She frowned for a moment, as if searching for the words. Finally she smiled shyly. "I said 'good little wolf'." Her smile grew. "You are doing good."

I nodded. "Your English is very good." I said lamely, not knowing what else to say.

"I am akokstén:ha," she said, touching her chest, "An old woman. Sometimes I forget to make my words known." She smiled shyly, so much like Ari. "I will try to do better."

I smiled at her. She was such a sweet lady. She reminded me a lot of Millie's grammie. I thought the two of them would get along well together.

Okwáho lit the bowl of herbs that Ari had prepared the night before and set it down in the center of the brazier. Smoke started rising in the air spreading throughout the cabin. "Aón:ria," she said. She closed her eyes and breathed in. "Aonrísera," she breathed out slowly. She indicated that she wanted me to do the same. "Aón:ria. Aonrísera," she repeated.

As I did, a calm seemed to descend upon me. I could feel my apprehensions drifting away with the wafts of smoke that danced around us. She whispered words that I couldn't understand nor could I even begin to remember them after the old woman spoke them. They were almost a song, a melodic chant. I began to feel light-headed as I breathed in more of the smoke.

Finally she spoke words that I did understand, "When they come, you should go with them. Use your mind and let the journey happen. I will be here with your body. Do not fear. I will keep it safe until you return."

Keeping my eyes closed, I nodded. Slowly, I had the sensation of stepping out of my body. I could see myself still sitting upon the cushion but now it seemed that I was standing off to the side, as an observer in a dream, perhaps. The door of the cabin opened as though from a strong wind, but I felt no breeze. Standing in the doorway were the White and Gray wolves, shrouded in their bluish-white, ghostly light. They barked softly at me and I glanced down at the Medicine Woman and she nodded with a knowing smile. "Go child," she said, nodding encouragingly. "Your journey begins."

As I stepped toward the door I morphed into a wolf and joined the ghostly pair. We ran across the clearing and entered the surrounding forest. They led me deep into the woods until we came across a hidden pond; a small waterfall was on the other side, feeding the tiny lake. It was night now, but I knew it shouldn't be. I was certain that not that much time had passed. Yet, the moon was shining brightly down upon us. The Gray and the White sat upon their haunches and howled up at the silver sphere high up in the heavens. I joined them, and together we paid homage to the moon.

The next thing I knew, none of us was in wolf form. Surprisingly we were all fully clothed. I was sitting beside my parents and they were smiling at me. I could feel their love and pride and I was happier than I'd ever been since I had lost them. We hugged and cried for several long minutes. I had so many questions that I wanted to ask, but my mind was a jumbled mess; I didn't know where to begin. I wasn't sure if I even knew how.

Mom squeezed my hand and spoke softly, her voice just as I had remembered. "There is little time, Kat. There is so much that we would like to share with you but that will all have to wait. We came to warn you. You are all in danger. Dark forces are joining together to take everything from you. Trust the Wolf within you to know whom you can rely upon. Her instincts are sharp and they will not let you down. You are the protector that the others will need in order to survive. Through misguided deeds, enemies will be in your midst. Trust yourself Kat. Trust the Wolf. She will not lead you wrong."

I shook my head, "I don't understand," I said frantically.

They were starting to fade away. "Please, don't go! I want

you to stay! I need you both!"

I opened my eyes and I was sitting across from Ari's grandmother. The old woman smiled sadly. "It is not all that you hoped, but understanding will come to you in time." She seemed to have known all that had transpired.

Tears streamed down my face as I looked around the room, hoping to see the White and the Gray wolves but they were not there. There was no clue that they ever had been. "Was I dreaming?" I asked in bewilderment as I ran a hand through my hair. "It seemed so real. I can still feel their embrace. I tried to hang on to them, to keep them with me, but I… I just couldn't." I was breathing heavily, and for a moment I thought that I was going to hyperventilate. The old woman handed me an earthenware cup of water. I took a sip, it was cold and refreshing, just what I needed. I glanced down at the bowl sitting in the middle of the brazier, gray ash was all that remained of the herbs it had contained. The hot coals of the brazier had grown cold. *How much time had elapsed?*

The cabin door opened and Ari and Aunt Abigail entered. Both of them gave me looks of uncertainty. Ari immediately started to remove the bowl from the brazier and to tidy up. Aunt Abby smiled at me. "So? How did it go?" She looked from me to the old Medicine woman.

I couldn't answer, and I glanced at the old woman who stood smiling at us both. "It was successful," she said in her raspy voice. I looked at my aunt and shrugged.

We were both silent as we walked back through the woods towards where we had left the Chevy. A considerable amount of time had passed by, the sun was beginning to set and darkness was claiming the forest around us. Finally, as we reached the pickup, Aunt Abigail stopped me with a hand on my arm. "Care to talk about it?"

I shrugged helplessly. "I'm not sure I can." I shook my head.

"It doesn't seem real, but yet it does. I can't explain it. One minute I was sitting across from this sweet little Mohawk woman and then I wasn't. I could see my body still in the lotus position but it was like I was observing it all from afar. Like I had stepped out of my body completely. Like I was a ghost or something. It was almost like I was having an out of body experience. Then I changed to the Wolf and joined the White and the Gray. They took me deeper into the woods, and suddenly it was night." I shook my head again. "It all sounds so crazy, I know."

She smiled. "Maybe you just need a little more time to process it. I'm sure it'll become clearer to you."

"I certainly hope so," I said. As I climbed into the pickup I looked over at her. "The one thing I do know is that the White and the Gray wolves *are* my parents. They are watching out for Bobby and me. I'm not sure how it's possible, but it is."

She fired the truck up. "Well, now you know. At least that's something."

I gave her a long look, and then said, "Have you ever gone on a Spirit Quest?"

Aunt Abby shook her head. "No, I haven't. Okwaho has always wanted me to, but I've never gotten up the nerve."

"But you thought it was a good idea for me to go on one, huh?" I wasn't sure how I should feel about that.

She shrugged with a sly smile.

Chapter Fifteen

Keegan Rourke

By the time we got back to Aunt Abigail's cottage the sun had long since set. Grandpa was sitting on the porch and he wasn't alone. A large, muscular man with a face chiseled from granite was sitting in the other rocker. He had a long scar that ran down his forehead and cheek, giving him a menacing appearance. He wore his blond hair short, in a tight crew cut. He sported a thick goatee of reddish-blond around his mouth. A black silhouette of a wolf head tattoo was emblazoned on the right side of his neck. He stood as we climbed out of the truck. Smiling he said, "Sam tells me you're in need of my help."

When I had first heard of Keegan Rourke I didn't like him. Especially after I had heard about what he had done to my grandparents. I liked him even less now. Something about the way he looked at us made my skin crawl. I certainly didn't trust him.

I glanced at Aunt Abby and raised my basket, "I'll take this inside." I was in no mood for a conversation with this man.

Aunt Abby indicated the basket she held, "Wait, I'll join you." She smiled at the two men on the porch, "These are time-sensitive, I'm afraid." She stepped around them and followed me into the cottage. Clearly, she wasn't interested in making friends with Keegan Rourke, either. At least I wasn't alone.

As we stood in the kitchen I could hear Grandpa and Keegan continue to talk. Keegan was laughing. "I see that I'm not truly welcome here. You'd think that they'd be a little happier to see me. I am here to save them, after all."

"You're here to help deal with Sebastian Barrister, that's all. My Pack isn't quite ready to take on an ancient vampire."

Keegan chuckled again. "What about you, Sammy? Are you at least grateful that I came as you asked?"

I could tell that Grandpa was tense. "Look, Keegan. I asked for your help. I'm glad you came."

Keegan sighed. "Well, how could I not come to your aid? You practically begged for my help."

"Is that how you see it?" Grandpa's voice was tinged with rising anger.

Keegan chuckled. "Relax, Sammy. I was only kidding with you." He sighed. "Though I think those women could be a little more appreciative, if you know what I mean."

"Stay away from them Keegan," Grandpa's voice was full of warning.

"That ain't any way to be, Sammy Boy I'm here to help. I thought we were friends."

I could see Grandpa shake his head through the screen door. "The friendship we had ended a long time ago. You made sure of that."

Keegan laughed as he stepped off the porch. "There's a lot of water 'neath the bridge between you and me, Sammy Boy. You should learn to forgive and forget. I'm gonna go for a little run, kinda scout things out. You're welcome to tag along."

"I think I'll pass," I heard Grandpa say. His voice sounded as if he spoke with a tightened jaw. I could tell there was no love lost between the two men. Keegan's manner was so belittling. He clearly thought that he was better than everyone else. In my mind he wasn't fit to stand in my grandpa's shadow. I was already doubting whether or not we needed his help in this fight.

Aunt Abigail stepped out onto the porch after Keegan had gone. She handed my Grandpa a whiskey. "You look like you could use a drink."

Grandpa accepted it gratefully. "Well, that's Keegan Rourke. What do you think about him?"

Aunt Abby pressed up against his back, and caressed his chest with her right hand. She lightly kissed his shoulder. "You want my honest opinion?"

He chuckled. "No. I don't think that's really necessary." He turned and kissed her.

"I just hope you didn't make a mistake in bringing him here," she said.

I stepped out onto the porch, unable to resist any longer. "During the *Spirit Quest* that the Mohawk Medicine Woman sent me on, I was warned by Mom that an enemy would be in our midst." I pointed to the woods where Keegan had disappeared. "He certainly fits that bill."

Grandpa looked at me with a furrowed brow. "Hold on a second. You spoke with your mom on some *spirit quest?*"

I glanced from him to Aunt Abby. "I know it sounds crazy, but it seemed so real. Dad was there too. They're both *wolf spirits* now. Surely you remember them. Back in 1884 they kept you from killing Bobby and me."

He gave Aunt Abigail a haunted look. "Is this really possible?"

She chuckled lightly. "Oh Sam, this is The Hollows. Anything is possible!"

§

It started out as a lazy Sunday. I awoke well after ten and was still in no hurry to climb out of bed. If it hadn't been for an insistent bladder, I could've lain there all nice and cozy for at least another hour, maybe more. Tomorrow I wouldn't be able to, because of school. As I begrudgingly pulled the covers off and sat up, I thought it seemed odd. The cottage was unusually quiet. There were no noises coming from the kitchen, no spoons clinking upon the sides of coffee mugs, no fork or knife clanging against a plate, no voices speaking softly in an attempt not to awaken the sleeping. Nothing. It was as though I were alone in the cabin. That was odd for a Sunday.

When I emerged from the bathroom, I was completely dressed in a soft flannel shirt and a ragged pair of jeans; one knee exposed. I was comfortable. Grandmother would never approve, and that thought alone made me grin. This was not Wellington House; she had no say here. I was no longer in her charge.

That is what I loved about living in the cottage with Aunt Abigail and Bobbybear. She didn't really care how I dressed – as long as I wasn't indecent. She drew the line there, but I was fine with that. I had no desire to expose myself. I laughed suddenly. Wasn't I doing that very thing each time I transformed? There had been times when I wasn't alone; the Wolf Pack and I had been on many patrols together. But it never seemed awkward being naked around the guys. At first it did, I'll admit. Especially when they would just stare and seeming to almost drool. Silas had broken everyone from that habit; he was used to being around naked dead bodies, both male and female, helping his dad at the mortuary. I shook my head as my thoughts continued to wander.

The Pack had made me the Alpha in Grandpa's place while he was off recruiting Keegan Rourke. I was new to the Pack, and it had taken a while for me to learn to depend on them, and vice versa. We all knew that with Sebastian Barrister stirring the cauldron of the Coven trouble was brewing. It already had affected us in very damaging ways. Now, with Tucker on the opposite side of the Pack, we really needed to come together as a more efficient fighting unit. We had hunted together. We were becoming a family. Cho and Silas were like brothers to me, and I was their sister. And then there was Brock…

Our relationship had started out on the wrong foot, but it had continually improved as time went by. Now we were actively seeking one another's company. I don't know if what we had was love, or just a fun version of it. We definitely were enjoying ourselves. Who knew what was in store for us?

Thoughts of Brock vanished with the opening of the cottage door. I had put on a fresh pot of coffee and had just poured my first cup. I needed the caffeine to jumpstart my body. Turning toward the door I gasped suddenly at the unexpected intrusion. I hadn't expected to see Keegan Rourke just barging in on me. I was thankful that I had at least gotten dressed. "Don't you believe in knocking?" I said, knowing my voice was a bit caustic, but I didn't care. He had no right. I could only hope that he didn't detect my fear.

He had a wide grin on his face as he entered the kitchen, placing one hand on the counter the other on the edge of the island. "Well, certainly not the 'hello' I was expecting, but it'll do, I suppose."

I turned my attention back to my coffee, adding far less than a teaspoon of sugar to blunt the bitterness. "If you're looking for my Grandpa, he isn't here. You should probably try his cabin." I didn't even know if he knew where Grandpa's cabin was, but I didn't really care. I just wanted to be left alone with my coffee. I wanted him gone. He was making me feel uncomfortable.

He smiled at me, as though sizing me up, appraising me somehow. "I didn't come here to see Sammy Boy. I was hoping to catch your aunt, actually." He glanced toward her bedroom before turning his eyes back to me.

I sipped my coffee. It was very hot and I could feel the scald on the roof of my mouth. I had taken a larger sip than I had intended. "She's not here, either. She's probably over at Wellington House with my brother." I could feel the panic starting to rise deep within me. I feared I had said too much. Now he knew I was alone. "She'll be back soon," I said rather quickly.

He nodded to himself as he casually took a step closer. "Sooo," he dragged the word out, "you're all alone then?" He chuckled as he shrugged. "I guess you'll have to do, then."

I stepped around the other end of the kitchen island, wanting the separation that it offered. "Well, unfortunately I don't really have the time at the moment. I was just fixing to leave."

He glanced at the coffee pot and then at the cup in my hands. He smirked. "Sure looks like you planned to be here for a little while longer." His eyes sparkled with mischief as he called my bluff. Okay, so he wasn't stupid. Just scary.

I swallowed. "Look, I think you should go now. We have nothing to talk about."

"Oh, sure there is, darlin'. You've been leading this pack of scrappy misfits for a while now. We could talk about that." His smile widened. "Maybe I could give you some pointers." His eyes drifted over my body, making me feel *very* uncomfortable.

I shook my head. "I'm good. But thanks anyway. Grandpa's back in charge of the Pack."

He pursed out his lips, nodded and continued to walk around the island, sliding his hand over the granite. "Well, we don't have to talk about business then. We could talk about somethin' else. Pleasure, maybe." The grin on his face was pure evil. Even his eyes had hardened.

The sound of a horse neighing outside drew our attention. We both paused, uncertain. My heart was racing, pounding inside my chest. The front door of the cottage flew open and Ari quickly stepped inside. She looked from Keegan to me, her eyes narrowing as she stepped up beside me. "Sorry I'm late," she said pointedly.

I smiled in relief, happy that she was here. "Don't worry about it, you're here now. That's all that matters." I didn't care why she had come; nor did the fact that she had simply barged in upset me. I was just grateful for her timely intrusion. He couldn't do anything with both of us present. There was safety in numbers. My heart was beating rapidly.

Keegan crossed his arms over his chest in annoyance as he frowned darkly. Clearly Ari's arrival had upset his plans. "You going to introduce me to your friend?"

"Ari, this is Mr. Rourke. He was just leaving."

Keegan's left eye narrowed, he looked us over menacingly. Finally he nodded. "Perhaps I should be heading out. He turned after a moment and stormed out of the cottage, the screen door slamming behind him. Ari's horse whinnied uncomfortably as he strode by.

I stepped toward the island and placed my coffee cup down. My hands were shaking and I spilt a good portion of it all over the countertop. "I'm sooo glad you showed up when you did. That man gives me the creeps!

She started sopping up the spilt coffee with a paper towel. "I saw him up near Valen's Ridge and wanted to keep an eye on him. From what I've seen, he is not a very nice man."

I nodded as I ran a hand through my thick hair. I was very near tears. "I don't think he is. He scares me."

After tossing the paper towels into the garbage she turned and gave me a big hug, pulling my body tightly against hers. "Well he's gone now. Are you gonna be all right?"

I nodded as I wiped the tears from my eyes, and then it dawned on me. "Wait a minute. Did you ride up on a horse?"

She smiled at me. "I did."

"You know," I said with a smile, "every little girl's dream is to be rescued by a white knight in shining armor."

She looked down at the clothes she wore. "Settle for a brown-skinned girl in denim?"

I beamed at her. "Even better!"

Chapter Sixteen

Two Girls and An Appaloosa

We stepped out of the cottage and I immediately fell in love with Ari's horse. He was the most beautiful appaloosa I had ever seen! His head, neck and chest were almost completely black except for a few white speckles here and there. The hindquarters of the horse were all white, except for a smattering of black spots. The horse's mane and tail were dark, as were the legs. Just above each hoof was a pure white stocking.

"Oh my gosh, he's gorgeous!" I patted his powerful neck and he seemed to like my presence. "What's his name?" I asked, smiling at Ari.

"He is *Sewahió:wane*, which means 'Apple' in my language." She shrugged, "Kinda corny, I know."

"No, no it isn't. I love it!" I laughed as the horse nuzzled me with its nose. "Can I feed him?"

She nodded. "He loves apples, if you can believe it."

"I think we may have some!" I rushed off and went inside

the kitchen. Opening the fridge I spotted the apples in the fruit bin. I quickly grabbed one and took it outside. Ari had mounted the horse in my absence and was sitting rubbing his neck. I hesitated. "You're leaving?"

She smiled at me. "No. I figured we could go for a little ride if you want"

I held up the apple in the palm of my hand and Sewahió:wane took it gingerly from me and started munching away. I smiled up at Ari. "That'd be awesome."

She held out her hand to assist me up, and it was only then that I realized that she was riding bareback. "You don't use a saddle?"

She shook her head. "I prefer direct contact with Sewahió:wane. Makes us feel like we are one. He's never even had a saddle on, only the bridle. Wrap your arms around my waist; you'll be fine. We'll take it slow until you get the hang of it." Ari pulled the reins to the right and we were off. She made a little clicking sound and I could feel her nudge the horse with her heels. He responded by stepping up his pace to a trot.

Instinctively I tightened my grip on Ari's waist. She placed a hand over mine and I could hear her soft chuckle of amusement. She made that same clicking sound as she nudged the horse again. Sewahió:wane picked up speed; we were now in a full canter. For a second I was sure I was going to bounce off his back, but Ari tightened her grip on me. She leaned her head back so that I could hear her better, the black strands of her hair caressed my face softly. "Move *with* the horse," she instructed. "Let your bodies meld together by moving in harmony."

I copied her movements and soon I no longer felt as though I were merely riding the horse. *We were one...* I could feel a wide, joyous smile stretching across my face. This was exhilarating. I felt the strong muscles of the horse stretch and flex beneath me and I immediately understood why Ari preferred to ride bareback. It strengthened your connection to the horse in ways that a saddle never could.

We rode deeper into the wood. Though I had been in this part of the forest many times, it seemed so new and different now. From atop the horse I was seeing it from a whole new perspective. It was enlightening in a way. I started laughing, feeling carefree and very much alive. I hadn't even noticed that Sewahió:wane was now in a full gallop.

The horse flew across the stream in two strides and continued to weave his way through the tall pine, heading uphill. As the trees started growing closer together, we slowed to a walk, but continued to climb higher. We seemed to be following a path now, and the spaces between the trees grew slightly wider. We skirted clusters of rock, brush and trees. Sewahió:wane's familiarity with the trail gave him sure footing; he seemed to love the strenuous effort of climbing.

Finally, we came to a stop and Ari helped me to dismount. She slid down after me and tossed the reins over the horse's back. "I want to show you something," she said. Taking my hand she led me through the tall pines.

"What about Apple?" I asked. She hadn't even picketed the horse.

"He'll be fine. He knows not to wander off," she said, unafraid.

She led me along, still holding my hand. We came to a stop in a small clearing surrounded by bushes holding blackberries, strawberries and even blueberries. She plucked a plump blackberry off a shrub and popped it into her mouth. "You seriously need to try these!"

I selected a nice-looking blackberry and pushed it past my lips. It was the largest I had ever seen. I closed my eyes and savored the bite. "Mmm, delicious!"

She picked a couple more and ate them. "I know, right!"

We crossed the clearing where the strawberries were growing and picked a few. They weren't nearly as good as the blueberries had been, but still, they were dark red and very sweet. "This is my favorite spot in the entire forest. My own little slice of Paradise," she said with a radiant smile lighting up her face.

We walked a little further and stood out on a high outcropping of gray rock. Below I could see the stream we had crossed, it came to a point where it dropped down into a good-sized pond, creating a wide waterfall as it fell. *I knew this pond!* It was the same one I had watched the guys playing in after a morning run, but it was the first time that I had seen it from this perspective.

Ari smiled at me. "I saw you with the guys, that day. I laughed so hard I almost peed."

I could feel the blush rising to my face. That had been the first time that we had all been naked, together. I happened upon them and started watching them play around in the water. Tucker had come up behind me, grabbed my arms and brought me out of the brush for the entire world to see. I had been completely embarrassed.

"You were watching from up here?" I asked.

Ari nodded. "Where the berries grow is so beautiful when the dawning sunlight shows through the pines and the dew sparkles like tiny diamonds over everything. I pick a mix of berries and then come out here and have my breakfast. Usually the guys show up and morph back into human form." She smiled shyly. "I like to watch them as they play and wash themselves after they've hunted." Her cheeks flushed slightly with her naughty confession.

I knew exactly what she was saying. It was a pleasing sight to behold. I decided that a change of subject was needed. "How did you find this place?" It was all I could think of.

Her smile grew. "A little birdie told me."

A little laugh escaped from me. I could actually picture a little bird landing on her shoulder and chattering away. I looked at her in amazement. "I feel like I'm in some Disney animated movie with either Cinderella or Snow White and all the woodland creatures are speaking to you."

She looked like she didn't have any idea what I was talking about. "Seriously?" I asked. "You've never seen a Disney movie?"

Ari shrugged and shook her head. "You've seen where I live. I don't have a television. There aren't any movie theaters in The Hollows. We're kinda sheltered from all the Big City conveniences."

"Wow," I replied, feeling shocked to my core that she was completely unaware of Disney. I had never fathomed that her life was so different from my own – my former life, anyway.

Ari giggled softly. "It's not so bad. I like my life. I wouldn't really change a thing."

I quickly put a hand on her arm. "Don't get me wrong, I think you have an amazing life. You're so in tune with nature. What you can do is incredible."

She laughed. "What I can do? You're the one that can become a wolf!"

I reached out and squeezed her arm as I laughed. "But I can't fly – you can!"

We could suddenly hear male laughter coming from below us. We peered over the side of the rock and could see the guys coming out of the woods. The three of them were completely naked and covered in blood. From our vantage point we could see everything clearly, but they didn't have a clue that we were watching them

Ari smiled at me mischievously. "I told you this was a great spot."

I grinned back at her. "Yes, you most certainly did."

Sitting upon the rocky outcropping, we watched Brock, Silas and Cho for a while longer and then Ari lightly touched my arm. "We should leave. I need to be getting back to my akhsótha." She quickly stood and offered me a hand.

We headed back through the clearing and found Apple

munching on grass not far from where we had left him. Even he seemed ready to go. Ari swung up onto his back fluidly and then helped me up. As we trotted along, twisting through the pine, she leaned back and turned toward me. "Does Cho like anyone in particular? I mean; does he talk about any of the other girls?"

"OhMyGod, do you *like* Cho Ming?" I said excitedly. I couldn't keep the smile off my face.

Ari sighed. "Never mind. Forget I asked." She lightly shook her head. A could see a rosy glow rising upon her cheeks.

I placed a hand on her shoulder and gave it a little squeeze. "I've not heard him talk about any girl. He's always talking about food. That guy is always hungry!"

We rode along in silence for a while and finally I leaned toward her, so that I could speak softly into her ear. "Do you want me to find out if he likes you?"

She didn't respond right away.

"Ari?"

Her nod was nearly imperceptible. "Is that a yes?" I asked.

She nodded again, this time it was clear. "Sure. Why not?" she said hesitantly.

I laughed. "This is so cool!"

When we got back to the cottage Ari helped me to dismount and I looked up at her. "Don't go just yet," I said placing a hand on her leg. "I want to treat Sewahió:wane to another apple."

Ari chuckled softly. "He will like that."

I went inside and quickly grabbed another red apple from the fridge. I went back outside and held it in the palm of my hand for Ari's horse. He eagerly accepted it. "He's such a beauty," I said as I patted his neck firmly.

She smiled down at me. "He usually is shy around others. I believe that you have won him over."

I looked up at her feeling happier than I had in a long while. "He's incredible. You and Sewahió:wane are welcome to come by anytime you want. I've really enjoyed spending time with both of you."

She chuckled softly. "I am happy to have met you."

I smiled. "Same here, Ari."

Chapter Seventeen

Gotcha!

Not long after Ari rode away, Aunt Abigail and Bobbybear returned from Wellington House. Bobby was all excited. "Wow! Was that a horse? Did you ride it? Who was that on the horse? What kind of horse was it?" He was practically jumping up and down in excitement.

"Slow down, Bobbybear!" I chuckled. "One question at a time." I glanced over at Aunt Abby apprehensively with a crinkled brow, "So, how did it go?"

She shook her head. "We'll talk about it later." She walked around the kitchen island and opened the refrigerator. She sighed heavily. "How does a breakfast dinner sound?"

"We're not eating at Wellington House?" I asked with a raised brow. Something had clearly happened between Aunt Abigail and Grandmother; my aunt seldom cooked anything.

She glared at me. "No. We are not."

I gave her a quizzical look. Evidently Aunt Abigail and

Grandmother had talked, and apparently it hadn't gone well. I made a mental note to ask her about their conversation at a more opportune time. I turned to my brother. "Yes, that was indeed a horse you saw. I did get to ride him. His name is Sewahió:wane. That's the Mohawk word for Apple. He's an appaloosa, that's why he has that unique coloring. He belongs to my friend Ari. That's who you saw riding away."

"Cool!" Bobby exclaimed. "Will I get to ride him next time? Please say that I can!" He glanced over at Aunt Abby, not waiting for a response. "Can we get a horse? That would be way cool!"

She patted his bottom. "Run along and play, let Kat and I chat a bit."

He gave me a hopeful look. "I really hope I can ride Apple next time."

I chuckled softly. "Go play, and I'll talk to Ari about it tomorrow at school."

"Cool!" he said as he turned and ran to the bedroom. He reappeared in the doorway a short time later. "Why do they call him Apple? Is it because he's an appolooga or because he just likes apples?"

I laughed. "It's appaloosa. And yes, he happens to love apples."

"Wow! Can I feed him next time?" he asked.

I chuckled again. "You sure can. He'll eat right out of your hand and won't even bite you."

"Cool!" The smile on his face was absolutely huge. He ran off toward the bedroom to play.

I leaned against the counter as Aunt Abigail started cracking eggs. "I had a visitor this morning."

She nodded. "Ari. I gathered that."

I shook my head. "No, before Ari. Keegan Rourke stopped by."

"Keegan Rourke!" she gasped. "What did he want?" she said frowning.

"He actually came here looking for you. When I told him you weren't here, he said that I'd do. I could tell that he wasn't really interested in having a conversation. If Ari hadn't shown up when she did, I don't know what I would've done. That man scares me, Aunt Abby." A chill ran through me and I wrapped my arms across my chest. "He kept looking at me all weird like."

She bit at her bottom lip and shook her head. I could see tears welling up in her eyes. She sighed heavily. "He scares me too."

"You know," I said, "on my *Spirit Quest* Mom told me that through misguided deeds an enemy will be in our midst. Do you think she was referring to Keegan?"

Aunt Abigail shrugged and then wiped the tears from her cheeks. "He's certainly not a friend. I don't trust him. I never wanted him here. I wish your grandpa had never gone for him. He may just be another enemy that we have to deal with before this is all over and done with."

I wrapped my arms around her and placed my head on her shoulder. "I know. But what can we do? He isn't going to just go away on his own, you and I both know that."

She nodded. "We'll have to make him go."

I pulled away from her and looked at her warily. "How are we going to do that?"

She shrugged as she stirred the eggs. "I'll come up with something. I just need to give it some thought."

"Are you going to tell Grandpa?" I asked.

She paused and sighed heavily, weighing whether or not it was a good idea. "Let me see what I can come up with first. If he finds out what Keegan is really up to, he might do something irrational."

"You don't think Grandpa can make Keegan leave?"

Aunt Abby shook her head. "Not without a fight. You saw the size of him."

I shivered. Keegan Rourke was about twice the size of my

grandpa. I didn't really think that it would end well if the two of them went at it. *But what if the Wolf Pack put up a united front? If we all stood against Keegan, maybe he'd simply leave... it seemed to work with Ari and me.* I glanced at my aunt and told her what I was thinking.

She shrugged. "I suppose that could work." She sighed. "Talk to the guys tomorrow and see what they say." She poured the egg mixture into the skillet. "You want to get me the sausage links?" She placed another smaller skillet on the stovetop.

I went to the fridge and took out the sausage. I handed them over to my aunt and she opened the package and started adding them to the other skillet, browning them. I added water and coffee to the coffee maker and started the pot. In short order, the smells of a breakfast dinner filled the cottage with enticing aromas. Bobbybear came out of the bedroom and made a beeline for the kitchen table. He was obviously hungry.

Aunt Abigail smiled at him and said. "How about setting the table? It'll just be the three of us."

He rolled his eyes and groaned, but managed to keep the smile on his face as he set about his task, anything to speed things along. The smells emanating from the kitchen were making us all hungry.

I quickly buttered and sliced the toast and carried the small platter to the table. Aunt Abigail followed behind with the bowl of scrambled eggs and a platter of nicely browned links of maple flavored sausage. I returned to the kitchen and brought Bobbybear his hot cocoa and a cup of coffee for both Aunt Abby and me. As I sat down across from my brother I asked, "So how did your Hide and Seek go with Sara?"

He rolled his eyes and shook his head. "She always wins! I don't know how she does it."

I glanced at Aunt Abigail and we both started laughing, almost causing tears to fall. Bobby crossed his arms and frowned. "What's so funny?" he asked with an exaggerated pout.

"She's a ghost, Bobby!" Aunt Abby said.

"Duh!" I chimed in, bringing another chorus of laughter from all of us this time, including Bobbybear.

After we had finished with dinner I swatted Bobby on the behind and sent him off to the tub. "School tomorrow. Make sure you wash behind your ears."

He sighed. "Do I have to?"

"Unless you want me to do it for you," Aunt Abigail said.

"Nuh uh! I can do it all on my own!" he groaned.

"Then do it, young man!" I said pointing to the bathroom. "Go easy with the bubble bath and don't make a mess all over the floor like you did last time."

He stopped and turned toward me, his eyes wide. "I didn't splash water all over the floor. That was Sara."

Shocked, I looked from him to Aunt Abigail. We both turned our stunned faces toward Bobbybear. He giggled and pointed at us, his face red with laughter. "Gotcha!" he said.

After I had put Bobbybear to bed, I found Aunt Abigail sitting in a rocking chair out on the porch. She was staring off into the darkened forest, a glass of whiskey in her hand; the bottle was on the small round table next to her. I eased the screen door closed behind me and sat down in the other chair and waited. She was lost in her thoughts and hadn't even acknowledged my presence when I finally broke the silence. "Sooo, you had a talk with Grandmother, I presume."

She blinked. "I'm sorry?" she took a sip of the whiskey.

"Grandmother? You talked to her about the accident?" I prodded.

Aunt Abigail downed the rest of the whiskey and refilled the glass before she faced me. "I did," she said.

"And?" I prodded.

She took another sip of the whiskey. She blinked as she swallowed it. I could tell it burned on the way down. Slowly, she started to relate her tale…

Abigail was angry. If what Kat had said was true, then her own mother was responsible for her twin sister's death. There was no other explanation that fit. She had sent her to the City to bring her grandchildren back to The Hollows before the accident had happened. How had she known about it? There was only one way she could have known. She had orchestrated the incident just as Kat had claimed.

Her anger drove her to Wellington House in search of answers. She took along a small penlight and the black satchel that contained the tools she hoped she wouldn't need: a wooden stake, and a rubber mallet. She avoided contact with Margaret, who was in the kitchen preparing tonight's meal, and headed upstairs, unnoticed. She climbed the narrow steps to the attic storage room, avoiding the creaking step and entered the dusty room at the top of the stairs.

She scanned the floor with the flashlight and confirmed her suspicions, footprints that led to the wardrobe where the old clothes of a bygone era were contained. Here, she could see evidence that the wardrobe itself had been slid aside, revealing a hidden panel. Abigail had almost completely forgotten this hidden room. She and her sister, Miranda, had found it when they were ten, their mother hadn't even known of its existence until then. Abigail smiled. "Gotcha!" she whispered.

She bit her bottom lip and sighed. Holding the penlight with her teeth, and gripping the satchel tightly, she searched the wall for the hidden release that would swing the panel inward, probing with the fingers of her free hand. It took some time; Miranda had been the one to discover it initially. Finally, she felt the slight depression with her fingertip and pressed. The panel started to move, scraping softly across the floor.

The room beyond was the same size as all of the other bedrooms in Wellington House. Along the far wall she spied the coffin. She ran a finger across the seat of the room's only chair, a plush, high-backed *chair from the turn of the previous century. It was dust free. Not surprisingly, the entire room was immaculately clean. Margaret had evidently been tasked with keeping the room neat; Mother hated the dust that accumulated everywhere; yet she didn't seem to mind it collecting in the storage room or the basement.* Odd.

She sat in the chair, placing the satchel upon the floor at her feet, and stared at the coffin, knowing that inside her mother was sleeping. She considered waiting for her to awaken, but quickly discarded that notion. She needed to get Bobby back to the cottage, if she could find him. By now Kat was probably wondering what had happened to them all.

She stepped up to the coffin and took a deep breath as she grasped the lid in both hands. Exhaling slowly, she lifted. It was surprisingly heavier than she had imagined it would be. She also was surprised that it made very little noise as it opened. She had been expecting a loud screech like in the movies… maybe that would come with the passage of time.

Her mother, Elizabeth Wellington, looked absolutely beautiful as she slept, all the troubles and cares, the worry and frustration that she had carried with her in life, seemed gone now. Here she was at peace. She was wearing a black, gossamer gown, and her skin appeared to glow with a pale radiance against it and the plush, royal purple interior of the coffin. She smiled, purple was her mother's favorite color. Abby glanced toward the chair she had been sitting in, her eyes drifting down to the floor where the plain black satchel waited.

She wondered, briefly, if she should take the wooden stake out and hammer it into her mother's chest with the rubber mallet, and put an end to this unnatural existence. She sighed heavily. It was not something she could do, and she knew it. Miranda had been the stronger of the two. Randi could have driven the stake through her mother's heart without even flinching. Pounding it home with solid, determined strikes, and then smile at a job well-done.

Abigail turned her attention back to the sleeping figure and placed a hand on her mother's shoulder, squeezing gently. "Mother, we need to talk."

As Elizabeth Wellington's eyes shot open, Abigail gasped and stepped back. She quickly covered her mouth so that she wouldn't scream. She was actually surprised that she had been so easily startled, but then again, she had never cared for watching horror movies alone. This reminded her of those... She turned, wanting desperately to flee. Behind her she heard the soft rustling of her mother's gown as she climbed from the coffin.

"Why have you disturbed me, Abigail?" her mother asked. She could hear the slight hint of reproach in her tired voice.

Abigail took a deep breath and let it out slowly, steeling her nerves, as she turned to face her mother. "We need to talk about the accident that killed Randi and Stephen."

She could see her mother's jaw tighten. "Her name was Miranda," she corrected. "So, you have talked with Katherine, I see."

Abigail nodded. "I have. She has helped me to see things a little more clearly. I know now that you did something to cause that crash. How could you murder your own daughter and the man she loved? Why would you do such a horrible thing?"

Elizabeth Wellington closed her eyes tightly and took a faltering step backward; she flung out a hand and grasped the edge of the coffin. It was the only thing that kept her from falling. Abby could see tears fall from her mother's eyes and streak down her face even in the dim, golden glow of the lamplight that illuminated the room, keeping total darkness at bay.

"I didn't mean for Miranda to die." She shook her head, her voice sounding defeated and broken. "I didn't. Stephen, yes, I wanted him dead, I won't deny it. He stole my daughter from me, took her so far away. They were never coming back to me. I figured with him dead she would be forced to return to me. She would bring her children home where they all belonged. She wouldn't have a choice. I sent you to assist her. But then I received word that the collision was far worse than it should've been due to black ice on the Interstate."

Grieving, she eased down to the floor, no longer trusting herself to stand. "I was wrong, Abigail. I should never have orchestrated any of this. I see that now. But I had hoped that once Miranda returned with her children, things would be better. I could give them a good life here at Wellington House. Perhaps Miranda could even be convinced to rejoin the Coven. Marybeth Collingsworth was already attempting to steal the Coven from me. She was gaining support. The daughter of the High Priestess was expected to receive the blessing of the Triple Goddess. I couldn't fulfill that with Miranda gone. You had left the Coven and burned all your bridges behind you. I was desperate. I was foolish, I see that now."

Abigail shook her head. "The Coven would never have accepted Randi. The wolf in her would be a stain that they couldn't overlook. She would never have received the Blessing of the Triple Goddess. You were foolish to think that they would."

"I know. But if Robert had managed to kill his grandfather back in 1884 the curse would've been lifted. Your sister would have remained pure. She would have received the Blessing. All would be as it was meant to be. I so wanted that. For her, for me, for all of us."

She sobbed mournfully. "I was wrong, Abigail. I should never have attempted any of this nonsense. Sebastian Barrister convinced me it would work. I never should have believed him. But I didn't know that he was working so closely with Marybeth. He had his own agenda. Together they wanted to take the Coven down a darker path. I was in their way. They wanted to eliminate me."

"Oh, Mother…" Abigail said as she sat down on the floor with her mother. Tears fell from her eyes, gliding softly down her cheeks. "I wish you had just come to me."

Elizabeth Wellington hugged her daughter close and spoke through her sobs. "I am so sorry, Abigail. I wish that I had too. I never wanted any of this. I only wanted my family back. Now I've ruined everything. You all hate me, and I deserve it." She pushed Abigail away and pointed at the black satchel. "You can end it here. I don't

deserve to continue. I won't fight you, Abigail. Finish me."
"Oh, Mother. Stop it. We'll figure something out."

Aunt Abby shook her head. "I couldn't kill her. I no longer even wanted to. I was still mad at her, but I just couldn't drive that stake through her heart." She downed the whiskey and stared off into the night, holding onto the empty glass tightly.

I reached over and rubbed her shoulder and sighed. My mind was a jumbled mess. I wondered if I had been there would I have been able to do what my aunt could not. It wouldn't really solve anything. My parents would still be dead. Could I take Grandmother away from Bobbybear by driving a stake through her heart ending her existence? I frowned after a moment. "Why does Grandmother do it? Sleep in a coffin, I mean. Why doesn't she simply shutter her windows and sleep in her own bed. It seems like it would be a lot more comfortable."

Aunt Abigail chuckled softly. "You know, I asked her that same thing."

My brows furrowed together. "What did she say?" It seemed important, somehow.

She sighed. "Now that she's a vampire her sense of hearing is very acute, so's her sense of smell. I can only guess that they've sharpened to make up for her inability to taste. She says that she tried to sleep in her own bed, but the sounds of the day kept her awake, even the little things. Sleeping in the coffin helps to muffle out the world around her; but even that took some getting used to." She laughed. "Mother's always been a bit claustrophobic."

That made me laugh. Pretty soon we were both in tears.

Chapter Eighteen

The Way to a Man's Heart

I pulled the Chevy up to the curb in front of Millie's house and shut off the ignition. As I climbed out of the pickup her grandmother greeted me from the porch. "Good morning, my dear. How was your weekend?"

I smiled as I stepped through the gated picket fence. "Good morning, Mrs. B! How are you doing today?"

She smiled broadly and lifted her knitting into the air so I could see. "Think it's going to be a blanket instead of a sweater," she chuckled.

I grinned. "Well I'm sure it'll be a beautiful blanket."

Millie smiled from the screen door. "Hey girlfriend!"

I swept my hand toward the beat up truck. "Your carriage awaits, M'lady!"

She was having difficulty managing her backpack and the crutches. I quickly swooped in to her rescue. "Let me get the backpack for you, Millie."

She smiled at me as she stopped and pushed her glasses up the bridge of her nose. "Thanks. I don't know what I'd do without friends like you."

I slipped an arm through the shoulder straps of her backpack and was nearly thrown off balance by the unexpected weight. "Good Lord, Millie! What do you have in this thing?"

She giggled. "Just a couple of odds and ends. You'll see." She hobbled out onto the porch and kissed the top of her grandmother's head. "Have a good day, Grams."

"You girls have a nice day too. Try to stay out of mischief."

Millie giggled again. "Don't worry about us, Grams. We'll be just fine." As she stepped off the porch she stopped and turned to me. "Oh, try not to jostle that backpack too much."

My spider sense started tingling. "What's in here, Millie?" I was starting to get a bad feeling.

She giggled. "Oh, nothing, really. It's just a little something that I dreamed up with a little help from my Grams and her friends. I want to show those bitches that they've messed with the wrong girl."

I stopped. "Millie, what've you got planned?"

"Relax, Kat. It's completely harmless, I promise. Nobody will get hurt, and everyone will get a good laugh." She rolled her eyes, "Except for the ones who get pranked, of course."

"Are you sure you want to do this? This could make things much worse you know." I wanted to talk Millie out of doing something she might regret. The very last thing I wanted was to incite things to get further out of hand.

She reached out and tried to take the backpack from me. "You don't wanna be a part of this? Fine. I'll fly solo."

I sighed. "Okay, fine. Have it your way." I refused to hand over the backpack. "Let's go before I change my mind."

"That's the spirit." Millie smiled, "Welcome to Team Vengeance!"

I held the door of the truck open for Millie and helped her

climb in as best I could. It wasn't easy given the weight of the mysterious contents in her backpack. I could hear the crinkle of paper bags and it made me a bit nervous.

As I got behind the wheel of the Chevy I slammed the driver's side door closed. Before I started the ignition I looked at her. "Have you ever heard Cho talk about any of the girls at school? You know, like any he might possibly be interested in?"

She frowned. "Well in all the time that I've known him, which isn't all that long, mind you, I've never heard him talk about anything other than food. Why? What's this about?"

I grinned. "Ari kinda mentioned that she's into him."

Millie's eyes went wide in surprise. "What? When did this happen?" She shook her head. "I miss one day and I miss out on all the new gossip!"

I fired up the ignition. "Don't worry, it didn't happen while you were absent. I only found out about her interest in Cho yesterday."

This time she slid her glasses down her nose on purpose. She stared at me over the rims. "You and Ari hung out yesterday?" She sounded hurt.

I could tell her eyes were starting to water, so I reached over and gave her knee a squeeze. "Don't worry, Mills. You're still my best friend! You're like a sister to me, really."

"Really?" she said as she pushed her glasses back into place with a meek little smile. "You're not just saying that, are you? You know, to make me feel better."

I slid across the seat and gave her a quick hug. She could be surprisingly insecure at times. "Nope. You really are like the sister I never had. Even Bobbybear thinks of you that way!"

"Aaw," she said with a happy little giggle, "I love you guys too!"

"So, what do you say? Wanna help me with a little bit of matchmaking?"

She quickly nodded, almost bouncing on the seat. "This is

going to be so much fun! I've always thought it would be fun to play matchmaker!"

I pulled away from the curb. "I just hope that Cho likes Ari. I really do think they'd look good together."

Millie nodded. "Oh I do too. Ohmygosh!" she gasped suddenly.

"What?" I asked, easing my foot up off the accelerator, thinking she'd forgotten something important. It wasn't too late to turn the truck around.

"What are we gonna do about poor Manny? I think he's sweet on Ari."

My eyes widened. "I hadn't thought about that. He does kinda dote on her. I think he does like her but I don't think she thinks of him in that way. I think she believes that they're just good friends."

"Oh, Kat! What are we going to do? I don't want to hurt Manny, he's such a sweetheart."

"Well," I said, "I guess we'll just have to find someone for him as well."

"Good luck with that," she said rolling her eyes.

I pulled into the school parking lot and found a spot for the pickup as close as I could to the main entrance for Millie's sake. As I grabbed her backpack she placed a hand over mine and stopped me. "We'll leave this here for now. I'll take care of it after school. I'll get Silas to help me if you don't want to be involved. For now, I just want to concentrate on getting Ari and Cho together."

I shook my head and sighed. "I really wish you'd change your mind about this," I nodded at the backpack. Whatever you've got planned is only going to make things worse."

Her jaw tightened. "Worse than the fact that I may have to walk with a limp from now on? They started this, Kat, under the pretense of extending the olive branch. I was willing to forgive years of abuse by my tormentors, to just shrug it off and move on. But no, they only wanted to hurt me further. It's a wonder that you weren't hurt by their dirty little shenanigans too. We've got to show them that we're not just gonna sit back and take their crap any longer. They wanna fight, we'll give them one!" She indicated the backpack with a nod of her head. "Maybe this will make them think twice. I promise you, this will hurt no one. You know me. I wouldn't do something like that."

I nodded, holding up my hands. "Okay, okay. I'm in. We'll wait until after school." I glanced at the backpack one last time before I closed the pickup door. Back in the City someone might steal the bag from the truck during the course of the day, but this was The Hollows, it was probably going to be perfectly safe.

The Wolf Pack was in the side courtyard where everyone seemed to congregate in the morning before first bell. Manny and Ari were there too, huddled together away from everyone else. I gave them both a smile and a friendly wave, which they both returned. Ari had a frightened look in her eyes as she frantically waved me over. I quickly kissed Brock on the cheek, waved at the others and said, "Hi guys! I'll be right back." Millie stayed with Silas, grinning like the Cheshire Cat.

Ari grabbed my arm and pulled me a step or two away from Manny. Obviously she had something pressing on her mind, but she didn't want Manny to overhear. "Look," she whispered tightly, "I've changed my mind. Please don't say anything to Cho."

I glanced over at where the guys were standing, and Millie was saying something to Cho and pointing at us. All the guys were now staring in our direction, widening smiles on their faces. "Uhm," I said softly, "I think it's already too late. I told Millie about our conversation this morning, and well," I shrugged, "I think she may have already said something."

Ari seemed to pale right before my eyes. She put a hand up to her lips and her fingers were trembling. "I think I'm going to be ill," she said nervously. She gripped my arm tightly and her eyes went suddenly very wide, like she'd seen a ghost. "Ohmygod! He's coming this way! What do I do?"

I smiled at her. "Relax. He's not going to bite you, or anything. Just take it easy. Everything's going to be just fine. Cho's really a very sweet guy."

Cho stopped as he got next to us. He had been eating an apple earlier and was still chewing the last bite he'd taken. He swallowed. Wiping the back of his hand over his lips, he smiled. "Hi," he said softly, sounding a bit nervous.

Ari smiled weakly. "Hi." She shoved a plastic container into his hands. "Here. I made this for you. It's *Mohawk Indian Corn Soup*. It's best if you eat it hot." She quickly stepped around us and ran toward the school building without a backward glance.

I gave Cho a look of uncertainty and shrugged. I squeezed his arm reassuringly and smiled. "Let me go check on her."

As I passed Millie and the others, she looked at me as though we had just witnessed a huge disaster. "What happened?" she said, pushing her glasses up the bridge of her nose.

I shrugged as I continued past them. "Beats me."

I found Ari in the girl's restroom standing at a porcelain sink, wetting a paper towel with cold water. She folded it twice, squeezed out the excess water, and then touched it to her forehead. She barely even acknowledged me as I stepped up beside her and placed a comforting hand upon her shoulder. "Are you okay?" I asked, concerned.

She closed her eyes briefly and then opened them and nodded. "I… I'm fine. Thought I was gonna be sick for a minute." She clutched the sides of the sink. "Still think I might pass out," she laughed nervously.

I rubbed her back. "I shouldn't have said anything to Millie. I had no idea she was going to say something to Cho so quickly. I really thought we could ease into things."

Ari shook her head. "No. It's all right. I… I shouldn't get so worked up." She swallowed. "God, I'm so thirsty!" She cupped her hand under the faucet and filled it with cold water and quickly took a sip. She chuckled suddenly and shook her head. "I never should've made him the soup. That was a dumb idea."

I chuckled. "Oh, I don't know. The guy does love his food."

She sighed. "My akhsótha said I should take him some soup. I shouldn't have listened to her. She's used to the old ways. Guys these days are different."

"I don't know about that. Guys are guys. I don't think they know how to be any different."

She chuckled again. "Good point."

The first period bell sounded.

Ari looked at me and inclined her head toward the door. "You should go. I don't want you to be late on account of me."

I smiled at her. "I can wait for you."

She shook her head and frowned. "No, go ahead. I'll be along in a minute."

"You sure?" I asked.

Ari nodded with a smile. "Yes. Niá:wen, Kat." She smiled shyly. "Sorry. That means thank you."

I smiled at her. "How do you say 'You're welcome'?"

She smiled. "Io."

I smiled back at her and nodded. "Io, Ari." I left the bathroom and to my surprise found Cho waiting across the hall.

He had a tentative smile on his face, his eyes shown with worried concern as he stepped closer. "Is Ari okay?"

I smiled. "She's fine, Cho. She'll be out in a minute. We should get to class."

He barely shook his head. "You go ahead, I'll wait for her."

I touched his arm. "That's sweet." I turned and headed down the hall to my first period class, English with Mrs. Crombie; fortunately it was only a few doors down.

Cho and Ari managed to just come through the door as the second bell sounded. Mrs. Crombie glared at them both as she stood up from behind her desk. "Nice of you two to join us. Take your seats, and let's get started."

Ari took the desk straight across the narrow aisle from me, a bright smile on her face. That was a good sign. Evidently things had gone well for both of them once she emerged from the bathroom.

Cho hesitated up at the front of the class and pulled a bright red apple out of the pocket of his Letterman's jacket. He placed it on Mrs. Crombie's desk. "Here, I brought this for you," he said with a dazzling smile of his own.

She seemed touched by his gift, but the entire class chuckled softly, seeing what she had not. A huge bite had already been taken out of the apple; it was facing toward us all. Mrs. Crombie cleared her throat, still completely unaware of the state of the apple. "That's enough of this nonsense, class. Open your books to page twenty-two, and let's begin."

Cho and Ari managed to sit close to one another in the next two classes, taking desks at the back of the class. They moved their desks closer together, narrowing the aisle between them even more. Both of them were sporting huge smiles as they looked into one another's sparkling eyes. They seemed oblivious to everything going on around them. They were fortunate that the teachers all failed to notice their inattention. Love was clearly in the air—or at least a budding romance.

As I stood in the lunch line waiting to pay, I saw Cho removing the plastic container that Ari had given him earlier that morning from the microwave. He was grinning from ear to ear as he carried it to the table where the Wolf Pack was sitting; Ari was there too, sitting across from him.

I sat next to Brock and glanced over at Cho's soup. The tantalizing aroma was definitely mouth-watering, and certainly more appealing than what I had on my own tray. I nudged him with my elbow. "Trade?"

He shook his head and hovered over the container protectively. "No way!" He smiled at Ari. "What did you say this was called?"

"Mohawk Indian Corn Soup. It is a traditional recipe of my akhsótha, my grandmother."

He frowned, searching the soup with his spoon. "But I don't see any corn."

Ari smiled shyly. "That's because my akhsótha prefers hominy instead of the corn."

He nodded as he scooped up a spoonful. "What's this?" he asked, frowning again.

Ari laughed. "Rutabaga."

Cho shrugged. "I've never had rutabaga before." He ate the spoonful and his eyes went wide. "It's delicious."

"You're not just saying that?" she asked shyly, a blush coloring her cheeks.

He shoved another spoonful into his mouth. "Nope. It is the best thing I've eaten in a long while. And believe me, I've eaten a lot of things lately."

Everyone laughed.

I looked across the lunchroom and noticed a figure sitting all alone, his back to us, sitting hunched in brooding silence. I reached across the table and touched Millie's hand, and I indicated Manny with a nod. She turned and glanced at her friend. I heard a slight gasp escape her lips. "Oh no. I was afraid of this. He's all alone…"

Silas pushed himself away from the table and stood. He picked up his tray and turned away from us. "He doesn't have to be."

One by one we followed him over and joined Manny at the table. He stared at us, wide-eyed and uncertain, but then a smile appeared at the corner of his mouth. It took a moment, but soon there seemed to be a sparkle returning to his dark eyes.

Millie met me at my locker after the final bell. "I sent Silas out to retrieve my backpack. He's gonna help me with it. Why don't you go pick up your brother and then come back for me? It shouldn't take us long. I'll meet you at the truck."

I sighed as I closed my locker. "Are you sure you want to go through with this?"

She nodded. "Yes. Tomorrow morning is going to be fun! Just you wait and see. It's gonna be hilarious."

I shrugged as I walked away. "I hope you know what you're doing."

Chapter Nineteen

Millie's Revenge

Fifteen minutes later, Melissa LaRoche rushed up to the driver's side of the Chevy as I climbed in and closed the door. She reached through the open window and grabbed my arm. She had a frantic expression on her face as she breathlessly asked, "Can I have a quick word with you before you leave?" She glanced fearfully back toward the front of the school, giving me the impression that she was afraid to be seen. Her eyes swept over the parking lot. Bobby had already slid to the middle of the bench seat and Millie had climbed in after him; they were waiting to leave.

I frowned, not certain she could be trusted. "What do you want?"

She swallowed as she nervously glanced over the hood of the truck, and then back at me. "I never wanted any of this. I tried to talk them out of it, honest I did." She glanced at Millie as tears seemed to fill her eyes. "I'm sorry you were hurt. But

I couldn't stop them. They're too strong. If they knew I was talking to you they'd hurt me too," she twisted her hands in anguish, her expression was pained.

"Why should we believe anything you say?" I was angry. Bitter. She had already conspired to hurt my friend, and only by sheer luck had I escaped injury. I wasn't about to give her another opportunity to do even worse. *Fool me once, shame on you; fool me twice, shame on me.* I was ready to send her on her way with a few choice words.

Millie quickly spoke up. "Let's hear her out."

I turned toward her. "Are you serious? After what she's done?"

Millie slid her glasses back into place. "We can use all the help we can get. You've said it yourself, we have loads of enemies."

I turned back towards Mel and opened the door, she stepped back. "Fine," I inclined my head towards my brother, "But he doesn't need to hear any of this."

I heard Bobbybear's disappointed, "Ah man!"

She nodded and we both walked away from the truck. "What's this all about?" I asked, crossing my arms over my chest.

Melissa swallowed. "It all started with the ceremony that the Coven had. Something happened that night, something really strange. There was this energy. I don't quite know how to describe it," she shook her head. "I've been to a couple of Wiccan ceremonies before, but this one was different. The High Priestess made a big show of trying to impress this guy Barrister." She shivered. "He gives me the absolute creeps!"

I nodded. "I know, I was there watching. I felt the energy you're referring to also."

She frowned at me. "You were? I didn't see you. But Shelby did, I guess. The guys took off after something, but I didn't get a good look at what or who it was. Shelby said we weren't alone. That's when that man, Barrister, and Tucker took off, with all the Sons of the Raven."

"You're not telling me anything new. They were all after me. I barely got away. If a friend hadn't helped me, I might not have."

She nodded. "But after they all left, Shelby seemed different. Changed somehow." She shook her head. "I can't explain it."

"Try," I said.

She winced. "There was a darkness in her that I'd never seen before. It's like she was possessed somehow. That wasn't supposed to happen. It was an innocent ceremony. Something really bad is fixing to happen. People are going to get hurt— maybe even worse than what happened to Millie. I don't know what, but I don't want any part of it."

"People have already gotten hurt, Melissa," I said.

She glanced toward the truck and nodded. "I… I know. And I am sorry. I just wanted you to know about Shelby. She's been changed. I'm scared." She squeezed my arm. "Really scared. I'm thinking about quitting the Coven."

"Is that why Shelby wasn't in school today?" It hadn't occurred to me until just now that she hadn't been here all day.

Melissa nodded. "I think so. Look, I've gotta go before someone sees me talking to you. I think whatever's gonna happen is going to happen this Friday night. I just wanted to let you know." She started to walk away.

"Thanks," I said. She'd given me a lot to think about.

She turned and nodded and then started to trot off, back toward the school. I could feel the hairs on the back of my neck begin to prickle. Tucker had told me that I had a week to decide whether to join him or not. Time was quickly running out. A cold shiver ran through me. Giving me goosebumps.

I climbed back into the truck; both Millie and Bobby watched me closely, waiting for me to tell them what Mel had said. I still didn't want to say anything in front of my brother. He was far too young to deal with all of this nonsense. I glanced at Millie and lightly shook my head. She nodded once and stared out the windshield as I fired up the truck.

When I pulled up to Millie's house she quickly got out and handed her backpack to my brother. "You wanna take this into the house for me? You can grab a cookie from Mister Frog if you want." Mister Frog was a ceramic cookie jar that Millie had made when she was little. Even though her skills had been lacking at the time, the cookie jar was cute.

"Awesome!" Bobby said as he slid out of the truck. He hurried off to complete his task of raiding Mister Frog.

Millie looked at me, she was doing that turtle thing with her neck, sticking it out, expectantly. "So? What did Mel have to say?"

I sighed. "She's scared. She believes that Shelby was somehow possessed during the *Drawing Down the Moon* ceremony."

"Wait. I thought that was supposed to be a harmless ceremony."

I nodded. "Usually it is. But with Sebastian Barrister involved, who knows? Melissa claims that something big is planned for this Friday. She wanted to warn us."

"Do you believe her?"

I shook my head. "Who knows, Millie? I know Tucker gave me a week to either join him or pay the consequences. I think that whatever the Coven has planned is all a part of that."

"What are we gonna do?" she asked with a worried expression.

"I need to talk to Aunt Abby and Grandpa. Hopefully they'll know what to do."

She nodded. "Well, let me know what you find out."

"I will."

Bobby climbed back into the truck, his mouth full of cookie. "Your Grams needs to bake some more cookies! Mister Frog is all out."

She reached in and tousled his hair. "How many did you eat, you little booger!"

He giggled. "Four!" Cookie crumbs shot from his overfull mouth as he laughed.

Her eyes widened. "Four! Your grandmother is going to hate me for spoiling your dinner!" She looked up at me as she stepped away from the truck. "Drive safely, Kat."

I nodded. "I will. I'll see you in the morning."

She waved. "Bye, Kat. Bye, you little stinker!"

Bobby waved enthusiastically. "Bye, Millie! See you tomorrow!"

As I drove home my mind was filled with thoughts of dread. Tucker's 'invitation' was more like a thinly veiled threat against everyone I cared about, and certainly one that I could never accept. I didn't want the power that he was offering. I really was only just learning to deal with lycanthropy; I refused to add vampirism to the mix. I had come a long way since I first transitioned in Aunt Abigail's basement, but I still had much more to learn. The Spirit Quest had shown me that much.

Melissa's concern about whatever was going on with Shelby seemed genuine, but was it really? I didn't know her very well at all. She had seemed nice enough when I was alone with her that first day she'd walked me to class, but when she was around the other Daughters of the Coven, she was another person altogether. Could she just be setting me up for another fall?

My instincts told me to trust her. She was truly concerned about her friend and didn't want anything bad to happen to anyone else. She seemed genuine when she said she regretted her part in what happened to Millie. *But was it merely a ruse? Could she be trusted?*

I honestly didn't know.

Bobby and I both had our windows rolled down and the rush of the cool mountain air felt good upon my face. I looked at my brother and smiled. He had a hand out the window, his fingers splayed wide. The wind was blowing his brown curls all about his face. He was smiling happily, his eyes closed. My hair was blowing like crazy as well, but I didn't care. It felt good. The strong scent of pine was intoxicating.

I could see clusters of *scarlet bee balm* growing at the edge of the forest and was tempted to stop and pick some, but I decided against it; we were already running later than usual, and I was certain that Grandpa wouldn't approve. Aunt Abigail liked to use the *bee balm* to make an herbal tea that she called *Oswego tea*, a traditional tea taught to the early white settlers by the Oswego Indians. I knew that *scarlet bee balm* had a lemony-orange taste similar to *bergamot orange*; but it could be quite delicious if you knew what you were doing. And Aunt Abby did.

We pulled up to the cottage and climbed out of the Chevy. I glanced at my brother. "You have any homework?"

"Nope," he kicked a pebble with his shoe. "I was able to finish everything in class. It's all stuff that Mom taught us already."

I pulled him against me as we walked up to the cottage. "I know, kiddo. Hang in there, you're bound to learn something new."

He sighed. "Yeah, but until then, school is boring. I wish I didn't have to go. I wish I could be homeschooled again."

We stopped on the porch and I knelt in front of him. "You're not still having trouble with those bullies are you?"

"Nuh uh," he shook his head. "They leave me alone now. Everybody does."

"Oh Bobby, you'll make new friends soon. You just have to give them a chance."

He shook his head. "I don't want any. I have Sara. She's all I need." With that he went on into the cottage and I heard him raiding the refrigerator for an apple.

Aunt Abigail turned to me and smiled. "How was your day?"

"It was pretty good. Millie and I played matchmaker for Ari and Cho." I grinned. "They were so cute together! Every time I looked at them today I couldn't help but smile."

Aunt Abby had a pleased look on her face. "Aw, that's nice. I really like Cho. He's a sweet boy, and Ari is a pretty sweet girl too, once you get to know her."

She gave me a sideways glance as she arched a brow. "What is it? I get the feeling that there's something else that you haven't told me. Trouble with the Daughters of the Coven, or Tucker?" She crossed her arms over her chest and waited for me to elaborate. A small, cunning smile stretched across her lips. You couldn't slip anything by her.

I crossed my own arms and leaned against the counter. "How did you know?"

She chuckled softly. "It's written all over your face, Kat. Besides, you get those creases of worry on your forehead and those little furrows between your brows when something is troubling you. You're pretty easy for me to read."

I shrugged. "Guess I'll have to work on my game face."

"Spill it," she said, nudging me with her toe against my shin. She sipped from a glass of iced tea.

"Is that *Oswego tea*?" I asked.

She shook her head. "Lipton," she said. "There's more in the fridge if you're interested.

I shook my head and sighed. "As we were about to leave the school Melissa LaRoche came up to the truck and told me that the Coven was planning something big for this Friday. She also claimed that she felt something dark had taken possession of Shelby at the *Drawing Down the Moon* ceremony. Sebastian Barrister tainted it, somehow, just as you feared he might."

She took a long, deep breath. "Well, I can't say that comes as any surprise. We knew his involvement with the Coven wasn't going to end well. Did she say anything else?"

I shook my head. "Not really. She said she was sorry for what had happened to Millie, and she didn't want to be a part of any of the Coven's plans. She's thinking about leaving the Coven."

"You think she was being truthful?"

I shrugged. "She sounded really sincere. But then again, I really don't know her all that well. Time will tell, I guess."

"Hmm," Aunt Abby said thoughtfully. "I'd better let Sam know to be on alert."

"Oh," I said as an afterthought, "speaking of Millie, she's planned some sort of retaliation against the Daughters of the Coven. She says it's harmless."

Aunt Abigail frowned. "I don't think that's a good idea. She doesn't need to stir them up any more than they already are. If you play with bees and wasps you're likely to get stung."

I shoved my fingertips into the front pockets of my jeans, and shrugged my shoulders. "It may already be too late. Whatever she's planned is going to happen tomorrow morning. Silas helped her set it up."

Aunt Abby shook her head. "I thought they both had more sense than that."

I bit at my bottom lip, and kept my silence. I didn't know what Millie had planned, but I wasn't looking forward to tomorrow.

§

Millie was leaning on her crutches, eagerly waiting at the curb in front of her house as I pulled up. She opened the door and climbed in rather awkwardly. The crutches weren't making it easy for her. "I was beginning to think you weren't coming."

I stared at her. "Look, I've been thinking, maybe it isn't such a good idea to antagonize Shelby and her friends. It could really stir things up, and we need more time to prepare for whatever the Coven has planned for Friday. If you start things with them, it is just going to make everything that much more difficult for all of us."

I could tell that I had made her mad by the angry way she looked at me. Her jaw tightened and she shook her head. "It's too late. What's done is done, and it can't be undone."

"Millie…" I reached a hand out to her.

"I know!" Millie said as she slid her glasses back into place. "I started having second thoughts this morning, but it really is already too late. As soon as they open their lockers…" she shook her head, "Let me just say this, you don't wanna be standing close by. Trust me."

I closed my eyes and lowered my head to the steering wheel. "Oh God, Millie. What did you guys do?"

She had a nervous little giggle. "You'll see."

§

We entered the school building and I started to head for my locker, but Millie reached out and put a hand on my arm. "You might want to hold off a bit." She had a nervous little smile on her lips.

About ten feet away from us Sherrie Marshall was twirling the combination of her locker. Millie's hand tightened on my arm, and I could see the corners of her lips begin to twitch; her hand felt a little clammy against my skin. As Sherrie opened her locker I saw a string attached to the door and the paper bag. The bag was pulled off the top shelf of her locker and it swung, striking the door. It erupted, sending a cloud of pale yellowish powder in the air.

The smell was immediately horrendous.

Down the hall I could see the same thing happening again and again, as the rest of the Daughters of the Coven opened their lockers. The stench of rotting meat, or dead bodies left too long in the sun, filled the air. People were screaming, gagging and puking as chaos ensued…

Millie pulled on my arm, practically dragging me outside with her to fresh air. How she managed it with the crutches was beyond me. Through my watery eyes I saw Silas and the rest of the Wolf Pack huddled together near one of the large trees that grew in the courtyard. They had never even entered the building.

"What was that, Millie?" I asked.

She grinned. "Ground up *Corpse Flower*. Smells horrible, doesn't it?"

Just recalling the horrid smell made me want to gag as we joined the others. We watched students pouring out of the building, some had the yellow powder on their clothes, others were untainted, but nearly everyone was either gagging or puking. Mass confusion dominated the school. Finally an announcement came over the P.A. system telling all students to remain in the courtyard until further notice.

After nearly an hour and a half, another announcement finally blared over the intercom, telling us that due to circumstances beyond their control, school was cancelled for the rest of the day and wouldn't resume until Friday, while the stench was removed and a thorough investigation into the incident was made. Principal LaRoche guaranteed that the culprits would be found, and serious consequences would result.

I looked at Millie. "This could be big trouble for you. They could expel you from school. They could even have you arrested. Millie, this *wasn't* some harmless prank."

She rolled her eyes and batted a hand in the air. "No one was hurt. Besides, there's no way that they can prove anything."

"What about fingerprints?" I said, crossing my arms over my chest.

"We were careful," she said, taking my elbow.

I twisted out of her grip. "How did you get the combinations to the lockers?"

"Silas got them from Norma Shelton. She won't tell. She can't stand the Coven. Her mom is a dear friend of Gram's. Marybeth Collingsworth and her cronies have threatened Grammy and all of her friends; calling them really horrible names."

I shook my head. "I've got a bad feeling about this."

"Oh pish posh. You need to learn to relax, Kat. Everything's gonna be just fine."

I placed a hand on her arm. "Tell me something. What's the use of getting revenge on the Cheer Squad if they don't know who it was that got them back?"

Millie laughed. "Trust me, Kat. They know; they just won't be able to prove it."

§

"So, you want me to drop you home?" I asked Millie.

She shook her head. "Not right away. We're planning on hanging out for a bit down by the creek. You wanna come along?"

I glanced down at my watch, Aunt Abigail had already dropped Bobby off at elementary school, and it was too soon to pick him up unless I wanted to sign him out early. Bobbybear would be thrilled, but I doubted that either my aunt or my grandpa would be too pleased. I didn't care. I decided that Bobby could use a break. He was already well ahead of the other kids his age thanks to the home schooling that Mom and Dad had given. It would be a good chance to spend some time with him. I looked at Millie and said, "I think I'm gonna treat Bobbybear to an early day. Since school's started we haven't spent a whole lot of time together. I miss him. We need to reconnect."

She put a hand on my arm. "That sounds fantastic. I'm sure he'll be thrilled." She glanced to where the Wolf Pack was gathering. "I'd better go before I get left behind." Millie gave me an awkward little hug, almost knocking us both over with her crutches.

I headed out to the parking lot and climbed into the Chevy. I didn't put the key in the ignition right away; I just sat there with my hands on the steering wheel. I could see two of The

Hollows' patrol cars pulling into the parking lot, and slowly moving toward the school entrance through my rearview mirror. The police were on the scene and would now begin their investigation. I could only hope that Millie and Silas didn't get into any serious trouble for her prank.

I watched as Officer Tiffany Jones climbed out of her patrol car and went to the trunk to retrieve the roll of yellow Crime Scene tape. Things were about to get serious. I fired up the Chevy and eased out of my spot, heading for the school down the street. The sooner I picked up Bobbybear and headed home, the better.

I pulled up into the little car loop at the front of the office and switched off the ignition. I sighed as I opened the door of the pickup and dropped down to the pavement; already this day was exhausting. It was one of those days that you just wanted to go home and jump into bed and pull the covers up over your head and shut the rest of the world out. Pretend it had never happened.

I went into the office and smiled at the secretary behind the counter. He was a thin man, probably in his late twenties. He wore thick horn-rimmed glasses with black frames, and coke-bottle lenses. His hair was slicked back with a ton of hair gel; I doubted a tornado could force a single hair out of place. "I'm here to check out my brother. He's Bobby St. Claire. I believe he's in Mrs. Somers' class." I produced my School ID so that he could verify I was on the list to pick up my brother.

"You know your aunt just dropped him off?" he said, looking suspiciously down his long nose at me.

I nodded. "Yeah, and I'm picking him up. He's got a dental appointment and she must have forgotten." It made me feel good that he was at least questioning things. Nobody was going to slip in and cause mischief on his watch. It was comforting to know that he took his job very seriously.

He slid the early release clipboard to me. "Sign this, please.

I'll contact his teacher. It'll just be a few minutes."

"Great," I smiled and quickly filled the form out, signing the appropriate box.

After he contacted Mrs. Somers he handed back my ID. "Something going on at the High School? I saw the police pull into the parking lot."

"Some kids pulled a stupid prank on a few of the students. I don't really know what it's all about." Saying I knew nothing about what was going on was clearly a lie, but it seemed easier than the truth at this point. No sense giving him any reason to question me further.

He shook his head and smirked. "Kids these days…"

I nodded. "I know, right?"

Bobby came in through another door and looked at me in surprise. "Kat? What are you doing here?"

I rolled my eyes and grabbed his shoulders and steered him out the door. "Don't tell me you forgot about your appointment too!"

He stopped suddenly, almost causing me to walk all over him. "What appointment?"

"Come on, Bobby! We're gonna be late!" I grabbed his hand and practically pulled him to the truck. As I opened the passenger door for him I leaned in and whispered, "Just get in the truck so we can get out of here, unless you really want to stay!"

He quickly tossed his backpack onto the seat and climbed in. "Nope!"

As we drove away from the school Bobby gave me a curious look. "Why aren't you in school?"

I glanced briefly at him and smiled. "Millie pulled a dumb prank on the girls that broke her leg. She and Silas put some really smelly powder in their lockers. It stunk up the entire hallway when they opened their lockers to get their books for class."

"Wow!" he said with a wide grin. "I wish I could've smelled it!"

I quickly shook my head. "Be glad you didn't. It was really horrible." I glanced at him with a serious look. "You can't tell anyone Bobby. If you say anything then both Millie and Silas can get into some serious trouble. The police are already investigating what happened. You don't want either Millie or Silas to get arrested, do you?"

He frowned. "Who am I gonna tell? I don't have any friends at school." He shook his head and then he giggled. "Did anyone puke?"

I nodded. "Several people. Even I almost puked, and I wasn't anywhere near it. It was so bad that they cancelled school for a couple of days so that they can do a really thorough cleanup and so that the cops can investigate things. Everything will be back to normal by Friday."

He slapped the seat with both hands. "Ah man! I wish someone would put that in my school!"

His face brightened suddenly. "I wonder if she has any left over?"

I shook my head. "No way, buster! You can get into big trouble doing stuff like that. The police are taking it very seriously. If they discover who the culprits are, they could arrest them and take them off to jail. Some pranks should never be pulled, even if they're only meant to be harmless and funny."

He frowned, his face taking on a very serious look. "Are Millie and Silas going to get into trouble, you think?"

I shrugged. "I hope not. But the cops were just beginning their investigation when I left."

Chapter Twenty

Betrayal

The large wolf watched from just deep enough in the woods so he wouldn't be seen. He had shed his human form before he ever got anywhere near the cottage. There were those present that could easily pick up his human scent, but were likely to miss the woodsy smell of the wolf, unless they were actively searching for it. *But why would they?*

In his current state he might be overlooked by the Wolf Pack. They would think of him as an ally if they saw him, a friend keeping watch against the enemies that were moving against them. Little did they know, he had already struck a bargain with the vampire, Sebastian Barrister. If he turned against Sam St. Claire and his pack of mangy dogs he would be well rewarded; the Witch and the she-wolf would be his! He hoped that Sammy Boy would remain alive just long enough to see his loved ones suffer. All Barrister really wanted was the boy for his own dark, nefarious reasons. The rest were inconsequential to his plans.

They were completely expendable.

It wasn't that Keegan really wanted the Witch and the she-wolf for his own guilty pleasures. He couldn't care less about them. But rather, he just enjoyed making Samuel St. Claire's long life as miserable as he possibly could. Sam had taken Kathy away from him, caused her to fall in love with him, leaving Keegan heartbroken and alone. In the end, he had made them both pay. And he wasn't done yet. He would destroy everything and everyone that Sammy Boy cared about, leaving him a broken man, just as he had been. And he would enjoy every last minute of it…

But to attack now would be suicide. He had no doubt that he could take them on one at a time, but as a pack they were much stronger. The Wolf Pack was gathering at the cottage to formulate plans of their own as they sought to protect themselves from the Coven and the vampire. Besides, he needed to go to Barrister and complete his transformation. The Vampire had agreed to turn him as Tucker Morrison had been, thereby increasing his own strength. He would be a powerful hybrid without equal – save for the Morrison pup. But he would deal with him when the time came. This forest wasn't big enough for two powerful hybrids!

As he started to turn away, he heard movement deeper in the woods. A familiar scent assailed him. It was Cho Ming; he could smell a hint of that little Mohawk girl's perfume still lingering on the boy. He morphed back into his human form and grinned. He was never one to let a target of opportunity pass him by.

Keegan was a big man yet he moved soundlessly through the trees. He could hear the lovesick pup singing softly about his little Indian maiden as he walked through the forest. He could see the boy pull a weatherproof pouch out of a nook in a nearby tree; he was preparing to get dressed. "I wouldn't bother," Keegan said as he stepped into the small clearing.

Cho practically jumped out of his skin. "Don't *do* that, man!

You nearly scared me to death." He eyed the huge naked man that was stepping toward him. "You're that Rourke dude that Sam went for. You're gonna help us fight Barrister." He visibly relaxed, not seeing an immediate threat.

Keegan chuckled. "That's me, kid." He looked toward the north. "Been a change in plans for tonight. The Pack is going to meet us at Sam's cabin instead of the cottage. Evidently they've learned that Barrister has a lair up near Valen's Ridge. They want the Pack to do a little investigating. I was told to wait for you."

Cho shook his head and laughed. "Man, I was just by there not too long ago, wish I'd known."

"Sam believes that the vampire and the Coven might go for your little Mohawk friend and the old Medicine Woman. You know, kinda make a statement."

"Ari?" Cho had a worried look on his face. He didn't know whether to run to her now, or go with Keegan and regroup with the Pack. He nodded; there was safety in numbers. He swallowed. "Let's get moving then." He shoved his pouch back into the nook of the twisted pine tree.

Keegan morphed back into his Wolf form, causing Cho's eyes to widen in surprise. The size of the beast before him was enormous. He'd never seen a wolf quite so large; but then again, Rourke was a giant of a man. He grinned. "Sure glad you're on our side!" He quickly took wolf form and trotted after the larger wolf…

Cho stopped at the edge of the forest, Sam's cabin was in the clearing just up ahead. He morphed back into his human form and scratched the side of his head. The cabin appeared to be deserted. "That's strange," he said as he glanced at the larger wolf coming up behind him, "it doesn't look like anyone's here." He frowned. Something wasn't right.

The large wolf growled, the fur beginning to bristle on his back. His head lowered and his shoulders hunched. He seemed about to attack.

Cho took a faltering step backward. "Whoa dude! What are you doing? We're on the same side!"

Drool dripped from the wolf's mouth. He snarled menacingly.

Cho swallowed. He frantically tried to put as much distance between them as he could. He desperately wanted to get into the cabin and bolt the door. To escape…

The wolf leapt through the air, knocking Cho to the ground. The beast's powerful jaws found the boy's neck, cutting off his frantic screams.

Chapter Twenty-one

Down in Numbers

I watched Grandpa standing on the porch of the cottage, staring off into the night. He shook his head. "This isn't like Cho to be so late. He's more than an hour overdue." I could tell that he was worried. We all could.

Aunt Abby tried to make him feel better. She rubbed his back lovingly and smiled. "He's probably still with Ari. You know how young love can be." She ran her fingers through his hair, forcing his lips to hers. She kissed him soundly.

Brock laughed. "Ari probably made him stay for dinner. You know how distracted Cho can be when it comes to food. He'll be here once there's nothing left for him to eat. You'll see."

Grandpa sighed, an anxious look rooted in his eyes. He was like a father to the pack. We were all his children in a sense. He would continue to be concerned about our welfare until he knew we were all safe and accounted for. That's what parents do. That's what leaders do; leave no one behind.

Silas looked up from the rocking chair. "You want Brock and I to go look for him? We can take a quick run through the woods."

Grandpa shook his head. "No."

Brock stepped off the porch and turned. "Silas is right. We could just take a quick run."

Grandpa slapped the porch post. He didn't like his orders to be ignored. "I said no." He shook his head. "Besides, you guys are probably right, Cho just got sidetracked by his new love interest. I'm sure he's fine. He'll show up soon enough."

The sound of an engine made its way toward us. It was Keegan Rourke pulling up in a dark blue Dodge Ram truck, a large white camper on its back; the kind with a sleeper over the cab of the truck. He pulled up in front of the cottage, stopping the vehicle just inches away from crashing into the wishing well. I heard Aunt Abby gasp nervously; she had seen it too. Keegan stepped out of the truck. "What do ya think of my new ride, Sammy Boy? Got all the comforts of home!"

"About time you showed up," Grandpa said tersely.

Keegan spread his hands out to his sides. "Well, you know me, always like to make an entrance. Besides, I wanted to check out the shower." He scanned the porch. "Looks like you're down in numbers," he said with a grin. "Who's missing? That little China boy?"

"He'll be along," Grandpa said.

Keegan laughed. "Well then, what are we waiting for? Let's get started, shall we?"

I felt a cold shiver shoot down my spine. I hadn't really thought that Keegan Rourke would be coming. But why wouldn't he? I knew that Aunt Abigail hadn't told Grandpa about the other day, and Keegan's visit. If she had, Grandpa would've already done something about it, surely. That thought sent another feeling of unease washing over me. Keegan was absolutely huge. Schwarzenegger huge. And he was dangerous.

Aunt Abigail stepped close to me, giving Rourke a smoldering glare as he stepped to the edge of the porch. She was not pleased by his presence either; I could practically feel the heat coming from her. He seemed not to notice her menacing expression, or he obviously didn't really care. He smiled, and inclined his head toward us. "Evening ladies. How about you be good little girls and fetch us something to drink?" He glanced over at Grandpa. "I've worked up a thirst today, how about you?"

I could tell that she was about to hit him with a scathing remark; I had felt her bristle beside me when he'd called us 'good little girls', but Grandpa didn't give her the chance. "We all need clear heads to formulate a plan. Lives are at stake, more than just our own. If Barrister isn't stopped, everyone in The Hollows could be at risk."

Keegan's eyes narrowed. "Fine. This is your little war. We'll do things your way." He grinned, and then added, tucking his thumbs in his belt, "For now."

Grandpa gave Keegan a steady look. "If you're not happy with the way things are done, you are free to leave any time. We'll manage without your help."

Keegan sighed and shook his head. "I couldn't do that, Sammy Boy. If anything bad were to happen to your little pack, why I'd never be able to live with myself. I'd be all torn up inside."

§

We were all either sitting or standing around the kitchen table and it was growing late. Cho still hadn't shown up. Aunt Abigail offered to put on a pot of coffee, but no one was interested. This wasn't like Cho. We all had the feeling that something terrible had happened.

Keegan leaned back into his chair, forcing it up on just the two back legs. I had to fight the urge to kick it out from under him. "Do we even know where this Sebastian Barrister is holed up? Seems to me he'd be a lot easier to defeat if we drove a stake through the bastard's heart while he was sleeping. Then the Coven would be easy to destroy."

"We're not out to destroy the Coven," Aunt Abigail said forcefully. "Their High Priestess is taking them down a dark path. Once we defeat Barrister I'm hoping they'll see the error of their ways. It isn't too late for them."

He chuckled. "It's easy to see how you all got in the mess you're currently in. You're all just too damned soft. You need to strike swift," he slapped the table with the flat of his hand, "strike hard," he pounded the tabletop again, "and finish this. Let everyone know who is in control of The Hollows! Leave no doubt."

I couldn't take it anymore. "We aren't out to control The Hollows. All we want to do is put an end to this evil vampire that is threatening the lives of everyone."

He slammed his chair back onto all four legs, startling everyone. "Does that include Tucker Morrison and your Grandmother? Tell me now and I will end them all."

I glared at Grandpa. "I can't believe this guy! Why did you bring him into this? He won't be happy until he's the last man standing. Surely you see that!"

Grandpa sighed. "We just want Sebastian Barrister out of the picture. I think we can handle the others."

Keegan stood up and shook his head. He pointed a finger toward my grandpa. "If you think you can do this without getting blood on your hands, you're a bigger fool than I thought. If you don't want my help, that's fine by me. I'll sit and watch it all play out. Sooner or later you'll all come begging for me to save your asses! And then we'll do it my way."

He glared at us all and then walked outside, slamming the screen door behind him. A moment later we heard the roar of the Hemi engine as he drove away from the cottage.

Brock shook his head and clapped his hands. "Well isn't that just great. We've managed to drive away the only help we had."

I shook my head. "We don't need his kind of help." I glanced over at Grandpa. "Did Aunt Abigail tell you about his visit here Sunday? He was hoping to find her here all alone, but instead he found only me." I could tell by the expression on his face that he didn't have a clue as to what I was talking about; she hadn't told him anything. I pressed on, despite the warning glance from my aunt. "He was all too happy to find me alone. No telling what he would've done if Ari hadn't shown up when she did."

Grandpa shot Aunt Abby an angry glare. "Why am I just now learning about this?"

She sighed. "I didn't want you confronting him. I was afraid of what he might do."

"Damnit, Abby! I can take care of myself! I don't need your protection!" he said angrily.

Her intensity matched his. "Seriously? Can you? Against him? He's a monster! He scares me half to death. He seems hell-bent on hurting you any way that he can. I am more afraid of what he might do to Kat or to me than I am of Sebastian Barrister! At least with Barrister we know what he is capable of doing." She stormed out of the room and slammed her bedroom door behind her.

It was suddenly very quiet in the cottage. I looked at Silas and Brock; they were still sitting at the table as though they were afraid to say anything, or even move. The tension had risen several degrees and no one wanted to risk another volatile confrontation by saying or doing the wrong thing. I looked at Grandpa tentatively. "I'm worried about Cho. He should've been here by now."

Grandpa sighed heavily as he ran his hand over his face. He looked exhausted. "I know." He glanced at Brock and Silas. "You guys still wanna go for a run? I'll accompany you." They both nodded and stood.

"I'm going too," I said. I hoped that I sounded forceful enough, but I couldn't really tell.

Grandpa shook his head. "I don't think so, not this time."

"I wasn't asking for permission," I said crossing my arms over my chest. "I'm going to go out and help search for my friend, either with the three of you, or all on my own. But I am going."

"Kat..." Grandpa sighed heavily.

"No!" I said much more forcefully. I started unbuttoning my blouse and heading for the door. "I'll be outside waiting on you guys."

I heard Grandpa practically growl behind me. "Has she always been like this?"

The guys chuckled. "Pretty much."

I was standing just on the other side of the wishing well with my arms crossed over my chest, covering my breasts, waiting on everyone else. Grandpa looked at me and shook his head, as he chuckled softly. He had a wry smile curving the corner of his mouth. "I don't know where you get that stubborn streak from. Listen, I want the three of you to stick together. No one is to go off alone. Understood?"

I nodded. "Yes sir," I said giving him a curt nod. "What are you going to do?"

He inclined his head toward the Chevy. "I'm gonna take your aunt and your brother to see your Mohawk friends. Hopefully Cho will be there. We'll meet back at my cabin in a couple of hours."

I nodded. "Okay."

He stared at me with a furrowed brow. "I mean it, Kat. Search the woods for two hours and then be back at my cabin regardless of what you find."

The guys stepped off the porch and morphed into wolf form. As Grandpa turned to go back inside, I transformed as well. The Wolf was all too eager to be set free, and I had to mentally push against her will to keep her in check. This wasn't a joy run that we were setting out on. We were searching for our missing brother. Cho was out there somewhere and we desperately needed to find him. He could be seriously hurt. I could only hope and pray that he was all right. Hopefully Grandpa and Aunt Abby would find him safe and sound, still with Ari and her grandmother. But I had a bad feeling in the pit of my stomach. *Something was dreadfully wrong.*

The three of us started off into the woods, Brock leading the way. He took us to the spot where the guys normally hid their extra clothes; it wasn't far from where I kept my own stash hidden. He transformed again and reached for the waterproof pack that contained Cho's clothes. Opening it he pulled out a white t-shirt. On the chest of the shirt was a picture of a large taco with the words *'Every day is Taco Tuesday!'* Typical Cho. He held out the shirt for Silas and I to get the scent. When we had it, we each barked once. Brock took a sniff and returned the shirt to the bag and then to the nook in the tree.

Before he transformed, I noticed two very different wolf tracks on the forest ground. I barked twice, drawing their attention. One was Cho's. The other was much larger. There was no doubting who the print belonged to.

Keegan Rourke.

They had been here together. We followed the trail, dreading what we might find.

§

As we approached the isolated cabin the tinny smell of blood, like that of wet metal, was thick in the air. The nearly full moon hung high in a night sky that was relatively free of clouds, giving us plenty of light to see by. I paused as we neared the edge of the clearing that held Grandpa's cabin. Cho's body, naked and torn to shreds, was lying ten feet from the cabin's door. I heard

Brock's deep growl beside me, and the mournful whine that escaped Silas. None of us could believe what we were seeing.

His body had been clawed and bitten savagely as only a monster could do. We were horrified to discover that his head was completely missing. What was left of his neck was horribly shredded. A pool of congealing blood darkened the ground.

We shed our wolf personas and looked at one another with saddened eyes, unable to keep our tears from falling. The gruesome death of our friend was frighteningly brutal. We had not expected to find him this way. It was a devastating blow that left us sickened and shocked to our core.

"Maybe it isn't Cho," Silas said with a tremulous voice. "I mean, without a head it could really be anybody. We don't know…" Even as he said it, he knew the truth. We all did. Our friend, our dear brother, was gone. He had been savagely murdered.

Brock wiped the back of his hand over his nose. "I need to find a shovel. Give him a proper burial."

"No," I said with a shake of my head. "Grandpa will want to see this."

Silas sniffled. "Can we at least cover him? I… I can't look at him like that any more."

"Sure," I said, touching his bare shoulder lightly with my fingertips. "I'll get a sheet to cover him. You guys ought to get dressed. We all should. The others will be here soon."

I opened the cabin door and gasped sharply. Cho's head was sitting in the middle of the kitchen table, his lifeless eyes wide and staring. Unseeing… The message was clear. We were all in very real danger.

I knew that when my grandpa and my aunt came they'd likely have Bobby with them. Though I felt that Grandpa needed to see exactly what had happened to Cho, my kid brother certainly didn't. Brock and Silas were reluctant to remove the head from the cabin, so it was left to me. I gingerly placed it next to Cho's body, and covered it all with a clean sheet. Afterwards we all went into the cabin and quietly dressed in the spare clothes that Grandpa kept on hand for us.

While the guys waited outside, I decided to scrub the blood from the tabletop. I didn't want there to be any evidence of Cho's death inside the cabin where my baby brother would be. It wasn't easy to get the blood out of the table, it was already starting to seep into the weathered cracks in the wood, refusing to let go, but I did the best that I could. Finally, as I heard the sound of the Chevy along the rugged patch of dirt road, I finished. I rinsed the washcloth as best I could and then just left it in the sink. I stepped outside feeling weak at the knees.

Three people were riding in the Chevy that I could see; my brother was not among them. Ari was sitting in the middle between Aunt Abigail and Grandpa. At first I felt a surge of panic, worried that something may have happened to my brother. But as Aunt Abby stepped out of the truck she put a hand in the air, "Bobby's fine. He's with Ari's grandmother. He'll be safe there."

Relief flooded over me and I plopped down upon the rocking chair that sat on the porch.

Grandpa stepped out of the truck next. "Ari said that Cho left in plenty of time to make it to the cottage. He should've been there."

Brock nodded, and indicated the blood-soaked sheet in the middle of the yard. "He's here."

Ari's eyes went wide as she took it all in. She ran toward the covered body before anyone could stop her. She lifted the sheet and gasped sharply, tears immediately springing from her eyes. She very nearly collapsed from the shock of what she'd seen. I quickly moved to comfort her. She covered her mouth with a trembling hand. "Who would do this?"

Aunt Abigail shook her head and covered her mouth as she let out an agonizing moan she fell against my grandpa's body.

Tears fell from her eyes.

Grandpa looked at Brock. "Who did this to him?"

Brock took a deep breath and let it out slowly. "I'm pretty sure it was Rourke."

Aunt Abby twisted her body against my grandpa and pounded his chest with her fist as she buried her face in the crook of his neck. The harrowing sound of her cries was more than I could stand, but I had to be there for Ari.

§

"We need to get the police involved," Aunt Abigail said. "Cho was murdered by Keegan Rourke. They can arrest him."

Grandpa shook his head. "And just what do you think the police are going to do? They aren't equipped to handle crap like this. They'd never be able to take Keegan in; he wouldn't allow it. Many more innocents would die. Besides, what real proof do we have that Rourke murdered Cho? We all may know it, but there's no way we can prove it in a court of law."

"So what are you suggesting? Sweep it under the proverbial rug and just pretend that it never happened? What about Cho's parents? Have you stopped to consider them in all of this?" Aunt Abigail said as she paced back and forth. "What are you planning on telling them about their son?"

Grandpa sighed. He ran his hand through his hair. "Jeezus, Abby! I don't have all of the answers. What do you want from me?"

She clenched her jaw tightly. "Justice. Justice for that poor boy, for his parents, for Ari, for all of you! Sam, Keegan Rourke murdered Cho and then lied to us all about it. He acted as if he didn't know a thing about it when in reality he had already committed the crime! He needs to be stopped! Clearly he is not on our side. What's to stop him from killing somebody else?"

Grandpa just sat there with a blank look on his face. He

seemed to be at an utter loss as to what to do. I had never seen him so distraught. He was clearly struggling with the demons within that threatened to rip his grasp of sanity away from him. I was frightened for him, for us all. I couldn't comprehend his indecision. I knew he was blaming himself for Cho's death. Had he never brought Keegan Rourke into this, Cho might still be alive.

I wasn't sure how we were going to recover from this.

§

The service for Cho was two days later, Thursday afternoon, in The Hollows' Public Cemetery, the same place where my parents had been buried several months earlier. Unlike then, today was a brilliantly sunny day, perfect for outdoor gatherings, picnics, family reunions, but not funerals. These belonged on dark, dismal days where even the thick clouds seemed to cry with falling rain. Perfect for mourning. But today was warm and inviting. Somehow it made it all seem so surreal.

I was pleased to see a good turnout for Cho's funeral. He had obviously been well liked; his carefree, jovial manner had made him many friends. He was also a favorite of the Faculty at Hollows High. So I wasn't surprised to see Principal LaRoche, Mrs. Crombie and the others in attendance. I had mixed feelings about seeing Shelby and the rest of the Daughters of the Coven there, along with the Sons of the Raven, but everybody liked Cho, apparently even his enemies.

I held on tightly to Ari's hand as they lowered Cho's coffin into the ground; she seemed completely devastated by the way Cho had died, it was almost as if she was shutting down, closing herself off. The official police report stated that Cho Ming had been attacked and killed by a wild animal, likely the same beast that had attacked the couple on the side of the highway two weeks earlier. I knew better. I was convinced that Tucker had been responsible for the attack on the road just outside of The Hollows. He'd practically admitted to it. But I blamed Keegan Rourke for Cho's murder. Proving it all was another matter entirely. Besides, how could I go to the police with any credible evidence without exposing the Wolf Pack? *Would they even listen? Or perhaps just turn a blind eye to it all, refusing to acknowledge the supernatural elements that permeated throughout The Hollows?*

As the somber ceremony came to a conclusion, I stiffened as Keegan Rourke stepped up to offer his condolences to the Ming family. It felt as though ice water had started flowing through my veins as I heard him state that he would hunt the beast responsible for their son's death. He would see to it, *personally*, that the family received justice. Through their sorrow and grief I heard them thank him for his generosity.

I wanted to scream.

Millie touched my arm and indicated the figure standing at the foot of Cho's grave with a minute nod of her head. "Why is he here?" she whispered.

I followed her gaze and saw Tucker standing there staring down at the coffin. He and Cho had been best friends, practically inseparable until Tuck had been turned into a creature of the night, a hybrid. His jaw was clenched tightly; his entire body seemed tense, ready to snap. I was surprised to see that his cheeks were wet with genuine tears of grief. The dark sunglasses kept me from seeing his eyes. But it was obvious he was hurting.

I eased my hand out of Ari's and touched her arm briefly before walking away. I stopped at Tucker's side and put a comforting hand on his shoulder, giving it a little squeeze. I could feel the slight jolt of his sudden awareness as he acknowledged my presence. "You know who did this," I whispered. "If we don't put a stop to it, this will only be the beginning. We need your help Tucker. Before we all end up like Cho." I searched the impenetrable mask of his face hoping for any sign that he was hearing me. "I know you don't want that. You didn't want this."

He brushed my hand from his shoulder and looked at me from behind those dark glasses of his. His bottom lip seemed to quiver with the intensity of the emotions and the anger locked up inside of him. He didn't say anything. He glared at Keegan Rourke, his jaw tightening with his intense rage. He said nothing. He just turned and walked away.

I watched him go not knowing what else I could do to either comfort him or get through to him. *Had he heard anything that I had said? What was he thinking? It was obvious that he felt intense grief for Cho's loss. Could this, perhaps, lead to Tucker's salvation?* I could only hope that it would. We were going to need help in the battle ahead.

Chapter Twenty-two
The Collingsworth Manor

After leaving the funeral for his friend, Tucker stepped deep into the woods at the edge of The Hollows Cemetery and morphed into his wolf form, not bothering to remove his suit first. Oddly, the tearing of his clothes brought him some perverse satisfaction. He was angry and needed to clear his head. Sebastian Barrister had obviously lied to him. He had assured him that none of his friends would be hurt—at least not until after he had the chance to turn them into a hybrid as he was. Barrister had told him he could form his own pack. He should've known it was a lie. Sam always said that you couldn't trust a bloodsucker! He was right. He realized now how foolish he had been.

The more he thought about Barrister, the angrier he became. Clearly he was not as big a part of the vampire's plans as he had believed. He would show them! He didn't need Sebastian Barrister any more. He could take control of The Hollows without his help. He was already stronger than any of the other wolves, including Keegan Rourke, despite the man's incredible size.

The thought of Rourke made him pause. Admittedly, he was a dangerous man, and likely twice as deadly while in wolf form. But he was a loose cannon, and couldn't be trusted. *Would Barrister really consider making him a hybrid?* That was a horrifying thought. He could definitely be a big problem. He needed to stop Rourke before it was too late. The Hollows wasn't big enough for two alpha male hybrids. And he was responsible for killing his friend. For that, he would pay!

§

The Collingsworth Manor was located at the northern edge of The Hollows, in what was commonly referred to as *Snob Hill.* Several other large houses were nearby, all occupied by wealthy members of the Coven. He had not been surprised at all when Elizabeth Wellington had been so easily removed from the coven hierarchy. Marybeth Collingsworth had gathered the priestesses loyal to her, kept them close, and simply shut the old woman out. The new power structure within the Coven intimidated those who had been devoted to Elizabeth, bending them to their will. Marybeth kept everyone in line through fear of reprisal. No one wanted to face Sebastian Barrister's wrath and be turned into a creature of the night, as the former Coven leader had been. If someone as powerful as Elizabeth Wellington could fall, so too could those less capable.

Fear was a powerful tool.

But if he could take out Sebastian Barrister, he could make them all cower to him. As the only hybrid he would be unstoppable. Marybeth Collingsworth would either pledge her support to him, or she would be replaced. Ironically, many of the Coven were already looking at Shelby as the High Priestess in Waiting – especially after their silly ceremony of *Drawing Down the Moon*. He smiled. Shelby was already taking a greater interest in him since he had become a hybrid; she was inexplicably drawn to power. The wolf couldn't help but smile as his male counterpart envisioned her in his arms.

§

He took his clothes from the waterproof pack and quickly pulled on a pair of sweat pants. He had briefly considered just barging into the Manor without anything on, but decided against it. He didn't want to hear Marybeth Collingsworth rant endlessly about his manners or the lack there of. He smirked; he knew that Shelby probably wouldn't mind. He pulled on a white muscle shirt and turned toward the house; his brows creased in anger. He wanted answers. He wasn't going to leave until he got them.

He pushed past Bertrand, or Beecham, or whatever his name was, and strode into the parlor where everyone was gathered. Seeing everyone else, including Keegan Rourke, already here celebrating when he had not even been invited, fueled his anger even more. He walked up to Sebastian Barrister and thrust out his chin. "I thought my friends weren't going to be harmed until *after* they had the opportunity to join me!"

Sebastian's eyes grew cold, his jaw tightened. "Perhaps you should take a moment and collect yourself. You seem to have forgotten your place, not to mention your manners."

Keegan Rourke chuckled softly; he was standing off to the side with Shelby and her mother, clearly he was enjoying himself. Tucker whirled on him. "I'll deal with you later," he snarled through clenched teeth.

Keegan thrust his drink into Shelby's hand and stepped quickly forward, confronting Tucker. He shoved his chest roughly with both hands. "Why wait?"

Tucker bristled, clenching his fists tightly.

"Enough!" Barrister's tone of voice left no room for further argument, his eyes burned with molten fire. "Clearly the two of you have issues that you need to resolve, but this isn't the time, nor the place for such frivolity. Need I remind you both that we are guests in Collingsworth Manor? I suggest you make your apologies to the Lady of the house."

Tucker turned back to Barrister, his eyes smoldering with anger. "I demand answers!"

In a flash, the vampire appeared before Tucker and clutched him by the throat, lifting him easily into the air with only his left hand. It was useless to struggle, and after a bit, he ceased trying. Barrister pulled his face closer to his and spoke in a commanding timbre that seemed to resonate throughout the room. "You forget your place, dog! You are in no position to demand anything. You exist to do *my* bidding, to carry out *my* plans. Do I make myself clear?"

Tucker growled but it came out as a strangled rumble. The vampire's grip tightened on his throat. His eyes burning bright red as his fangs grew long and sharp. He repeated, "Do I make myself clear?"

Tucker nodded as best he could, and the vampire released his hold upon his neck. Tucker fell to the ground, growling in angered humiliation. The vampire's claws had broken his skin and drawn forth a small amount of blood; it could very easily have been far worse. He realized just how strong Barrister was. He wouldn't underestimate him again.

Sebastian turned his attention back to Keegan. "Marybeth wishes for you to send a message to the gypsy charlatan. You will go there tonight and deal with this Bradford woman. We'll show the Wolf Pack that they cannot protect everyone. We'll chip away at their resolve, weaken them from the outside."

Keegan raised both eyebrows. "What about the girl?"

Sebastian glanced over at Marybeth. She sipped her glass

of wine slowly and then said, "Do with her as you will. She must pay for her little childish prank that she pulled against the Daughters of the Coven. Let everyone know that their actions carry very real consequences."

Sebastian looked back at Keegan and nodded, but said nothing.

Keegan Rourke smiled. *This was going to be fun!* he thought.

Tucker turned and left the room. He'd heard enough. He refused to be a part of this any longer. Sebastian Barrister would destroy everyone who opposed him. He couldn't allow that.

Marybeth Collingsworth placed a hand on Sebastian Barrister's arm. "It would seem that you've angered him. I don't think he can be trusted any longer."

Keegan nodded, crossing his arms over his thick chest. "I agree. I think his loyalties are shifting."

Barrister nodded his head thoughtfully. "Perhaps you are right." He looked at Shelby, drawing her attention with his gaze. "Can you remove the enchantment from his ring?"

She nodded. "Of course."

Sebastian Barrister finished his glass of wine. "Do it."

§

Shelby Collingsworth lit the match and held it on the end of the black candle melting it enough for a single droplet of hot wax to dribble onto the center of the table. She then stood the slender candle on the puddle and held it there until the wax cooled and hardened, holding it in place. As the flame of the match neared the tips of her fingers, she lit the candle before blowing the match out. A black fire flickered on the end of the tapered wax. She placed her hands flat upon the table, fingers splayed wide, the tips of her thumbs and index fingers touching, as they surrounded the narrow candle. She closed her eyes as she turned her thoughts to Tucker Morrison, and the ring he wore. Her lips scarcely seemed to move as she whispered, "Dark Mother, hear my call. Remove the blessing bestowed upon his protective talisman. He has been deemed unworthy. Dark Mother, hear my call." A breeze blew through her hair, causing the dark flame to dance wildly upon the wick it consumed, but the candle remained lit. She opened her eyes and smiled as she pinched the flame between thumb and forefinger, leaving behind a rising swirl of thin smoke in the air.

§

As Tucker ran through the forest in wolf form, he felt stricken with unyielding pain all over his body. It was almost as if his skin was burning. He knew immediately what was happening to him. Sebastian Barrister had ordered his protective talisman be destroyed, and the witches had complied. *Shelby had betrayed him!* He knew he was running out of time. Sunset was still too far away. There were caves nearby where he could seek shelter until the sun went down, but that wouldn't save his friends. He refused to allow any more innocents to die. He had to make it to Abigail's cottage as quickly as possible.

Chapter Twenty-three

Tucker's Warning

After Cho's funeral, we had returned to the cottage in a somber mood. Deciding that a little celebration of Cho's life was in order, we had stopped off at the grocery store and bought burgers and hotdogs to cook out on the grill; and what better way to celebrate Cho than with one of his favorite foods? I saw Grandpa step into the woods. His shoulders were hunched and he seemed angry. I glanced at Aunt Abigail and asked, "Is he all right?"

She sighed heavily. "He will be. He just needs time to process everything. He feels responsible for Cho's death. He blames himself for that, and for what your grandmother did to Tucker. The gravity of it all is beginning to settle upon his shoulders, I think."

"But there was nothing he could've done about Tucker. Cho yes. Had he not brought Keegan Rourke into this mess Cho might still be alive."

"That's what's got Sam so angry. He knows that Keegan is responsible for Cho, but he still blames himself."

"You want me to talk to him?" I really didn't have any idea what I'd say. *Yeah, you brought Keegan into this mess, knowing full well what he was capable of, but you did it anyway. Cho died because of your bad decision. Now put it behind you and move on. We've got bigger problems ahead.'*

Aunt Abby shook her head. "No, I don't want you to talk to him. He's not in the mood to hear from anyone. He just needs time alone with his demons." She inclined her head toward the door. "I'm gonna go slice tomatoes and onions for the burgers. You and Millie want to give me a hand inside while the guys get the grill ready?"

I glanced over at Millie; she was sitting on Silas' knee as he slowly rocked back and forth in the chair. Brock was sitting in the other, but he wasn't rocking. "I'll get everyone moving," I said.

Before I could say anything, Brock lunged from his chair and stepped off the porch. "What the *Hell* are you doing here?" he said angrily.

Everyone turned to see who it was that had gotten him so stirred up. It was Tucker in wolf form. I could see immediately that something was wrong. Small tendrils of smoke were rising up out of Tucker's fur. Panicked, I called out to my aunt.

She came to the screen door and her eyes went wide. Tucker had stopped, and morphed back into human form. You could see bits of flesh burning all over his body. "Quickly! Get him inside and draw the curtains."

Brock whirled on her, ready to fight. "Are you crazy? No way!"

"Do it, Brock. Now!" she said forcefully, leaving no room for further disobedience.

Millie and I drew the curtains closed as Silas and Brock helped Tucker to the sofa. Aunt Abigail returned from the bedroom carrying a wool blanket and quickly covered Tuck. "What happened?" she asked, as she knelt in front of him and began to inspect his wounds.

Tucker chuckled halfheartedly. "Guess the other side decided they no longer need me. They removed the enchantment on this," he held up his hand showing us the ring. The stone that once glowed with a slight red hue was dark, dulled by the lack of magic.

"Serves you right," Brock said with a sneer.

Tucker just shook his head and chuckled weakly.

"Now's not the time for this!" Aunt Abby snapped. She gave me a worried look and the shake of her head was barely even perceptible. Tucker had already taken too much damage and now, even out of the sunlight, his flesh still seemed to be burning away. A re-enchantment of his ring would take far too long. More time than he had.

Tucker nodded knowingly as he stared at my aunt. "It's all right. Brock's right. I deserve this." He reached out and squeezed my hand, his own felt hot and incredibly dry, almost chapped, feverish. He swallowed. "Barrister is sending Rourke to Millie's house. You need to get there as quickly as you can."

Millie gasped sharply. "Oh no! Grams…"

Aunt Abby nodded quickly. "You guys go. Do what you can to stop Keegan. I'll do what I can for Tucker."

Brock and Silas headed for the door, Millie was right behind them. I hesitated for a brief second, looking down at Tucker. His lips quivered and he closed his eyes tightly for a moment. When he opened them, tears flowed down his cracked cheeks and he looked at me with such heartbreaking sorrow. He shook his head. "I… I never wanted… any of this." He frowned as he tried to shrug. "I guess I let the power go to my head."

I glanced at Aunt Abby and then touched him lightly on the shoulder. "We'll fix this," I said, sounding more confident than I felt.

Chapter Twenty-four

The Bradford's Home

Keegan Rourke stood on the sidewalk in front of the yellow, two-story Tudor style house on 2016 Maple Street. He reached into his shirt pocket and consulted the scrap of paper; this was the place. He wadded the paper up and flicked it into the shrubs that surrounded the wrap-around porch. He grinned as he chewed on the wooden toothpick that was stuck in his mouth and took a deep breath. The Coral Bells were just beginning to blossom, smelling faintly of chocolate.

He pushed open the gate of the picket fence and didn't bother closing it behind him. He wasn't planning on being here that long. He laughed. He seriously doubted that the little old lady or her plump granddaughter would give him much of a fight, but he planned on taking as much enjoyment as he could, regardless.

He whistled as he stepped onto the porch and headed to the door. He opened the screen door and grasped the knob of the solid front door; it turned easily in his hand. People were so damned trusting. He pushed it open and said, "Knock, knock!" as he went inside. He grinned. *No one locked their doors in this little town, how convenient!*

§

I glared at Brock as we drove down the highway heading toward The Hollows. "Can't you make this thing go any faster?" I hated complaining when I knew that I couldn't do any better.

He pushed his foot hard on the accelerator, coaxing more speed from the old Chevy. "I'm going as fast as I possibly can."

I could tell Millie was agitated; she was practically bouncing beside me. "Oh God, please hurry! Gram's all that I have!" Tears streamed down her cheeks.

"Ssh!" Silas tried to comfort her as best he could. "We'll be there soon enough!" I saw the worried glance that he gave Brock. We were still too far from town.

The sun was already beginning to set. Brock stepped on the button located on the floorboard and the headlights brightened. The trees along the sides of the road seemed to be blurred as they went flying by. I could only hope that we'd get there in time. I was worried. Keegan was a cruel man.

§

"Anyone home?" Keegan said as he looked around. A set of stairs to the house's second level was on the right; to the left was the parlor, a narrow hallway leading to the kitchen and the back of the house stretched out before him. He glanced into the parlor but it was empty. He swept his hand over the tabletops, knocking lamps and framed pictures onto the floor. "Oops," he said, chuckling softly.

He pulled his hunting knife from the scabbard on his belt,

grabbed a cushion off the sofa and stabbed it with the knife, ripping it haphazardly. He tossed stuffing everywhere. "Come out, come out, wherever you are… Keegan wants to play!"

He turned toward the entrance to the foyer and grinned. He could hear someone coming down the stairs. He sheathed the knife as he heard the old woman's voice call out, "Millie? Is that you, dear?" He stepped into the darker shadows of the parlor and waited, as his own excitement grew.

§

As we sped along the mountain highway at an alarming rate, the panic in all of us was building. We were all terribly worried about Millie's grandmother; she was just a tiny thing, certainly no match for a monster the size of Keegan Rourke. We could only hope that we could get there in time. Suddenly flashing blue and red lights swirled inside the cab of the pickup. Brock glanced into the rearview mirror and immediately started to slow the truck. "Crap!" he said through clenched teeth. Millie sniffled and tears started down her cheeks. I took her hand and squeezed it, hoping to give her a small measure of comfort. I gave Brock a worried look as he steered the Chevy onto the shoulder of the road and came to a stop.

Officer Tiffany Jones stepped up to the driver's side door and shined her flashlight over each one of us. "Do you know why I pulled you over?" she asked.

Brock nodded. "Yes. I was speeding."

She nodded. "Yeah you were. I clocked you doing ninety-two. I didn't know this heap of rust could go that fast without falling apart."

Millie began to sob uncontrollably.

"What's wrong with her?" Tiffany asked shining the flashlight on Millie.

I sighed. "Look, officer, we need to be going. Her grandmother is in very real danger. Just give us a ticket and let us be on our way."

She shined the light in my eyes and studied us silently for a minute. "I think I'm going to need all of you to step out of the vehicle."

Brock shook his head and sighed heavily. "We really don't have time for this, Tiff. If you don't let us go, her grandmother will be murdered. Follow us if you want to, but we need to be going."

I could see her indecision as the flashlight wavered in her hand. She glanced up the road and then back at her patrol car. "What's the address? I can at least call it in, get somebody to do a wellness check."

"Twenty-sixteen Maple," I said. "Please hurry."

Tiffany nodded, slapping the door with her palm as she stepped back. "Go before I change my mind."

Brock didn't hesitate. He smiled at her as he put the pickup into first gear, "I owe you one," he said.

She reached for the hand-mike clipped to the right epaulet of her uniform. "Dispatch, we have a possible 10-64 in progress at 2016 Maple Street. Be advised that the resident is elderly and alone. I am 10-17 that location."

§

Esmeralda Bradford stopped at the foot of the stairs and gasped. She could see that someone had overturned an end table in the parlor and broken a lamp. Her pictures were scattered on the floor, bits of shattered glass everywhere. "Who's there?" she asked nervously. She saw movement in the darkness and the shadowy silhouette of a man—a very large man—moving toward her. She quickly turned and started back up the stairs. She could hear him chuckle behind her as he pursued, taking the steps two at a time.

Tears sprang to her eyes as she attempted to flee. She wanted to scream but her voice caught in her throat, only a horrified groan escaped her lips. She was just happy that Millie hadn't yet returned. At least she would be safe.

She could hear him stomping up the stairs beneath her. She was almost to the second floor landing, and then she could turn left and go down the short hallway to her room and lock the door. She felt him grab her foot with a strong grip and she fell, hard, against the steps. It felt as if at least one rib had cracked. She gasped for breath and the pain was excruciating.

He chuckled again. "Where's your granddaughter? I was hoping she'd be here too. No sense her missing out on all the fun!"

"You…" she clenched her eyes closed as a sharp stab of pain filled her chest, "…leave my granddaughter… alone!"

He shook his head and laughed. "No can do, granny! No can do." He started pulling her down toward him, causing the back of her head to thump roughly upon each step. Dark spots flashed across her vision. She had to fight with everything she had to remain conscious. If she succumbed, he would kill her without hesitation. She could only fight him off if she remained awake. She raked her fingernails over his arm.

§

Ari Tekahionwake had arrived at Abigail's cottage for Cho's Wake, but the others had already gone. Abby and Tucker told her what Sebastian Barrister had planned for Millie and her grandmother. They said that they only hoped that the others would arrive in time to save the old woman.

Tucker was in considerable pain. His skin was literally drying up, becoming chapped and flaking away in little burning embers. He stood, looked at them both and said, "I am sorry for all the pain I've caused. Forgive me." They watched him walk out into the bright, fading sunlight and cast the wool blanket aside. He spread his hands out away from his sides and tilted his head up to the orange sky as he dropped to his knees. He seemed to welcome what was coming with a sense of relief. They could see the tiny flames burning his body, like pinpoints, turning him into dust. A breeze picked up and blew the ashes, the last remnants of Tucker Morrison, away into the coming darkness, scattering them among the trees of the forest.

Abby and Ari exchanged horrified looks. "That poor boy," Abby said, raising a hand to her lips.

Ari swallowed. "I need to go. I can get to Millie's quicker than they can!" With that, she ran out into the yard and transformed into a sparrow, her clothes fell to the ground in a heap. She quickly flew up through the towering pines…

She flew along the mountain highway and saw the police cruiser force the speeding Chevy to the side of the road. There was no way they were going to make it in time now. More determined than ever, Ari flapped her wings harder. She had a lot of distance to cover, and time was running out.

§

Sirens shattered the illusion of calm, in the night that claimed The Hollows as Ari landed in the front yard of the two-story yellow Tudor home. She could see the front door was open and she saw Keegan Rourke ascending the stairs. She ran to the porch and grabbed the first thing available to her—silver knitting needles from a basket of yarn. She cast the knitting aside, opened the screen door and lunged forward, striking the huge man in the back with the long needles.

He roared angrily, loosening his hold on the old woman's foot as he turned to face this new assailant. Recognition reflected in his eyes. *It was that Mohawk tramp that had interfered with him at the cottage!* His voice thundered, "YOU!" He swung his massive fist, connecting with her cheekbone. She slammed into the wall and slumped, almost immediately to the steps, dazed and confused, it was all that she could do to keep from tumbling down the stairs.

He towered above her, his excitement growing as he looked over her naked body. He chuckled. "Tonight's my lucky night!" he proclaimed with a huge lascivious grin.

The old woman somehow managed to stand. She saw that the giant before her was about to take his vengeance out on the poor girl that had come to her rescue. She couldn't allow that! A flash of light reflected off of something protruding from his back. *'Are those my knitting needles?'* she wondered. They looked as though they were about to fall out of him. She lunged forward and shoved them deeper.

With a grunt Keegan faltered and stopped suddenly. His hands fell to his sides. He peered down at the pointed needles protruding from his chest. *"Sonofabitch!"* he said as he pitched forward and toppled down the stairs, his eyes rolling up into his forehead.

The staircase was bathed in flashing blue and red lights as the patrol car pulled up in front of the house. Sheriff Maynard Thompson was the first through the open door, followed by Deputy Malcolm Hennessey. Both men had their guns drawn. They holstered their weapons as they took the scene in. "Are you ladies all right?" the sheriff asked. He took off his jacket and placed it over the naked girl. The junior officer knelt over the body of Keegan Rourke and felt for a pulse. He shook his head.

The old woman sat down on a step, exhausted and in a good deal of pain. Each breath she took hurt immensely. Ari joined her and wrapped an arm around her shoulders. "I got here as quickly as I could."

The woman smiled and squeezed the girl's knee with a trembling hand. "Thank you."

The Sheriff keyed his mike. "Dispatch, inform the Medical Examiner we have a 10-67 on scene. Also request you send an ambulance, we have two with minor injuries."

The intercom crackled and a voice responded, "10-4."

As the Chevy pulled up outside, Millie covered her mouth with a trembling hand. "Oh no! Are we too late?" panic shook her voice. Silas climbed out of the truck and retrieved Millie's crutches from the bed of the pickup.

I quickly slid out of the truck behind her and said. "I don't think so." I placed a hand on her shoulder and we followed Silas and Brock into the house.

Chapter Twenty-five

Consequences

Millie's grandmother refused to be taken to the hospital to be checked out. Instead, she insisted that the medic that came in the ambulance wrap her torso with bandages. In reality, there was nothing more that could be done. Ari was sporting a massive bruise on her left cheek where Keegan Rourke had slammed his fist into her, but she was otherwise unharmed. After the Coroner removed the dead body, the sheriff left his deputy and Officer Tiffany Jones on the scene to finish up.

As the deputy departed, Tiffany was standing outside with Brock, Ari and me. The others were inside with Mrs. Bradford. She put her notepad into her breast pocket and then clicked the top of her pen before sticking it in as well. She looked us over. "Either of you care to explain?"

I glanced at Brock and then stared at her as if I didn't have a clue as to what she was talking about. "Explain what, exactly?" Ari just tightened the blanket around her body and stared off down the street, clearly she wasn't interested in saying anything. Besides with the blow that she'd taken to the jaw it was probably difficult to speak.

Tiffany nodded. "Look, I get it. This is The Hollows. A lot of freaky shit happens around here that can't easily be explained. But I just can't help but feel that you guys know more than you're letting on."

I shrugged and gave her a blank stare. "I'm not sure I'm following you."

She sighed. "I just want to help."

Brock shrugged. "We're all good. I need to be getting Kat back home. Tomorrow's a school day and it's getting late."

I tensed. Tomorrow was Friday. I could only wonder if, in light of recent events, whether or not the Coven was still planning on doing something. I shivered at the thought. I looked up and noticed that Tiffany was eyeing me shrewdly. I couldn't afford to say anything about my fears to her. I mean, what could she possibly do, anyway? I forced a yawn. "I am pretty tired." I leaned into Brock's body and smiled as he wrapped his arm around my shoulders.

Tiffany shook her head as she opened the door of her patrol car. "The Hollows is my home too. I just want to do all that I can to protect everyone who lives here. I really don't like being on the outside. I feel helpless, you know?"

I almost laughed, thinking she wouldn't really like being on the inside, either. I quickly turned my face and pressed against Brock's chest, not wanting to give her anything else to question.

We watched as Tiffany turned off her flashing lights and drove away from the curb. She headed off into the night to continue her patrol. Brock sighed and said, "You know she only wants to help."

I nodded. "But what can she do, really?"

He sighed. "I don't know. I just hate the feeling that she's out there trying to do her job and keep everyone safe, but she doesn't have a clue as to what she's really up against." He shrugged. "Not knowing could get her killed."

"So what," I said, looking up into his eyes, "you wanna tell her everything? Tell her to start carrying silver bullets in her gun and a wooden stake on her belt to fend off rogue wolves and vampires?"

Brock gave me a look that clearly said he was still unsure. I stood up on the tips of my toes and kissed his cheek. "You've got a big heart, Brock. It's obvious. But do you really think that Tiffany is ready to go up against the supernatural? Sometimes I'm not even sure we are, and we're a part of the whole thing."

He sighed heavily as he ran a hand through his thick hair. "I know what you mean." He sighed again. "Come on, let's get you home. I want to check on Tucker anyway."

Ari gave us both a hesitant look. "About that..." she said. "He kinda walked out into the fading sunlight and just vaporized himself. I think he was in so much pain that he couldn't take it anymore."

Brock fell back against the truck, pulling me with him. "Shit!" he said in disbelief.

It felt like I was just punched in the gut unexpectedly. I was pretty shocked by this news too. I didn't know what to really say. "Oh no," I said, covering my mouth with my hand.

Ari nodded, sorrow filled her eyes. "I'm sorry."

§

As the three of us headed back toward the cottage, I glanced over at Ari. She was staring straight ahead as a breeze blew through the open window and whipped her long, black hair in chaotic slaps against her face. Brock had a brooding look pinching his face as he drove along the mountain highway. The mood in the truck was somber. I couldn't take it anymore.

I brushed my own tumultuous hair out of my face, pushing

it behind my ear and turned toward Ari. "I thought you were going to stop by the cottage so we could all celebrate Cho's life?"

I could see the tears build in her dark eyes, but they didn't fall right away. Only when she nodded did they slowly track down her face. "I did. That's how I knew about Tucker."

I frowned, trying to comprehend what she was saying. "But if you did, then how could you possibly have beat us to Millie's house?"

She turned to face me, her lips curved into a slight, shy smile. "You had to follow a winding road through the forest. I could fly in a straighter line. I knew that if I took flight I could possibly get there ahead of you. Good thing I did, too."

I smiled and squeezed her arm. "My little heroic sparrow."

She rolled her eyes and sighed as she chuckled softly. Wiping the tears off her face, she said, "It's not a big deal."

I put a hand onto her arm. "Sure it is! As a kid I always wished I could fly!" I grinned. "Well, that, and turn invisible."

"Invisibility isn't really a good thing," she said softly, "I've practically been treated by the other girls as invisible all my life. Until Millie and Manny came along, anyway."

Brock glanced over at her. "That's because you've never tried to make friends. You're always aloof. You should try and step out of the shadows more."

Ari shook her head. "That is not as easy as it sounds." She sighed and turned to stare out the window. "I tried doing that with Cho, thinking things might be different… and it hasn't ended well."

I quickly slid closer to her and wrapped my arm around her shoulder. "Oh, Ari…" I didn't know what else to say. Silence descended upon us and we drove the rest of the way to the cottage with each of us alone in our thoughts.

As Brock stopped the truck in front of the cottage, Ari quickly opened the door and stepped out. She let the blanket fall from her shoulders and then quickly changed into a bird without saying anything and flew off into the night, heading northward through the tall pines.

Brock gave me a little peck on the cheek with his lips and said. "I'll leave you with the truck. Think I'll take a moonlight run to clear my head. I'll see you tomorrow."

I watched him walk into the forest, peeling his shirt off as he went, and nodded. "Good night," I said, but got no response. I turned toward the cottage where I could see a dim golden glow from a lamp in the living room. Aunt Abigail was waiting for me.

I found her curled up on the sofa, a blanket pulled up around her neck, fast asleep. I knelt down beside her and touched her shoulder. Her eyes opened and she smiled, embarrassed that she had drifted off. "What time is it?" she asked as she sat up.

"It's late," I said.

Aunt Abby looked at me with her face scrunched in worried concern. "How's Millie's grandmother? Is she all right? Were you able to stop Keegan?"

I sighed. "Ari got there in time to save her." Over the next hour I related everything that had transpired and she did the same, telling me how she had watched Tucker vaporize himself in the dying sunlight. It was still hard for me to believe that a little old woman and a small Mohawk girl could stop someone as big as Keegan Rourke.

We sat on the sofa, sipping mugs of hot *Oswego tea* as we talked. Finally, with nothing more to say, we headed off to bed, both of us exhausted.

§

I woke up the next morning feeling like I hadn't gotten any real rest. I wanted to just roll over, cover my head with a pillow, and just sleep the day away! It had seemed like this week had taken an eternity to end. I was thankful it was Friday, and after today I'd have the next two days to rest and recuperate. The school year had only just started and already I couldn't wait for it to be finished. Now I knew how Bobbybear was feeling. Poor kid was completely miserable.

By the time I finished getting dressed for school in the bathroom, my breakfast was ready. Aunt Abigail gave me a look over her cup of coffee that had me wondering what she was thinking. Bobby was nowhere in sight. I sat down at the table and looked at my aunt. "What's up?" I asked. "Where's Bobbybear?"

She took a sip of her coffee. "He's not feeling well. I think I'm going to keep him home today."

I looked around. "Oh? Where is he?"

She inclined her head toward her bedroom. "He's lying down in my room. I figured I'd give him a snuggle once you leave."

"Really?" I said, suddenly jealous. "Sorry if I'm in the way." I swallowed a bite of marmalade-covered toast and frowned. I wasn't really very hungry despite the fact that I hadn't eaten anything since before Cho's funeral.

She smiled. "It isn't at all like that. Your brother saw what happened to Tucker and he's a bit upset. I think he had bad dreams all night. I'm surprised he didn't wake you."

I shrugged. "I guess I was more exhausted than I thought." I pushed my plate away, I'd barely eaten three bites but I didn't feel up to having any more. "How'd grandpa take the news about Tuck?"

Aunt Abby shook her head. "He doesn't know. I think he stayed up at the cabin."

I sighed. "It's not good for him to wallow in his grief all alone."

She nodded with a knowing smirk. "Try telling him that."

I shook my head, angry that Grandpa was acting so childish. Even Bobby was acting more mature. We had things to do!

We needed everyone to pull their own weight, not wander off sulking…

"Well," I said as stood up, "I think I'm going to head on out. I want to check on Millie's grandma, make sure she's doing alright. Poor thing's been through a lot. And I'm kinda curious how Shelby and the gang are gonna react to all that's happened. Should be an interesting day at school." My eyes widened. "I'm sure we'll hear all about Millie's prank and the police investigation today, too."

"Indeed," Aunt Abby said with a raised brow. "You'll have to fill me in once you get home."

I laughed. "Oh I will!"

§

A dense fog hung close to the ground, filling the gaps between the tall pines, and hugging the mountain road. As the sun began to rise it was causing a bright glare that was almost too much to bear. I drove slowly, apprehensive about the conditions on the highway. The asphalt was wet, and I knew that the Chevy needed a set of new tires. I could feel the tension in my shoulders and I was gripping the steering wheel tightly. I didn't like driving like this. And I was tired. I stifled a yawn.

Finally, as I drove closer to The Hollows, the sun began to burn off most of the fog. It had receded enough so that now it only hugged the trees at the edge of the road. I was able to relax more, and pick up speed, making up for a little lost time, though I was still coming into town earlier than normal. I had plenty of time to stop off at Millie's.

As I pulled up in front of the yellow two-story, I saw Silas, Millie and her grandmother all sitting out on the porch. They appeared to be having breakfast. My stomach growled in protest. Evidently three miniscule bites of toast were nowhere near enough to satisfy my growing hunger. And I knew the wolf was probably ravenous, but she'd have to wait.

Millie waved gleefully as I walked around the front of the Chevy and through the gate of the picket fence. "Just in time for cupcakes!" she said. "Have you eaten yet?"

I grinned back at her. "I think I can be persuaded to indulge in a cupcake this morning." As I stepped onto the porch I knelt down beside Mrs. Bradford. "How are you doing, sweetie?"

She smiled, and gingerly touched her side where it was all wrapped up. "I'm doing okay, I suppose. It only hurts when I breathe. I had a little trouble sleeping, but I guess that can only be expected."

Millie touched me on the shoulder, "But that didn't stop her from baking this morning! I swear, the woman is absolutely unbelievable!"

I looked at Silas. "I'm surprised to see you here so early."

He chuckled softly as he took a bite of cupcake. Millie rolled her eyes. "He never left. Said he was gonna keep watch all night."

I winked at him. "You rock, Silas!" We bumped our fists together and then exploded them in the air.

Mrs. Bradford shook her head. "All a little overboard if you ask me." She pinched his cheek, giving it a little jiggle. "Such a handsome boy, though!" Silas turned a deep shade of crimson that I thought was rather cute.

The old woman frowned. "I do worry about that girl though; the one who saved me from that monster. She took a pretty nasty blow to the face."

"Ari? Oh she's fine, really. A bit bruised maybe, but I think she'll heal nicely." On the drive back to the cottage last night, Ari seemed okay, but looks could be deceiving. She had taken Cho's death pretty hard, and now this had happened. I truly hoped that she was going to be all right.

Millie's grandmother got all misty eyed for a moment, and her bottom lip quivered. "Such a sweet girl, helping out a stranger like that. If she hadn't come along…" She closed her lips tightly, unable to say anything else. She frowned suddenly. "And why was she naked?" she shook her head.

We all exchanged looks but kept quiet about Ari's lack of clothing.

Millie gave her a huge hug. "Oh, Grams! I do love you so much. And Ari is a very sweet girl. I'm sure she's glad she could help. Maybe I can get her to come by after school so you can thank her properly."

Her grandmother's face brightened. "Oh that would be nice!"

We sat around on the porch eating cupcakes and chatting away and before we knew it we needed to leave for school. Millie looked at her grandmother with a worried expression clouding her face. "Are you sure you're going to be okay here alone? I could stay if you want, it wouldn't hurt for me to miss one more day."

She batted a hand in the air. "No, I'll be fine. Mabel and the others will be coming by later for some coffee and cake. They'll probably end up staying well into the afternoon. You know how they can be sometimes. And besides, I promised them I'd break out the Tarot and do a reading." She winked at me. "Those silver-haired ladies just love that, you know."

Millie leaned in and kissed the top of her head. "Okay, Grams. Just promise me you won't overdo things. Try and get some rest. You need to heal."

She batted another hand in the air. "Oh pish posh. You worry too much my dear." She sounded slightly annoyed but then her face softened. "I promise not to swing from the chandelier." She winked at Silas and whispered conspiratorially, "But that's only because this old house doesn't have a chandelier!" she giggled. Silas and I both laughed.

Smiling, Millie shook her finger at the old woman. "Oh you behave, Grams!"

Silas chuckled as we loaded into the Chevy. "I really love

your Grams. She's such a sweet woman."

"Feisty," I added.

Millie sighed. "Lord help me, but she is adorable." Millie cocked her head and gave me a strange look. "Why was Ari naked, anyway?"

I sighed. "It's really not my secret to tell, so you both have to promise not to say anything." I waited until they both had given me a confirmation nod before I continued. "Ari is able to transform into a sparrow, much like Silas and I can into a wolf. She was able to fly here quicker than we could drive. Good thing too."

Millie looked astonished as she nodded. "I'll say!"

We arrived just as the first bell sounded. As we were heading into the school building, Principal LaRoche met us at the door. "Ah, there you all are. I need to see the three of you in my office, right away." He turned and walked off, leaving no room for protest.

We quickly exchanged looks. I had a bad feeling that it was time to pay the piper for Millie's prank. But the reason I was being included escaped me. Birds of a feather, I guess…

We entered his office and took the seats he indicated. He sat behind his desk and eyed us all with calculating eyes. "Did either of you happen to see Mrs. Shelton when you came in?"

We all shook our heads and he continued. "Of course you didn't. Norma Shelton no longer works at the school." He gave us all a knowing look. "That is due to her involvement in your little prank earlier this week."

Millie leaned forward and started to speak, "But she didn't—"

Principal LaRoche raised a hand, cutting her off. "She admitted to supplying you with the combinations to the lockers. That is a violation of the school's privacy policy. Now, as for the three of you…"

Millie looked at me with tears filling her eyes. "It's my fault, no one else's. Punish me, not them."

"No!" Silas said hastily. "I helped with the prank too."

Millie smiled weakly. "But really, Kat had no part in it."

Principal LaRoche leaned back in his chair. "I assume that this was some form of 'payback' for the incident on the field. That was an unfortunate accident. But it did not warrant a reprisal that shut down the entire school and forced a police investigation. They wanted to make arrests, but I talked them out of it. In the end, they agreed to let me handle your discipline."

"What happened on the field wasn't an accident," Millie said as tears rolled down her cheeks. "Those girls meant to hurt me."

Principal LaRoche glanced at me. "So I've been told."

Millie moved to the edge of her seat and placed a hand upon his desk. "They would've hurt Kat too if they could have."

He cleared his throat. "Be that as it may, effective immediately, the three of you are suspended from school for the next two weeks. You are not permitted on school grounds during that time. That includes the school parking lot. Questions?" He glared at each of us in turn.

Millie sobbed. "It isn't fair to punish Kat. She tried to talk me out of this, but I wouldn't listen to her. She's innocent. She really shouldn't be punished for this."

He stood up and walked around the desk and opened the door. "Then perhaps you should have listened to her. That's all I have. Gather whatever you need from your lockers and go. I'll see you in two weeks."

Tears rolled down Millie's cheeks as we stepped out into the hallway. "I'm so sorry, Kat. It isn't fair, but I tried to tell him you didn't have anything to do with that stupid prank, he just wouldn't listen. His mind was already made up. I think his daughter and those other girls got to him. They probably told him you were involved." She put a hand on my arm and gave it a little squeeze. "I'll make them pay for this, I swear."

I jerked my arm out of her grasp and rolled my eyes. I glared angrily at her. "No Millie! Enough is enough! Can't you see that your actions have serious consequences? We've been kicked out of school for two whole weeks! We're just fortunate that we didn't get taken into police custody."

She shook her head. "So what? We're just supposed to take their crap and not fight back? That doesn't seem fair. I've put up with their shit for far too long. I don't want to take it anymore. I'm not gonna take it anymore!"

I sighed. "You just need to be smart about it. That's all. Anything on school grounds can get us suspended. Next time we might get expelled completely, and I for one, don't want to have to repeat the year."

"Sooo…" she grinned. "What's the plan?"

I quickly ran a hand through my hair. "I don't have one. Not yet. Besides, we've more important things to worry about than petty pranks against Shelby and her friends. Two of my friends are already dead because of this stupid war. We need to find a way to end it before anyone else gets killed."

Chapter Twenty-six

Dilemma

After dropping Millie and Silas off back at Millie's house I headed for home. I drove along the mountain road with a myriad of thoughts running through my head. The driver's side window was down and the wind was whipping my hair into a frenzy around my face. I leaned my left elbow on the door and tried to tame my hair with my hand. I wasn't having much luck.

There was still so much to consider. Surprisingly, Keegan was out of the picture, thanks to Ari and Millie's grandma. Sebastian Barrister had ordered Tucker's sun-talisman to be disenchanted, which was a death sentence for a vampire, apparently even a hybrid, during the light of day. I no longer had to worry about Tucker's ultimatum but there was still the Coven to deal with, as well as the Daughters of the Coven and the Sons of the Raven. I had no idea exactly what they were planning but I was certain that it would not be good!

But the Wolf Pack had problems of our own. Cho had been

murdered. Grandpa had wandered off, despondent, blaming himself for bringing Keegan Rourke into the mix. We had lost Keegan as an ally – if he ever really was one. Grandpa had been so certain that Rourke was needed in order for us to have any chance against Barrister. *Were we now doomed?* Surely not! There had to be a way through this! I simply refused to give up hope.

Melissa LaRoche had told me that she was done with the Coven, that she no longer believed them to be on the right path; claiming that they had strayed too far from the Wiccan beliefs. That led me to believe that the Daughters of the Coven were not as strong as they seemed. They could be fracturing from within. Perhaps this was a good sign. It was possible that we might be able to exploit this to our advantage. Could Melissa be a new ally? Only time would tell.

Marybeth Collingsworth and Sebastian Barrister had sent Keegan Rourke to deal with Millie and her grandmother. *Why? What possible threat could the two of them be?* I knew that even when my grandmother was leading the Coven that they had looked down upon Mrs. Bradford, mainly due to her Gypsy blood and her Tarot readings. *But could that be all there was to it?* I didn't think so. *What possible threat could Esmeralda Donea Bradford really be to them?* It didn't make sense. I'd have to look into this a bit further, I decided.

I glanced off into the forest as I drove along. I was coming upon the site of the accident and the place where I had seen the female vampire in the woods. She was still out there somewhere. She needed to be found and dealt with before she became a bigger problem. Right now she was probably feasting on the blood of animals, but it wouldn't be long before she felt the need for something far more substantial; like human blood.

Sebastian Barrister had made it clear that Bobbybear somehow featured heavily in his plans. But I still needed to figure out how? *Why was my little brother so important to the vampire? Was it his strong connection with Sara, a girl who died in 1884?* I shook my head. It didn't make any sense to me and I was starting to feel a dull ache in my temples just trying to sort it all out.

But somebody had to do something. Our enemies weren't just sitting back waiting for our next move. They were actively stirring the pot, moving their chess pieces across the board. If we didn't start taking steps to thwart their agenda we might find it was already too late. I couldn't allow that to happen. I was certain that Bobbybear was once again in very grave danger. It was up to me to save him. I could feel the tears well up in my eyes as fear swept through me. *How?*

I found myself wishing again, that we'd never been forced to come to The Hollows.

Chapter Twenty-seven

The Raven

I could see Aunt Abigail sitting on the front porch of the cottage, sipping her morning coffee when I pulled up. Her brows furrowed curiously as she watched me exit the truck and slam the door closed behind me. I shrugged. "Millie's prank got the three of us suspended from school."

She shook her head. "But you didn't have anything to do with that, I thought."

I plopped my backpack onto the porch and sat on the other rocker. "Yeah, well Principal LaRoche didn't see it that way. Evidently since I had gone to him claiming that the cheer squad—including his darling daughter, had deliberately hurt Millie, he was convinced that I was equally to blame. I think he's blaming me for not doing more to stop Silas and Millie, and because of that, I have to share the punishment."

"You want me to have a talk with him? I'm sure that I could straighten him out." She smirked. "And if not me, I could put in a word with your grandmother."

I rolled my eyes. "God no! Besides, it's just for two weeks. The time away from school will give me the chance to do something about all the craziness that's going on." I gave her an intense look. "We need to be doing something before someone else gets seriously hurt. These guys are playing for very real stakes. I guarantee you that Sebastian Barrister won't give up on his plans just because Keegan was killed." I was pretty certain that there was no stopping. Keegan Rourke was just a pawn to him in a much larger game, just as Tucker had been. Both were sacrificial lambs offered up for the slaughter in his sinister eyes.

"What do you propose?" she asked over the brim of her coffee cup. Her elbows rested on the arms of the rocker.

I shrugged. "I don't really know. But we need to do something. Grandmother says she wants to regain control of the Coven, but is she doing anything to achieve that goal? Grandpa's wandered off, moping, just when we need to regroup and formulate a plan of our own. We're down in numbers. Keegan betrayed us, but he's been taken out of the picture. I can assure you that our enemies aren't just sitting around. We need to be doing something! Sebastian Barrister is coming for Bobbybear. He flat out told me that. How are we going to stop him? You're a witch, can't you cast a spell or something?" I placed my elbows on my knees and dropped my head into my hands. I began to sob. I felt so helpless. I was not beyond hanging cloves of garlic around the windows and doors of the cottage, if it would help. I refused to give in and let the vampire win. Letting him have my brother was not an option. I would die first.

Aunt Abigail took another sip of her coffee and then carefully set the cup down on the table between the two rocking chairs. She stared off into the forest and sighed slowly. "First off, you are correct. We need to be doing more. We cannot wait for them to make their next move. We need to be proactive, not reactive. Remember, I am not like the witches of the Coven. I'm a Healer. I practice what would be called *green witchcraft*, drawing my powers from nature and the earth. There are protection spells that can be cast to keep out negative energies; this would include those individuals that mean to do us harm. Sebastian Barrister would not be able to take Bobby from the cottage. But you must bear in mind that this spell has its limitations. The witches of the Coven could combine their powers and eventually find a way in. That whole 'strength in numbers' thing works in this instance too, I'm afraid."

"Anything's better than nothing at this point," I said. In all honesty I had hoped for more. I had envisioned my aunt standing within swirling winds, a magical aura surrounding her as she cast balls of fire and lightning against our enemies. But, alas, that was not to be; she wasn't the all-powerful sorceress of my dreams.

"How powerful is the Coven?" I asked after a moment.

"The power that they wield can be quite extraordinary, especially if they work together." She shrugged. "Now that they have Barrister on their side, I suspect that gives them a bit more potency, especially casting dark magic."

"What about the Daughters of the Coven?"

She raised her brows. "Normally I wouldn't be too concerned with them. They are merely beginning acolytes, able to cast only minor spells of little consequence, nothing too dangerous. But, since Barrister corrupted the *Drawing Down the Moon* ceremony he has called upon the powers of the Dark God's influence. They could be alarmingly more precarious."

I nodded, recalling how Melissa LaRoche had said that Shelby had been changed after the ceremony. It had frightened her. "What about the Sons of the Raven?" I hadn't seen them do much of anything. They seemed to be typical boys, smart-mouthed and mischievous, bullying those who were weaker, but little more.

Aunt Abigail smiled. "They aren't too much of a worry; even

less so than the Daughters of the Coven. I mean, they can be a handful but they have no mystical powers of their own. They are little more than the Coven's minions handling things that require a bit more physical strength and brute force."

I frowned. "So what's with the title, then?" I made quotation marks in the air. "Sons of the Raven?"

She leaned forward and picked up her coffee cup, giving it a little tilt. She frowned at its lack of brew. "The Raven was a very talented Warlock. Legends claim that if he were to combine his powers with the High Priestess of the Coven, together they would be unstoppable. The sons of Coven members took to calling themselves Sons of the Raven." She shook her head. "I guess it made them feel more important."

"You say 'legends', what happened to the Raven? Why didn't he and the High Priestess merge their powers?"

Aunt Abigail shook her head as her eyebrows rose up her forehead. "He simply disappeared. The day that the Raven and the High Priestess were set to wed, he vanished. The wedding was to take place at the *Drawing Down the Moon* ceremony, after the High Priestess received the Blessings of the Moon Goddess; but the Raven never showed. No one has ever seen him since. That was over a hundred years ago."

"I wonder what happened to him?" I said.

"Who knows?" Aunt Abby stood, taking up her coffee cup. She frowned. "You could've probably researched him at the library in town if it hadn't burned down. This all happened back in the late eighteen hundreds."

I felt a cold chill sweep over me. "Really? The eighteen hundreds, you say? Could you be more precise?" My mind was starting to churn.

She gave me an odd look. "I don't know. I think it was some time in the 1880s though."

I swallowed. Sara Robinson had died in 1884, mauled by a wolf in the woods — my own grandpa, as it turns out!

Grandmother had sent Bobbybear back in time with liquid silver in the hopes that he could kill the wolf. Had I not gone back in time to save him, Bobbybear would've been killed too. I could only wonder if I had seen this mysterious Raven on the great estate while I was back in time. There had been a large gathering honoring the former Governor, the Raven could have been among the partygoers… But who was he?

Frowning, I reached out and touched Aunt Abigail's arm. "Do you happen to know who the Raven was? Surely he had a name."

She looked at me like she thought I had lost my mind. "Good lord, Kat, how old do you think I am? Talk to your grandpa, he was around back then." She started for the door and then stopped and turned. "Why do you ask?"

I shrugged. "I don't know. I guess I just love a good mystery. The Raven simply vanished, never to be seen again. What if he left because of what happened to Sara? The Robinson family left The Hollows and moved away. Maybe the Raven was a family member."

She laughed. "I think you're grasping at straws. Besides, how could this help us anyway?"

"Honestly, I don't have a clue. It just seems important somehow."

I couldn't explain it, but I had the nagging suspicion that the Raven's identity was important. But even if we determined who the Raven was, how could it possibly matter? He would have been long dead by now, anyway. Still, it continued to bother at my thoughts. I needed to have the mystery solved so that I could focus on more pressing problems. I made a mental note to talk to my grandpa. It would give me a good excuse to go to his cabin and check in on him. I was worried about him. No one had seen him since we returned from Cho's funeral and he had wandered off. It was high time he rejoined the living—before there were fewer of us.

I followed Aunt Abigail into the kitchen and watched as she poured herself another cup of coffee. I bit at my bottom lip, suddenly feeling my nerves starting to get the better of me. She gave me a knowing look as she turned and took a sip of her coffee. "What's up?" she asked. There was no getting anything past her.

I almost laughed. "Well," I dragged a finger across the countertop, "I was thinking about going for a morning run. You know, to clear my head."

Her nod was barely perceptible. "You want to check on Sam."

I shrugged. "Well, if I happen to be up near his cabin, I thought I might stop in and see how he's doing… maybe convince him to come back. We need him now more than ever."

She closed her eyes and took a deep breath. When she opened her eyes they were moist and a single tear escaped down her cheek. She nodded. "That would probably be a good thing. I've been tempted to drop in on him but figured I'd give him a bit more time." She wiped her fingertips over her eyes and forced a smile. "While you're doing that, I'll get to work on the protection spell for the cottage."

I opened the screen door and started out, but I hesitated. Turning back to my aunt, I said, "Is there anything you want me to tell Grandpa? If I see him, I mean."

She sighed. "Tell him that the troops will scatter and die if their leader runs from the fight."

I blinked in surprise. I hadn't expected her to come up with something so profound. "Anything else?" I asked.

She nodded. A slow smile formed on her lips. "Tell him I love him."

I stepped away from the cottage and walked deeper into the woods, undressing as I went. By the time I got to the 'Changing

Tree' as I liked to call it, I was nearly completely naked. I peeled off my bra and panties and tucked them away in the waterproof bag with the rest of my clothes. I returned the small duffle bag to the nook in the tree. My gaze was drawn to another of the bags, the one that belonged to Cho. It had obviously been closed in haste, neglecting a portion of his t-shirt that had caught in the zipper. A fleeting thought flashed through my mind as I reached for it, not wanting the clothes inside to become drenched if it should rain. I hesitated as my fingertips brushed the canvas, and I felt overwhelmed with sadness knowing that my friend was dead and would no longer have need of the last garments he had ever worn.

I stepped away from the tree and tilted my head upward. The morning sun felt warm on my face and bare skin, despite the breeze that whispered softly through the pines. A small smile curved the corner of my mouth as I imagined that the hushed sound of the wind through the lush, green needles were Cho's assurances that everything would be all right. I thought of the ghostly aura that surrounded the wolf spirits of my parents and I wondered if Cho had his now as well. Would his own spirit continue to run through the woods that he knew so well? Would my wolf spirit return to watch over my brother when my time came? I could only hope that I could continue to be there for him as my parents were for me. I turned toward the north, took a deep breath of the intoxicating fragrances of the pine, and began to run, morphing into the wolf as I darted through the brush.

It had been a while since the wolf had been out on a run. I could feel her desire to be turned loose pulling at my mind. She wanted total freedom and she was being very forceful about it. I eased up on control, but not completely. I knew that if I allowed her to run with too much reckless abandon it could be hours before I could rein her in. We didn't have that kind of time; neither of us could lose sight of the big picture. So I let her run at her own pace, and only gently nudged her toward my grandpa's cabin.

I could see Grandpa's cabin through the trees as I dressed into the clothes that were stashed nearby. The place looked deserted. The windows were dark and the front door was slightly ajar, no sign of smoke arose from the lone chimney. There was no sound to be heard, certainly none giving hint of a human presence. *Where could he be?*

I stepped from the secluded copse of trees and approached the cabin cautiously, almost afraid of what I might find. My eyes glued to the spot on the ground where we had found Cho's headless corpse, and a shiver ran violently through every fiber of my being, calling forth countless goose pimples. Already, the day was becoming incredibly warm, the sky was cloudless and the bright sunlight seemed unbearably hot. Beads of sweat trickled down the sides of my face.

I forced my head up toward the open cabin door as I continued to walk forward. My throat felt incredibly dry and I swallowed, hoping to bring relief, but it was useless. The last time I had been inside the cabin I had found Cho's head waiting for me. "Grandpa?" I called out, but the voice that came out sounded like some frightened little girl in a horror movie. I put a fist to my mouth and cleared my throat, but the dryness remained. "Grandpa?" I tried again. It was still sounding like a scratchy whisper that I doubted anyone inside the cabin could hear even with the door open.

I stepped onto the porch and nudged the door with my foot. It creaked loudly as it swung open, allowing more sunlight to enter the dark abode. "Grandpa?" I whispered. "It's me, Kat. Is everything all right?" I peered inside, almost afraid to actually enter the cabin for fear of what I might find.

But the cabin was empty. There were signs that it had recently been inhabited. A skillet was in the sink with remnants of scrambled eggs still clinging to the bottom of the pan. A plate was there too, along with a fork and a butter knife. I touched the side of the half-filled coffee pot; it was still warm. Grandpa had obviously eaten breakfast before he left. *But where had he gone?*

Darkness filled the cabin as a tall figure stood in the doorway. Turning, I saw that it was Grandpa. I put a hand to my breast. "You startled me!" I said breathlessly.

He frowned darkly, his annoyance clearly evident. "I don't need you checking on me."

I shook my head. "I… I'm not… well, maybe I am. No one's seen you since Cho's funeral. You just disappeared. We've been worried sick."

"I'm fine. You should go." He stepped aside to allow me to pass, but I stood my ground. Crossing my arms over my chest I cocked my head to the side. "You can't get rid of me that easily."

"I don't want you here," he said flatly.

"Well that's just too bad, cause I'm not leaving until we talk about what's going on. You can't just run off and sulk. We need you. We're fighting a war in case you've forgotten." I was angry. His attitude was starting to really piss me off.

He leaned against the doorjamb, causing the wood to creak in protest. "You're all better off without me around. I'll just get somebody else killed."

"Don't say that. It's not true and you know it!" I said, feeling the frustration starting to rise within me.

"What about Cho?" he said with a wave of his hand. "His death is on my hands!"

"No!" I said emphatically. "You didn't kill Cho. Keegan did. He's responsible."

Grandpa gritted his teeth. "But I brought Keegan into this. If I hadn't, Cho would still be alive."

"You don't know that, Grandpa. We have lots of enemies.

We've already lost Cho. We can't afford to lose you too. They've already started attacking us. Barrister sent Rourke to attack Millie and her Grandmother."

"Crap!" his tightened fist struck the wall at his side.

"Millie wasn't there. Her grandmother was alone. Fortunately Tucker decided to switch back and come to our side, but it cost him his life. He was able to warn us about Keegan before he died."

"Tucker's dead?" He shook his head, wincing with regret. "Is the old woman okay? Did Keegan hurt her?"

"She suffered a few broken ribs, a knot on the back of her head, but she's going to be fine. Ari got there in time to save her. Somehow they were able to kill Keegan."

Grandpa swept a hand over his face and sighed heavily. "Well that's surprising. Neither one of them strike me as capable of killing someone like Keegan. They're both so small."

I nodded. "They stabbed him through the heart with silver knitting needles. He was pronounced dead on the scene."

Grandpa chuckled. "Well, that's good. At least we don't have to worry about him anymore." He looked at me as he pushed himself off the wall and straightened. "What else have I missed?" He frowned suddenly. "What is today, anyway? Friday? Why aren't you in school?"

I rolled my eyes and shook my head. "It's a long story."

After telling him all about Millie's prank, and our subsequent two-week suspension, I looked at him and said, "Now I have a question for you."

He sighed as he went into the kitchen and opened a cupboard. He pulled an empty bottle of whiskey down and frowned, giving it a little shake. He tossed it into the garbage bin under the sink. "Shoot," he said, "I'm all ears."

"Who is the Raven?"

His eyes widened. "The Raven? How the hell would I know?"

"Apparently he goes as far back as you do. He was supposed

to marry the Coven's High Priestess back in the eighteen-eighties but he suddenly disappeared. You're the only one I know of that is old enough to know what his real name might be."

"And this is going to help us, how? Exactly?"

"Honestly, I don't know. But I somehow feel that it may be important."

"He's probably dead now, anyway."

"Not everyone that lived during that time is dead. You're here, so is Sebastian Barrister. Why not this Raven character?"

Grandpa shook his head. "That's all we need! The Raven was supposed to be a powerful warlock. He was always trying to make a name for himself, started going by 'Raven'. He up and disappeared one day. Everyone just assumed he left The Hollows for the big city." He shrugged. "I never really thought much about him. I had other concerns at the time."

"He disappeared hours before his wedding was to take place. Supposedly it would have increased both his and the Coven's power tremendously," I added. "I doubt he'd just leave. It doesn't really make much sense."

Grandpa nodded. "No, that doesn't seem likely. He was always power hungry. In fact, he was Sebastian's younger brother, Rutherford Barrister."

I felt as if I had just been punched in the gut.

Chapter Twenty-eight

Incident at the Morgue

Doctor Patrick Monaghan folded his newspaper closed, and placed it beside his breakfast plate. He smiled at his wife as he stood, and kissed her cheek. "I'm afraid that I'll have to cancel our luncheon today, I've an autopsy on the body that was brought in last night."

Mary squeezed her husband's arm. "Would you like me to bring a sandwich by a little later?" It was usually the only thing that he could manage during a meticulous autopsy; something he could eat while he worked. Otherwise, he'd forget to eat altogether.

He chuckled softly. "That would be nice, my dear. Shall we say around eleven?"

She smiled at him as she cleared the table. "Just make sure you come upstairs on time. You know how I don't like going down there after you. Dead bodies give me the willies."

He chuckled softly. "I will, my dear. Besides, it is only the one dead body. I doubt he can hurt you now."

She shook her head adamantly as she shivered uncontrollably. "Makes no difference to me."

He grabbed his walking stick and his derby hat from the peg by the front door and kissed her again as she held the front door open for him. He stepped out onto the wide porch of their modest home on Willow Tree Lane, and smiled congenially at his neighbor of thirty some odd years, Mrs. Mabel Thatcher. She was a sweet little blue-haired widow, close to ninety if he recalled correctly. "Good morning Mrs. Thatcher. How are you doing this glorious Friday morning?"

She smiled as she waved a gloved hand in the air, her rather large purse hanging from the crook of her arm. Clearly she was on her way out for her Tarot reading. She loved discussing her readings in the early evening as they sat out on his porch, enjoying a glass of wine. "I'm doing well, Doctor Monaghan. Thank you for asking. How's Mary today?"

He nodded. "She's got a touch of bursitis this morning, but otherwise she is doing just fine."

A concerned look crossed Mabel's wrinkled face. "Tell her to drink more orange juice! She's not getting enough vitamin C. If she doesn't have any on hand I can pick some up after I return from my afternoon tea."

"That won't be necessary Mrs. Thatcher. Mary has just squeezed a fresh batch of oranges. She'll be fine, I'm sure."

The old woman nodded with a frown. "Squeezing them oranges is what's probably brought on her bursitis!"

He chuckled softly. "Ironic, isn't it?"

Mrs. Thatcher arched a brow as she chortled softly. "Oh, it is." She paused and studied him for a moment. "Heard sirens making a ruckus last night. Anyone we know?"

He cocked his head slightly. "You know I'm not at liberty to say, Mrs. Thatcher."

She nodded knowingly. "Can't blame an old woman for trying, Doc."

He couldn't help but smile. All she really wanted was a nice piece of gossip to share with her friends, and who could blame her, really? He waved as he turned to go. "You have a good day, Mrs. Thatcher. Tell the girls I said 'hello', would you?"

Smiling broadly she batted a hand in the air. "You know we aren't girls anymore." She chuckled softly.

"No, I suppose not. Have a good time all the same." He touched the brim of his hat and gave her a curt nod.

He always enjoyed his morning walk to the mortuary, especially when there was hardly a cloud in the sky and the sun was shining brightly. A gentle breeze blew along the street, and he noticed the crisp chill in the air, despite the warmth of the sun. A storm was brewing. He'd have to send Silas to check on Mrs. Thatcher's roof after school to make sure that his patch job was still good. The old woman was sweet and friendly most of the time, but if you did something to get on her bad side, the whole town would know in a matter of hours. Besides, Mrs. Thatcher was awfully fond of Silas. She treated him better than she had her own sons when they were young. Of course the Thatcher boys had always been a couple of hellions. It was a wonder she had survived them.

The rest of his morning walk was uneventful. Ten minutes later he was inserting his key into the front door of the Mortuary. A thought nagged at his mind, causing him to frown. *What kind of a monster would attack an elderly woman in her own home?* Dr. Monaghan shook his head. If you asked him, the bastard deserved what he got! He closed the front door behind him and hung his cane and his derby hat on the rack by the entrance. He crossed over to the counter and picked up the clipboard detailing his latest arrival.

ROURKE, KEEGAN,
DECEASED MALE, APPROX. AGE 44,
CAUSE OF DEATH:
STABBED THROUGH BACK WITH TWO
KNITTING NEEDLES PIERCING THE HEART,
RESULTING IN INSTANTANEOUS DEATH.
DRUG RAGE SUSPECTED.

He scowled. He absolutely hated it when they made an assumption as to the cause of death; that was his job to determine. He scratched his chin as he set the clipboard down and donned his lab coat. He briefly considered starting a pot of coffee but decided against it; he wanted to get this over with as soon as possible. By all indications the autopsy seemed fairly straightforward. But you never really knew what you might find once you opened somebody up.

He flipped the basement switch at the top of the stairs and waited for the flickering of the fluorescent lights to steady before he started down. He could hear the hum of the long bulbs as they warmed and brightened. He crossed to his workstation and began to set out the tools he would need for the autopsy. It was just after 8 a.m., by 8:10 he was ready to begin.

§

Mary Monaghan entered the mortuary and peeked into her husband's office. She frowned at his absence. He was probably still down in the lab performing the autopsy. She glanced at the watch on her wrist; it wasn't quite eleven. She sat the lunch basket onto the center of his desk and then took a seat across from his leather office chair. She opened her purse and took out the folded newspaper and began to work the crossword puzzle as she waited for him to come up.

By 11:17 he still had not joined her. She frowned in

aggravation. Sometimes he could get lost in his work and lose all track of time. She stepped out of his office, crossed the lobby and stood at the top of the stairs. "Pat? It's after eleven. I'm here with your lunch."

There was no response.

Annoyed, she shook her head. He knew she didn't like going down there. "Patrick! Patrick, are you coming?"

The fluorescent lights went out, shrouding the basement in complete darkness. She frowned. *Why would he do that?* From somewhere down below the sound of a tray with stainless utensils clattered loudly upon the floor, causing her to jump. "Patrick? Are you all right?" She hit the light switch at the top of the stairs, but the lights refused to illuminate. "Patrick?" She took a step downward, craning her head to see better, but it was just too dark. "Patrick, it's Mary. Do you need help?"

There was still no response.

Sighing heavily in frustration, she opened her purse and extracted a small penlight. She turned it on and started down the steps.

§

By the time that Silas stepped through the front door of his home he knew that something was amiss. He had expected to be greeted by the smells of dinner coming from the kitchen, but there were no tantalizing aromas filling the air. A quick run through the house told him he was alone. He frowned. He knew his dad had the autopsy on Rourke, but that shouldn't have taken him all day. And even if it had, it didn't explain his mother's absence.

Something was wrong. The feeling kept nagging at him. His dad was always pretty punctual. He preferred his dinner at the same time every day, 6 p.m.; it was now close to 5:30. His mom should've been nearly done preparing their evening meal. A quick look in the kitchen confirmed that she hadn't even started cooking yet. Silas frowned. This wasn't like her…

Forty-five minutes later he couldn't take it anymore. Something was definitely not right. He grabbed a jacket and headed back out into the growing darkness. The jog to the mortuary took him only a few minutes. He was relieved to see that the lights were still on.

He stepped inside and headed for his father's office; the door was open and the lights were on. He saw the untouched lunch sitting in the center of the desk. His mom's crossword puzzle was there beside her purse, unfinished. The hairs on the back of his neck started to rise.

Silas stood at the top of the stairs and hit the light switch, but the lights refused to illuminate the darkened basement. "Mom? Pop?" he called out, not really expecting an answer. The silence was deafening. He swallowed as he started down the stairs.

Someone entered through the front door, and he turned. "What are you doing here?" he asked, unable to keep the surprise out of his voice.

Tiffany Jones, still in uniform, smiled. "I'm looking for your father. I wanted to see if he had the autopsy results on the vic brought in last night."

Silas nodded. "I'm sure he sent his findings to the station already."

She shook her head. "That's just it, he hasn't."

Silas frowned, giving his head a little shake. "Something's wrong."

"What do you mean?" she asked with an arched brow.

"Mom and Dad are usually so punctual. Everything happens at the same time, every day. But not today."

Tiffany nodded. "That's why I'm here."

"Same," Silas said. "No one was at home, so I came here." He shook his head again, a worried expression troubling his eyes. "But it looks like the place is deserted."

Tiffany indicated the basement with a nod, "No one's down there?"

Silas half turned and shrugged. "The lights are off."

"Is there a switch someplace?"

He almost laughed. "Tried it already. They don't seem to be working."

She pulled her Mag-light from its holster on her belt. "Let's have a look."

His eyes went wide as she drew her service revolver as well. "Is that really necessary?" he asked, pointing at the gun in her hand.

She shrugged. "It makes me feel better."

Silas nodded. "You want me to go down first?"

Tiffany shook her head. "No. I want you to stay up here. We don't know what we're dealing with."

Silas frowned. "It's a morgue."

Tiffany wasn't in the mood. "Just stay behind me at least."

He allowed her to pass and then began to descend the steps behind her. The only sound to be heard was their own footfalls. Tiffany panned her light, sweeping the darkness of the lab. She stopped suddenly, and illuminated the wall along the steps below them. A bloody handprint, too small for a man's, smeared upon the flat white paint. This certainly wasn't a good sign. She heard Silas gasp behind her. "Focus!" she whispered harshly.

A puddle of blood was at the base of the stairs. She swept the light over it, pointing it out to Silas. "Be careful where you step. You don't want to disturb any evidence."

She turned the beam of her light upward striking the ceiling in the center of the basement. She could see that the fixture was missing a single bulb. She scanned the light slowly across the ceiling. Two other fluorescent bulbs were missing in the other two fixtures. "They were deliberately removed," she said.

Silas touched her shoulder. "I think I saw them sitting on the embalming table when your beam swept over it."

She returned the beam of light back to the table in the center of the lab. Sure enough, three fluorescent bulbs were lying on top of the stainless steel table; but there was no body present. "Where's the body?" she asked, not really expecting an answer.

Silas shrugged. "If you'll hold the light for me I'll reinstall the bulbs so that we can see better."

"Go for it."

As he twisted the last light into place, the overhead lights flickered and hummed, chasing the shadows away with bursts of white light that brightened as they warmed. "Don't touch anything else," Tiffany warned. It was obvious now that a struggle had taken place. A thin tray that usually held Doctor Monaghan's surgical instruments had been knocked to the floor, scattering the scalpels and other tools necessary for an autopsy, everywhere.

Tiffany nodded at the large stainless door on the far wall. "Would Rourke's body be in there?"

Silas frowned and shook his head. "When they brought him in last night they would've placed him on the embalming table and wheeled him in there for cold storage. Pop would've brought him out here to do the autopsy."

"Is there another embalming table?" Tiffany asked.

Silas shook his head. "Just this one."

She gave him a stark look. "So where's the body?" she repeated.

Silas shrugged as he looked around. "Well, maybe Pop finished the autopsy and put him on a slab."

She looked at the wall containing several smaller stainless doors. "In one of those, you mean?"

Silas nodded.

She walked over to the counter at the head of the embalming table. A clipboard was there but it was mostly blank, only preliminary facts about the victim was filled in. "It looks like he was just beginning to start the autopsy. Very little detail has been written down."

Silas frowned and shook his head. "That isn't like Pop. He's very systematic."

Tiffany pointed at the countertop. Two knitting needles, coated in blood and other bodily bits was sitting on a stainless steel tray. "Why would he leave those like that? Why didn't he bag and tag them as evidence?"

"It doesn't make sense," Silas pulled at his bottom lip with his thumb and forefinger. He wore a dark scowl upon his face. Usually his dad was very systematic, very organized. This was just sloppy…

Tiffany shook her head. "I'm not liking this at all."

"You?" Silas said. "How do you think I feel?"

She crossed to the wall with the bank of smaller doors that Silas had referred to as 'slabs' and began to open each one; all six were empty. "This doesn't make any sense at all."

Silas swallowed, his eyes growing wide. "Where's the body?"

She holstered her firearm. "I need to call this in." She had the feeling that she was in way over her head as she reached for the mike clipped to her right shoulder. "Dispatch, request 10-33 Monaghan Mortuary."

Static was her only response. She keyed the mike again. "Dispatch, I require immediate assistance at the Monaghan Mortuary…" She shook her head, "I'm not getting any reception down here."

Silas pointed toward the back door of the lab. "That door should be closed."

Tiffany sighed heavily as she drew her service revolver again. "Where does that door lead?" she asked.

"The alley behind the building. It's where they bring the bodies in."

She took a deep breath. "Stay behind me," she cautioned as she stepped toward the door. Silas nodded.

As she reached the door, she nudged it open with the toe of

her shoe and immediately raised her weapon, sweeping it from side to side. She could see a figure lurking in the shadows. She took a calming breath and then said, "Freeze! Hollows Police. Place your hands in the air and slowly step into the light."

"Mom?" Silas said, recognizing his mother.

The figure turned and raced toward them, snarling viciously.

Tiffany was rocked back a step as the shock hit her. The woman ran into the light, arms outstretched towards them, her eyes glowing with a dark red hue. Tiffany could clearly see the light from the lab reflecting off the sharp incisors. Her weapon lowered slightly. "What the…?"

She was shoved aside by Silas, as he yelled, "No! Don't shoot her! That's my Mom!"

As Tiffany recovered her balance she gasped sharply. A large wolf struck the old woman in the chest, knocking her backward. Vicious snarls from both creatures splintered the night. Fearing for her own and Silas' lives, she raised her weapon and fired until the revolver was empty…

Tiffany knew that she had hit both the targets with multiple gunshots, but it didn't appear to have had much affect. It had slowed them momentarily, enraged them, but the end result was the same; the targets disappeared down the alleyway in the same direction. "Shit!" she said as she quickly got to her feet. She reloaded her revolver as she scanned the alley. *Where the Hell had that wolf come from? And where the Hell was Silas? Had he gone back inside?* He was unarmed so she couldn't blame him; it was the first sensible thing he had done all night.

She keyed her mike and started to call for backup, but she stopped without saying a word. *What was she going to say? No one would believe her!* She was still trying to make sense of what had just happened. It was like something out of a horror novel, or one of those late-night macabre horror shows hosted by *Elvira*. As she made her way to the door she looked at the scraps of torn clothes littering the ground. *Silas had worn these!* She was sure of it. But they appeared to have been ripped off of him. *What had happened to him? Was he hurt, possibly dying?* "Silas?" she called out, hoping she would get an answer.

Only silence greeted her.

What the Hell was going on?

After a quick search of the mortuary, she knew she was alone. She holstered her service revolver and keyed the mike on her shoulder. "Dispatch, this is Unit 2. Immediate assistance requested at the Monaghan Mortuary. Multiple shots fired, suspects still at large, three persons missing… wild animals involved." She shook her head as she dropped her hand from the mike. "Christ! It sounds crazy even to me."

"Dispatch, Unit 2. 10-22 my last."

"Are you sure you want me to disregard your last transmission, Unit 2?" came Dispatch's static reply. The reception still wasn't the best.

Tiffany sighed. "10-4, disregard." It all just sounded so crazy. They'd think she was nuts!

Chapter Twenty-nine

Answers

Tiffany Jones rolled her police cruiser to a stop in front of the Monaghan residence. The only light coming from the house was through the kitchen window on the north side. She stepped onto the front porch, her right palm resting on the butt of the revolver holstered at her hip. She pounded on the screen door with the side of her left fist. "This is The Hollows Police doing a wellness check. Is anyone home?"

There was no reply. She opened the screen door cautiously and tried the knob of the front door. It was locked. She closed the screen as quietly as she could and moved to the side, peering through the large bay window of the living room. The only thing she could make out was the light coming from the kitchen. Someone was there; she could see their shadow spilling across the dining room floor.

She stepped off the porch and walked around to the north side of the home. She eased up the three steps leading to the kitchen door and peered through the flimsy lace curtain. Silas was there. To her surprise he was completely naked. It looked like he had three bullet wounds on the right side of his chest, but it could be a trick of the shadows. She tried the knob and it turned freely in her hand. She opened the door and stepped quickly inside. It was only then that she confirmed the bullet wounds in his chest. "We should get you to a doctor before you bleed out," she said.

Silas spun around, clearly surprised. He looked down at his chest, as the bullet wounds seemed to heal and fade away. "I… I don't know what you're talking about," he said meekly. There was no way of his getting out of this. She had seen too much already.

Tiffany's eyes were anime large. "What the *Hell* is going on here?" She gave him an incredulous look as the last of the bullet wounds disappeared completely. "How is that even possible?"

Silas gave her a weak smile. "I can explain."

Her eyes narrowed. "Damn right you will."

Silas nodded. "Mind if I get dressed first?"

She swept her eyes over his body and smiled. "That's probably a good idea."

He indicated the counter behind him. "If you want to make some coffee, I'll be back down in a minute."

Blushing slightly, Tiffany jerked her head up and nodded. "Yeah. That sounds like a good idea. I could really use a cup right about now."

As she went about getting the coffee started, it gave her time to think and refocus. She had the feeling that Silas knew more about what had happened at the morgue than he let on. He had said that the woman in the alleyway was his mother, but she hadn't appeared exactly human. Tiffany frowned. *Had it just been a trick of the light and her overactive imagination that had caused her to see fangs and glowing red eyes?* She didn't think so. *And where had that wolf come from? He hadn't been in the morgue; they had already searched there, yet the beast had emerged from behind them. And how had Silas managed to escape, unscathed, with only his clothes torn to shreds? Had she hallucinated the wolf and actually shot Silas by mistake?* That was a troubling thought. But none of this explained what she had witnessed moments ago.

Silas was more than he seemed.

As she heard him coming down the stairs, she was thankful that the coffee had finished brewing, it gave her something to concentrate on. After pouring two cups, she turned, relieved to see that Silas was fully dressed; he had only to finish buttoning his plaid shirt, which he seemed in no real hurry to do. She smiled tentatively. She couldn't say that she objected to his unbuttoned shirt. *The guy had some nice abs!*

He smiled as he accepted the cup she offered. "I didn't think to ask if you wanted sugar or creamer?" she said hesitantly.

He took a sip of the coffee. "This is fine the way it is. Thank you, Tiffany."

She preferred hers with a bit of sugar, but decided against it. She needed it strong and robust, untamed. She took a sip of the hot coffee and cringed slightly at the unexpected bitterness. "So," she said looking into his eyes after searching his face, "care to explain what the heck is going on?"

Silas took another sip of his coffee and then set the cup down on the countertop. "Let's just say that you're not the only one seeking to protect and serve The Hollows."

She put her cup down and crossed her arms over her chest. "I've never been a fan of these cryptic word games. You need to get to the point. Fast. Before I run out of patience."

He chuckled softly as he raised his hands in the air, fingers spread wide. "Take it easy, Tiff."

That set her off. She slammed both hands against his chest and shoved him backwards; he scarcely moved. It was like striking a wall. "A girl doesn't like being told to take it easy. I suggest you get on with it before I haul your ass in. You can explain things down at the station."

Stunned, Silas had an amused smile curving the corners of his mouth. "On what charge?"

"How about fleeing an active crime scene, for starters? I'm sure I can come up with some other reasons if you want." She hoped he wouldn't call her bluff. She couldn't think of anything else at the moment, other than charging him with interfering in an active investigation.

He grabbed his coffee cup and took a seat at the kitchen table. "What do you want to know?"

"Let's start with the bullet wounds. How did they just disappear like that? That isn't possible. At least it shouldn't be." She saw the expression on his face and knew that he was fixing to deny everything. She put a hand in the air. "I know what I saw. Those wounds looked to be from a Glock. My Glock. Did I shoot you at the morgue?"

He sighed, his eyes searching her. Finally, he said, "Yes, you did. It hurt like hell too." He chuckled softly.

She shook her head. "But how? I didn't even see you. It was only that wolf and that other creature."

He studied her for several very long seconds. Finally, he said, "The wolf was me. I'm a Lycan. I can transform into a wolf at will. I did it to save you from the vampire."

Tiffany blinked in surprise. "Vampire? You said that was your mom! Are you telling me your mother is a freaking vampire?"

He sighed as he nodded. "Apparently so."

"Bullshit!" She was angry now.

Silas ran a hand through his hair. "I wish it was."

Tiffany repeatedly tapped her index finger on the tabletop as her mind raced. "Sooo… you're a wolf and your mom is a vampire. What about your dad? What the hell is he?"

Silas shook his head slowly. "He was human this morning. They both were." He studied her for a moment, not sure she was believing anything he was telling her. "I think when my Pop started the autopsy on Keegan Rourke, he was attacked."

"By whom?"

Silas shrugged. "My guess is that when Pop removed the silver knitting needles from Rourke's heart, Keegan attacked him."

Tiffany shook her head in denial. "That isn't possible. I saw Keegan Rourke's body at the Bradford residence. There was absolutely no pulse. He was definitely dead."

Silas shook his head as tears began to form in his eyes. "I guess he was a hybrid like Tucker. That's the *only* explanation that fits."

"A *hybrid?* What do you mean by that?"

"A werewolf/vampire mix," Silas said.

She frowned. "You're telling me that Tucker, Tucker Morrison, was a hybrid? Some mix of vampire and werewolf?"

He nodded.

"And you believe that this Keegan Rourke was one too?"

"I'm certain of it now. It's the only explanation that fits."

"Look," Tiffany reasoned, "I'm no doctor, but I studied anatomy in High School. I know that those knitting needles pierced Rourke's heart. There's no way he could survive that. No one could."

"I'm pretty certain that the silver knitting needles killed the wolf part of him. Silver is actually toxic to werewolves. The longer it stays in the body, the more damage it does." Silas shrugged. "But it wouldn't have *any* effect on the vampire part of him. I don't know, maybe it paralyzed him somehow. Silver actually hinders the healing process of a vampire, it slows it down, dramatically. I think that once the needles were removed by my pop, it set the vampire free, and he attacked."

"And you believe that Rourke is responsible for turning your mother into a vampire?"

"You saw her."

"And your dad?"

Silas shrugged. "I think Rourke turned my pop, and then either he or Pop drained my mom. No way to know for certain. But this is all my best guess."

"How do you know so much about how silver affects vampires and wolves?" she asked.

He smiled. "My girlfriend used to work in The Hollows Library before it burned down. She reads a lot about this kind of stuff." He shrugged. "Guess some of it soaked in."

"Okay," she said with a nod. She frowned. "So how many of these creatures are out there?"

Silas sighed heavily. He shook his head and shrugged. "I don't really know."

"Are there any more like you?" she asked.

He pushed his coffee cup across the table. "There're a few of us. The Pack that I'm a part of, we try and protect The Hollows, keep it safe."

"Shit!" Tiffany shook her head. Her mind was racing. "I need to know who they are."

"There's more that you need to know first. Do you feel like taking a ride?"

Chapter Thirty

A New Ally

Aunt Abigail and I were sitting on the front porch of the cottage, drinking a fresh cup of hot coffee as we waited for the sun to rise. I had just returned from a morning run in the woods and we were just relaxing and talking about my parents; their life in The Hollows, and things we had done in the City when they were alive. It was nice to hear about their lives before they married and moved away. And it seemed that my aunt was enjoying listening to me talk about their lives after they left. We could see headlights of a car coming through the woods to the north of Wellington House and we paused, distracted by the unexpected interruption. We had no clue who it could be, really. Grandpa's truck was here, and the Bentley was still in the garage at Wellington House.

We sat with eager anticipation as the patrol car pulled up in front of us. Aunt Abby and I exchanged looks of uncertainty, she with an arched brow. When I saw Silas get out of the vehicle with Tiffany Jones, I knew that something was wrong. He had a pained expression on his face, and his eyes seemed haunted by something he had seen. My first thought was that something had happened to Millie or her grandmother. I jumped up and practically flew off the porch. I could feel my heart quicken as it thundered inside my chest. "Is everything all right? What happened?"

He raised his hands placatingly and spoke as though he were exhausted. He must have read my mind. "Millie's fine. So is her grandmother. But I think we do have some serious problems ahead of us." His eyes were red-rimmed and puffy. It looked like he had been crying or something.

I glanced from him to Tiffany. She had a thoughtful expression on her face as she slowly nodded her head. "What's this about?" I asked.

"We think both his parents might be dead," she said.

"Undead," Silas amended, swallowing the lump in his throat. He sounded anguished, barely keeping it together.

Tiffany shook her head and rolled her eyes. "Whatever."

I placed a hand on Silas' arm. "How is this possible? Did Barrister attack your folks?" It occurred to me that our enemies were striking where we were most vulnerable, chipping away at us with the desire to shake our resolve and weaken us. They were hitting us where it would hurt the worst—our families. The Wolf Pack couldn't defend everyone, we weren't that strong, and our numbers were swiftly dwindling.

Silas shook his head. "No… I don't think it was Barrister."

I dropped my hand from his arm. "If not him, then who?"

He swallowed, glancing from me to Aunt Abby. "It's Keegan. I think when my pop went to perform the autopsy on Rourke he somehow attacked him. The first thing Pop would've done was to remove the silver knitting needles from his heart."

Astonished, I turned to my aunt. "How is this possible? I know that Keegan was dead. I saw it myself. He had no pulse when the EMTs checked. He was pronounced dead on the scene." I quickly looked at my aunt. "Didn't you say silver was toxic to werewolves? That's what you said when Grandpa had been shot by Harrison Beckett."

Aunt Abby bit at her bottom lip. "If the knitting needles were silver and they pierced his heart, it would kill the wolf, but *not* the vampire. I think that, possibly, Sebastian Barrister had made Rourke a hybrid, like Tucker. That would certainly explain everything."

I shook my head. "But if his heart was pierced why didn't it destroy the vampire too?"

"Silver has no effect on a vampire other than to slow their healing. It kinda serves as a paralysis. Besides, vampires have no beating heart, no pulse. They drink blood to survive, but they cannot pump it through their veins. I think they absorb it, somehow."

I frowned, clearly missing something. "Why does a wooden stake through the heart work and not a knitting needle?"

Aunt Abby smiled a quirky little smile. "It all has to do with the wood having once been a living thing. There are those who believe the wood has to be Ash—like the Tree of Life, but that just isn't so. I wouldn't worry too much about it. It's a fun fact but has no real value to us at the moment."

I ran a hand through my hair, my mind swirling. If this were all true, then Keegan Rourke was still out there, a threat to us all. I glanced at Tiffany. "What's your place in all this?"

She put her hands on her waist, her right resting on the butt of her revolver. "I swore to protect and serve my community. That's what I intend to do." She glanced at Silas and then returned her gaze to me. "But with everything that Silas has told me, I think that I may need your help."

I frowned. "What has he told you?"

Silas answered before she could. "Everything," he said.

Tiffany nodded. "It has actually cleared up a whole lot for

me. Even in High School I could tell that there was something strange going on in this town, but I could never figure it out. I just assumed the stories about witches were just small-town lore. That the numerous wolf sightings in the woods were simply because they were in their natural habitat; I never considered the fact that they were Lycanthropes; people I actually knew." She gave me a steady, appraising look. "Kinda makes me see everyone in a whole new light."

I gave her a small smile, not wanting to expose too much. "Well, not everyone you see is a Lycan, just remember that."

She returned my smile. "But you are." She glanced over at Aunt Abigail. "And I would suspect that you are not."

A small chuckle escaped my aunt. "No, I am not a Lycan, but I have many close friends who are."

Tiffany nodded. "Fair enough." She turned back to me. "I understand that Tucker Morrison is a *hybrid*. I'm going to need to speak with him."

I could only blink in response and I turned to my aunt, not knowing what to say. She shook her head, clearly better prepared for this than I was. "I'm afraid that won't be possible. The High Priestess of the local Coven removed the spell from the talisman that protected him from sunlight. When he came to warn us about what the Coven and the vampire were up to, he had already received too much damage from the sun. He chose to end his own existence."

Tiffany frowned. "That's almost a little too convenient, don't you think? Where's the body? Did you report his death?"

Aunt Abby shrugged. "Who would believe a word of it but it's true; I saw him disintegrate right over there," she pointed to the spot near the Wishing Well.

"Am I just to take your word for it?" Tiffany asked bluntly.

"That's entirely up to you," Aunt Abby said with a raised brow. "But I wasn't the only one to witness it. You can talk to Warise Tekahionwake. She was here when it happened, so was my nephew; but I would rather you not question him. He's still pretty traumatized by the whole thing. He's only six."

Tiffany jotted Ari's name down on her notepad. "It's not that I don't trust you, I just feel like it is better to touch all bases. I hope you can understand that."

Aunt Abigail nodded. "Absolutely."

"Do you know where I can find her?" she asked, sounding all-official.

She nodded. "She lives with her grandmother up near Valen's Ridge. Well, a bit deeper into the woods east of the Ridge. It isn't easy to get there, really. There is a road from the north, but it is a fairly good distance."

Tiffany put her notepad and pen back into the left breast pocket of her uniform. "I'll find her." She turned and started to get back into the patrol car. "I want to trust all of you, really I do. This is all a lot to take in. I'm not even sure that I can give credence to it all. I mean werewolves, vampires and witches all seem so… so unbelievable."

I smiled at her. "Trust me, I know exactly how you feel!"

She nodded. "Take care of yourselves. I'll do what I can, but I can't make any promises." She glanced at Silas. "You need a ride back into town?"

He shook his head. "No. I'll be fine."

§

Tiffany drove slowly back to the mountain highway, trying to make sense of everything that she had learned. She had gone to the Monaghan Mortuary hoping to obtain the autopsy report on Keegan Rourke. Never in her wildest dreams had she expected to stumble into a nightmare steeped with the supernatural. So many other things that she had always puzzled over since High School now made much more sense.

As she neared the bend in the road where the accident scene

had been, she slowed and steered her police cruiser to the side of the road. She spoke into her mike, "This is Unit 2, currently 10-7."

Dispatch's static-filled response answered. "10-4 Unit 2. Please advise when you are available."

"10-4." She returned the mike to the hook on the dashboard and shook her head, wondering what the heck she was doing. Now that she knew that Tucker Morrison was responsible for killing the man and his wife, she wanted to look at the scene again. She had parked the cruiser in nearly the exact spot that the Mercedes had been. She climbed out of the patrol car and pulled the long flashlight from her belt loop.

Even though it was past sun up, this area was still pretty dark; the golden rays of the sun wouldn't reach here for another hour at best. She waved the beam of light over the asphalt; the dark stain was still there where the male vic had bled out. She followed the bloodied prints of the wolf toward the center of the road. She could faintly see where Tucker must've transformed back into human form. If you knew what you were looking for, and now she did, you could see the impression of a human footprint. When she had first been on the accident scene it had appeared to be a smudge. Now she knew better.

Tiffany walked to the edge of the highway and peered down at the slope that led down into the forest. You could see where the woman's heels had torn up the ground in her haste to get away. She only had one shoe on, having lost the other when she tripped over the carcass of the dead deer. She scanned the beam of light in the forest. Something was out there, moving in the trees. She had seen a fleeting glimpse of white among the lush greenery. Of course, it could just be her imagination, but she didn't think so.

She glanced at her wristwatch and sighed heavily. "Quit being so silly," she chastised herself. Turning slightly sideways, she began to descend the incline of the slope careful not to slip and fall. "Hello? Is anybody there?" she called out. "This is Officer Jones of The Hollows Police Department. Hello?"

"Help me! Please. I'm hurt," came the voice of a woman. She sounded frightened, anguished.

Tiffany was relieved to hear the woman, she had half expected to find some sort of monster. Clearly this woman needed help. She scanned the forest looking for anything that might give her a clue; the voice could've come from any direction, it was difficult to tell. "Hello? Ma'am, where are you?"

"Help me. Please. Help me."

Tiffany's heartbeat quickened inside her chest. She could sense her anxieties heighten. It was still too dark to see much of anything clearly. *This poor woman has been out here alone, scared, maybe injured…* She tried to speak calmly, not wanting to frighten the woman any further than she already was. "I'm trying to help you, ma'am. But I can't see you. I need your help so that I can assist you. Tell me where you are…"

"Over here. Please, help me!"

Tiffany scanned the beam of light to her left. She was almost certain the voice was coming from that direction. She pushed on through the thick vegetation. "I'm coming. Just hang on!"

"Please… help me… I'm so hungry… I'm frightened…"

Now the voice seemed to be coming from her right. She shook her head. This was crazy! *When was the sunrise going to light up this neck of the woods so she could see better?* "Where are you?"

Nothing. No response.

"Ma'am?" Tiffany asked

The sound of feminine laughter and the rustle of shrubbery came from behind her. Tiffany turned. Her breath caught in her throat at the sight of the disheveled woman in front of her. Her clothes were torn and dirty, covered in mud, blood and who knew what else. Blood was smeared across her chin; her hair was uncombed and looked like a rat's nest. But it was her eyes that alarmed Tiffany the most. They were red, almost glowing.

Tiffany swallowed. "It's okay ma'am. You're not alone anymore. I'm here to help you." She couldn't think of anything else to say.

The woman laughed. "I don't want your help. I just want your blood!" Her incisors grew in an instant; saliva dripped from her open mouth. Arms outstretched, she moved quickly toward her prey.

Tiffany recalled the creature she had seen at the morgue as she backed away. She dropped her flashlight and pulled her service revolver. "Stop!" she yelled frantically. "Stop or I'll shoot!" The vampire continued to advance, hunger flashing in her bright eyes.

Tiffany fired repeatedly, seeing six shots strike the woman's chest with little affect. She turned and ran, trying desperately to make it back to her cruiser. She stumbled and fell, sliding upon the dew-slickened ground. She could hear the creature still coming after her, she was getting closer. Tiffany rolled over on her back, her eyes wide and fearful. "Please, no! You don't need to do this. I can help you!"

The vampire chuckled softly. "It'll all be over soon."

Tiffany had somehow lost her gun. *Had she thrown it at the creature?* She searched the ground frantically for anything to use as a weapon. Her fingers closed on a hefty branch. She quickly thrust it up, feeling the creature slam into it. It pierced the vampire's chest, and miraculously found her heart. In an instant the vampire turned to dust and was gone. It was almost as if she had never been. Tiffany watched in horrified disbelief as the chalky particles drifted to the ground around her.

She stared at the tapered branch in her hand; the pointed end of the limb had killed the vampire. *Of course,* she thought, *wooden stakes do that!* She giggled somewhat hysterically to herself. She had been truly fortunate to find the branch on the ground just as she needed it. She knew she would have to be better prepared for the next time. She couldn't trust her life with sheer luck. She tossed the limb aside and slowly got to her feet. She glanced at her uniform and frantically brushed her hands over the remnants of the vampire. "Eew!" she said disgustedly. She looked around. She needed to find her service revolver and her flashlight.

Chapter Thirty-one

Gram's Warning

After Tiffany drove off in the police cruiser Silas plopped down on Aunt Abigail's sofa. With his elbows on his knees, he sighed wearily. He was exhausted. It was obvious that he had gotten very little sleep. I sat down next to him and wrapped an arm around his shoulder. "We can't be certain that your dad was turned. You didn't actually see him."

Silas shook his head. "I had hoped that Pop had gotten away, but I'm almost positive that he didn't. If he wasn't at the mortuary he would've been at home, so I went there, hoping to find him, but he wasn't there either."

Aunt Abby handed him a shot of whiskey. "Here. Drink this, it'll calm your nerves."

He accepted the shot glass from her but he didn't take a sip. He just stared at it as though he were looking for answers, but even I knew that there were no answers to be found in that small glass. He frowned and swallowed. "My gut tells me that they're both gone now." Tears ran down his face. My heart broke for him.

"Is there any place that your dad might have gone, if not home?" Aunt Abby asked softly.

Silas downed the shot of whiskey and winced. "Pop was a creature of habit. He went to work every day and came straight home afterwards. He loved spending time with my Mom; she was his whole world. If he somehow managed to escape from Keegan, he would've gone home. I'm sure of it."

Aunt Abby exchanged looks with me and sighed. "Then you may be right. I think we have to assume that Rourke has turned both your parents. Sebastian Barrister is growing his army while our numbers are dwindling."

I glared at her with an intense look. I couldn't believe that she was saying all of this in front of Silas. What he needed to hear was anything that would give him hope; but here she was shattering that chance.

He reached out and placed his hand over mine, giving it a reassuring squeeze. "She's right. There's no sense in sugarcoating it. Sebastian Barrister is using our loved ones against us, knowing it'll be difficult for us to fight them." He shrugged. "I mean, I don't know if I could fight my own parents. I faced my mom in the alley behind the mortuary but there was no way I could've hurt her. I went at her in wolf form, but that was only to keep her from harming Tiffany. I wanted to help my mom, but she was already beyond that."

I was beginning to feel utterly helpless. We weren't doing anything to stop our enemies. The Wolf Pack was in complete disarray. Grandpa was still at his cabin. He had yet to return to us. Brock had gone off radar too; it was difficult to know where his head was these days. Could it really be that I was the only one feeling a sense of urgency? I couldn't escape this feeling that we needed to be doing something more. Anything at all was better than what we were currently doing.

Silas looked at me as he stood. "Do you think you could take me back into town? With Keegan still alive I want to check in on Millie and her grandmother, just to make sure they are okay. This whole thing with my parents has really put me on edge. I don't think I can handle any more trauma at the moment. I need to know that Millie and Grams are both safe. I'll stay with them for the time being, maybe I can protect them if Rourke comes back."

I nodded. "Sure. I can do that. Just give me a minute."

Aunt Abigail arched a disapproving brow, but she kept her silence. I could tell that she wasn't keen on the idea of me going out. The Coven and Barrister were stepping up their attacks and even the daylight hours weren't going to be safe for long if they were wearing protective sun-talismans. After dropping Silas off at the Bradford's I would be alone. That thought didn't sit very well with her.

He smiled. "Okay, great. I'll be outside."

As he stepped outside, I turned to my aunt. "Go ahead, say what's on your mind. I can tell that this whole thing is bothering you."

She stopped wiping the kitchen counter and tossed the rag down. She turned to face me. "That's right, it does bother me. Why do you have to take him into town? Why can't he just take the truck himself? I don't see why you should place yourself in harm's way unnecessarily."

I sighed. "It isn't like that. He needs company right now. Both of his parents are missing. His mom has been turned into a vampire and it stands to reason that his dad has been as well. He's my friend, but he's more than that. He's like a brother to me. I can't just abandon him when he needs me most. And I really want to check on Millie and her Grams too. Keegan is still out there. I need to know that they're both safe. Besides, if I take him into town I can bring the truck back. We may have need of it."

She sighed heavily as she closed her eyes and nodded. I could tell by the quiver of her chin that she was near tears. I wrapped my arms around her and hugged her tightly. "I'll be fine, honest. I'll drop Silas off, check on Millie, and then come straight back."

She sniffled and quickly brushed a hand over her face as she pulled away from me. "Okay. Go. Do what you have to do. I'll cast some protection spells to make the cottage safer. But I want you to come back as quickly as you can. Don't take any side trips."

I rolled my eyes. "I won't Aunt Abby. I'll come straight home. Promise."

Aunt Abby crossed her arms and tucked her chin down toward her chest. "I mean it, Kat."

I scoffed. "Have a little faith, will ya?"

"I mean it, Kat. I know you," she said.

I couldn't help but roll my eyes again and chuckle softly. "Okay!"

As I climbed behind the wheel of the Chevy, Silas leveled his eyes at me. "If this is going to be a problem, I can just get to town on my own."

I batted a hand in the air as I turned the key in the ignition. "Don't be silly, Silas. Aunt Abby was just being overprotective. She feels obligated to point out the possible dangers. She's fine with it."

"Are you sure?" he asked.

I reached up and twisted the rearview mirror so that I could see my face. "Is everybody seeing something in my face that isn't there? Why can't you guys trust me a bit more?"

Silas laughed. "We can tell that your mind is churning behind your eyes. Something's definitely going on. You're up to something."

I put the mirror back into place and shook my head. "I don't know what you mean!" It was impossible to keep the grin off my face. I busied myself with driving the truck, refusing to look over at him for several minutes.

As we neared the bend in the road where the driver of the Mercedes had been killed, we could see Tiffany's police cruiser on the side of the road. The morning sunlight was sparkling across the dew-covered ground. I slowed down and pulled over onto the shoulder behind the police car. Tiffany was nowhere in sight. Both Silas and I scanned the woods for any sign of her. "This can't be good," I said as I switched off the ignition. I knew what was out there. Danger!

As we started to climb out of the pickup, Tiffany emerged from the woods. I could see grass stains on her beige uniform pants and a few pine needles were stuck in her hair. I searched her eyes warily. "Is everything all right?"

She stuck her hand through Silas' open window. "Do you have a pocketknife?"

He nodded. "Yeah, why?"

She snapped her fingers impatiently. "Give it to me."

When he didn't comply right away she slapped her hand against his chest. "Now, Silas!"

He leaned back and fished the pocketknife out of his pants and handed it over to her. It was a red Swiss Army knife with all the bells and whistles. I didn't even know he carried one. She studied it for a second and then shoved it back at him. "I need a sharp blade." She snapped her fingers impatiently.

Silas glanced at me and then selected the long blade with a serrated edge. Before he could give it to her she slapped the door with her hand. "I'm not skinning a damned fish, Silas."

He quickly nodded and selected another blade. "Will this work?" he asked.

She took it and nodded. "Thank you." She walked to the driver's side door of the patrol car and opened it, removing her police baton from between the front seats. She sat down and began to sharpen one end of the nightstick.

Silas glanced at me incredulously. "What the hell?" he asked.

"I climbed out of the pickup and walked up to the cruiser slowly. "Is everything all right, Tiff? What's going on?"

She shook her head as she continued to whittle upon the black baton, sharpening one end to a nice point. "I got lucky."

"What do you mean?" I asked nervously.

"I was attacked by that bitch of a vampire; the wife from the Mercedes. If I hadn't grabbed a tree limb I'd be dead right now."

Silas had walked up behind me. "You mean 'undead'," he said.

She glared at him, clearly not amused. "Whatever." She inspected the sharpened end and nodded with satisfaction. She stood up and put the baton through the loop on her belt, then handed the knife back to Silas. "I'm not going to take a chance like that again. I want to be prepared." She frowned at me. "I shot that bitch 15 times. I saw the bullets hit her. I emptied my magazine and it did nothing to stop her. What the hell?"

I sighed. "Bullets won't stop a vampire."

"What about silver bullets?" she asked.

Silas frowned. "Silver bullets can kill a werewolf, but not a vampire."

She nodded. "Good to know." She climbed back into her police cruiser. "You kids stay safe." She pulled away from us, stirring up a small cloud of dust in her wake.

Silas looked over at me. "She seemed pretty rattled."

I nodded. "I know exactly how she feels."

We climbed back into the Chevy and continued down the road in silence. I knew the fear that Tiffany must have felt having experienced the same thing myself. The only thing that had saved me from becoming a victim of the female vampire was the rising sun. Tiffany had emptied her Glock to no avail. At that point all of her training had likely gone out the window. The wild look she had in her eyes by the time she got back to the highway was one of complete and utter terror. It wouldn't be surprising if she packed up her things and simply went as far from The Hollows as she possibly could.

Who could blame her?

We made it to Millie's house without further incident. Silas held the gate of the picket fence open for me and together we stepped up on the porch. I was surprised to see that Millie and her grandmother weren't sitting out on the porch as usual; the weather was certainly pleasant enough; the sun having warmed the chill away from the night before. And then I thought about Keegan Rourke.

Had he returned and sought his revenge?

Silas softly rapped his knuckles upon the screen door and we waited quietly. Much to our mutual relief Millie soon appeared and greeted us with a huge smile. "Hey ya'll, come on in. We were just talking about you two!" She stepped back a few feet balancing on her crutches as she waved excitedly.

Silas and I exchanged curious looks. "I hope it was all good," I said with a chuckle.

Millie's exuberant smile faded. "Well, that's the thing. It wasn't all that good. Gram's been peering into her crystal ball practically all morning. Yesterday afternoon she read the Tarot for her lady friends," she glanced at me, "you know, all those blue-haired sweeties she knows…"

"Their hair is silver!" Grams shouted from the parlor.

Millie rolled her eyes and lifted her hand to her lips as she whispered, "Yeah, and the sky is actually pink! Anyway, she scared them all off with her readings. It was something about darkness embracing The Hollows, you know, real doom and gloom stuff." She placed a hand on my arm, "Do you know she told Mabel Thatcher that she shouldn't go home, it wasn't safe."

Silas frowned. "What did Mrs. Thatcher do?"

Millie batted a hand in the air. "She just told Grams that she was crazy as a loon. She lived in a respectable neighborhood and there were good people on both sides of her. She and the other ladies left shortly after that, claiming that Grams was spouting nonsense. Yet they eat it up when Grams gives them favorable news." She shrugged. "People can be so fickle!"

"Maybe I should go check on Mrs. Thatcher," Silas said with a glance in my direction.

Millie rolled her eyes. "I don't know what's going on with Grams here lately. She's been coming up with all kinds of weird stuff. I think that Keegan's attack has really shaken her up more than she'll admit." She lowered her voice to scarcely more than a whisper, "Frankly, I'm kinda worried about her."

Millie's grandmother stepped into the foyer, shaking her finger at her granddaughter. "Listen here young lady, I know what the cards told me sounds bad," she glanced at Silas and me, "that's why I consulted my crystal too."

"Oh Grams, please…" Millie begged.

Grams took hold of Silas' arm. "You check on Mabel. You'll see!" She placed her other hand on my arm. "That sweet Mohawk girl's in trouble too. Those bird-brains are out to cause mischief for her and her grandma."

"Bird-brains?" I asked, not sure I was following her.

Millie shook her head and rolled her eyes dramatically. "She means the Sons of the Raven."

"Bird-brains!" Grams confirmed with a nod.

I glanced at Silas and then turned back to Millie and her grandmother. "You should both know that Keegan Rourke isn't dead. He survived—at least a part of him did, anyway. The Lycan part of him was killed, at least we believe so. But, evidently, he was a hybrid like Tucker. We believe that the vampire survived. He's still out there somewhere."

Silas nodded. "He killed my folks. I believe they're both undead now. Vampires like Barrister."

Millie's face turned ashen.

Grams put a trembling hand to her lips. "Mabel…" she whispered softly.

I gave Grams' hand a little pat. "Silas and I will go check on Mrs. Thatcher to make certain she's all right. But first we need to make sure that you both are safe. We don't want Keegan to return for some form of revenge."

Millie gasped. "Do you really think he will?"

I shrugged. "He might."

Grams squeezed Millie's arm. "Go with them. I'll be fine."

Millie shook her head. "No, Grams, I'm not leaving you here alone."

Grams batted a hand in the air. "I'll be fine. Besides, I want to consult my crystal again. Dark times are upon this community. You should all go check on Mabel. You'll see soon enough that I'm not talking foolish. Now go. All of you!"

Millie sighed and shrugged helplessly. "She's hung crosses all over the house after she did a Tarot reading. She's even got a vial of Holy Water in her pocket—Lord only knows where she got it."

I touched Millie's arm. "Are you sure you don't want to stay with her?"

Millie's eyes watered. "She won't allow it."

I sighed. "Well let's do this quickly so that we can get back. She shouldn't be here alone."

Mrs. Bradford sighed heavily. "I'll be fine, child! Go! Check on Mabel!" She pushed us toward the door.

Against my better judgment I handed Silas the keys to the Chevy. "You're driving."

As Silas steered the pickup from the curb, Millie shook her head, her eyes were moist with tears. "I've never seen Grams like this. She scares me." She gave me a forlorn look. "What if it's dementia?"

I gave her a hand a squeeze. "Why would you say that? It's not dementia. She's just a little on-edge, and who can blame her after what Rourke put her through? Just try to be a little more understanding and give it time. She'll be back to her old self before you know it."

Millie pushed her glasses back into place. "I certainly hope so."

In less than five minutes we pulled up in front of Mabel Thatcher's house. Silas turned off the ignition and handed me the keys. "Before we leave I want to check my home, see if Pop's returned."

"Which one's yours?" I asked. Both he and Millie pointed to the house on the right. "OK let's do it to be sure," I said. "This shouldn't take us very long."

Silas chuckled. "You don't know Mabel Thatcher then. She'll latch on and won't let you leave until you've eaten a slice or two of fresh cherry pie or some other dessert. And all the while she'll be talking your ear off."

Millie's stomach growled loudly. Embarrassed, she glared at us both, "What? Silas had to go off and mention pie, I haven't eaten breakfast yet!"

As we stepped through the picket fence, Silas reached down and picked up the newspaper from the middle of the sidewalk. He frowned. "That's odd. She usually picks up the Gazette straight away. Says she doesn't like her news to grow any colder than her coffee."

"Maybe the paper was delivered late," I suggested.

Silas and Millie shook their heads. "Never happens," they said in unison. I could only shrug in response.

Stepping up on the front porch we could see that the door was slightly ajar. Millie gasped. "Oh no!"

I quickly shook my head. "Let's not jump to conclusions." Fear knotted in my stomach; this couldn't be good.

Silas pushed the door open with his foot. "Mrs. Thatcher? It's me, Silas. Is everything all right?"

There was no answer.

"Mrs. Thatcher, are you there?" he asked.

Still, there was no reply.

Entering the house we found the living room in disarray. The sofa was pushed askew and a lamp was knocked to the floor. We found Mabel Thatcher lying on the floor in the dining room. Two small, perfectly round puncture marks were on her neck. Her skin was ashen and there was no pulse. I looked up at Silas and Millie and shook my head.

Millie started crying, nearly falling over as she buried her head against Silas' chest. He swallowed. "Do you think she'll turn?"

I stood slowly. "It's a very good possibility."

Millie gasped. "Why hasn't she turned already? Wouldn't she have done so by now?"

I shrugged. "If she's going to turn she'll probably do it by sundown."

"That's hours away!" Millie said. "Are we just supposed to wait and see?"

"We need to call somebody," Silas said. He ran a hand through his hair. "But who do we call with something like this?"

I took a deep breath and let it out slowly. "Tiffany," I said.

Silas nodded. "My folks have a phone. I can call the station and have them contact her from there."

"Take Millie with you, I'll stay here," I said.

Silas glanced down at Mrs. Thatcher with a look of uncertainty. "We could all go."

Millie gave me a pleading look. "Yeah, why don't you come with us? There's no point in you staying here alone. It's not like Mrs. Thatcher is going to wake up, or anything. You said yourself that she probably wouldn't turn until after sundown."

I shrugged, giving her an anguished look. "I know. I just don't want to leave her here all alone. She didn't deserve what happened to her."

Millie reached out and put a hand on my shoulder. "You're a really sweet person, did you know that?"

I chuckled softly. "It's the least I can do."

After Silas and Millie went next door to make the call, I glanced around the room and sighed. There weren't any photos sitting in frames anywhere to be found, not on shelves, nor on any of the walls. It was as if the old woman had no one to care about, nor anyone to really care about her. *Had she no family?* It saddened me to think that Mabel Thatcher was alone in life; I had no desire to have her be that way in death. No one deserved that. Not even my own grandmother.

Finally, I couldn't take the gloominess anymore and I stepped outside and sat on the porch steps. The morning sunlight felt comforting on my face, despite the slight chill of the morning. Millie returned after several minutes and joined me on the steps. She wrapped her arms around my shoulders and leaned her head against mine. We sat there in silence, not feeling the need for words.

Silas crossed the lawn and jumped over the picket fence between the two houses just as Tiffany was pulling up in her patrol car. She opened the driver's side door and stood with one hand on the hood of the cruiser the other on the top of the door. "What's this about?" she asked with a raised brow. "I'm officially off-duty right now."

Silas nodded. "We figured you'd want to see this. Mrs. Thatcher's been bitten."

Tiffany glanced from Silas to Millie and I. "What do you mean 'bitten'?" she asked.

I helped Millie to stand and I answered, "All of her blood's been drained by a vampire. Her body is inside."

"Shit!" Tiffany said as she leaned back into her car and pulled out her nightstick from between the front seats. She stuck it into the belt loop on the opposite side of her holster and closed the car door. "Is she going to turn into a vampire?"

I nodded. "That is a very high likelihood when the sun goes down."

She crossed the yard and moved up the steps past us. "You

kids stay out here," she said.

I reached out a hand and grabbed her arm, bringing her to a stop. She glared at my hand coldly, causing me to release her. "What are you going to do?" I asked.

Tiffany swallowed. "What needs to be done." She had a dead-serious look in her eyes as she turned from me and went inside.

When she returned, she had tiny beads of sweat above her upper lip. "It's done." She frowned as she looked at the sharpened end of her police baton and shook her head. "There wasn't even any blood when I shoved this through her heart."

I sighed. "Whoever did this to her was ravenous. Probably a newly created vampire."

Silas coughed uncomfortably. "Whoever did this entered the house through the front door. We found it open when we got here."

Tiffany put her nightstick away. "What made the three of you know to come here?"

"Grams told us. She saw it in her crystal ball," Millie said.

Tiffany shook her head. "Her crystal ball? Seriously?" We all just stared at her. "She rubbed her temples gingerly as though she had a massive headache coming on. "And what am I supposed to do with this information? No one's going to believe any of this. I'm likely to get laughed right off the Force."

"But it's all true," I said.

Tiffany shook her head. "It's a damned nightmare is what this is!" She sighed heavily. "I'm going to need statements from all of you." She pointed at Millie, "And I'm gonna need one from your grandmother as well."

It took a little over an hour to give my written statement to Tiffany. I had taken longer in town than I had planned and I knew Aunt Abigail was going to worry about what was keeping me. I had promised that I was going to drop Silas off, check on

Millie and her Grams and then come straight back. She was not going to be a happy camper about any of this.

I briefly considered picking some beautiful wild flowers growing along the side of the mountain highway, but quickly discarded that notion. It would only delay me further and I doubt that it would sufficiently lessen my aunt's foul mood enough to get me out of the hot water that I knew I was already in.

As I rounded a bend in the road I heard a loud pop and then the pickup shuddered violently. I fought with the steering wheel, trying to keep the vehicle under some semblance of control as I coaxed it to the narrow shoulder on the side of the highway. I had no doubt that one of the incredibly thin tires had finally given up its lease on life.

I climbed from the cab of the Chevy and found that the passenger side, rear wheel was practically torn to shreds. Fortunately there was a spare in the bed of the truck. I knew that I would need a jack in order to change the tire, but I didn't readily see one. I bit my lip as I frowned. "What the heck?" I said to myself as I ran a hand through my thick hair.

I let down the tailgate and climbed into the bed of the truck and lifted the spare tire up so that I could roll it out onto the ground. It was heavier than I had expected; I'd never had to change a tire before, so I really didn't have any idea what I was getting myself into. I still needed something to jack the truck up so that I could get the tire swapped out.

I glanced up and down the highway hoping to see someone else on the lonely mountain road that might be able to offer assistance, but there was no one. I thought about waiting for someone to come by, but that could take hours. The only other option was to either change the tire myself, or morph into the wolf and head for the cottage.

A thought occurred to me that the jack might be under the bench seat in the cab of the truck. It wasn't, but I could see that there was something behind the seat. "Bingo!" I exclaimed as I leaned the seat forward. The jack was there along with the four-way cross wrench that I would need to remove the lugs.

By the time I figured out how to work the jack, the sun was almost directly overhead. Aunt Abby was going to kill me, but what could I do? I couldn't really afford to just abandon the truck on the side of the road. It took almost all of my remaining energy just to loosen up the lugs so that I could get the shredded tire off. Things were not going my way. By the time I finally got the tire changed, I was soaked and dripping sweat. My hands were blackened and dirty. I tossed the jack and the lug wrench behind the seat and then pushed the back cushion into place. I blew out a long, slow breath as I climbed back into the Chevy and fired her up. My arms felt weak and very heavy. I was exhausted. But even more than that, I was proud of myself.

As I pulled up in front of the cottage I knew I was in trouble. Aunt Abigail was sitting on the porch and as I climbed from the cab of the truck she stood up and glared at me with moist eyes. She crossed her arms over her chest and said, "You're late."

I pushed the drivers' door closed and nodded. "I know, and I'm sorry. But you wouldn't believe everything that has happened this morning!"

She could see that my hands, arms, shirt and pants were covered in blackened streaks from handling the tire. Her expression seemed to soften. "Did you have a flat tire?"

I nodded. "What gave it away?"

She rolled her eyes and chuckled softly as she stepped off the porch and gave me a hug. "I was worried that something dreadful had happened to you."

I couldn't help but laugh. "Oh, Aunt Abby, let me tell you about my day!"

She eased me to arm's length and crinkled her nose. "Maybe you should cleanup first. You're completely soaked, and filthy.

You've got black streaks on your face as well."

"I have no doubt," I said with a shake of my head.

As we entered the cottage she turned toward the kitchen. "Are you hungry? I could fix you some lunch."

I declined. "Really, I'm not hungry at all. I could use something cold to drink though. Something with ice in it."

"Tea?" she asked.

"Sounds divine!"

"You go get cleaned up and I'll get some tea going."

I didn't argue. I made a beeline for the bathroom; a nice hot soak in the tub sounded like it could do wonders for me. I was beginning to notice aches in various parts of my body.

I closed my eyes and sighed as I eased down into the steaming water and bubbles that filled the tub. Already I could feel my body starting to relax. I scooped up two handfuls of soapy water and splashed it on my face, then scrubbed vigorously with a washcloth. I completely submerged and stayed under the water for several long seconds. Gasping for breath I sat up and reached for the shampoo. I really wanted to just soak for an hour but I had already lost too much of the day.

As I rinsed the shampoo from my hair I remembered what Millie's Grams had said about the Sons of the Raven. I had to warn Ari that she and her grandmother could be in trouble! I quickly pulled the plug out of the bottom of the tub and stood up. Wrapping a towel around me I called out to my aunt. She met me at the bathroom door a worried look on her face.

"Is everything all right?" she asked.

"Yes." I quickly shook my head. "I mean no! I think Ari and her grandmother are in trouble! Millie's grandma saw something in her crystal ball. It had to do with the Sons of the Raven. She was right about Mabel Thatcher, so I'm pretty sure that she's probably right about this too. We need to warn them!"

Chapter Thirty-two

Sons of the Raven

Ari could hear the low rumbling of the jeep and the whining creak of its chassis as the vehicle jostled along the rough terrain leading up to her akhsótha's cabin. At first she thought it was either Kat or Abigail, but she quickly discarded that notion. The sounds she heard were clearly not from the old Chevy that they usually drove. And Abigail never came up the rugged dirt road, it was too far out of the way, she simply preferred to cut through the woods on foot and gather various herbs when she came for a visit. Then she heard the hoots and guffaws of three or four young guys. She heard empty beer bottles shatter upon trees and rocks along the road. It was obvious that the guys had been drinking heavily. This wasn't going to be a friendly visit. This was trouble. She was glad that her akhsótha wasn't home. With any luck she'd be gone until after these fools had left.

She heard the jeep come to a stop in front of the cabin. She eased up to the window and peered out, careful not to disturb the curtain too much. She could see Danny Hancock behind the steering wheel of the vehicle. She never really liked him. He thought way too much of himself just because of his size. Fat, by no means, he was all muscle with broad shoulders and thick biceps. He had wavy brown hair that he always seemed to be running a comb through. He couldn't pass a mirror or a window without staring at his own reflection. He was always condescending and a bit of a brute. Jeremy Willis wasn't much better. He was a slightly smaller version of Danny. He wore his hair slicked back with some kind of gel that made his hair seem darker than it normally was; she could remember his hair being a shade or two lighter back in grade school, but now it was practically jet-black. Together they were a duo you tried hard to avoid if you were smart. They were always picking on those smaller than they were. They never passed up a chance to harass Manny if they could. When you threw Bradley Somers and Marty Selby into the mix they were far worse. Both were close in size to the other two; and both were equally charming. Bradley and his twin sister Breck could be nice enough if you removed them from the others. They were followers. Marty was the really mean one. He seemed to delight in hurting others. He was smallest of the group but that wasn't saying much; he was still a big kid, far bigger than those he chose to torment; she and Manny seemed to be his favorite targets.

Marty must have noticed the curtain move and he threw his nearly full beer bottle at it, shattering both window and bottle. "Have a beer!" he chuckled as he hopped out of the jeep. He came close to falling on his face.

Startled, Ari stumbled backwards, nearly falling to the floor.

"Come on out and play, Ari! We're just here to have a little fun!" Marty cooed as he reached through the window and pushed the curtain aside. He swayed slightly; clearly he had been drinking way too much.

"Go away!" Ari shouted; anger causing her brows to crease.

"That ain't no way to be!" Marty said defensively. "We came all this way to see you, least you could do is open the door and play nice."

"Go away, Martin!" Ari said. "You've already caused enough trouble."

Jeremy was at the door, trying to get in. "It's locked!" he said.

Danny laughed as he climbed from the jeep. "So? A big boy like you shouldn't let that stop him! Break it down!"

Jeremy shoved his beer against Bradley's chest. "Here! Hold this." He started throwing his shoulder against the door.

Marty chuckled from the window. "Oh come on, Jer! You gonna let a little door like that stop you?"

Jeremy growled. "Why don't you shut up and just climb through the damned window?" He threw his body against the door again. It wouldn't be long now; it was starting to give.

Ari looked around frantically. She ran her fingers through her straight black hair as she bit at her bottom lip. There was nothing she could do to stop them from gaining access to her home. Her only chance was to escape out the back. Without further hesitation, she sprinted toward the back door.

Marty was poised at the window. "She's getting away!" he yelled. His foot became tangled in the curtain and he fell, crashing down hard. A second later the door splintered and Jeremy plowed inside, tumbling to the floor.

Danny slapped Bradley's chest with the back of his hand. "Quick! Let's get around back before she gets away!"

Ari ran out the back door just as they were rounding the corner. She could hear Jeremy ripping through the house behind her like an enraged hurricane; they were coming at her fast. She feared that her akhsótha would return and be harmed, that alone kept her from taking flight as the sparrow. She needed to lead her pursuers away. Her only hope was with the woods in front of her. She knew the forest better than they did. If she could make it she had a chance!

Danny cursed angrily. These buffoons were letting her get away! He tossed his beer bottle at her and it exploded on the tree ahead of her, causing her to switch direction. He pulled the Smith and Wesson .38 Special from the back of his waistline and fired off a warning shot. The round *thunked* loudly into the tall pine just over the fleeing girl's shoulder. It brought her other pursuers to a halt. They turned and stared at him, shock on their faces.

He quickly fired two more shots as Ari darted through the trees. She screamed as one of the bullets struck her left thigh. She tumbled forward, rolling down a steep embankment. "I got her!" Danny roared jubilantly as he pumped the revolver into the air above his head. "Don't let that bitch get away!"

Hooting and hollering Marty and Jeremy tore through the brush in pursuit. Bradley shook his head and slipped back through the trees toward the cabin. Danny had crossed the line. He wanted no part of this. They were no longer out for a little fun at Ari's expense; clearly this was now a matter of life or death. He hadn't agreed to any of this.

Jeremy and Marty peered down the embankment where Ari had gone over; she was nowhere to be seen. "You sure you got her?" Marty asked swaying slightly; his breathing was hard.

Danny joined them. "Look!" he pointed to the leaves of the small shrubbery on the incline of the hill. "There's blood! I told you I nailed her!" he bragged.

Jeremy slapped his arm, grinning. "You got her, man!" His expression was full of glee.

Danny slid down the embankment. "She couldn't have gone far. We need to find her before it gets too dark!"

Marty looked over his shoulder. "Hey, where's Brad?"

Danny scowled. "Forget him! He's a pussy."

They could hear the sound of the jeep fading in the distance as it drove away. Jeremy shook his head. "That bastard took our ride!"

"Forget him, I said!" Danny roared. "We need to find Pocahontas before she gets away!"

Marty slipped and fell on his backside and slid down the small hill. He was laughing hysterically. "Pocahontas. Now that's funny!" he said, bleary-eyed.

Jeremy grabbed his shoulder and helped him up. "You're drunk. Come on."

Marty jerked his arm away. "I'll show you how drunk I'm not when we catch that injun!" He grabbed his crotch. "I'll teach her a lesson with this!"

Jeremy started through the trees. "I ain't havin' no sloppy seconds! You're after me!"

"Like hell!" Marty said as he stumbled forward.

"Spread out," Danny motioned with the revolver. "We can cover more area that way." He shook his head, clearly not happy with the way things were going.

Ari stopped and leaned against a tree. She was in serious trouble, and she knew it. She was breathing heavily and the pain in her leg was growing worse, already her jeans were coated in blood below the knee. As best she could tell the bullet had gone clean through, and her leg still functioned, but it was getting stiff. Sweat and tears stung her eyes as she ripped the left sleeve of her soft plaid shirt at the shoulder; thankfully it tore off easily. It had been her favorite, but it couldn't be helped. She needed to try and stop the flow of blood.

She scraped moss from the north side of a nearby rock and stuffed it in the holes of her jeans where the bullet had entered, and exited her thigh. It was difficult to keep it in place due to the blood flow; she could really use another set of hands, but that just wasn't an option; and she certainly couldn't ask her pursuers to help her. She quickly placed her makeshift bandage over the wound and pulling it as tightly as she could stand, she tied it in place. When she finished her hands were coated in blood and they were shaking pretty good. She had to move. She couldn't stay where she was; they weren't that far behind her. She had left a trail of blood in her wake that even a blind man could follow. Gulping in a few deep breaths, she pushed away from the tree trunk and hobbled as fast as she could through the forest. She had to lead them further away from the cabin if it were possible. She had to do all she could to protect her akhsótha. No matter the cost.

§

Okwaho Tekahionwake had been picking herbs when she heard the gunshot ring out and echo through the forest. Frowning, she placed the prong of wild ginseng into the medicine bag that she carried, and then she cocked her head and waited, listening. Two more shots followed the first, these two in rapid succession. She could tell that it was coming from the general direction of her cabin, and that worried her. Neither she nor her granddaughter possessed any guns. This, then, meant trouble. Ari was home alone.

She pulled the long strap of her medicine bag over her head and placed the satchel upon the ground. It was a shame to leave it behind but what choice did she have? She began to undress as quickly as she could. Folding her clothes neatly, she placed them on top of the medicine bag and then she turned and started running, naked, through the forest. She morphed into her namesake, an old wolf, and in an instant she plunged through the forest.

§

The large black wolf was foraging alone in the woods when he heard the first shot. When the next two rang out, the wolf barked, alerting the consciousness of the man within. It was clear that there was an unknown danger threatening the woods to the northeast. It was where the Old Wolf lived with her human pup. They had always been kind and friendly to both man and beast. They had fed him when he was hungry, cared for him when he was ill. Now they might need his help. The black wolf growled, exposing its teeth in a massive snarl as it abandoned its quest for the deer it had been pursuing. It turned in the direction from which the gunshots had originated. He was off in search of a new prey.

§

Ari stopped for a brief rest. She eased herself against the huge rock and blew out a long, exhausted breath. Even that hurt. Frowning, Ari glanced down at her makeshift bandage; the sleeve was soaked in blood. She felt weak, her hands were still trembling and she was sweating profusely. She was cold, but she felt as though she were burning up. None of this was a good sign. Her breathing sounded ragged and her leg was almost useless, she could barely bend her knee, and when she did the pain was excruciating. She didn't know if she could continue much further. She froze. In her peripheral vision she could see movement off to her left; it was Marty. She closed her eyes tightly as a wave of dizziness swept over her. "Please..." she mouthed the word.

"There you are!" Marty said as he turned and began to walk toward her. He considered calling out to the others but decided against it. He could tell that she wasn't going much further. This way he had some alone time with her before the others arrived to take their turn. He chuckled softly.

Ari swallowed. She couldn't believe how incredibly thirsty she was. As she tried to push off of the rock to escape, she faltered. The stiffness in her leg caused her to stumble and she fell to the ground. She cried out in agony as she landed, face first upon the ground, all the air was forced from her lungs.

Marty grimaced as he stood over her. "That must've hurt!" He chuckled again. He bent and rolled her over, grunting with the effort. "You don't look so hot." His eyes shot up his forehead and he grinned. A mischievous twinkle lit both eyes. "Well, you look hot – I've always thought you were a sweet looking girl. But what I meant was you don't look like you're doing so good." He patted his hand upon her wounded leg and he seemed to take a great deal of pleasure from the pain it caused as she flinched and scrunched up her face in agony. "Oops!" he said with another chuckle. "Guess I shouldn't have done that, huh?"

Ari could barely keep her eyes open as she glared up at him. She felt like she was going to pass out. She thought that that would almost be better if she did.

He began to rip her blouse open. "Let's have a look, shall we?"

"Whooo?" A large Great Horned owl called out from a nearby pine.

Marty glanced at the owl and chuckled. "Guess he wants to see too." He ran his fingertips along her cheekbone and down her neck. He slipped a finger under her bra strap at the shoulder, and lifted. "Black's a nice color on you." He started to pull it off her shoulder.

He heard a flutter of frantic wings behind him. He straightened and turned, his eyes growing wide with instant fear. The owl flew straight toward him, its talons ripping at his face, scraping across his cheek, very nearly taking his right eye. "What the hell?" He batted his hands in the air trying to desperately fend off the flying menace. He slipped upon the blood-soaked pine needles and fell backwards.

Ari could hear the sickening crunch as he landed beside her. His head had struck the huge boulder, where she had rested only a moment ago, and now he just lay there with his head at an odd angle. He seemed to be staring at her without seeing.

The corner of her mouth twisted up very slightly and then darkness claimed her.

§

Jeremy Willis stopped and leaned against a tall thin pine, its lowest boughs still a good two feet above his head. He frowned as he looked around him, and he shook his head. He had no idea where he was. He was lost. "Guys?" he called out, swallowing his fear. He waited for a response, but none came.

He heard a branch snap off to his right, and then another. Something was moving through the forest. "Guys? Is that you?" he called out again.

Everything grew quiet and still. Jeremy squinted as he tried to see what was out there, but he couldn't see anything except more trees and shrubbery. "This isn't the least bit funny guys! I'm not amused!" He was certain that he was being pranked. He'd show them. He picked up a nice sized rock and tossed it into the woods where the sound had come from. He heard the stone crash through the leaves and strike upon the ground where it rolled harmlessly away. "Keep it up and I'm gonna nail you with one of these!" He picked up another rock.

A low, vicious snarl sounded from directly ahead of him. Another growl came from his right. He could see two wolves emerging through the brush. Both seemed to be bathed in a ghostly blue-white light, their heads low, teeth bared, stalking him.

He dropped the rock. "Oh shit!" he turned and started running. He could hear the wolves thrashing through the woods in pursuit.

§

Danny heard Jeremy's frightened yell, but he couldn't tell where it had originated from, but he knew that it was some distance away. He was immediately concerned. He had never heard his friend scream like that, and they had been through some really crazy shit together over the years. It sounded like it may have come from up near Valen's Ridge. There was no telling what kind of predicament the idiot might have gotten into. He tucked the gun into the top of his pants and started climbing up the hill using both hands to assist his assent as he cursed softly.

He slipped a couple of times but eventually managed to get to the top of the hill. He shook his head and chuckled to himself. The ground leveled out for about twenty feet or so, and then began to rise again. "I hate the mountains!" he said as he wiped his brow with the back of his hand. With a heavy sigh he started to climb again.

He found it was easier to make progress if he climbed at an angle rather than trying to scale the hill going straight up. He froze suddenly. He had seen movement off to his left, above him. He pulled out his revolver and held it in both hands, bracing his feet as best he could. He started to relax when he saw that it was just a skunk. But the damned thing was scampering straight for him. "Oh no you don't!" he said and quickly fired off a shot.

He missed the skunk by more than a foot, but it didn't deter the creature even a little bit; it continued to head toward him. It seemed to be picking up speed. The last thing that he wanted was to get sprayed by an enraged skunk. It probably had a nest nearby and was protecting its family. Danny decided to leave well enough alone; Jeremy would just have to wait. He turned and started to make his way back down the slope as fast as he dared, half running, half jumping; anything to distance himself from the skunk. This was all more than he had bargained for.

His foot struck either a root, or perhaps a rock, and his whole body pitched forward, causing him to fly through the air. He flailed his arms wildly and at the last moment tucked his head down and twisted his body so that he could take the brunt of the landing on his shoulder, which he did. The brute force of the hard-packed ground nearly knocked the wind out of him anyway as he tumbled heels over head down the remainder of the slope.

When he righted himself, he realized that he had lost his .38 Special. Frantically he looked around, desperate to find the weapon. He saw a reflection of sunlight glint upon the stainless steel of the handgun; it was lying about ten feet away, up from where he was now, almost buried in pine needles. He tried to stand, but a sharp stab of pain jolted through his ankle. He sucked in a huge gulp of air as he winced and sat back down.

Bending his knee, he raised his pant leg so that he could see about his ankle. He exhaled in relief as he realized that it was nothing but a bad sprain – no bone was broken. Gingerly he crawled up the slope and retrieved his weapon. He heard movement off to his right and not more than eight feet from him was a large, black wolf, teeth bared in a vicious snarl. "I don't have time for this!" he hissed as he leveled the revolver at the wolf and squeezed off a shot. He saw the bullet strike the beast just behind the left shoulder. The wolf yelped in pain and disappeared into the brush.

Danny chuckled. "Stupid animal! That'll teach you to mess with me!" Carefully he got to his feet and tried to hobble down the slope to more level ground. It wasn't easy, but he managed it. He heard something coming down the hill toward him, fast, and he turned, raising his gun, thinking it was the skunk again. It wasn't.

It was the black wolf.

As the creature leapt toward him, saliva dripping from its jaw, Danny quickly lifted his revolver and squeezed the trigger. The hammer slammed down with a click. He tried again, twice, to fire his weapon, but it was no use. The gun was empty. It no longer mattered. The beast was on him. He could only scream.

Chapter Thirty-three
There Are Worse Things to Be

The old wolf followed the trail of blood through the forest. She found two bodies lying near to one another beside a giant boulder that seemed to support a leaning pine. The tree was bare, having died long ago. Okwaho morphed back into her human form and raised a trembling hand to her mouth, fearful that her granddaughter had gone the way of the pine. As she drew close she could see Ari's chest slowly rise and fall with each ragged breath she managed. The boy was not so lucky. His neck was badly twisted, forcing his head at an awkward angle. His sightless eyes seemed to stare into the Great Beyond.

Before long Okwaho was joined by the black wolf. She held her hand out to the black beast, palm down. The black stepped toward the old woman and bowed its head beneath the outstretched hand. The old woman scratched the top of the wolf's head. "I will go to the cabin and prepare," she said. "Bring her to me as quickly as you can."

The wolf barked once in understanding.

A moment later the old Medicine Woman was gone, replaced by a wolf with silver fur. She headed south through the forest. The black wolf glanced at the lifeless body of the boy and snarled before morphing back into human form.

The dead boy was close to his size. Sam St. Claire stripped the boy of his pants and shirt. He quickly dressed and then gingerly scooped Ari up into his arms. At first, she tried to pull away, to fight him off, but her eyes opened briefly and upon seeing who it was, she relaxed. Sam started through the woods, following the path that the silver wolf had taken. He walked as fast as he dared, not wanting to jostle her too much. He was worried. Ari felt cold and her complexion was very pale. She had already lost a considerable amount of blood. Time was of the essence.

§

Okwaho took one final look around her home. She had done the best she could repairing the damage done by those vile boys, but there was nothing she could do about the splintered front door or the shattered window. That would all have to wait. Soon Sam would bring her granddaughter home and then they would have to work hard to save her life. The old woman had never been so frightened. Ari had lost a great deal of blood and would likely need a transfusion in order to survive. Unfortunately that was a task that would be difficult to perform with things that were available. Tears stung at her eyes. The only other option was unthinkable, but she didn't want to lose her granddaughter. She was the only human family she had left.

The creaking sounds of a vehicle coming up the road put her on edge. She feared that it was more of those boys coming to finish the job. She vowed to give them a fight before she allowed them to do more harm to her sweet girl. She stepped outside, placing her hands upon her waist; she was ready for the inevitable.

To her surprise it was the rusty old Chevy pickup truck that belonged to Sam. It could only mean that Abigail was coming to help. *But how did she know that her services were needed? And would she be in time to do Ari some good? Or was it already too late?* She couldn't be sure, but it was good to see her nonetheless. The overhead light in the cab of the pickup was on, enabling her to see that Abby was not alone. Kat was with her.

This was a good sign. Ari needed all the emotional support she could get in order to survive. She would need those she cared about, and those who cared about her, to talk her into remaining in this life and to turn away from the pull of the next. Okwaho wiped her tears away and smiled. As the two women climbed from the truck she spread her arms wide to receive them. "How did you know of my need?" she asked, her voice thick with emotion.

§

Even against the white sheets Ari looked alarmingly ashen. Each breath that she seemed to struggle with was raspy, almost a death rattle. "You have to do something!" I pleaded with my aunt. I hated seeing my friend this way. It was frightening.

Aunt Abigail exhaled slowly; she had such a forlorn look on her face. "There's not much I can do at this point."

"Can't we take her to a hospital?" I was desperate to save my friend. She didn't deserve this. Whether I was being silly or not, I felt responsible for what had happened to her. Maybe if I had acted sooner we could've gotten here in time to save her.

My aunt shook her head. "I'm not sure she would even make it there. The closest one is just too far away."

I gestured with my hands in the air. "We can't just let her die. We need to do something!"

"She needs a transfusion," my aunt explained, "to have any chance at all."

I hastily rolled up my sleeve and thrust my arm towards her. "Take my blood!"

"Oh, Kat, that's very sweet of you." She shook her head. "But she can't be given just any blood. Besides, we don't even know what blood type she is. The wrong type could kill her just as quickly."

Grandpa rolled up his sleeve. "Use my blood."

Aunt Abby looked at him and smiled, "Sam…"

"I'm Type O, Abby. I believe that's Universal," he said.

A surprised look came over her face. "It is." She glanced down at Ari and nodded. "That might do the trick."

"So," Grandpa said, "what do you need?"

She ran a hand through her hair. "I believe that I have everything I need in my bag, actually." She glanced at Ari's grandmother and then back at Grandpa. "I just don't know what it'll mean to have your blood running through her veins. What will it do to her?"

He shook his head. "She won't become a Lycan, if that's what's worrying you. She'd have to receive my DNA, not just my blood for that."

Aunt Abigail gave him a strange look. "How do you know so much about that?"

He chuckled. "When you've lived as long as I have you tend to pick up a few things. For example I know that there is Lycan DNA in my body, not my blood. Lycanthropy can be genetically passed along, that's where Kat gets hers. But you can also become a Lycan through the medical transfer of DNA, or by simply surviving an attack from a Lycan."

Ari's grandmother shrugged. "That is how I came to be a Lycan. I was attacked many moons ago, well after my children were born. That is why Ari is not a Lycan, it is not in her bloodline."

I crinkled my brow. "But she can morph into a bird."

The old woman smiled. "There are worse things to be." She went back to her task of crushing berries that she had gathered deep in the woods with a mortar and pestle. It was an odd assortment of berries that were unfamiliar to me. As she smashed them with the stone pestle there was a reddish-purple hue and the pulp resembled a thick gelatinous goo; I had no idea what it was for. The Medicine Woman was murmuring in her native tongue, it sounded melodic in a way. *A prayer, maybe?*

After a time, she dropped a few more berries into the mortar and crushed them as well. Next, she took a small pouch that hung around her neck by a thin leather strap and poured a yellowish powder into the palm of her hand. She added this to the mixture and it seemed to thicken the goo considerably.

She dipped her fingertips into the mortar and then rubbed them across Ari's cheeks, just under her eyes. Then taking her left thumb she started at Ari's forehead and went down her nose, across her lips, chin and down her neck with more of the paste. She nodded once and then looked at Aunt Abby. "She is ready now."

The old woman stood up from the bed and took my arm. "Come, child. Let us leave so that they can do what needs to be done."

I glanced at Aunt Abby, hoping she would ask me to stay, but she didn't. She just smiled at me and nodded. "It'll be okay." Without protest I allowed Okwuho to lead me from the room.

There was nothing left to do but wait.

Chapter Thirty-four

Sinister Plans

Marybeth Collingsworth ran the brush through her daughter's thick, auburn hair as she stood behind her at the vanity. She found the task to be enjoyable, almost therapeutic in a way. Shelby never complained. It was nice, mother-daughter time, and they could talk about anything. No topic was off the table. Tonight's was a bit of a surprise to the High Priestess.

"Mother," Shelby said, looking at her mother's reflection in the vanity mirror with a slight frown creasing her forehead, "I have a question for you that has been bothering me."

"Oh?" Marybeth said. There was a bit of apprehension in her voice. Her hand paused as she waited.

"What does Sebastian Barrister want with Bobby St. Claire? He's just a little six-year-old boy."

Marybeth resumed brushing her daughter's hair. "It seems that the child has a special ability that Sebastian is in need of."

Shelby placed her hands on the vanity and twisted her body

so that she could see her mother more clearly. "What special ability could he possibly have?"

"Well," Marybeth twisted her shoulders back so that she could continue to brush her daughter's hair, "Robert St. Claire has the capability to speak with the dead. His best friend is a ghost, from what his grandmother says."

"A ghost? That's absurd."

"Elizabeth Wellington swears by it. She says that the boy has even gone back in time and played with her on numerous occasions. In fact, it was Barrister's idea to send him back to 1884 to kill the wolf that mauled the poor girl. The bond between the two is quite strong."

Shelby frowned. "That's odd. Why would Sebastian Barrister care about the girl? Was she related to him in some way?"

Marybeth shook her head. "That's not my understanding, no."

"Then I don't understand," Shelby said with a shrug. "Why care about a child that you don't know, especially if she died a hundred and thirty some years ago?"

"Well, it is my understanding that Sebastian Barrister's brother, Rutherford—who was known as The Raven, was set to wed the Coven's High Priestess in a ceremony that would give both extraordinary powers. He simply disappeared on his wedding day before the ceremony could take place. Sebastian believes that Sam St. Claire, the wolf that mauled young Sara Robinson, may also have killed his brother to punish Sebastian for some bizarre reason. Evidently Sebastian and Sam were always at odds. Anyway, Sebastian hoped that Robert could kill the wolf with liquid silver, thereby preventing his brother's murder."

"So I take it that Bobby failed?"

Marybeth chuckled softly. "Oh of course he did. He's just a six-year-old child after all. How could he possibly be expected to slay a monstrous wolf? It's absurd, really." She shook her head as she resumed brushing her daughter's hair. "I don't know what Sebastian was thinking, truth be told." She paused with the brush and shrugged. "Perhaps it is a deficiency caused by his condition. Extreme blood loss can cause strange things to happen, I'm sure."

"So what does Barrister want with the child now?" Shelby asked, trying to comprehend it all.

Marybeth shrugged. "Sebastian believes that the boy can contact his dead brother's spirit. Evidently he still has designs on fulfilling the marriage ceremony."

Shelby twisted again. "Couldn't he accomplish the same thing with a séance? It sounds like it would be a whole lot less trouble than the way he's going about it now."

"I suggested that very thing to him. He's already tried it apparently."

"And?"

Marybeth shook her head. "He was unable to make contact."

"And he thinks that Bobby St. Claire might be able to talk to his dead brother when he could not?"

"That's the plan. He believes that if the boy can contact his dead brother then Sebastian might be able to learn where Rutherford's earthly remains are buried. If he knows that, he may be able to bring him back."

Shelby's brow furrowed. "Wouldn't that require Dark Magic?"

Marybeth nodded. "The darkest."

"Then why does Sebastian need the Coven? We don't practice the kind of magic he'll need."

"My dear, he intends for his brother to wed a priestess, of course. He wants to fulfill the ceremony that was promised."

Shelby swallowed. She had an uneasy feeling rising in the pit of her stomach. "Who is to wed The Raven, mother?"

Marybeth smiled as she leaned forward and kissed the top of her daughter's head. "Why, that honor is yours, darling. That is why Sebastian used his influence at the *Drawing Down the Moon* ceremony. Surely you felt the Dark Goddess enter your body." She smiled at her daughter's reflection in the vanity mirror. "Everyone could sense the change come over you." Her face brightened as she smiled. "It was quite exhilarating to behold. I was so very proud of you my darling."

A look of horror crossed Shelby's face as she gasped softly. She could hear the Dark Goddess' laughter in her mind. She stared at her own reflection in the vanity mirror and for the briefest of seconds saw her eyes flash a bright green. She gripped the edges of the vanity tightly, fearing that she was losing control of her own life.

Since the *Drawing Down the Moon* ceremony she had sensed another presence in her mind. It was almost as if another was sharing her body from somewhere within. She had heard of people having multiple personalities but knew that this was not the case with her. This was something far more sinister.

Chapter Thirty-five

A New Lease on Life

I was surprised at how good Ari looked now that she had received the blood transfusion. Already the color had returned to her complexion, and her breathing had greatly improved. She was strong, a real fighter. She was going to pull through.

I opened the door and peeked into the room and was relieved to see that she was awake. I smiled at her as I carried a bowl of soup to her bedside. "Hey, how are you doing?" I asked tentatively.

She took a deep breath and blew it out slowly, her dark eyes sparkling brightly in the candlelight. She shrugged. "I've been better, but at least I no longer feel like I am knocking on Death's door."

"Are you hungry?" I asked, lifting the bowl for emphasis. "I brought you some soup."

Ari nodded. "I am starving!"

I placed the bowl on the nightstand beside the bed. "Here,

let me help you to sit up."

She gave me a look that clearly said she didn't want any assistance. "I can do it."

I watched her struggle for a bit longer and then I stepped in and helped to get her in a better position to be able to handle the soup without spilling it all over herself or the bed. Beads of sweat coated her forehead along her hairline. She exhaled a deep breath and smiled up at me apologetically. "I guess that I'm weaker than I thought. Thanks."

I smiled at her. "No worries, I'm happy to do whatever I can. It's going to take time to regain your strength. You lost a lot of blood."

She nodded slowly as a frown creased her brow. "About that…"

I picked up the bowl of soup and handed it to her. "Aunt Abigail says that you're going to be just fine. It might take some time, but you'll feel like your old self soon enough."

She must have read something into the look on my face. Or maybe my eyes had revealed to her that there was something that was bothering me. She seemed to study me for a moment longer. She asked, "Who was the donor?"

I sighed as I turned and faced her. "My grandpa is a Universal Donor. He's Type O. It's his blood that saved you. I offered but we couldn't be sure I was a match." I chuckled softly and shrugged. "To be honest I don't know what blood type I am."

She nodded, a slow smile appeared on her face as she reached out and touched my arm. "I appreciate the offer."

I slowly sat down on the bed beside her and put a hand on her good leg. "I'm just happy that my aunt had everything she needed in that little bag of hers. You gave us all quite a scare."

After a moment she smiled. "That is why my akhsótha painted my face."

I shook my head. "Why was that? What did it mean?"

"She was preparing me for the *Afterlife*. She didn't want me to go into the *Great Beyond* unprepared should the transfusion have failed." She chuckled softly as she saw the confused look on my face. "The face paint lets all the spirits know that a warrior is walking among them and they should not block their path. If they do, they risk their own spirit being taken by the angered warrior." She chuckled softly, a rosy blush coloring her cheeks. "I know it is a silly tradition, probably nothing more than Tribal mumbo-jumbo, but try telling that to my akhsótha. She has always held firm to the Old Ways."

I smiled. "I really like your akhsótha. She's a cool lady, and a very smart woman."

Smiling happily Ari took a spoonful of the broth and nodded. "She is."

"Can I ask you something?"

She studied me for a moment and then nodded. "Sure. What's on your mind?"

I sighed. "Why didn't you just morph into a bird and simply fly away? Why did you let them do this to you?"

"I felt that I needed to draw them away from my home. I didn't want them here when my akhsótha returned. I was hoping to save her. She's all I have."

We sat in silence for a while as Ari continued to eat her soup. When she was done she handed me the bowl. "Those boys who came here, what happened to them?"

I stood up from the bed and looked down at her. I shook my head. "They won't ever bother you again, Ari."

"Are they dead, then?" she asked softly.

I nodded. "They are."

Her eyes filled with tears and as she blinked, they rolled down her cheeks. She brushed them away with her fingertips. "I think I'd like to rest a bit," she said softly.

§

Members of The Hollows Sheriff's Department pulled up in front of the cabin in three different police cruisers as Grandpa was supervising the reinstallation of the front door that had been bashed in by Jeremy Willis. Brock and Silas had come a few hours earlier to replace the door and the broken window. After they finished hanging the door, the guys moved to begin work on the window.

Sheriff Maynard Thompson was a robust man with an unkind face. He had been taking notes since his arrival, grunting as he jotted down relevant information upon his pad of paper. Evidently Bradley Somers had filed a report with the local law enforcement as soon as he returned to town. He had admitted that they all had been drinking and were just out for a 'little fun'. When Danny Hancock pulled out the revolver and started firing off shots, he knew it wasn't going to end well so he simply took off, not bothering to try and talk the others out of the course of action that they had pursued.

Grandpa had told the Sheriff about the location of Marty's body, having discovered it when they found Ari unconscious in the woods. Grandpa had been asked to escort two of the deputies to recover the body, which he did with reluctance. Brock and Silas went with them. A thorough search of the forest would undoubtedly determine the fate of Danny and Jeremy as well, but it would take time.

Sheriff Thompson chewed on the end of his thick, unlit cigar as he returned his notepad to the breast pocket of his uniform. "I believe I have all the information that I need," he said as though he were bored. He inclined his head toward Tiffany as he spoke to Aunt Abigail and Okwaho. "Officer Jones here will take care of everything else." He sighed after a moment. "It's a shame, what happened. I'm sure these boys didn't really mean any harm. We all know how young boys can be. It's unfortunate."

"Oh?" Aunt Abigail said crossing her arms. "Then why did

they forcefully break in to this home? If you ask me, I'd say that Bradley Somers should be arrested for his complicity."

Sheriff Thompson took the cigar stub from his mouth and glared at her. "Well, no one's asked you for your opinion, ma'am. I'm interested in gathering the facts, not placing blame for supposed crimes."

"They busted down the door and shattered a window to gain entry into this home. What, exactly would you call that?" Anger flared in her eyes. "I believe that breaking and entering is a crime."

He placed the stub of the cigar back into his mouth and chuckled softly. "The door and the window seem just fine to me."

"They were just replaced."

He nodded. "So you say. Look, there is no evidence that either were destroyed as you claim. What reason would these fine young men have for the violent acts that you suggest? There just aren't any witnesses substantiating any of your claims."

"What about Ari?" Aunt Abby said, pointing toward the bedroom where Ari rested.

He shrugged. "From what I hear that girl is a tease and a flirt. I can produce numerous people that will attest to that fact. For all I know she enticed these boys out here and once she'd gotten them all drunk she got scared. You cannot expect boys with raging hormones to just stop. It ain't natural."

I couldn't take it anymore. "That's complete bullshit! They broke into her home and chased her through the woods. They even shot her!"

He took a deep breath and blew it out slowly. He shook his head. "I saw no evidence of a bullet wound on the young lady's leg. Not anything recent, anyway. Care to explain to me how that is even possible? I think you people are trying to spread a whole lot of your bullshit around and discredit these boys for no good reason. These boys are dead. I'll not allow you to smear their good name."

He took out his cigar and shook it at me. "Seems to me that you were recently kicked out of school for a stunt you pulled." He grinned at Aunt Abigail. "Sounds to me like you ought to keep her on a tight leash."

"What is that supposed to mean?" Aunt Abby snapped angrily.

He chuckled. "You're a smart cookie. You figure it out."

Sheriff Thompson turned and walked back to his patrol car. Opening the door he tipped his hat with a smile. "You ladies take care now." He chuckled softly as he climbed behind the wheel and drove away, kicking up a cloud of dust.

I looked at Tiffany and shook my head. "I can't believe you work for that man!"

Tiffany put her own notepad away and sighed. "Not everyone on the Force is like him. You have to believe that. I want to do what's right, but my hands are tied." She nodded toward the cabin. "Is Ari a wolf too? A Lycan? Is that why her bullet wound healed so quickly?"

I shook my head. "No. She's not a Lycan." I smiled. "But she is special."

Tiffany nodded. "I get it. You don't want to talk to me." She studied me for a minute. "But just know that I am on your side."

§

Over the next few days Ari regained her strength remarkably well. Aunt Abby, Grandpa, and her akhsótha had claimed that her ability to transform into a sparrow allowed her body to heal at an accelerated rate. It was obviously true. When she was in human form you could scarcely even see the scars on her thigh where the bullet had passed through. If you knew where to look you could still see the faint round marks, but even then it wasn't easy. It had been no wonder that the sheriff hadn't believed us.

After the others left I had stayed behind with Ari and her akhsótha, wanting to help out as much as I could. It was becoming increasingly more obvious that Ari was back to her old self and no longer needed my help. It was time that I headed home. I hugged both Ari and Okwaho and bid them farewell. Morphing into the wolf, I headed through the forest at a leisurely trot.

Chapter Thirty-six

An Unexpected Encounter

I didn't waste time heading home. The Wolf pushed against my mind, wanting more freedom to hunt and play, but I refused to relinquish control to her. The woods had become increasingly more dangerous lately. We had seen numerous hunters carrying rifles, determined to rid the forest of the deadly wolves that had slain Danny Hancock and Jeremy Willis. The mangled bodies of both boys had been recovered deep in the woods. Reports surfaced that Danny had succumbed to a vicious wolf attack. Jeremy had obviously fallen from Valen's Ridge, his body broken and horribly twisted. The investigation showed that he had been running from a pair of wolves. I didn't dare roam the forest during the light of day in wolf form. It was safer at night.

The citizens of The Hollows were enraged. They were out for blood. During our runs we had to make sure that we stayed well clear of the hunters, though it was unlikely that they carried silver bullets in their guns. The very last thing we needed was for armed men to start shooting at anything that moved.

The Wolf could smell the scent of man in the forest as she moved like a silent ghost through the tall, slender pines, and the occasional oak or hickory clump, as she headed toward the southeast and home. The smell of woodsmoke from the campfires of the men filtered through the gaps in the trees as the Wolf angled toward the river.

She paused in a clump of the straggly shrub known as Hobblebush, known for the branches that bent toward the ground, and took root. Men would often trip and lose their footing in these slender branches that 'hobbled' the unaware passers-by, causing them to trip and fall. If you weren't careful you could easily break a leg. Aunt Abigail always called it Witch-Hobble, but Grandpa referred to it by its more common name of Hobblebush; I guess either would suffice. Regardless, the bush offered excellent cover for the Wolf.

The thick, lush green leaves sprouted brilliantly white flowers with smaller white clusters in the center of the larger ones. Normally they only blossomed from May to June, but for some reason these were still in full bloom. Tiny berries that grew from the shrub were favorites of many forest creatures. The flowers themselves were often mistaken for honeysuckle, but really they were nothing alike.

I could hear men talking, their voices carrying a good distance in the quiet forest that surrounded their campsite. They had been drinking a good deal and their speech was slurred to the point that it was difficult to understand. I figured that it was best to pass them by as quickly and as quietly as I could; alcohol and guns seldom turned out well. The Wolf seemed eager to be off, so we continued to the river and found a shallow place to cross.

From where I was now, if I headed due east, I would make it to Grandpa's small cabin. But I continued to head in a southerly direction. I was anxious to return to the cottage. I hadn't seen

Bobbybear for several days and I was missing him a good deal. I couldn't wait to get back to him and snuggle against him as we both drifted off to sleep.

I entered the small clearing where my clothes were tucked away in the nook of an old twisted tree. I morphed back into my human form and reached for the waterproof bag that contained my clothes and began to get dressed. There was a chill in the night air and goosebumps quickly rose upon my exposed skin. I froze, hearing the snap of a dried twig from somewhere off to my left. Usually the Wolf was pretty good about picking up the presence of danger, either by her keen sense of smell or her sharp hearing, but now that I was back in human form, I hadn't.

Something was out there; I could just make out a shadowy form moving in the trees. I debated about calling forth the Wolf but hesitated. If it were a hunter searching for a wolf, I could just be putting myself into more danger. "Who's there?" I called out, my voice full of uncertainty.

Shelby Collingsworth stepped from the shadows of the pines and into the moonlight where I could see her clearly. She looked frightened. "Oh thank goodness, it's you!" she said, sounding relieved.

I blinked. "What are you doing here?" I scanned the forest, certain that she wasn't alone. Shelby seldom went anywhere without her entourage. My first thought was that this was a trap of some kind. With the Daughters of the Coven, you never really knew. I certainly didn't trust them.

Shelby had a pleading look on her face. "I need your help."

"You want *my* help?" My first instinct was to laugh, but I didn't. "With what?" My gut was screaming for me not to trust her. The last time I had, Millie had gotten seriously hurt.

She took a step toward me. "Is there someplace we can go? I hate these woods, too many wild animals running around." She blushed. "You know what I mean. But now there are fools with guns everywhere."

I crossed my arms over my chest, still thinking this could be some kind of trap; a ploy just to get through Aunt Abigail's protective charm that she had placed over the cottage. "We can talk here," I refused to budge.

Shelby rolled her eyes and shook her auburn curls. "Whatever. Look, we need to work together to end this before someone gets hurt."

"It's a little late for that, Shelby. Some of my friends have already been killed or seriously hurt by you and your little goonies."

She reached out and took hold of my arm, but upon seeing my glaring look, she dropped her hand. "I never wanted any of that to happen. You've got to believe me!"

"Really?" I said, almost laughing at the absurdity of it all. "What about Millie? You seem to have planned that."

She shrugged, blushing again. "Okay. You've got a point. But what happened to Cho and Tucker," she shook her head, "I didn't want that. No one was supposed to die."

"But they *did* die," I said. "So have others."

Shelby reached out and took hold of my arm again. "That's why we need to stop this! Sebastian Barrister is trying to bring back his dead brother. That's what he wants your kid brother for. He believes that Bobby has a really good chance of talking to his spirit and then he'll be able to find where his earthly remains are buried. He wants to resurrect his brother and fulfill some ancient prophecy."

"What prophecy?" I asked.

She sighed, biting her bottom lip. Tears began to form in her eyes; either she was truly frightened or she was just a really good actress. "You've never heard the story about the powerful Warlock that was to wed a High Priestess of the Coven? Their union would grant both unbelievable powers - powers that would reach far beyond The Hollows. They would be unstoppable. Maybe even invincible," she shrugged, "I don't know, exactly." She shivered.

Tears rolled down her cheeks. "Kat, I was selected at the *Drawing Down the Moon* ceremony. I am to be the Warlock's bride! You have to help me, Kat. I don't want to get married—least of all to some dead guy!"

"So this is all about what you want, is it?" I couldn't help but sound cynical.

"Kat… please… help me!" she begged.

I sighed, my mind racing. Finally I looked at her sympathetically. "I don't know what you want me to do. How can I help you?"

She wiped the tears from her face with the tips of her fingertips. She sniffled as she smiled. "Oh, thank you, Kat! Honestly, I don't know how to thank you properly!"

"How can I help you?" I asked again. I was getting impatient. I just wanted to get to the cottage and see Bobbybear.

Shelby stared into my eyes. "Slay the vampire. If Sebastian Barrister is destroyed then all this will just go away." She placed her hands to the sides of her head and winced as though she were in an incredible amount of pain, suffering a migraine, maybe. It seemed to pass just as quickly as it had come.

§

As Shelby and I walked up to the cottage we could see Grandpa and Aunt Abigail sitting on the front porch sipping wine as they sat in the rockers. I could see the smile disappear from my aunt's face as she recognized my companion. "What is *she* doing here?" her voice was scathing.

Shelby froze. It didn't take her long to know that she was not welcome here. "Maybe this isn't such a good idea," she said. "Perhaps I should go."

I put a hand on her arm and forced her to stay. "You came here for my help. If we're going to do this, we need theirs."

Shelby bit at her lip and nodded. Her eyes were clouded with uncertainty. "Whatever you think is best."

Aunt Abigail arched a brow as she looked from Shelby to me. "Do you want to tell me what this is all about?"

Grandpa stood up and put a hand on her shoulder. He knew as well as I did how quick she could lash out in anger. She was close to reaching that point now. His touch seemed to calm her some. I couldn't help but smile at him, and then I turned my attention to my aunt, explaining everything that I knew.

She listened patiently, nodding occasionally. It was almost as if some of this she already knew. I could only wonder what secrets she was keeping from me.

Grandpa was the first to speak. "It would help if we knew where Sebastian Barrister's lair was. If we knew that, we could strike against him when he is at his weakest, during daylight."

Shelby sighed and shook her head. "That wouldn't really do you much good, I'm afraid. His resting place is protected by powerful sigils that won't allow anyone to come close."

Grandpa glanced at my aunt. "Sigils?"

Aunt Abigail nodded. "Magical glyphs to ward others away." She shook her head. "It is very plausible. Marybeth Collingsworth is a High Priestess in the Coven. Her powers are equal to my mother's, or at the very least, close. That is why she was able to assume control of the Coven after my mother…" she shrugged, "…after her removal. I'm fairly certain that Marybeth has put the sigils into place."

Shelby nodded. "She did."

Grandpa looked at my aunt. "Could your mother remove these sigils?" he asked.

Aunt Abby shook her head. "No. Only the witch that placed them can remove them."

Grandpa ran a hand through his thick hair. "That's just great," he said. He shook his head after a moment and swore softly. Finally, he looked up at Shelby. "I still want to know where Barrister sleeps."

Shelby had a pained look on her face. "His coffin is in Collingsworth Manor. But he's not alone, not any more. He's turned others." Her eyes began to water. "I… I think he has plans to turn even more people; build an army of undead." She shivered.

Grandpa tensed. "We already know about Keegan."

She wiped a tear from her cheek. "I know that he wants to create even more hybrids."

Aunt Abigail gasped as she put a hand over her mouth. "Sam, we need to keep Brock and Silas safe. He might try to get to either of them to weaken our numbers even more."

Grandpa shook his head. "They'll be all right. Both have pretty good heads on their shoulders."

She put a hand on his arm. "When Dr. Monaghan started the autopsy on Keegan he removed the silver knitting needles. I think it killed the wolf in him, but not the vampire. He drained both of Silas' parents. He might be able to get to Silas through them."

Grandpa grabbed Shelby's arm tightly. "Do you know anything about the Monaghans? Where they are?"

Shelby nodded fearfully. "Barrister keeps them in his lair."

He released his grip on Shelby's arm and glanced at my aunt. "We could use more allies."

"Our last ally didn't pan out so well," she snapped, referring to Keegan.

I could see Grandpa's jaw tighten with rising anger. To his credit, he didn't respond.

I quickly spoke up before the tension in the air caused either to say something that they might regret. "Tiffany Jones knows everything. She wants to help us in any way that she can," I said. Grandpa was right, we needed allies badly.

He sighed. "Who's this Tiffany Jones? A Coven member?"

I almost laughed. "No. She's the female deputy that showed

up at Ari's cabin with the others."

"Great," he shrugged. "So we have one cop on our side, but that's not nearly enough. I don't think that she can do much against Maynard Thompson—he's always been against us."

Aunt Abigail squeezed his arm. "At least it's a start." He nodded. "All right." He pinched his bottom lip for a moment as he thought. "Why don't you have a chat with your mother? See if maybe there is something that she can do to help us with Shelby's… situation. After all, she was once head of the Coven. She might have an idea or two."

She nodded her head in agreement. "I was just thinking the same thing."

"While you're doing that," he said, "I'll run Shelby back into town. Then I'll swing by and gather the Pack. We'd probably best stick close together until this mess is resolved."

§

They rode in silence until the truck turned onto the highway leading to The Hollows. The sky was clear; stars twinkled softly as the light from the full moon glowed bright upon the blacktop. Sam glanced over at his passenger and studied her for a moment. She seemed like a very nice girl, not someone that you'd expect to be involved in such a sinister plot. He sighed as he turned his attention back to the road.

Shelby turned and looked at him quizzically. "Something you wanted to say?" Her voice was soft, sweet, so much like Kat's.

Sam chuckled softly. She was sharp, didn't miss a beat. "I was just thinking that you seem to be a very nice girl, but I can't help but remember what you and your friends did to that Bradford girl. That was just plain mean."

She nodded as she ran a hand through her auburn curls. "I know. Believe me, if I could turn back time and change things, I would. It wasn't very nice. I'm sorry that she was hurt."

"Maybe you should try and tell her that," he offered. "Peace has to start somewhere."

Shelby shook her head. "She'd never listen. There's too much water under the bridge. We've a long history between us, none of it very nice. It's hard to believe that we were once really good friends, but that was a very long time ago; first grade, I think. After that, we just seemed to drift apart." She shook her head. "Looking back, that was definitely my mother's doing."

He nodded. "Sometimes we do stupid things. It's almost human nature, I think. But we can always change the course we're on. We just have to make the choice to do what's right." He frowned suddenly, wondering what was causing her hand to twitch upon her leg. He glanced over at her, suddenly concerned about her wellbeing.

Shelby's smile slowly left her lips and her face went blank. Her entire body seemed to quiver as he glanced back at her; the green in her eyes seemed to darken as he watched. He reached a hand out toward her as he began to slow the truck. "Are you all right, Shelby?" he asked, a hint of panic rising in his voice.

She smiled again, but it wasn't the same, sweet smile of the girl from a moment ago. This was something else entirely; something dark and foreboding, something sinister. She clawed his arm savagely, ripping deep furrows into his forearm. "You cannot stop this!" she hissed.

He fought to get away as best he could, while still maintaining control of the truck, but there was nowhere for him to go. He inadvertently pressed the accelerator as the Chevy pickup swerved across the road in his struggles. It plowed down a steep embankment, crashing through slender pines as it dove off the highway. It bounced and rolled several times, and the scream of twisting metal split the eerie silence of the forest. Finally, when it came to a stop it was upside down, its tires still spinning. The engine hissed as it began to smoke, dripping fuel from a ruptured tank.

Chapter Thirty-seven

Trouble in Paradise

After Grandpa left with Shelby, Aunt Abby decided to go to Wellington House to talk with Grandmother in the hopes that she could offer more insight into Shelby's problem. I stifled a yawn, and then grinned sheepishly at her. I was exhausted. "You can let me know what you find out in the morning. I'm gonna go snuggle up against Bobbybear," I said.

She chuckled softly. "Sweet dreams, Kat."

I watched her leave the cottage and then I turned and headed for the bedroom, barely picking up my feet as I shuffled along. I was thankful that no one was here to chastise me for not walking properly, but I was tired and didn't really care. I began to undress as I went.

I could see Bobby's sleeping form taking up most of the bed. I finished undressing and then pulled the oversized t-shirt over my head. It had been one of my dad's. It had a few holes here and there, but I didn't mind, it was nothing revealing. It was extremely soft and went down to mid-thigh, and it was comfortable to sleep in. It was a small way of keeping my dad with me.

I lifted the covers and slipped into bed, pulling Bobby close against me. He wriggled his body even closer. My eyelids were heavy and it was difficult to keep them open. Finally, I stopped trying and drifted off to dreamless sleep.

Aunt Abigail awoke me, giving my shoulder an urgent shake. "Kat, wake up!"

"Huh?" my mind was groggy, refusing to concentrate. "What time is it?" I asked, squinting my eyes at the morning sunlight streaming in through the window. It had seemed like I had only just gotten to bed, but it was obvious now that I hadn't.

"It's almost ten. I need you to get up. Your grandpa never returned with the guys. I need you to see if you can track him down." Creases of worry lined her face and fear filled her eyes. She was on the verge of losing it.

"But Grandpa took the truck, surely you're not wanting me to go into the town in wolf form." I began to unravel myself from the twisted blankets, but it wasn't easy. Bobby was already up, probably in the other room.

Aunt Abby shook her head. "Of course not. Harrison is going to take you into town in the Bentley. He'll take you wherever you need to go and then bring you back here if necessary."

The thought of being in the Bentley alone with Harrison Beckett caused me to hesitate. The last time I had been alone with the man he had been drunk. Fortunately then Grandpa had come to my rescue.

Aunt Abby frowned at me as she looked at me. "I need you to get dressed as fast as you can, he's already waiting outside with the car."

I still wasn't happy but I dressed quickly and then went into the bathroom and brushed my teeth. I shook my head at the reflection in the mirror, not happy with the bags under my eyes. I could still use several more hours of sleep. No matter how hard I tried, I wasn't moving fast enough for my aunt. She glared at me as I emerged from the bathroom. "My God what was taking you so long?" she asked.

I squinted at her as I moved my head backwards. "Excuse me? It was like five minutes!"

She sighed and closed her eyes as she nodded. "I know. I'm sorry. You did great." She wrapped her arms around me and gave me a hug, kissing the side of my head. "Forgive me?" she asked, her voice breaking slightly.

I nodded against her. "It's OK, I get it." I stepped back out of her embrace and smiled reassuringly. "Don't worry, I'll find him. I'm sure he's all right."

"Hope so," she said wiping her tears away, "cuz I'm gonna kill him!"

I walked outside and could hear the soft purr of the Bentley as it idled. Harrison Beckett opened the back door with a hesitant smile. He seemed to blush. "Good morning, Mistress Katherine."

I glanced at Aunt Abigail and kinda rolled my eyes. This new Harrison Beckett was going to take some getting used to. "Morning, Harrison."

He closed the door securely after I had slid into the back seat and then he walked around the rear of the Bentley and got behind the wheel. He glanced up into the rearview mirror, still sporting a look of concern. "Mistress Katherine? About the other night… I just want to offer my sincere apologies. There's no excuse for the way I acted. I am deeply sorry."

I studied him for a moment and then sighed. I decided that it was stupid to make any more enemies. I said, "Let's just forget it ever happened, shall we?"

He seemed surprised. After a moment's hesitation he nodded.

"Very well, Mistress Katherine. Thank you, that is most kind of you."

"How's your head?" I asked, recalling how hard he had struck it against Wellington House.

He furrowed as he touched the back of his head with his fingertips. "I'll survive."

I could see his ears turning a bright red and I couldn't help but smile. Finally, I shook my head. "Let's just go to The Hollows. I'll direct you from there."

"Very well," he said as he started the car moving.

As we drove upon the dirt road that took us from the cottage and around the north side of Wellington House, I studied the manor silently. The old house was dark and foreboding; I couldn't help but shiver. When I looked in the rearview mirror I could see that Harrison was watching me closely.

I glanced back at Wellington House and sighed, trying to summon the courage to ask the question that was burning in my mind. Finally, I decided to throw caution to the wind and just jump right on in. "Why didn't you leave, Harrison? Why did you stay after what happened to my grandmother?"

He chuckled softly and glanced toward the manor before looking back into the mirror. He shrugged. "Where would I go?"

"There has to be other places you could work. Why stay here?"

"I wanted to leave," he confessed. "I even tried, but I didn't get very far before she found me and forced me to return." He shook his head slowly. "Margaret and I are trapped here. She won't allow us to leave." He chuckled again. "Besides, I don't believe that Margaret would leave if she had the chance. And now it is too late for me."

"How so?" I asked, leaning forward in my seat. I truly wanted to know.

After a long pause he said, "Once she has marked you, you

belong to her." He turned onto the blacktop and picked up speed as we headed toward The Hollows. I sat back against the seat and stared out the window as the pines zipped by. I closed my eyes and allowed my body to relax. My suspicions were confirmed.

Grandmother had bitten both Harrison and Margaret to ensure their continued loyalty.

Once we had reached The Hollows I decided to direct Harrison to Millie's house, thinking that Silas would likely be there rather than at his own home, given all that had happened with his folks. And I figured that if he wasn't there, Millie might know where he had gone. It was still possible that he was with my Grandpa. Whatever the case, I couldn't afford to get distracted like I had the last time; Aunt Abigail was already pretty frazzled, it wasn't going to take much to send her over the edge.

As the Bentley pulled up in front of Millie's home, I could tell that something was horribly wrong. Both Millie and Silas were on the front porch having a very heated discussion about something. I could see that Millie had been crying, her eyes were a little puffy and her cheeks were a deep rouge color. I saw Silas shake his head with vigor. This couldn't be good. I climbed out of the Bentley before Harrison even got around the car to open the door for me.

On seeing me, Silas and Millie stopped arguing. Silas stepped off the porch and threw a hand over his shoulder. "You need to talk some sense into her!"

I blinked, caught off guard by the unexpected hostility in his voice. "Whoa! What's going on with you two?" I looked from him to Millie. She was glaring at me, seething with anger. Something had definitely gotten her riled up. I had never seen her in such a state.

Millie shook her head. "It just isn't fair!" She turned and stormed into the house, struggling with the crutches. She slammed the screen door closed behind her.

I looked at Silas. "Mind telling me what this is all about?" I felt like I was caught in the middle of a raging storm.

Silas sighed heavily as he ran a hand through his hair. "Millie knows about Ari. She's jealous that Ari can shape-shift into a bird, we can turn into wolves and she can't do any of that. She's feeling left out." He gave me a haunted look. "Do you know that she actually wanted me to make her a Lycan?"

I blinked again, totally blown away by this bit of news. "All this because Ari can turn into a bird?"

Silas threw his hands up into the air, exasperated. "I don't know! There seems to be more to it but she won't talk to me about it. She said if I wouldn't do this for her, then I wasn't a very good boyfriend. She actually broke up with me. I tried to make her understand that what I really loved about her was that she was normal." He shook his head. "But that didn't go down very well. Now I'm in even more trouble because I said she was normal. That really set her off again! I don't know how to fix this."

I sighed, placing a hand on his arm giving it a reassuring squeeze. "Let me talk to her. I'm sure that I can talk some sense into her."

"As you can see, she's pretty upset about the whole thing. I don't know what you can say to calm her down. I tried everything I could think of. It seemed to only make matters worse." He looked me straight in the eyes. "But we can't do what she wants."

I rolled my eyes. "God, I know! She doesn't know what she's asking. I'll talk to her, but I need you to stay here while I do. We've got bigger problems brewing. My grandpa is missing."

"Missing?" he had a look of immediate concern on his face. "What do you mean by missing, exactly?"

Shelby Collingsworth showed up at the cottage last night asking for our help. Grandpa was going to drive her back into town and then pick up you and Brock. He still hasn't returned."

Silas shook his head. "I haven't seen him since we were all at Ari's place."

I searched his eyes. "What do you think it means? Do you think that he might have run into Keegan or Sebastian? Could they have done something to him?"

He frowned as he shoved his fingertips into the front pockets of his jeans. "It's certainly a possibility." He took a step toward the gate. "You talk some sense into Millie if you can. I'll check in with Brock. We'll meet up back at the cottage."

I pointed to the Bentley. "You want Harrison to give you a ride to Brock's?"

Silas chuckled and shook his head. "No way! It'll be easier if I don't. Trust me."

I shrugged. "Whatever you think is best. Oh, please be careful. Shelby said that Barrister is out to make more hybrids. Aunt Abby is afraid that he'll use your parents against you."

He had an anguished look in his eyes. He shook his head. "I won't let him use them against me. They're gone. I can't bring them back. I know that. In time I might even learn to live with it. But I won't let him get to me by using them. Eventually I'll make him pay for what he's done."

I nodded sympathetically. As he left I turned back toward the house and took a deep breath as I stepped onto the porch. I crossed over to the door and knocked. "Millie? It's Kat. Can we talk?"

After a moment she appeared at the door, but made no effort to open the screen door or invite me in. She crossed her arms over her chest and glared at me angrily. "It isn't fair, you know. Why does everyone get to be special but I can't? Is Ari a full-fledged member of your little pack now? Where does that leave me? I don't want to be just an honorary member. I've earned a spot!"

I sighed. "Can I come in so that we can talk about this? I

can't have this conversation with you through a screen door."

She turned the knob and then pushed the door open with the end of a crutch as she rolled her eyes. "Come on in."

I followed her into the parlor and we both took a seat on the sofa. Her jaw was tightly clenched and I could see the anger still flushing her cheeks as molten fires burned in her eyes behind her round lenses. I took a deep, calming breath, trying to choose my words carefully. "I really don't know why this has gotten you so upset. Nothing's changed. Ari has always been able to take the shape of a sparrow. She can even see through the eyes of other animals." I shook my head, "I don't know how, really, but she can." I shrugged. "She's a special girl."

She gave me a teary-eyed look as she slapped her hands against her thighs. Almost as though she were pleading with me she said, "I want to be special too! I'm tired of being just a fat, normal girl with friends that can turn into these amazing things." She shook her head. "How can I protect my Grammy, keep her safe when there are all these monsters out there?"

I took her hand and squeezed it reassuringly. "Oh, Millie! We'll keep you and your Grammy safe. You have to believe that we'll do all we can."

"But that's *my* job!" she said angrily.

I could see that my words had very little impact on her. She was still furious. Tears formed in her eyes as she slowly shook her head. "I was afraid this was going to happen. You and Ari are besties now, I get it, neither of you have time to spare with the chubby girl. I'm beginning to feel like an outcast all over again. It just isn't fair!"

I was in total shock. I couldn't believe what I was hearing. "Oh, Millie… no. That isn't it at all!" I tried to place a hand on her knee, but she brushed it away.

She quickly stood and pointed toward the door. "I think you should leave."

I blinked. "Millie…"

"Go!" she pounded the floor with her crutch as she slapped her thigh, still pointing toward the door. "I want you out of my house!"

I blinked back the tears that were forming in my own eyes as I stood. Nodding I said, "Okay, Millie. Perhaps you need a little time to wrap your head around this. Take the time, but please, don't do anything rash. I love you. You are special to me!"

She rolled her eyes and practically flew to the door. I was amazed how well she moved despite the cumbersome crutches. Pushing it open she raised her voice. "You are no longer welcome here! Just go!"

I felt numb as I stepped out onto the front porch. I cringed as Millie slammed the door closed behind me. I turned and eased the screen door closed. I closed my eyes tightly as the tears streamed down my face. I covered my mouth with a trembling hand and bowed my head in anguish. This was not how I had expected my day to go. Wiping my eyes, I stepped off the porch and walked to the Bentley. Harrison dutifully opened the door for me and I slid in, still sobbing. He closed the door softly and walked around the car and got behind the wheel. He paused, adjusting the rearview mirror in order to see me better. "Is there anything that I can do, Mistress Katherine?" he asked softly.

I shook my head. "Just take me home, please."

He nodded, readjusting the mirror. "Straight away, Mistress Katherine."

Chapter Thirty-eight

The Beast Within

As the Chevy pickup came to a stop, upside down, Sam could hear the sounds of twisting metal come to a halt. The engine made an awful hiss as it died, and small, snaking tendrils of smoke began to rise in the air. All he could smell was smoke and gasoline. He could see that the windshield was badly cracked, and what looked to be a large rock pushed the spider-webbed glass inward, blocking his vision. He glanced at the passenger side of the cab but Shelby was nowhere to be seen. *Had she been thrown clear? Had she even survived?* He couldn't be certain. He needed to get out of the truck so that he could search for her; she may desperately need his help. Then he recalled, fully, what had transpired. She had changed before his eyes into something sinister. *She had caused this!* He frowned. *It would serve her right if she were buried beneath the wreckage!*

It took him several minutes to crawl from the crippled truck; it certainly wasn't easy. The bench seat had shifted and was now at an awkward angle. How he had not been pinned against the steering column was beyond him. In the rearview mirror he could see that he had cut his forehead in the crash. He remembered slamming it against the glass on the driver's side door as he had been tossed about the cab. His right arm felt as though it were on fire. He could see the deep gashes caused by Shelby's sharp fingernails. *What the hell was that all about, anyway?*

Shelby had seemed possessed by some malevolent entity. *But where was she now?*

The deep, bloody furrows cut into his forearm burned. He could remember seeing the wound glowing with a soft greenish tinge, but it had quickly faded away. He could feel whatever it was racing like a wildfire through his veins. *What had she done to him?* He didn't know, but he had the incredible urge to hunt, to kill. The Wolf within him fought for dominance and he let the Black have his way. It was easier to deal with the pain coursing through him, and he knew it would help him to heal.

The silvery glow of the Moon still shown in the night sky, and the stars beckoned. He released the beast within, and howled mournfully. He limped through the trees in search of prey.

He found his way to a stream and stopped to drink. His thirst was almost as powerful as his hunger. Dipping his head he began to lap up the water greedily. The strange green glow of the Wolf's eyes was unfamiliar to him, but he gave it little thought.

A vision of a woman filled the mind of the Wolf… Her name was elusive for a moment, but the human part of him knew who she was. She was called Abigail… The beast within him snarled viciously. Had she been the one to hurt him? He couldn't be certain anymore. He was confused. *No… that couldn't be right… Abby would never hurt him.*

Sam felt his control over the wolf begin to recede. He was tired and hurt. The wolf made him feel stronger.

A rifle shot crackled through the forest. The bullet struck a

rock at the edge of the stream and ricocheted off harmlessly.
The wolf turned and ran. The forest was not safe.

Chapter Thirty-nine

Distressing News

Aunt Abigail stepped off of the porch and crossed to the Bentley as we rolled to a stop. She opened the door and frowned at me, worry still evident in her eyes. "Did you find Sam?" she asked, wringing her hands together.

I shook my head as I slid from the car. "No one's seen Grandpa. Silas is going to get hold of Brock and they'll meet us here. We can come up with something then."

"What's wrong?" she asked breathlessly. She could see that I'd been crying and immediately turned on Harrison. He took a step back, raising both hands in the air in innocent protest.

"It's Millie," I said with a choked voice.

"What? Is she all right? What happened?"

I chuckled softly as I wiped the tears from my face. "She wants to by a Lycan."

Aunt Abby stepped back. "A Lycan? What's brought this on?"

I wrapped my arms around her and she held me tightly. "She heard about Ari," I said. "She's feeling left out, or something. She broke things off with Silas because he refused to help her; to make her like us. When I tried to talk some sense into her she got really upset. She threw me out of the house, said I was no longer welcome."

Aunt Abby practically growled, sending a wave of shivers through me as her breath tickled my neck. "What the heck is she thinking? Doesn't she realize that none of you are Lycans because you wanted to be?" She shook her head. "I don't understand why she's acting so childishly."

I sighed. "She just wants to be able to protect her Grammy. Keegan's attack has left her feeling really insecure. Now that she knows that Ari can change into a sparrow she's feeling left out all over again. She's been an outcast nearly her whole life. I guess now she's back to feeling like she isn't good enough." I shrugged. "I really don't know."

As Harrison got back into the Bentley, we stood together on the porch. He waved as he turned the car around and headed for the garage at Wellington House. "Sooo," I said, "what did Grandmother have to say about Shelby's impending nuptials?" I couldn't help but grin a little bit. The idea of her having a planned wedding to a former dead person just seemed really bizarre.

Aunt Abby raised her eyebrows. "Mother seemed to take a bit of enjoyment out of it at first. But I convinced her that the poor girl was completely frazzled she decided to take pity on her. She said that the wedding will never take place, and that we shouldn't worry about it."

I frowned. "I wonder why she said it won't happen? Shelby seemed pretty convinced that it would."

Aunt Abigail shrugged. "She said that she had a plan to prevent it. When I pressed her for details she just sat there sipping her sherry with a little smirk on her face. It was really quite annoying. I couldn't take it anymore, so I left. I was hoping that Sam would be back with the guys by the time I returned."

§

It was late in the afternoon by the time that Silas and Brock showed up at the cottage. They had only recently dressed, and were still buttoning their shirts as they approached from the woods. The look on their faces clearly indicated that they were about to give us more bad news. I reached over and took Aunt Abigail's hand and squeezed it tightly, trying to bring us both some measure of comfort as we waited for what they had to say. My chest felt incredibly tight. My mouth was dry as I looked at them and asked. "What's wrong?"

Brock glanced at Silas before he said anything. Silas just dropped his head, not wanting to look us in the eyes. Brock cleared his throat. "We found the Chevy at the bottom of a steep incline. It was upside down and looked as though it had rolled several times."

Silas spoke quickly. "There was no sign of Sam. It looks like he morphed into his wolf form and left the scene of the accident. We found what was left of his clothes, all shredded. There was a small amount of blood on the scraps, but nothing major."

Brock sighed. "We didn't see any sign of Shelby."

"Why didn't you track Sam?" Aunt Abigail asked tightly.

"We tried," Silas said. "But it just became too dangerous. There were a lot of hunters in the woods. It seems like we weren't the only ones looking for him."

Tears formed in her eyes. "So that's it then? We're just gonna give up on him?" she asked.

I squeezed her hand. "No one's giving up on him. We'll find him."

She gave me a pained look. "He could be injured!" she said.

I shook my head, refusing to accept that he was seriously hurt. "They didn't find that much blood, just a few drops." I glanced at the guys for conformation, "I'm sure he's fine." Deep down I could only hope that he was.

The hunters weren't using silver bullets, so if they happened upon Grandpa in wolf form, they couldn't hurt him. Perhaps this was our silver lining of hope.

§

I stepped out onto the porch to get a breath of fresh air; we had been inside the cottage for what seemed like hours, trying to come up with some sort of plan. We desperately needed a plan to find Grandpa, a plan to help Shelby, and a plan to stop Sebastian Barrister once and for all. It was enough to make your head spin.

I could see the moon rising through the gaps in the tall, slender pines. This full moon was different. It looked almost crimson. As Aunt Abigail joined me with a glass of merlot in her hands, I asked, "Why is the moon so red?"

She took a sip of the wine and glanced up at the moon. "It's called a Blood Moon. It's caused by a total lunar eclipse."

I chuckled softly as I watched her. She looked up at the night sky with a furrowed brow. She seemed to be a bit unnerved. "Is something wrong?" I asked.

She blinked and then looked at me. "Don't you feel it?" she asked.

"Uhm, I feel a chill in the air…" I said with a slight shrug.

She took a deep breath and then turned her eyes up at the red moon. "There's an odd energy in the air tonight. I'm surprised that the Lycan in you doesn't sense the raw power."

I grasped my talisman and lifted it up off my chest, twisting the polished steel with my fingers. I wondered if I took it off would I feel the pull of the moon then? But I couldn't. It wasn't safe to be a wolf right now in these woods. Too many hunters were out, eager for a kill. I let go of the talisman and felt its weighty steel upon my skin.

I turned my gaze from the heavens and studied the thickening, dark shadows within the forest that I knew so well. Grandpa was out there, somewhere. I could only pray that he could find his way back to us without endangering himself. Hunters were firing off shots at nearly anything that moved, some not bothering to identify their targets before shooting their guns. But even if Grandpa were shot, it wouldn't be life-threatening for him. Hopefully this 'wolf-hunting-craze' would end soon, before innocents were slaughtered.

Chapter Forty

Blood Moon Ritual

The room at the northern end of Wellington House, on the ground floor was seldom used. In fact, no one but Elizabeth Wellington had entered the room in several years, not even Bobby on one of his many escapades of curiosity. Margaret had been in to clean it once, years ago, but had been forbidden to return. It was here that the High Priestess practiced her solitary magic. Though she had once led the Coven, she had always had magic that she kept just for herself, practiced and perfected in this room.

Powerful magic.

The walls of the room were solid oak, polished to a high sheen. The northern wall had the only window, but it was tightly shuttered most of the time. But not tonight. Tonight, Elizabeth needed the light of the Blood Moon to bathe the room with its crimson glow. Carved on the eastern and western walls were the various phases of the moon. A dark pentacle was painted on the floor, fully encircled. In the heart of the pentagram was a small altar carved from limestone. On it was a silver candelabrum that held three black candles that burned with a small, black flame. A silver necklace holding a white, almost clear crystal was sitting in a stone bowl, beside it was an old knife with a glistening blade of pure silver and a black leather hilt.

Elizabeth closed her eyes and lifted her palms into the air. She began to chant softly, her head swaying gently to the left and right.

> *"Candles of black and Goddess of old*
> *Release the powers that you hold*
> *With the blood that flows into this crystal cast*
> *Protection from the sun's glow*
> *And make it last."*

She took the knife and drew the blade across her left palm. Her jaw tightened as the pain registered in her mind. She turned her hand and held it over the bowl, and squeezed, allowing blood to drip onto the necklace. The crystal seemed to glow as the stone absorbed the blood. Smiling, Elizabeth praised the Moon Goddess for her generosity. She held her injured palm up into the red moonlight. The wound healed, not by the Goddess, but rather by the mere fact that she was a vampire.

Elizabeth Wellington crossed to the northern wall and shuttered the window. Now only the black flames of the candles and the faint glow of the Blood Stone shone in the darkened room. She returned to the altar and took the necklace in her hands and placed it around her neck with a smile.

This was only the beginning of her plan.

Chapter Forty-one

A Visit to The Hollows

Margaret heard the insistent tinkle of the summoning bell coming from the parlor. She had been tending to her morning ritual of dusting when she heard the ringing. She frowned, thinking that it was probably Master Robert playing with things he shouldn't. Well, she was not in the mood for his childish games. She decided to give him a piece of her mind.

She thrust open the double doors of the parlor, and spoke before she even saw him, "Stop that this instant, young man!" She very nearly choked on her words when she saw Mrs. Wellington sitting upon her favorite chair; bell in hand.

Elizabeth Wellington smiled with amusement as she set the bell onto the table next to her. "Pardon me?" she said with an arched brow.

Margaret gasped; realizing that the heavy curtain was pulled wide open and sunlight was streaming in through the window. "Mrs. Wellington! The sunlight!"

"Leave the curtain, Margaret!" Elizabeth said in a commanding voice.

"But you should not be in the sunlight with your… your condition!" Margaret said frantically.

"I said, *leave it!*" she said sharply. Then she allowed her voice to soften. "It has been far too long since I have felt the sun's warmth upon my skin."

Margaret hesitated. "Won't it…?"

"Destroy me?" Elizabeth batted a hand in the air. "I have seen to that minor inconvenience." Her hand touched the necklace with the faintly glowing red crystal that hung around her neck. She smiled. "Have Harrison bring the car around. I'd like to take a trip into town."

"Are you serious, madam?" Margaret seemed uncertain.

Elizabeth glared at her. "Have you ever known me not to be?" Her annoyance with the servant was rising.

Margaret shook her head fearfully. "No, ma'am."

"Then do as I have requested."

Ten minutes later Harrison Beckett pulled the Bentley in front of Wellington House. He climbed out of the car and opened the back door, waiting for his passenger. When Margaret had called the garage she hadn't said whom he was taking into town. His annoyance was clearly etched upon his face. He didn't like his morning coffee to be interrupted with such short notice. When the front door of Wellington House opened, he was clearly shocked to his core. He had not expected to see Elizabeth Wellington descending those steps in broad daylight. *How was it even possible? Sunlight was supposed to destroy vampires!*

He struggled for a moment. Unsure of whether he should try and protect her from the sunlight, or merely watch her burn. She smiled at him. "Good morning, Harrison! I hope you're up for a bit of a drive."

"But…?" he stammered, confusion written all across his face.

She chuckled softly as she climbed into the car and waited. Finally, the amused smile left her face and she glared at him. "Don't just stand there with your mouth open like that, Harrison. It is unseemly. Let's be off!"

He jolted out of his shock and quickly closed the door and then he stole a glance at Margaret, who was standing on the top step at the entrance to Wellington House. She was nervously wringing her hands in front of her. Clearly, she hadn't a clue as to what was going on either.

Harrison glanced into the rearview mirror and looked into Elizabeth's eyes. "Where to, madam?"

"Take me to the Sheriff's Office. I need to have a little *chat* with Maynard."

"Right away, Mrs. Wellington," he said as he put the Bentley into motion.

Twenty minutes later the car pulled up in front of The Hollows Police Station. Harrison quickly exited the vehicle and held the door open for Mrs. Wellington. He offered her a hand for assistance. He couldn't help but notice how unnaturally cold it still felt. He wisely resisted the urge to cringe.

"This should not take terribly long. Wait here," she said in a commanding voice.

Discreetly wiping his hand upon his trousers, he nodded. "As you wish." He watched as Elizabeth Wellington made her way into the building, her walking stick pounding out every step that she took. He squinted up at the morning sun as he ran a hand through his thick hair. This was certainly a strange day, he decided. He wondered if the strange color of last night's moon had anything to do with this odd behavior.

Fifteen minutes later, she returned to the car. He opened the door for her and then got behind the wheel. He glanced up into the mirror and felt uncomfortable. "Uhm…madam…" he pointed at his own lip nervously, "…you've got a little…"

Before he could finish she licked the blood off her lip. "Thank you, Harrison."

He had been about to hand her a handkerchief to remove the blood, but now there was no need. He quickly put it away. He swallowed the bile rising in his throat. "Where to now, madam?"

"Collingsworth Manor. I want to drop in on my dear friend Marybeth." Her eyes twinkled brightly. A bit of color seemed to have returned to her complexion, driving away some of the pallor that had been so prevalent before.

He nodded and pulled away from the curb. "Right away," he said, a small smile forming at the corner of his mouth. *A strange day indeed!* He drove to the north end of The Hollows and started up the winding drive of *Snob Hill*. Five minutes later he stopped at the gate outside the Collingsworth estate and keyed the intercom. "Mrs. Wellington to see Mrs. Collingsworth." After a short pause, a buzz sounded and the massive wrought iron gates swung open. He shook his head in surprise. He had figured that they would be denied, given the bad blood between the two women recently.

Stopping in front of the Great House, he hopped out of the car and opened the door for Mrs. Wellington. He had an inquisitive look in his eyes and a grin upon his face. "Care to tell me what's going on?" he asked.

She looked at him stoically. "Mind your place, Harrison. That is no concern of yours."

He blushed. "Yes, ma'am. My apologies."

After she had been admitted into the Manor, Harrison leaned heavily against the Bentley and sighed, already he was feeling exhausted. The days of Elizabeth Wellington confiding in him were over. A part of him was glad for that, but another part of him missed those days very much. Now, however, her activities were far more sinister than they had ever been. The less he knew, the better off he'd be.

He watched as the Sheriff and his deputies drove up the drive to the Great House. He was surprised to see that two of the deputies were driving a hearse. He watched them curiously as they all climbed from the vehicles. He studied the men in uniform, searching their necks for signs that they had been bitten, but saw nothing. He placed a hand on his own forearm, recalling where she had sunk her fangs in him after she had been turned. Undoubtedly they bore the same marks on their arms now too, but it was impossible to know for certain; they all had their sleeves rolled down.

§

It had been relatively easy for Elizabeth to exert her control over Marybeth Collingsworth. Her hypnotic glare had drawn her in, her strong, commanding voice bent the weaker woman to her will. Marybeth had happily pulled her collar aside, granting her neck freely to her former friend. Had Sebastian Barrister been more careful, he could have taken measures to prevent this from ever occurring. But Elizabeth had counted on his ego and his arrogance to make him sloppy. He had foolishly allowed this to happen.

Marybeth Collingsworth spoke the enchantment that would remove the sigil from above the doorway, allowing Sheriff Maynard Thompson and his men into the darkened chamber where the vampire slept. Three coffins were in the room, two of them little more than simple pine. Only one was built from solid oak and had brass handle grips.

She watched in silent fascination as the Sheriff and his men placed heavy chains around Sebastian Barrister's coffin. She felt she should do something to stop them, but she couldn't. Elizabeth Wellington had forced her compliance by taking control of her. Now she was helpless to resist.

Maynard Thompson secured the padlocks onto the chains that bound the coffin. He tugged on them to be certain that they were tight and would hold. They did. Satisfied, he turned to Elizabeth Wellington and spoke. "What about the others?"

She handed him the small black satchel. "I'm certain that they contain Doctor and Mrs. Monaghan. Neither deserves the fate that was forced upon them. End them and be quick about it. Afterwards you know what you are to do with the chained coffin."

He nodded. "Yes, your instructions were quite clear."

Elizabeth Wellington nodded. "Good," she said simply. "Then I will leave you to it." She turned her gaze to Marybeth. "Where is Keegan Rourke?" she asked.

Marybeth turned her glassy stare to face her. "Not here. He has a different place, I'm not sure where."

"Very well." Elizabeth grasped Marybeth's arm and guided her out of the room. "You look like you could use some sleep. Why don't you go on up to bed?"

"Yes," Marybeth said without emotion. "I'm not feeling quite myself. I believe that some rest would do me a world of good."

Elizabeth patted her hand. "I believe that you are right, my dear. Off you go."

Marybeth cocked her head to the side. "Off I go." She turned and headed for the stairs.

Satisfied, Elizabeth Wellington stepped out into the bright sunlight and took a deep breath. The warm sun felt good upon her skin, but it did little to drive the chill from her body. She smiled at Harrison as he opened the door to the Bentley.

"Where to, madam?" he asked crisply.

"Home," she said as she sat and drew her legs into the car.

Harrison nodded. "Very well, Mrs. Wellington." He closed the door softly and then got behind the steering wheel and fired the Bentley up. "How was Mrs. Collingsworth today?" he asked.

A slow smile crossed Elizabeth's lips. "I found her to be quite agreeable."

He continued to try and engage her into conversation as they drove along, but she seemed disinterested. Finally, he lapsed into silence and just let her be. She turned her attention to the window, watching the scenery zip by. *Yes, today is a strange day!* He thought to himself. *Very strange indeed.*

§

Elizabeth Wellington unlocked the double door at the northern end of Wellington House and stepped into the room. Sitting upon the white altar that rested in the center of the pentagram was the chained oak coffin that contained Sebastian Barrister. She ran her hand along the polished wood and smiled contentedly. One eyebrow arched high upon her forehead and she whispered softly. "Sleep well, Sebastian. You never should have crossed me. You chose the wrong witch to join your side. Marybeth cannot hold a candle to me. Now you will have all eternity to contemplate your foolish arrogance." She turned and stalked from the room taking long, slow strides, stabbing the floor sharply with her walking stick.

She took one last look at the coffin, an evil smirk on her face, and then she closed the door and turned the key in the lock. She laughed, quite pleased with her day.

Chapter Forty-two
Return to School

We could no longer afford to go into the forest in wolf form. The sheer number of hunters stalking wolves continued to grow in the wake of what had happened to the Sons of the Raven. And though we were immune to their bullets, we couldn't let the general society know that there were wolves out there that could not be harmed by anything other than silver bullets. It didn't matter that the Sons of the Raven had brought it all upon themselves; nobody seemed to care. Nor did anyone seem concerned that Ari had been a victim of those same boys. She was a Mohawk Indian and there were still far too many prejudices against her people. The truth was simply easier to ignore.

Those of us in the Wolf Pack had to face those same persecutions. We too, were among the minority in The Hollows. Now we were being hunted. Wolves were being slaughtered, their pelts hung upon road signs or staked to wooden poles for all to see. It was becoming somewhat of a frenzied atmosphere, and local law enforcement seemed to look the other way. It was almost as if they were encouraging the behavior; they were certainly turning a blind eye to it all. And with Maynard Thompson in charge, I wasn't surprised.

In the days that followed the *Blood Moon*, heavy rains fell relentlessly, washing away any hope of tracking Grandpa. His tracks and his wolf-scent had simply vanished along with him. There was little more that we could do, but wait and pray for his safe return. But as each day passed, it seemed even more unlikely. *Had he fallen prey to the hunters?* But if he had, wouldn't only his human corpse be found? In the event we were wrong that once a werewolf was killed the dead body would revert to its human form, we had to remain vigilant. We tried to keep track of all the desecrated wolf pelts that we found hanging as gruesome trophies, but none were the large, black wolf that was the form that Grandpa always took. It was just a small blessing.

Aunt Abby was in a perpetually dark mood. She would easily snap at the least provocation, generally it was unwarranted and she would become immediately apologetic. I completely understood but it was increasingly harder on Bobbybear. He started spending more time at Wellington House, even sleeping in his old room rather than returning to the cottage, much to the absolute delight of Grandmother; she had always welcomed him and truly seemed to be enjoying his company.

Now, thanks to the talisman that she had crafted, she spent less time sleeping her days away. She would even ride in the Bentley, taking Bobby to school and then picking him up afterwards. It was good to see that she was trying to make up for all the trouble she had caused, and I found myself rather pleased with the changes she'd made.

Brock would come by after school and give me updates on all the happenings during my continued suspension. Without the Chevy, he had borrowed his dad's Jeep, a 1986 red Laredo CJ7, rather than always showing up in wolf form. It was a beautiful Jeep, despite its age. The chrome grille and bumpers, along with the black fenders accented the bright red nicely. Aunt Abigail was growing increasingly restless. Finally she convinced Brock to take her up to Grandpa's cabin, hoping that he would be there.

He wasn't. But she decided to stay there, and clean the place up, hoping that he'd return. I stayed at the cottage; that way we had all the bases covered, yet there was still no sign of Grandpa. It was as though he had just ceased to exist.

Grandpa wasn't the only one that had seemed to just vanish without a trace. So had Sebastian Barrister. Brock told us that it was the entire buzz going around school between the Daughters of the Coven and what was left of the Sons of the Raven. Barrister's unexpected departure led me to believe that somehow his, and Grandpa's disappearance were related in some way. *But what did it mean?*

Grandmother seemed delighted by the fact that Sebastian Barrister had disappeared. She seemed to smile more. Perhaps with his absence, his control over her had lessened. She was happier than I'd seen her in a very long time.

§

I awoke almost an hour before my alarm clock was set to go off. I knew it was pointless to try and go back to sleep, my mind wouldn't allow it. Today was the end of my two-week suspension and already I was anxious to get back to my classes. And I missed my friends. I could only hope that Millie was back to her old self. I missed her the most.

Despite my inability to fall back to sleep, I didn't get up right away. I continued to lie there in bed, staring up at the ceiling I hadn't slept very well, thoughts of school, Aunt Abby and Grandpa kept pulling at my mind. And I missed not having

Bobbybear and Mr. Grizzle as snuggle partners.

I was lonely. And miserable.

I longed to let the Wolf out and give her freedom to run. *I missed the old days.*

Brock leaned on the horn of the Jeep as he rounded the corner near Wellington House's garage. It irritated me when he did that, and he knew it. I think he just loved teasing me, no matter how much I scolded him about it. And then there was his lame joke about waking up the dead that I had to endure. He seriously needed to get new material. Bobby had a better sense of humor than Brock, hands down, and he was only six; Brock just acted like he was. That thought made me chuckle. *God I desperately needed company!*

I threw the covers off of me and sat up, still reluctant to climb from the bed. There was a chill in the morning air, but that was nothing new. You'd think that I'd be used to it by now, but clearly I wasn't. The Jeep's horn blared again as Brock pulled up out front. I sighed heavily as I got up and stretched my arms with my hands reaching for the ceiling. Standing on the tips of my toes it remained untouched with more than a foot to spare.

I headed for the bathroom to relieve myself and to get ready; Brock's heavy hand on the horn was starting to stress me out. Clearly he wouldn't stop until I forced him to.

When I came out of the bathroom I could smell the rich aromatic blend of fresh coffee and bacon filling the cottage. To my surprise Brock was standing at the oven cooking scrambled eggs. He smiled at me as I reached for a mug. "Good morning, Sunshine," he said. "I figured you might like a hearty breakfast before we head out."

I poured myself a cup of coffee and then wrapped my arms around his shoulders and kissed him firmly upon the lips. "You sure know how to make a girl feel special," I said. I frowned at him, almost pouting. "What are you after?" I teased.

He chuckled softly. "Me?" He shrugged. "I just figured that

since you're all alone here you might appreciate a little extra attention."

"Mmm?" I smiled, nibbling at his earlobe. "That it, huh?" I could tell that it sent a shiver coursing down his entire right side, and he tried to raise his shoulder and cock his head to keep me from doing it again. I laughed as I reached down and squeezed his butt cheek, giving it a firm pinch.

He gave me a look that clearly said I was headed for trouble if I kept it up. "You're awfully flirty this morning."

I arched a brow as I took a slice of bacon and bit it in half. I shrugged. "I've been stuck here all by myself. I need to have a little fun before I go stir crazy."

He turned off the stovetop and emptied the pan of eggs onto a plate. "Your breakfast is ready," he said with a grin.

"You're not having anything?" I asked, accepting the plate and heading for the table.

"That's all the eggs," he said. "But I'm good. I'll just have a slice of toast and some bacon." He'd cooked the whole package of bacon and there was no way I could eat it all—well, I probably could, but it wouldn't be the wisest thing, certainly not the healthiest.

"I'll share my eggs with you," I offered.

He kissed me on the lips. "I'm good. Sit. Eat your breakfast." He poured himself a cup of coffee and then joined me at the kitchen table. "Your refrigerator is almost bare. The milk was expired. You need to do some serious shopping."

I shrugged. "Bobbybear usually uses all the milk before it spoils, but he's been staying at Wellington House."

He nodded. "Sooo, how about I take you grocery shopping after school?"

I shook my head. "That isn't necessary. It's just me here. I'll manage with what's in the cupboard."

He leaned back against the chair and sipped his coffee. His eyes twinkled and he had a mischievous grin twisting his lips.

"Well, I was thinking I might just stay the night tonight. You know, keep you company."

I almost choked on my breakfast. I reached for my coffee and took a huge sip to wash the food down, scalding my tongue and the roof of my mouth in the process. I stared at him as I wiped my mouth with a napkin. "But I don't even like you."

His grin grew. "I can't stand you either."

I could feel the heat begin to rise within me. "I suppose you could take my Aunt's room. She won't be here, she's still up at the cabin."

He shook his head. "That just won't do. I'd only be staying here to keep you safe and out of trouble. I'll need to keep my eyes on you."

"Oh," I said with a shrug, "keep me out of trouble, huh?" I smiled at him mischievously. "I guess I can make that work."

I pushed my plate away and stood up. I walked around the table and straddled his lap. Wrapping my arms around him I kissed him soundly. His lips responded to mine as he held me firmly against him.

"We should go," he said, his voice sounding raspy. He had a longing in his eyes that told me he was just as hungry as I was. I kissed him again and then slid off his lap. If I hadn't, we might not make it to school.

§

I gave Brock a steady look as he drove the Jeep along the mountain highway. I couldn't keep from smiling at him. He still had that boyish grin on his face, almost as if he knew what I was thinking. He probably wasn't far off, if the truth were told. I wrapped my arms across my chest; the air whipping around the windshield was frightfully cold. I wished that I had thought to wear a jacket. I found myself missing the Chevy even more. There were no doors, or a top on the Jeep to block the wind. It had bucket seats, so I couldn't even snuggle up against Brock for warmth. I knew if I tried to speak, my teeth would only chatter.

I was almost as nervous now about returning to school as I had been on my very first day. At least then I knew I'd be seeing Millie and the gang. I had been eager for school to start, having only ever been home-schooled. But now I was uncertain what I would find. Hopefully, during our time apart Millie had reconsidered her desire to become a Lycanthrope and we could get back to the way things were. I needed things to get back to normal. My world was falling apart, it seemed to be unraveling at the seams.

I started laughing, thinking that nothing had been normal since the death of my parents and I found out I could turn into a wolf. Brock gave me a strange look. He must be thinking that I'd completely lost my mind due to all of the solitude. "Are you all right?" he asked.

I wiped the tears from my eyes and nodded. "I'm fine. I was just reflecting on how crazy my life has become."

He nodded. "I get it. You went from being a Big City girl to a shape-shifter in a tiny mountain town." He shook his head, "Honestly, I don't know how you do it."

I laughed again. "It's not like I had a choice."

He glanced at me and then returned his attention to the road. "Would you change things if you could? Go back to the city life? You could wear that talisman Abby made you and live a relatively normal life."

I shook my head. "No way. That life doesn't exist anymore. I think it died with my parents. I truly think that this is where I'm supposed to be now."

He reached over and squeezed my hand. "Well, I'm glad you're here. I'm glad we're together."

I studied him for quite some time. "I am too," I said.

It was true. I was happy that Brock and I were together.

I didn't want to be with anybody else. Even on that first day that we'd met, I had been strongly attracted to him, despite his demeanor—he hadn't been very nice as I recall. Every time I saw him, I felt a fluttering sensation in my stomach that only grew. As we got to know one another better, our mutual attraction strengthened. Now I couldn't imagine life without him.

"I love you," I said.

He smiled but didn't say anything.

I waited, to see if he would respond, but he didn't. He wouldn't even look at me. He continued to watch the road. I know he'd heard me. I felt like I had been punched in the gut. I had been expecting – or hoping, that he would say those words back to me, but he didn't. He only smiled. *What the hell did that mean?* I shouldn't have said those words to him. Now I wish that I hadn't, but it was too late for that. I could feel the fear knot in the pit of my stomach. I turned and watched the pines along the side of the road flash by in a blur. I couldn't look at Brock for fear that I might start crying. We drove the rest of the way in silence.

As we pulled into the parking spot at Hollows High, I hopped out of the Jeep without a word. I just felt the need to get away. But Brock wasn't going to let that happen. "Is something wrong?" he asked.

I shook my head. "No. Why would there be anything wrong?" I couldn't keep eye contact with him.

"You seem angry," he said.

"Nope. I just need to report to the Principal's Office so that I can get reinstated. The sooner I get that over with the better."

He stood up, stepped over the passenger seat and dropped down beside me. He went for my hand but I pulled it away. "I'll walk you there," he said.

I stepped away and shook my head. "No. I know where it is. I'll see you in class." With that I turned and walked briskly away, leaving him standing there. I just wanted to scream, but I couldn't even do that; there were too many people standing around. The last thing I wanted to do was cause a big scene. I had enough to deal with.

I made my way to Student Administration and found that Silas and Millie were already there, waiting to be seen. "Morning guys!" I said, forcing a smile to my face. I could feel the thick tension that already permeated the air. Neither of them could look at the other.

Silas seemed glad to see me. "Good morning, Kat," he said, returning my smile.

Millie was not as pleased. She leaned upon her crutches and looked away, ignoring me. Clearly she was uninterested in talking to either of us. I glanced over at Silas and he shrugged. He wasn't getting anywhere with her, either.

"Millie…" I said, reaching out to touch her arm.

She stepped away from me, her eyes full of angst. "Don't!" she said in a caustic voice.

I refused to just give up. Her friendship meant too much to me. She and I had already been through so much together. "Can we talk about this, Millie? Please?"

The door to the Principal's office opened and Principal LaRoche gave us a curt nod. "Good," he said, "you're all here. Come on inside, let's get this over with. You three don't need to miss any more class than you already have."

He closed the door behind us and then took his seat behind the desk. He waited until we were seated in the three chairs across from him before he said anything. "I sincerely hope that the three of you have thought long and hard about the little stunt you pulled. It was childish and could easily have turned into something much worse. There is no place at Hollows High for that kind of nonsense. It will not be tolerated. Any other pranks by the three of you will result in your immediate expulsion. Do any of you have anything to say?"

Shaking our heads we kept our silence. 'Sorry' just didn't seem adequate enough.

He nodded. "One of the girls on the Cheer Squad came forward and admitted that the incident that occurred out on the practice field injuring Miss Bradford, was in fact, done intentionally. With that in mind, I have abolished the Squad for the remainder of the school year."

Millie frowned, leaning forward in her seat. "But you're not punishing them?"

He glared at Millie until she shrank back. "Had this information surfaced before your retaliation, those involved would have been either suspended or expelled. However, in light of your actions, I have elected to just move on to other concerns facing this school. As you may be aware, several students have been mauled in the woods resulting in the tragic loss of life. The community as a whole is suffering. I suggest that you put all of this misfortune behind you. Buckle down, concentrate on your studies, and let's get through this school year without further incident."

As the bell sounded, he stood and walked to the door. "I'll be keeping my eye on the three of you." He opened the door and we stood. "Oh, and one more thing." He looked at Silas. "You're participation in all sporting activities for the remainder of the year has been revoked. Any and all gear that you may have needs to be turned back in to Coach Simpson by the end of the day. All extra-curricular activities are likewise suspended for you ladies. Actions have consequences people. That is all. Now get to class."

Millie moved amazingly fast as she left the office and quickly disappeared in the throng of students trying to make their way to class, leaving Silas and I to walk together. "So she's still upset with us, I see," I said.

Silas arched one eyebrow and grinned. "You picked up on that, huh?"

I put a hand on his arm and gave him a sympathetic look. "I'm sorry about all this. I'm sure she'll come around. Just give it some time."

He sighed as he shrugged. "That remains to be seen. Still no word on your Grandpa?"

I shook my head. "Nothing. Aunt Abby's gone to stay at his cabin, hoping he might show up there. I'm holding down the fort at the cottage in case he shows up."

"How's that going?" he asked as we stopped at my locker.

"It's kinda lonely, actually. Bobbybear's been staying at Wellington House so I've got the place to myself."

I twirled the combination dial and opened my locker. I took out the notebook I needed for first period and then shoved my backpack into the locker. "I'm about to go stir crazy."

Silas had already put his backpack away and had everything he needed for class. We turned from my locker and went the short distance down the hall toward first period. "How are you holding up?" I asked.

He shrugged. "I'm having a little trouble sleeping at night. The house just seems too quiet now." He chuckled softly. "I'm not saying my parents were loud or anything, but not having them around just amplifies the silence. I don't like it. The place just feels empty. Not at all like home. The hardest thing of all though, is not knowing anything new concerning my folks."

I shook my head. "That's has to be rough."

Mrs. Crombie welcomed us back to class with a warm smile. "The two of you will need to see me after school briefly so that I can give you the work you've missed. Unfortunately you won't receive grades for the makeup work, but it'll help bring you up to speed with the rest of the class. I need it turned in by Monday." She gave me a little wink. "That shouldn't be a problem for you, Kat."

The morning continued to drag on with Millie disappearing as soon as the bell rang after each class. She was obviously not going to give me the opportunity to talk with her. So I stopped trying. Hopefully I could corner her at lunchtime. Besides, it might give me a chance to avoid Brock just a bit longer; I was still upset with him. Sooner or later I was going to have to face him, he was my ride home, after all.

I turned from the lunch line with my tray in hand and glanced at the Wolf Pack's usual table. Brock and Silas were already there. I wasn't surprised to discover that Millie wasn't. I scanned the cafeteria and saw Ari sitting at a table with Manny. To my surprise, Melissa LaRoche was also there, sitting very close to Manny. But I didn't see Millie anywhere.

At first I wondered why Mel was sitting there and not with the Daughters of the Coven, but then I recalled the conversation that we'd had in the school parking lot. She said then that she was done with the Coven. I guess it was true. She had always seemed like a sweet girl, but yet she had participated with Shelby's stunt on the practice field. I had no doubt she was the one that confessed Shelby's plot to hurt Millie to her father. It only made sense.

I sat down beside Ari and smiled. "Hi guys!"

Mel gave me a hesitant smile. "Hi, Kat. Glad to see you're back in school."

I pointed my index finger toward her and Manny, shifting it between the two of them. "Sooo… how long has this been going on?"

Manny blushed.

Mel shrugged. "I told you I was done with the Coven. As soon as I told Shelby she cast me out of the group. So I kinda became an outcast." She leaned in and bumped shoulders with Manny. "He kinda rescued me."

Manny nodded. "She joined me and Ari at our table." He smiled at her. "And I'm really glad that she did."

"Cool," I said. I glanced at Ari. "Have you seen Millie?"

Ari frowned. "She's been shooting me these really intense

looks all morning. What is that all about anyway? I didn't think that I'd done anything to upset her, but obviously I have."

I shook my head. "It's not you. Not really. She's…" I glanced up at Mel and then shrugged as I looked back at Ari, "just being silly about things."

Ari frowned. "Did she break up with Silas? I noticed that they aren't glued to one another like they had been. I thought it was pretty odd."

I sighed as I looked down at my tray of food. I scrunched up my nose; I really wasn't hungry. "Millie just has a lot on her mind, I guess." I stood up. "I think I'll see if I can find her."

Ari quickly got to her feet. "I'll go with you." She glanced at Manny and Mel. "I think these two lovebirds would rather be alone, anyway." Mel giggled and Manny grinned at her, blushing even more.

As we walked out of the cafeteria Ari looked at me and said, "Is it true? Did your grandmother take back control of the Coven?"

I stopped walking and stared at her, completely shocked by her statement. "Where did you hear that?"

"It's all the Daughters of the Coven can talk about. Apparently your grandmother had a heart-to-heart chat with Marybeth Collingsworth and convinced her to step down. Shelby isn't too pleased from what I gather." She gave me a bewildered look. "I'm really surprised that you didn't know."

"Well, to be honest, I've had a lot going on. I knew my aunt was going to talk to my grandmother and enlist her help with a problem that Shelby had, but I certainly wasn't expecting this to come out of it." My mind raced. With Grandmother assuming control of the Coven again it was possible that Shelby's little problem had gone away. I wondered if this was also why Sebastian Barrister had left unexpectedly.

Had Grandmother somehow thwarted his plans? Why didn't he just stop her? Couldn't he control her? That thought made me laugh out loud. Could anyone really control Grandmother? Not likely, and certainly not for very long.

We found Millie out in the school courtyard. She was sitting with her back to us, so she didn't see us coming. Her crutches were leaning against the bench upon which she sat; I knew if I could grab them she wouldn't be able to escape us. I put a hand to my lips to warn Ari to keep quiet. She nodded with a smile.

As I grabbed the crutches I pulled them over the back of the bench and Millie let out a squeal of panic, not sure what was happening until it was too late. She quickly stood and whirled around to face me. "Give them back!" She attempted to grab them from me, almost falling.

I held them at arm's length and took a step away from her. "Not until we've had the chance to talk."

She rolled her eyes and started to hobble away. "Fine. Keep them. I don't care."

"Millie!" I said frantically. "Please stop. Don't do this!"

To my surprise, she stopped and turned. Her eyes had filled with tears, and they were starting to roll down her cheeks, coming to a stop against her round lenses. She glanced at Ari and then looked at me. "Can I have my crutches back?"

I started to hand them over, but then I hesitated. "Will you talk to me?"

She sighed heavily. "If I must."

I gave her back the crutches and she stuck them under her arms. She leaned upon them heavily as she stared down at the ground. Finally she looked up at Ari and said. "So, I hear that you can become a little bird and that you can fly."

Ari glanced quickly at me and then back at Millie. "That's right. I'm sorry I never told you. I just didn't want you to think that I was a freak or something."

Millie's lips parted. She seemed truly shocked. "I would never think anything like that."

Ari cocked her head to the side. "So are we still friends?"

Millie smiled hesitantly and then she nodded. "Of course we are. And I'm really glad that you aren't dead."

Ari practically threw herself against her and for a moment I thought they both might fall. Ari wrapped her arms around Millie and said, "I am too! If Kat's grandpa hadn't shared his blood with me I wouldn't be."

Millie nodded. "I know." She pulled out of Ari's grasp and looked at her. "And I'm really happy that he did. Honestly." She glanced at me. "It's just that after Keegan's attack on my Grammy I got really scared. I mean, I should be able to protect her and keep her safe, but I can't. Not really. All my friends can do these really amazing things and I can't do anything like that. There's nothing special about me."

I watched as more tears spilled from her eyes and rolled down her cheeks, splashing against her glasses. "When I brought it up to Silas, he…" she started really sobbing, "…he laughed at me! And that really hurt! You know?"

I stepped in and gave her a hug. "Oh, Millie, I'm so sorry! He never should have laughed, but I'm sure he didn't mean anything by it. He loves you. We all do."

Ari shrugged and winced. "Well… I *like* you. But…"

Millie pulled her into our little group hug. "Aw you love me and you know it!"

Ari laughed. "Yeah, I do."

As we all headed back toward the school building Millie asked, "So what's going on between Manny and Mel? Are they like together together?"

Ari nodded as she held the door open. "Inseparable."

Millie shook her head. "I swear! You miss two weeks and everything changes!"

I laughed. "Tell me about it."

Millie stopped and cleaned her glasses on the hem of her blouse and then returned them to the bridge of her nose. "Is it true what I hear about your grandma? Is she really back in control of the Coven now?"

I raised both brows. "That's what I hear!"

"So?" Millie said, "What's that mean for us, going forward?"

I shrugged. "I don't really know. I think I'll have a little talk with Grandmother and find out exactly what is going on. It would be nice if this whole war between the Coven and us were finally over. Too many people have already paid the price."

I stopped walking suddenly and they both turned and looked at me expectantly. "What's wrong?" Millie asked after seeing the troubled frown on my face.

I blushed and shook my head. "I may have screwed up," I said wincing.

Millie and Ari quickly exchanged looks and then Ari touched my arm. "How?" she asked, sounding concerned.

I looked from her to Millie and then back again. "I told Brock that I loved him on the way to school this morning."

Millie almost lost one of her crutches. "You didn't!" she said with a gasp.

I nodded, still wincing. "I'm afraid so."

Millie blinked. "Well, what did he say when you told him?"

"That's just it," I said. "He didn't say anything. He just smiled and practically ignored me." I closed my eyes and shook my head, putting a hand over my face. "It was the longest ride to school I've ever had."

Ari frowned. "So what are you gonna do?"

I shrugged. "I have no idea. He was planning on spending the night at the cottage tonight, but now I don't think it's such a good idea. I mean, what'll I say? What'll I do?"

"What about your aunt? Is she okay with him spending the night?" Millie asked.

"Aunt Abigail's up at my grandpa's cabin. I've got the cottage all to myself."

"No Bobbybear?" she asked, surprised.

I shook my head. "He's staying at Wellington House."

Millie's eyes went wide. "I like Brock. He's a nice guy. But I really don't think you should be spending the night alone with him."

I growled in frustration. "I know. But how am I gonna get out of this without ruining everything?"

"Easy!" Millie's face brightened. "Tell him that you're spending the night at my house so that we can talk. He'll buy that, especially after all that's happened lately." She touched my arm. "And you're more than welcome to stay, Grams would love to see you." She glanced at Ari. "You could stay over too, you're my Grammy's hero after all! We could make it a girl's weekend!"

I laughed. "As lovely as that sounds, I'm afraid I can't. I need to be at the cottage in case my grandpa shows up."

She frowned, pulling her head back. "He's not staying at his cabin with your aunt?"

"Oh, you haven't heard. Grandpa went missing about the same time that Sebastian Barrister disappeared. We're hoping he'll show up soon."

Millie gasped in surprise. "Barrister's missing too?" She looked from me to Ari. I'm sorry to hear about your grandpa. I honestly had no idea." She pushed her glasses back into place. "Do you think that it's all somehow related? Barrister and your grandpa both missing at the same time, I mean?"

"Who knows?" I said with a shrug. "Grandpa was giving Shelby a ride back into town. He was going to get hold of Silas and Brock and bring them back to the cottage to consolidate our forces and come up with a plan. His truck was found off the highway with no sign of him anywhere."

"Wait," Ari said, "he was giving Shelby a ride into town?"

I nodded.

"Seems to me she should know something," Ari said crossing her arms over her chest.

Why I hadn't thought about talking to her was beyond me. How did she get back into town? Grandpa had clearly gone off the road on his way to The Hollows, otherwise the guys would've been with him when the accident happened. They clearly weren't.

"You've got a point!" I said, and then I sprinted for the cafeteria to talk to Shelby.

Chapter Forty-three

Shelby's Denial

When I got back into the cafeteria, Shelby was just dropping her tray off at the scullery. She rolled her eyes as she saw me approach. She made some snide remark that I couldn't quite hear, but the three girls with her giggled and eyed me with huge grins. "Is there something that I can help you with?" she asked. It was evident that she just wanted to walk away from me without giving me the time of day.

That wasn't going to happen.

"What happened to my grandpa?" I asked.

Shelby gave me a look of disdain as she scrunched up her face. "How should I know?"

She tried to walk away from me but I reached out and grabbed her arm and pulled her toward me. The surprise on her face was priceless. "You were the last one to see him," I said.

She glared at my hand and then jerked her arm free. She arched a brow. "Was I?"

"He was taking you back into town after you came to us for help. He never made it into town, clearly you did. I just want to know what happened."

Shelby glanced at the other girls that were standing around. She shook her head. "Don't be ridiculous! Why would I come to *you* for help?" She glanced at the other Daughters of the Coven and laughed. "She's delusional!" she practically snorted.

She poked a finger into my chest. "If you *ever* lay a hand on me again, it'll be the last time. I promise you that!" She started walking away, the other girls in tow.

I was angry now. "Well I hope you have a nice wedding then!" I couldn't think of anything else to say. Now I wish I'd just kept silent.

Shelby turned abruptly, a smirk on her face and an evil glint in her eyes; they appeared to darken, suddenly being replaced by a deeper shade of green. They returned to normal just as quickly as they had changed, leaving me to wonder if it had been simply my imagination. No one else had seemed to notice. Shelby said, "You can't have a wedding if there isn't a groom."

Brock and Silas walked up, just as Ari and Millie entered the cafeteria. Brock touched my arm. "What was that all about?" he asked.

I sighed heavily. "She knows more than she's telling."

He nodded. "Maybe. But you can't approach her like that when she's got the others around her. She had to save face, you didn't really give her much of a choice."

I scowled as I rolled my eyes and shook my head in frustration. "I know."

He reached into his pocket and took out the keys to the Jeep. "Listen, Silas and I have stuff to do, so I'm not gonna make it tonight. You take the Jeep. It's a stick just like the Chevy, so you shouldn't have any trouble with it."

I glanced at Silas as I took the keys, he wouldn't meet my gaze. I looked back at Brock. "What about your dad? Isn't he going to need his Jeep?"

Brock shook his head. "Nope, he won't miss it. It's yours until I need it back."

"Sooo… I'm not gonna see you at all this weekend?"

Brock glanced at Silas and then he smiled at me, shaking his head. "No. Silas and I have this… *thing* that we need to attend to. It might take us all weekend, I'm afraid. I'll just see you on Monday." He leaned in and planted a kiss on my forehead before he walked away.

"That didn't sound good," Millie said.

Ari rubbed my back. "You gonna be okay?" She was giving Brock a very dark look as he walked away.

I shook my head and tossed the keys in the air and caught them as they came back down. "Yeah. Why wouldn't I be? I just got a new ride!"

Chapter Forty-four

Magic in the Air

The rest of the day dragged slowly by. In each class I received a ton of make-up work that needed to be handed back in Monday, first thing. It was the assignments that I'd missed during my suspension. It wasn't going to be graded, per se, but if I wanted to pass the class, it was one of Principal LaRoche's requirements. Thank goodness it was Friday! It meant I had all weekend to get it done. I didn't think it was going to be much of a problem, but Millie was mortified.

"I'll never get it done," she moaned. "I wish I had listened to you when you tried to talk me out of that stupid prank!"

"That's water under the bridge, Millie. We can do this!" I said in an attempt to boost her confidence.

Her shoulders dropped. "You can probably do it. I'm not so certain that I can."

"Sure you can!" I said enthusiastically. "We'll do it together. It'll be fun!"

Ari agreed. "I'll do whatever I can to help. Some of it is really pretty easy."

I quickly nodded. "We can all spend the weekend at the cottage."

Millie frowned. "I can't leave Grams all alone. Not after all that's happened."

"Okay," I said, "I guess I could stay at your place until we get the work done."

Millie's face brightened. "Could you?" She glanced at Ari. "What about it?"

Ari shrugged with a smile. "I guess I can make that happen. I just need to grab a few things."

"That's not a problem, so do I," I said. "We can drop Millie off at her house," I told Ari. "And then I can drive you home so that you can grab everything you need. I'll do the same, and then we'll just come back."

Millie's smile slowly faded. "But what about your grandpa? What if he shows up at the cottage and no one's there?"

I shrugged. "Then I'm sure he'll head for his cabin. He'll find Aunt Abby there. It'll be fine. Really." I could only hope that I was right. It made sense to me. If Grandpa were able, he'd make it happen. *But what if he wasn't?* I shook my head, forcing all the negative thoughts away. I tried to remain positive. *Thoughts create!*

We all climbed into the Jeep with me behind the wheel, Millie in the passenger seat, and Ari in the back. I took a deep breath as I silently told myself that I could do this. Millie touched my arm. "You okay?" she asked.

I nodded. "Oh, yeah. Sure. I was just taking a moment. This will be my first time driving the Jeep, that's all."

Millie gave my arm a little squeeze. "You've got this."

Ari slapped the roll bar with her hand as she leaned forward. "Let's roll!" she said with an excited Woot!

We all laughed. I put the key into the ignition and turning it, the Jeep roared to life. In a matter of seconds, we were on our way. I found driving the Jeep was a lot smoother than the beat-up old Chevy had been. For one thing, we were a lot higher up than we had been in the pickup. It felt like we were flying with the air whipping all around us. It was funny that I hadn't really noticed it when Brock had driven. I guess doing the driving forced me to be more aware. And now with the sunshine it was a lot warmer than it had been this morning.

We pulled up in front of Millie's house and we climbed from the Jeep and made our way inside. To our surprise, Millie's grandma was standing at the foot of the stairs with a couple of bags packed. "What's all this?" Millie asked, pointing at the luggage.

Grams batted a hand in the air. "Well, if you girls are spending the weekend at Kat's place, I'm not going to sit around here all alone. Gertie has invited me to stay at her place for the weekend." She grinned as she leaned toward us conspiratorially. "It'll be fun!"

Millie cocked her head to the side. "What makes you think we're staying at the cottage?"

Grams batted a hand in the air. "Oh, please! You know I consult my crystal on a daily basis!"

I glanced at Millie. "So? What's the plan?"

Millie laughed. "I guess I just need to pack a few things!"

Gertrude Wilson pulled up in her sedan and Grams headed out the door. "You girls have a nice time!" she called out, smiling broadly. Ari and I each grabbed a bag and carried it out to the car for her.

Grams gave us both a hug. "You girls are so sweet!"

"Have a nice time, ladies!" we said.

They drove away as Millie joined us.

As we climbed back into the Jeep, Ari asked, "Did your grandmother really see us going to the cottage in her crystal ball?"

Millie glanced at us and smiled. "I told you she has Gypsy blood in her veins. She takes her Tarot and Crystal Ball *very* seriously. She's *not* a charlatan by any means despite what members of the Coven claim. She's the real deal."

As we started down the street, Ari touched my arm. "Why don't we check on your aunt first? While we're there I can quickly fly home and gather my stuff. I can ride Sewahió:wane back and leave him with her at the cabin. That way she's not completely trapped."

I looked at her through the rearview mirror. "Are you sure?"

She nodded. "Absolutely."

"Who's Sewahani?" Millie asked, scrunching up her face.

Ari laughed. "Sewahió:wane," she corrected. "It means 'Apple'. He's my appaloosa."

Millie turned and touched her arm. "Wait! You have a horse!? Why am I just learning this about you?"

Ari laughed. "You knew I had a horse! I told you ages ago."

"How come I've never seen him?" Millie asked.

Ari laughed again. "Probably because you've never come to my home before."

Millie's face brightened. "So is that an invitation?"

Ari nodded. "It can be."

§

Aunt Abigail was sitting on the porch of the tiny cabin with a glass of Iced Tea in her hand as we drove up. For some reason she didn't seem surprised to see us. "Nice ride," she said simply.

"Compliments of Brock's dad," I said.

She nodded, taking a sip of tea. "What are you girls up to?"

As Ari hopped from the Jeep she transformed into a sparrow, her clothes fluttered to the ground at our feet as she flew off toward her place. Millie's jaw dropped. "Holy shit! How cool is that?" She pointed through the pines where the tiny bird had flown. "She's so graceful!"

I laughed as I shrugged. "Yeah, it's kinda her thing. I'm kinda envious of her."

"Why?" Millie asked. "You can turn into a wolf!"

I laughed as I gathered Ari's clothes. "But I always thought it would be cool to fly."

Aunt Abigail laughed. "I always thought it would be fun to be invisible." She placed her glass of tea aside and nodded at Millie. "Aren't you tired of those things yet?"

"What? Oh! You mean the crutches?" Millie shrugged. "Yeah, but it's not like I have a choice."

Aunt Abby smiled at her. "Oh, but you do. If you let me help you."

Millie quickly nodded. "What? Sure. What do I need to do?"

Aunt Abigail laughed. "Relax. It'll take a little time."

Millie had a huge smile on her face as she glanced at me. She grabbed my arm excitedly. "This is so cool!"

As we stepped up onto the porch I stuck my fingertips into the front pockets of my jeans, and gave Aunt Abby a hopeful look. "So, have you had any news about Grandpa?"

She nodded. "As a matter of fact I have. It seems that Melissa may have been right when she told you that something happened at the *Drawing Down the Moon* ceremony. Your grandpa said that Shelby just seemed to *change* in the pickup, right before his eyes. She attacked him and clawed his arm. Her fingernails were coated with something that really messed him up. He had to revert to his wolf form, but still it took a while for it to work out of his system. He had to avoid all those idiots in the woods with their guns. Thankfully they seem to have finally grown tired of that nonsense. The Wolf had taken complete control over his mind. Fortunately, it also helped to speed up his healing. Once he felt stronger, the Wolf eased off. So he came here."

I felt a shiver run down my spine as I recalled Shelby's eyes in the cafeteria and the way that they had glowed. I considered saying something but I didn't. I glanced toward the cabin door. "Is he here? Can I see him?"

"He's out on a run right now. He wanted to check in with Okwaho to make certain all the hunters weren't harassing her. He should be back a bit later."

I sighed. I was a little disappointed that Grandpa was gone. I had been worried about him and had missed him a great deal. "Well, that's a relief." I cocked my head to the side as I blinked and brushed tears from my eyes. "So, can you really heal Millie's broken leg?"

She nodded confidently. "I can."

Millie grinned. "So what are we waiting for?"

We all laughed. Aunt Abigail stood. "Let's go inside."

She directed Millie to sit on top of the kitchen table. Millie looked at the table dubiously. "You sure it'll hold me? I'm not exactly a thin girl, you know."

"It's sturdier than it looks, trust me," Aunt Abigail said patting the tabletop. I noticed that she had blushed slightly, but I shrugged it off. I probably didn't want to know how she knew that the table was so sturdy.

I gave Millie a hand getting up on the table, it wasn't easy, but we managed. "Scoot back," Aunt Abby said, placing a hand on Millie's shoulder. "I need your broken leg up on the table."

Millie rolled her eyes. "I just hope I don't get a splinter in my butt!" Her glasses started slipping off the end of her nose and she had to stop and push them back into place, then she resumed her backward scooting.

As Millie moved into place, Aunt Abigail opened a cabinet in the kitchen. I had always thought that it was a pantry, but it wasn't. It smelled like her basement, full of herbs and other mystical ingredients. Evidently she kept a supply here as well. I guess it only made sense that she would. She pulled out four, long tapered white candles and handed them to me. "Place one at each end of the table, and one on either side, if you would be so kind."

I took the candles and the box of matches that she gave me and dribbled hot wax upon the table, and then placed the candles as she had instructed. Millie gave me a nervous look. Clearly she was having second thoughts. "Uhm… you know, I only have about four more weeks with the cast. I think I'll be fine."

"Relax, Millie. You can trust my aunt."

Millie batted a hand in the air. "Oh, it isn't that. It… it just seems like a lot of work. I don't want to trouble anyone. I can… I can just…"

Aunt Abby frowned at her. "Stop being such a silly goose. It'll be fine."

Millie laughed nervously. Beads of sweat trickled down the side of her face. "I need to pee!" she said.

"Hold it," Aunt Abby said. She mixed some green powder into a small glass of water and stirred it with a finger. The water glowed with a bright green fluorescence, which she quickly drank down. I heard her chant something, but couldn't really comprehend what she was saying. It was soft, sweet, and melodic. She leaned in front of Millie's face and exhaled. "Breathe it in!" she said sharply. Millie complied; inhaling the green wisps of smoke, she immediately relaxed. I could see that her eyes had glossed over. Now it was as though she were either in a trance and heavily sedated, I couldn't really tell which.

Next, Aunt Abigail placed one hand above the cast and the other upon Millie's foot. She closed her eyes and continued with the soft singsong mantra that remained elusive to me. When I tried to concentrate on what she was saying, I couldn't. To me, the words had no meaning. They didn't even make any sense; they were like another language completely, but it sounded very pretty. There was something magical in the air.

When she took her hands away, her palms glowed with that same green light, but dissipated in a matter of seconds. Now, the glow came solely from underneath the cast on Millie's leg. It seemed to flicker as the flames on the candles grew. The wax seemed to melt faster. Aunt Abby stepped back and placed a calming hand on my arm when I started to speak, she shook her head. We stood in silence as the candles burned low and the light slowly faded away.

Millie blinked rapidly. "I… I feel… strange. My leg tingles, like it does when you sit too long and it goes to sleep."

Aunt Abby nodded, and she spoke softly. "It is part of the healing process. It will begin to dissipate, just let it happen."

After a few minutes Aunt Abigail walked around the table, snuffing out the flames of the candle stubs. She went back to the cupboard and searched through the vials. "Ah," she said softly, and smiled. "There you are." She grasped a small bottle containing a powdered mixture of pale pink, purple and white. She handed it to Millie. "When you get back to the cottage I want you to run a bath, and sprinkle all of this in the steaming water. Bathe in it for at least an hour."

Millie crinkled her nose, taking the vial. "What is it?" she asked.

"Ground Motherwort. Its nurturing and curative properties are excellent to soak in. It will help speed the healing process of your leg," Aunt Abby said.

"That's it?" Millie asked.

She nodded. "Oh, and try to stay off your leg for the rest of the night, just to give it a chance to strengthen a little bit more."

"What about the cast?" I asked.

"Oh!" Aunt Abby seemed surprised, as though she had forgotten all about it. "It can come off."

Grandpa appeared in the doorway of the cabin. "Better let me handle that," he said. The sound of his rich baritone brought a smile to my face.

I rushed into his arms, practically throwing myself against him. "Grandpa! I'm so happy that you're all right!" Tears sprang from my eyes.

He chuckled softly. "I've missed you too, kiddo."

Millie waved. "Heya, Mr. St. Claire. Sorry about sitting on your kitchen table."

"Hello Millie," he said. "Let me get that saw."

Panic flickered in Millie's eyes. "Whoa! Saw? What do we need a saw for?"

Aunt Abigail laughed. "Relax, Millie. He just wants to remove the cast. You'll be fine."

She had visibly paled. "Uhm… shouldn't we let a professional handle that? I mean, what if he slips?"

I was forced to hold Millie's hand as Grandpa carefully cut into the plaster cast. He made two vertical cuts along the length of the cast, starting high up on the calf. He never cut all the way through, just down so that it was very thin where he had run the saw blade. Once he was satisfied he grasped the cast in his hands and pulled. It came apart easily, freeing her leg and foot.

Sweat broke out on Millie's forehead and ran down the side of her face. "I feel like I'm gonna pass out," she said.

Aunt Abigail handed her a glass of cold water. "Here, sip this," she said.

Millie took a small drink and smiled. "Thanks," she whispered. "I feel much better now. Whew! Thought I was gonna lose it for a minute there!" she chuckled as she pushed her glasses up the bridge of her nose.

Aunt Abigail frowned. "You need to get those fixed."

Millie giggled. "It's not like I haven't heard that before!" She wiggled her toes and then giggled again. "Oh my!"

As Grandpa helped Millie down from the table, we heard the whinny of Ari's horse outside. She was just sliding down from Apple's back as we went outside the cabin. She carried a small leather knapsack over her shoulder. Seeing Millie walk on her crutches without the cast she raised both brows. "Did I miss much?" she asked with a smile.

Millie smiled. "Sure have! We've had the most magical time!"

We all laughed.

As the sun was beginning to set, Grandpa had put a pot of venison stew on the stovetop to warm up. The enticing aroma wafted out of the cabin as we all sat outside enjoying the cool air of the early evening. We talked about the weather and other nonsensical stuff as we waited, enjoying a break from our worldly troubles. Finally, it was time to eat.

I smiled up at Aunt Abigail as she handed me a bowl of stew. "Thanks," I said appreciatively.

"You're welcome," she said as she sat down beside me on the porch step. "Listen, do you think you can do without me for a few more days? I'd kinda like to hang out here with your grandpa a bit longer."

Steam arose from the spoon of stew and I blew upon it to cool it some before sticking it into my mouth. I nodded. "Sure. We're gonna have a Girl's Night at the cottage when we get back, and then tomorrow Millie and I have to do a bunch of make-up work if we want to pass this year. So we've got enough to keep us busy. Ari's gonna help."

Aunt Abigail nodded. "I know I didn't leave a lot of food in the house, but you can always eat at Wellington House, I'm sure your Grandmother wouldn't mind."

I chuckled softly, almost spitting out my food. "We're good. Tomorrow we'll run into town and do some shopping for necessities."

She arched a brow. "No junk food."

I laughed. "I said necessities."

She chuckled as she bumped her shoulder into mine. After a moment she said. "You know, I think things are finally going to work out."

"Don't jinx us!" I laughed.

She laughed. "Okay, maybe a little junk food."

Chapter Forty-five

Girl's Night

Keegan Rourke moved silently through the forest, his shoulders slumped in brooding anger, his hands tightly fisted at his sides. He could no longer assume wolf form and move through the pines with the lissomness to which he was long accustomed. What he had once taken for granted was now lost to him— stolen by the old woman with Gypsy blood and the small Mohawk girl. They alone had managed to tame the beast, and for that, he vowed to make them pay.

He peered at the witch's cottage through the heavy boughs of the pine, his jaw clenched in fury. The place appeared to be deserted. But he was a patient man. He had eternity on his side. They would come. And then he would strike, the speed of the vampire would help him to disable his enemies.

He grinned, feeling his incisors growing. Perhaps he could wait inside the cottage, spring at them from the dark shadows when they least expected. He stopped suddenly. Not because he wanted to, but simply because he was unable to take another step closer. It was as though some invisible barrier kept him away. He snarled with increased irritability. *The witch's magic!* She too would be made to pay.

There had to be a way through this invisible wall. He just had to find it. But every time he attempted to draw closer to the cottage he was repelled. And each time he was struck with a powerful jolt – almost an electrical charge.

Headlights were bouncing through the trees along the road from Wellington House. He quickly stepped back into the shadows of the forest so that he could remain unseen. To his surprise it was a Jeep carrying the three girls: Sam's granddaughter Kat, the plump Bradford girl, and the Mohawk. He grinned and saliva dripped from the corners of his mouth. His luck was changing. It always seemed to turn his way when he needed it most.

He chuckled softly. He was going to enjoy this.

§

By the time we arrived at the cottage it was already quite dark. I started the bathwater for Millie and added the bottle of Motherwort powder just as Aunt Abigail had instructed. Before closing the bathroom door Millie said, "If you don't hear from me in an hour, you'd better come and check on me. If I drown in my sleep I swear I'll haunt you!"

I couldn't help but laugh despite the fact that I'd already had enough ghosts haunting me. I certainly didn't need any more.

Ari had already started a fire going. The warmth coming from the crackling flames and the snap and pop of the pine logs was helping to relax me. I sat beside her on the sofa and sighed. After a moment I hopped up, startling her. "What's wrong?" she asked, starting to rise.

I shook my head and grinned. "Don't get up! I just thought,

'*what's the sense in having a Girl's Night without some refreshment?*' Sooo…" I opened up a cupboard in the kitchen and pulled out a bottle of Jack Daniels. It was nearly full. "How's about we have a little drink?"

Ari laughed and her eyes lit up. "Do you think we should?"

"Why not?" I asked, grabbing three glasses. "It's just the three of us and we're not going anywhere. Aunt Abby won't mind, as long as we don't get too carried away. Besides, she was young once."

Ari grinned mischievously. "All right, count me in!"

I poured three glasses and handed one to her. I sat mine down next to the bottle on the coffee table and the other I took for Millie. I crossed to the bathroom door and knocked softly. "You okay in there?" I opened the door without waiting for a reply.

Shyly, she quickly covered herself as best she could. "Are you kidding me? An hour can't have gone by already!" she sounded shocked.

I laughed as I twirled the amber liquid in the glass. "Thought you might want to have a little drink while you soaked."

Her eyes lit up. "Is that whiskey?" she asked reaching out her hand.

"Yup!" I replied giving up the glass. "Don't take too long in here or we'll drink it all."

Millie took a huge sip and said with a hoarse voice, "You better not!" Her eyes started watering. "Wow!" she said. "This stuff is horrible!"

Closing the door, I said. "Don't bathe forever, you'll miss out on all the fun,"

"Guys!" I heard her muffled reply. "Not fair!"

I eased back down on the couch and picked up my glass. Ari clinked her glass against mine. "Here's to Girl's Night!" she said softly. Her eyes seemed to sparkle in the firelight.

"Cheers!" I said.

I could feel the burn of the whiskey all the way down to the pit of my stomach as I took a sip. I glanced at Ari and smiled. "So how have things been since you returned to school?"

She nodded. "Pretty lame actually. I've missed not having you guys there. Manny and Melissa have been very into themselves and I've been giving them their space. Brock has been pretty popular playing the school jock card, not really my thing. Honestly, I've been pretty lonely." She reached out and placed her hand on mine. "I'm really glad that you're back."

Maybe it was the booze, but it seemed like there was something more to the way she held her hand on mine and the way she looked at me. I felt my heart do a little flutter thing inside my chest and it startled me. I quickly took another sip of whiskey.

I was suddenly eager to change the subject. "I'd like to get to know you better, Ari. Tell me about you."

She chuckled softly. "There's really not much to tell. You already know most of it. I'm a shy Mohawk girl that has very few friends." She shrugged. "That's about it."

I smiled. "Tell me about your parents. I've never heard you talk about them."

She sighed as she took another sip of the whiskey. I could see her dark eyes were wet with the beginning of tears. "My mother died giving birth to me, so I never knew her. My dad wasn't able to cope with my mother's death, so he went down to the city to work construction." She glanced at me and smiled shyly. "A lot of my people do. My rakshótha – my grandfather – actually helped to build the Twin Towers, but that was a long time ago. My father died in a construction accident not long after he left. So it has been just me and my akhsótha for a long time now."

I reached out and touched her hand. "Oh, Ari, I'm so sorry."

She raised her glass in the air. "We've all lost somebody. It is a part of life."

The bathroom door opened and Millie stood there, wearing a robe, leaning on one crutch. The other hand held her empty whiskey glass. "Wait for me!" If her glass had been full she would've spilt it all over the place; she wasn't very graceful as she made her way to the sofa on just a single crutch.

I refilled our glasses and we raised another toast to Girl's Night. After taking a sip Millie said, "I would've been out sooner but I noticed some black dust on the windowsill. I cleaned it up. You're welcome, by the way. You really need to clean better. If your aunt saw that, she'd throw a fit, I know Grams would!"

I could feel panic rising within me. I touched her arm, almost spilling my drink. "Tell me you didn't!"

Millie frowned, giving me a dark look. "Easy, girl. You almost knocked my glass out of my hand."

I got up from the couch and ran into the bathroom. The windowsill was pristine. I covered my mouth with my fingers. "Oh, no!" I whispered hoarsely.

Millie shook her head. "It's no big deal. I just took some damp toilet tissue and ran it over the dust. It came right up. It's no big deal."

"What did you do with it?" I asked.

She shrugged. "Flushed it."

Ari looked at me curiously. "What's the matter?"

"That wasn't ordinary dust," I said. "Aunt Abigail placed it there on purpose. All the windows have it. It's to ward off evil. It was a protection spell that she had put in place. It was to keep evil from entering the cottage. Now the spell is broken, and the cottage is vulnerable."

Millie turned bright red. "Well how was I supposed to know that?"

I sighed as I ran my hand through my hair. I shrugged. "It's okay. There's no way you could've known. It probably doesn't matter now anyway. Sebastian Barrister is gone. I think the worst of this is over."

The front door flew open and a massive figure stepped inside. I dropped my whiskey glass onto the floor and it shattered, spilling everywhere. My eyes were wide with terror. Keegan Rourke flashed an evil grin. "Thanks for the invite, girls!" He snarled at us, flashing his growing fangs. Millie screamed. I couldn't move, and apparently neither could Ari. We were at the mercy of the vampire.

He took a step toward us, his hand cupped in savage claws with long, dark nails. He stopped suddenly and my eyes were drawn to the wooden point sticking out of his chest. He glanced at me with hate raging in his suddenly wide, orange eyes. He looked down at his chest as realization dawned on him. His face twisted in anger. *"Fu—!"* he roared and then he evaporated into a cloud of dust, leaving Tiffany Jones standing there holding out her sharpened nightstick.

After a moment she smiled. "Thought you might need a little help," she said.

The vampire's spell was broken almost immediately we were no longer frozen with our fear. I glanced down at the remnants of dust at her feet, and then looked back at her. "How did you know to come?"

"Long story," she said as she put the baton away. "Aren't you ladies a little young to be drinking?"

Millie quickly downed her whiskey and coughed, her eyes watering. "Are you gonna arrest us?" she could barely talk and her voice was raspy.

Tiffany shook her head. "Not if you share."

I went to the cupboard and got two more glasses. After filling everyone up, I handed a glass to Tiffany.

She accepted the glass with an appreciative nod and quickly took a sip. "That's good," she said. "It's been a long night, I need this." She raised her glass in a silent toast and then took another sip.

"So? What made you come here?" I asked.

"I was on patrol and the dispatcher relayed an urgent message from Silas Monaghan. He and Brock Jacobins had just come from the Collingsworth residence and learned a couple of disturbing things. One, his parents had been found in coffins by Sheriff Thompson. The deputies with him had staked them, leaving nothing behind but dust-filled coffins. Silas was pretty upset but also seemed relieved that his ordeal was over. He and Brock said that they had been told by Marybeth Collingsworth that Keegan Rourke was staying out of a modified camper attached to his truck. I actually found it in the woods not far from here. He had the windows painted black on the camper to keep out the sunlight, I guess. I figured that he was on his way here, so I figured I'd come too." She shrugged, "Looks like I got here just in time."

Ari lifted her glass. "We're grateful that you did."

I took a sip of my whiskey and refilled Tiffany's glass. "So that's it, then. It really is over."

Epilogue

Transcendence

Bobby looked up at his grandmother and frowned uncomfortably as he tugged at his collar. He hated having the top button of his shirt fastened; it felt too tight against his throat. "I can hardly breathe," he winced as he complained. He made a show of it by bulging out his eyeballs as far as he could and sticking out his tongue. It was a futile effort devised to illicit a laugh from the strict old woman next to him. But she wasn't buying into it.

She rolled her eyes at him as she pulled on the lower hem of the jacket of her Victorian ensemble, a long skirt that went to midway down her calf and matching pale blue coat that puffed slightly at the shoulders. Her blouse was white with ornate lace ruffles at her neck and both wrists. She wore high, black boots that were tightly laced. He couldn't see the top of them, but he assumed they went almost to her knees. "Nonsense, Robert." She slapped his hand away from his collar and smiled thinly. "You look very dashing."

His lip twisted into a grimace. He didn't think he could run in these old shoes, certainly not very fast. "My feet hurt," he said. "I think my feet have grown or maybe the shoes have shrunk."

"The shoes haven't shrunk," she said as she pulled the parasol out of the antique armoire. "You're just getting too big," she said giving him an appraising look. He was sprouting like a weed, but she supposed that it was normal. She guessed that was what little boys did.

He shifted his feet nervously. "I hope this works."

She paused briefly. "Of course it will work. Why would it not?"

He shrugged. "I don't know."

She took him by the hand and led him over to the doorway. "Are you ready, Robert?" she asked as she straightened the hem of her jacket again.

Bobby nodded as he stuck a finger in his collar and scowled. "Uh huh," he said. Upon seeing her glare he quickly amended his comment. "I mean, yes ma'am.

She opened the door and they walked into the room. The musty scent of almost two hundred years of accumulated dust filled the air. The filth coated all of the furniture in a thick layer. She nodded at her grandson. "Close the door, Robert."

He placed his hand on the edge of the door and swung it closed with a slight smile and a sigh. This was his favorite part; it made his stomach do a flip-flop and his head felt light, almost as if it would float away – if it weren't firmly attached at his shoulders. A moment later, all of the dust that had built up over the years, faded away, replaced by a varnished sheen. He felt the familiar stirring deep within his belly and it made him think of when he and his family had visited Coney Island and gone on the rollercoaster. They had so much fun that weekend! He smiled at the memory, but it soon faded. A short week later both his parents were dead.

§

I walked along the forest path leading up to Wellington House from the cottage. Golden rays of sunlight filtered through the thick boughs of the sturdy pines, warming my skin as I felt the sun's glow upon my face. It felt good. Chipmunks scampered across my path, their cheeks puffed out with seeds for storing. I could hear birds twittering, from somewhere unseen. The forest was at peace, no longer threatened. The hunters had abandoned their quest for wolf hides.

I smiled as I breathed in the heavy scent of pine and continued along my way. I could finally relax. Sebastian Barrister had vanished. There was no sign of him anywhere. Keegan Rourke was dead. War with the Coven had been averted, and Grandmother had assumed control once again. Enemies wanting to kill us at every turn no longer threatened us; peace was restored to The Hollows. I was looking forward to what tomorrow might bring.

I had been neglecting my brother a lot lately, but my intention had been to shield Bobbybear from the horrors that confronted me. It was time to remedy that. Time to make good on my promises to spend more time with him.

I heard Bobby's tender laughter off to my right as Wellington House came into view. He was playing near Grandmother's garden, and he wasn't alone. I could hear girlish squeals of delight mixed with his.

"Do not trample my garden," I heard Grandmother warn halfheartedly, her voice sounding slightly amused by the gaiety that was flowing from the youngsters.

I walked softly, determined to surprise them, but it wasn't meant to be. Bobby was playing tag with Sara Robinson, both of them giggling as children often do when having fun. Sara ran up to me and touched my bare arm. "Tag," she said as she quickly darted away, "You're it!" Her hand was not the cold whispering touch of a ghost; it was soft, firm and warm, very much alive.

I glanced at Grandmother as she tended her garden in the last rays of sunlight. She wore the talisman that magically protected her skin and I could see the warm red glow from the heart of the crystal. She still had the pale skin of the undead; the pink and radiant color of the living was a thing of the past where she was concerned. Her cold touch still chilled me, and I had to fight hard not to shiver every time.

Bobby and Sara collided with one another and fell to the ground in a heap, laughing hysterically. The impact had been hard, and by the sound of it I was surprised that they were not seriously hurt. I gasped sharply, looking from Bobby to Grandmother, as comprehension dawned. Sara wasn't a ghost. I put a trembling hand to my lips, knowing that they had traveled into the past and drastically altered events. The consequences could prove catastrophic. "What have the two of you done?" I said, breathlessly.

§

Rutherford Barrister stepped through the open door and paused, listening intently, not wanting to be discovered. He glanced back toward the room he had just left and smiled thinly. It had changed. Dingy sheets were draped over the furniture and layers of dust covered everything in sight. Footprints, marking the passage of three others could easily be seen upon the floor. They belonged to the old woman, the boy and the girl. Now his were added to the mix.

He reached into his pocket and withdrew the small copper coin that the boy had dropped upon the lawn just outside of the Robinson manor. He looked at first one side and then the other. The one had a likeness of Abraham Lincoln with the words IN GOD WE TRUST emblazoned above his head. Behind his neck it said LIBERTY and under his chin was presumably the date. 2021. He chuckled softly to himself. *Was this really possible?* He wondered. Had he truly transcended Time? *Had he travelled*

137 years into the future? Tonight was to have been his wedding night – he had been on the verge of fulfilling his dreams of power and greatness. *Was all that lost to him now?* Not if he could help it.

§

Shelby Collingsworth walked through the forest; her white gossamer gown seemed to float on the air as she moved through the tall, slender pines. The light from the rising moon made the garment appear to glow in the dark forest as she stepped beyond the trees and stood on the high outcropping of rock at Valen's Ridge. She raised her hands into the air, as her eyes turned to dark green pools that seemed to gleam in the moonlight. "Come to me!" she whispered into the night. Her soft voice wafted through the trees, almost silently.

§

Sam St. Claire awoke with a start, as if snapping out of a dream. He turned and stared at the sleeping figure next to him. "Did you say something?" he asked softly.

Abigail didn't respond.

"Come to me…" he heard the faint whisper again.

He got up from the bed and went outside. The night was clear. Countless stars shared the night sky with the silvery ball of the full moon. He morphed into wolf form and howled a soft, mournful plea to the night. The Black Wolf turned and headed through the forest at a swift run.

Shelby smiled as the large wolf joined her on the outcropping of rock. She put her hand on the wolf's head, and scratched between his ears. He leaned his head against her leg, his eyes glowed a bright green as he stared off into the night. "Good boy," she said in a voice clearly not her own.

To be continued in:

Valen's Ridge

The Hollows: Book 3

Mohawk Pronunciation Guide
Mohawk Vowels:

Character used:	*Mohawk pronunciation (as in...)*
a	father.
a:	father, only held longer.
e	get, or the a in gate.
e:	gate, only held longer.
i	police.
i:	police, only held longer.
o	note, only held longer.
o:	note, only held longer.

Mohawk Nasal Vowels:

Nasal vowels don't really exist in English. They are pronounced just like the oral ("regular") vowels, only using your nose as well as you mouth. To English speakers, a nasal vowel often sounds like a vowel with a half-pronounced 'n' at the end of it.

Character used:

en

en:

on

on:

Mohawk Consonants:

Character used: *Mohawk pronunciation (as in…)*
(also sometimes used:)

h   hay.

k (g)   gate, soft k in skate, or hard k in Kate.

kw (gw, khw)   gw in Gwen, or the qu in queen.

r (l)   r in right in some dialects, but like l in light in others.

n   night.

s (sh, c)	s in sell. Before y or i, the Mohawk pronunciation sounds more like the sh in shell.
t (d)	d in die, soft t in sty, or hard t in tie.
ts (j, ch)	ts in tsunami. Before y or i the Mohawk pronunciation sounds like the ch in char.
w	w in way.
wh	Some Mohawk speakers pronounce this sound with the voiceless "breathy w" that many British speakers use in words like "which," but others pronounce it like the f in English fair.
y	y in yes.
' (?)	A pause sound, like the one in the middle of the word "uh-oh."

Mohawk word:	*English translation:*
shé:kon	hello
hen:,wakata karí:te	I am doing well
akhsótha	grandmother
rakhsótha	grandfather
ká:to	come
sátien tánon	sit down

aón:ria	breathe in
aonrísera	breathe out
ioiá:nere'	good
ohstón:ha	little
ohwáho	wolf
akokstén:ha	old woman
sewahió:wane	apple
niá:wen	thank you
Io	you're welcome
kanatakón:ha	sparrow

About the Author

Tom was born in Kermit, Texas in 1960 and raised all over the Great American Southwest, never staying in one place for too long. His father worked for the El Paso Natural Gas Company, a job that necessitated frequent moves for increased opportunities.

Tom graduated from High School from an American Boarding School on the island of Mallorca, Spain in 1978; his family was living in Algeria at the time. After graduation, he spent the next twelve years in the Navy. Diagnosed as an insulin-dependent diabetic, he was forced to change careers. He worked in the construction industry as a Union Pipefitter often working on launch complexes at the Kennedy Space Center.

Tom currently lives in Satellite Beach, Florida with his wife of over forty years. From a very young age, he dreamed of becoming a published author and never stopped scribbling away on notepads. This is his fourth novel published by Purple Parrot Publishing, proof that 'Dreams don't have to stay that way.'

https://www.tomhornauthor.com/